Tara,

Death and
Other Things

I literally could not have done this without you. I can never thank you enough

Christopher Hall

Chris

DEDICATED TO THE MEMORY OF

Joseph Donvito

Clifford Hall

Kevin Kenney

David Russell

Paul James Salerno

CONTENTS

PART ONE:
THE UNIVERSE LAUGHS

CHAPTER ONE

It is dark...darker than it had been the night before. Darker than the bluest night in this town, one that existed for decades, centuries even, way before those that currently walked its streets had been born. Before they took their first step, and last steps. Before Richard was hit by that bus on Eighth Avenue, an avenue where the wind battered its windows and tumbled trash and leaves into the street, where rain would come and go, yet always leave its mark, where people were born and left immediately; heading out on the first train to the first place that didn't know their name, where they could reform themselves, make a new life, create a new name, leave behind that abusive father or girlfriend, live out the dreams that were crushed along with the garbage when it rained. This place, this place, it ate people alive; those few left made it by on guile and grit, squinting their eyes to keep score in a place as hostile as a kill box, hoping that one day the rain would stop, that the sun would shine through, that for once the darkness wouldn't be as black, that the blue became brighter, the sun no longer afraid of the rain, the day new and refreshing instead of the God's honest same. This place, it's stubborn in its ways, yet everyone got up in the morning and went about their days, punching clocks and sitting in traffic and carrying a brown bagged lunch; where girls got pregnant and kids dropped out of school, homeless men hoped to impress someone with their singing voice just enough to get a nickel, a quarter, if they hit that high note, this is the blackest world—and it is raining again.

1

"I've waited too long, I can't do this anymore. We fight too much. You're dismissive, childish and unwilling to change. You're still that boy in the hockey jersey sitting on the couch with your friends drinking beer. You feel distant. I look in your eyes and see nothing when you stare back, but you light up from the smallest hello from a stranger. You talk to them and you smile and your eyes glow; I feel like a coat rack that you carry around. I don't fucking get it—I don't get you. Are you unhappy? Do you even care anymore? I can't tell. You tell me I'm selfish; that all I care about is myself. Look in the mirror. See your blank eyes, see the one who is really being selfish. I've done everything...but I can't call you without getting that quiet stinging in the back of my mind that the person on the other end of the line is loathing every word I'm saying, while saying otherwise. You are too complex, too moody, too polemic. You exist in the extremes. I can't live here with you anymore. Do you know how badly you hurt me that day when you told me all I think about is myself and how I used our relationship to my benefit? You crushed me; I wish you never say those words to anyone ever again. This has bothered me almost every day since you said that and finally I've decided at some point, I just have to let you go. I'll think about you, but I don't love you anymore. I don't know how you feel or what you're thinking and right now it doesn't even really matter. You are the cancer in my soul that needs to be cut out, so..." Marie trails off, running her index finger around the rim of her coffee cup.

This coffee shop is empty. It's late; rain runs slowly down the windows of the front doors. A busboy cleans a table across the way, one of the few other things breathing. This old diner, this hollow place.

Andrew looks up, staring at Marie with those vacant eyes she has studied for so long. He starts to open his mouth, tugging at his blue jacket, but then reconsiders. He looks back down at the table. He adjusts his silverware, straightening the fork he was just fiddling with, then he glances up at her again.

Looks at her truly for the first time in a while. He doesn't see the same person he has carried in his mind for the last few years. She wasn't that girl at the party anymore. Her hair was tied back in a bun, tiny bags under her eyes from stress, her fingers a little fatter. She still looked great, older than before, but this look changed Andrew's mental image of her within seconds, aging Marie half a decade. He carried that old image for so long, while that image aged gracefully in the years following. She was different—maybe he was, maybe he wasn't.

Andrew and Marie continue to sit in stunned silence, fidgeting on either side of their booth, unsure of what exactly to do, each one thinking about running for the door, or throwing their now cold plate of food against the wall. They didn't know what to do.

The bus boy walks up to the table with a hot pot of coffee and offers, "Coffee?" Andrew nods his head and the bus boy fills his cup to the brim, with some spilling out and pooling in the saucer beneath it. Andrew exhales, either to catch his breath or to blow the hot steam off the cup.

Marie stays locked on Andrew, waiting for something, anything, any sort of response.

"Nothing? You can't say anything now? Not even a 'fuck you,' an 'I hate you,' nothing? Please say something, please let me know that you're even listening," Marie says.

The bus boy walks back across the diner toward the cash register, where the counter jockey's eyelids flutter after a long day.

"That guy is having the worst day of his life," the bus boy says. The cashier shakes his head awake. He looks over toward Andrew and Marie.

"Yea, I've seen that before; that booth has seen the death of a few relationships. The lonely last supper of a couple where the girl tells a guy just how shitty he's been, or that she knows he's cheated on her. Hopefully she throws a drink in his face and storms out of here, there's nothing on TV"

Silence reigns.

The rainy front door bursts open. A man with a ski mask on his mug pulls a gun out of his trousers and puts it right in the cashier's face.

"Give me all the fucking money in the drawer," he says to the cashier whose hands were so high in the air he was damn near touching the ceiling. The gunman wheels around to the bus boy and barks, "And you! Open the fucking floor safe! You guys are making eight dollars an hour, don't be a fucking hero!"

Andrew looks at Marie, who quietly pulls off a ring from her middle finger and places it in her left pocket. As the cashier opens the drawer and puts everything in a doggie bag and the combo was being turned on the safe, the gunman dashes over to Marie and Andrew's table with a bag.

"Empty your goddamn pockets!" he screams.

Andrew gets out of his chair and starts to empty his pockets, "Listen man, just take it easy, she doesn't have anything, I'll give you everything I have, just take it and go."

The gunman looks down at Marie who peers back up at the man whose eyes are anything but vacant. He now points the gun at Marie. Marie trembles back into her booth, her eyes wide.

Andrew raises his voice, stepping closer to the gunman.

"Listen man I told you, she doesn't have anything, just leave her alone," Andrew says to the gunman. He turns to look back at Andrew, then toward the bus boy and cashier, he quickly darts a few feet in their direction, yelling at them to move faster. He moves the gun back toward Andrew, his eyes blinking fast.

"She your girlfriend?" he asks.

Andrew looks down at Marie and then back at the gunman.

"No... but I'd ask you to just leave her alone. We can go to an ATM and I can take out as much money as you want—I'm just asking you man-to-man to leave her alone," Andrew pleads.

The gunman grabs Marie by the arm and yanks her upwards, her momentum carrying her toward the floor, "Empty your fucking pockets!"

Before Marie's knees hit the ground Andrew spears the gunman, both of them fly over a nearby table and to the floor. Marie rolls out of the way, just dodging the two men as they tussle on the ground.

Then, ear shattering bangs. BOOM, BOOM. The gun goes off twice, Andrew convulses, falling off the gunman and hitting the floor. The gunman straightens his mask and pulls money out of Andrew's pocket. He jumps to his feet and runs toward the front of the coffee shop, grabbing the doggie bag full of cash as he blows through the door and into the rainy night.

Andrew clutches at his chest as he lies on his side, pain ringing where the silence once stood. Marie rolls Andrew over onto his back, seeing wounds on his chest and right arm. She takes off her jacket and presses it down on his chest. She peers back at the cashier who is wailing into the phone. She looks at Andrew's eyes, the vacancy is gone, replaced with a bit of fear and straining. Andrew peeks down at his chest, murmuring out, "I'm sorry."

Andrew grimaces, gritting his teeth as he starts to see blood pooling on the old carpet of this decades-old establishment. He glances at his chest, the red hole cutting through his white undershirt.

"And I thought you did a lot of damage," he says.

Marie lets out of a laugh through the tears. As the employees hurry around the shop, Andrew just keeps staring at Marie.

"You look so beautiful tonight."

Minutes later, the paramedics rush into the coffee shop, moving Andrew from the floor to the back of an ambulance to the doors of an emergency room at Williamson General Hospital. The ceiling above Andrew keeps changing; it's as if he is flipping through a set of photographs. His blinking slows, he feels a little empty, but a little lost, his ears hearing things as if he is under water and someone is shouting from above; he starts to see things. Maybe this is what death feels like. He feels the crash opening of the surgery doors beneath his feet and soon he sees a bright light above him, not the afterlife, at least not yet, but the surgeon's bat signal. The light that says your body is going to be opened up a little bit more. That the big dig is moving from Boston into your carcass. The light starts to get a little bit bigger, a bit more encompassing, a smidge brighter. Andrew closes his eyes. The light is gone.

Marie paces rapidly, moving like a tornado outside the door Andrew entered. She feels disoriented, blue, a bit strange. Everything vanishes without a trace; all she can do is stare. All she can do is replay the words and scenery. The way the plant in the corner was brown on its edges, showing signs of not being watered in a while. The room sucks in on her, threatening to pancake her. She shakes her head; trying to knock these images off their pedestal, refocus her mind's eye. That's when she looks up.

Andrew opens up his eyes again. The light shining as bright as before, the dull pain in his chest getting duller. He rolls his eyes, trying to glance at anything but that light. He can't move. He can't think of something to think of. He is truly gone. His eyes begin to fade. He closes them once more. The pain was gone.

Marie spins into a seat in the emergency room. She pulls the ring out of her pocket and places it back on her middle finger. She stares at it. The gold is dirty. A scratch mares the side. She sees shoes out of the corner of her left eye. The shoes are loud. They hit with the sound of a stampede. She doesn't look up from her ring.

"Marie?" comes from the mouth attached to the head, attached to the torso, attached to the legs, attached to the shoes. Marie looks up to see Andrew. He's wearing his blue jacket, blood staining the left side.

"I'm sorry," he mouths. Marie looks at him strangely. She then looks at the hospital doors. A nurse was soaked in blood, staring right at Marie. Marie's eyes travels back to Andrew, but he's no longer there. In his place is the surgeon, with the familiar blood staining the left side of his hospital scrubs.

"I'm sorry," he repeats.

Marie stands up from her chair, her arms limp, her legs crippled. She stumbles away, toward the automatic doors of the emergency room. Out into the circular driveway she continues. She collapses onto the sidewalk, hanging from the edge of the curb.

"Are you okay?" a voice says. She slowly cranes her neck, laying eyes on a man of a medium build, dark hair and glasses. He repeats his question. Marie turns back around without answering.

The man in glasses pulls out his cell phone, dials a number and places it to his head. He hears the first ring.

The call soon travels to an end table cluttered with magazines and days-old bottles of beer. The phone vibrates left and right, swaying the liquid in the bottles back and forth. A hand reaches from the couch to grab it. Mark cracks his neck and then answers the phone.

"Don't hang up...you need to get here," the voice on the other end of the line says. Mark rubs his eyes and straightens his back.

"Planes, trains or automobiles—you should get on one of them and get here," the voice continues. Mark looks at the people laid out across the rundown beach house floor, all passed out for a variety of reasons.

"I'm gonna be home Tuesday," Mark replies.

"He doesn't have that long."

Mark heads toward the stairwell. "Alright, I'm coming."

Charlie, the voice on the other end of the line, hangs up his phone and looks back down at Marie. Her head sits still, looking out toward the edge of town, down toward the water. The light tower peeks out above the downtown district, its light combing back around the corner every few seconds.

Charlie thinks about making another cursory overture to the girl he saw sitting motionless on the curb of the hospital. Sadly, he has sat in that spot many times—he's felt whatever this girl was going through. Not really being much of man of words, he turns around and walks back toward the hospital.

He enters the automatic doors and gives a wave to Dolores, the night receptionist, who sits like she sits every night, head down, indulging in a crossword. He enters the ICU and scrubs his hands with sanitizer. Then he sees the hallway, that hallway, that fucking hallway—a prison without bars but with and more bedpans. A long, dank, combination of death and near death. The smell of urine and feces fills the air, a smell that no longer fazes Charlie, a smell that he has become all too familiar with these last few months.

As he makes his way down this hallway that time forgot, he looks at his watch. It reads 3:42 a.m.

"Where is she?" he mumbles to himself. Charlie continues to make strides toward the hospital door, its eerie shadow enveloping the nearby nurses' station. This hospital room is the only one with its lights on at this late hour.

Charlie leans and peeks into the room where he sees Jane sleeping in a chair. Her arms crossed, head leaning to the right, blond hair tussled in the same direction. Charlie takes a seat on the windowsill and looks at James.

James is in the last stages of cancer. His body ravaged—skinny arms, legs and torso. His hair shorn short, far from the long well-kept hairdo of yesteryear. He got old in the last year, his hair more gray than it has ever been. James' heart monitor pulses quietly, another sound that seems almost second nature to Charlie. It was sound that is a part of this area as much as the nurses speaking loudly and the squeaking of tennis shoes as the orderly passes nearby. It's a strange place, a place that is nothing but wrong. A place where the only up side is that someone survives a few more hours, maybe a few more days. There are no miracles in this place. No Hail Mary's that come true. It's hard not to feel weary in a place like this.

"Mom," Charlie whispers.

Jane quietly opens her eyes. She stretches her arms and rights her body, rubbing the cramp out of her neck.

"I got in touch with Mark, he's on his way," Charlie offers. Jane looks back at Charlie and says, "You were able to get him on the phone?" Charlie nods, collapsing into a nearby chair.

9

Now on the road, Mark changes lanes and passes a swerving SUV. As he passes the "Welcome to New York" sign, Mark continues to fly in the left lane. Hiding on the side of the road, a cop turns on his lights. Giving chase to Mark, the cop accelerates.

Mark can only mutter a "shit" as he pulls over to the side of the road. As he pulls out his license and registration, the officer approaches Mark's window.

"Do you know why I pulled you over?" the officer asks, pointing his flashlight into the car.

"No sir, would you care to inform me?" Mark asks back, not obnoxiously but not far off. "Have you been drinking tonight, sir?" the officer quickly replies.

"No sir..." Mark looks up at the officer's nameplate, it reads Officer Wright, "...Officer Wright."

"Where are you going at this time of night?" Wright asks. Mark says in no uncertain terms, "My father is in a hospital."

Wright looks up from the license and into Mark's eyes, "Is that the truth son?"

"Unfortunately officer...that's the truth," Mark replies. Wright hands Mark back the license. "Go see your father, just be careful out there."

Mark grabs his license and places it back in his wallet, "Thanks officer; you have a good night."

Wright heads back to his police cruiser and turns off his siren lights. Mark puts his car in drive and continues his way down the highway.

Officer Wright watches as Mark's vehicle becomes just a speck on the horizon—its red tail lights no longer visible. He grabs his coffee out of the cup holder and shakes it about. Putting it to his mouth, he downs the remaining liquid. Placing the cup back into the center console, he slowly pulls back out onto the highway.

Wright has been driving these highways for a long time. The lines around his blue eyes show the years. The grizzled stubble on his chin the product of being too hung over to shave this morning. He's in his early 50's, still policing the road at an age when officers usually settle into a desk job. It's the middle of the night and all he has is the sporadic noise that comes through the radio. This quiet New York suburb is dark, the faint lights of the city just visible on the horizon. He continues down this highway in the middle of the night.

His stomach grumbles, he's hungry, he hasn't eaten today. He was tired of having oatmeal every morning in his apartment. Tired of making the same thing every day, alone in that place. Tired of the routine. He should have been better than this, he thought. He should be sleeping. Waking up early to take kids to school, punching the clock and then heading home for his son's baseball game. He never settled down, he stayed out in the cold. He drives these quiet roads alone late at night in both his professional and personal lives. Wright never got it together. He tried to stay the wild card, the maverick, for as long as he could. He thought he had all the time in world to settle down and live a life until the day that he didn't. He blew relationships that could have produced something fruitful. He wasted opportunities of getting that desk job and nice pension by being the loudmouth at the bar who used his position to be an asshole. His later life was marked with self destruction including a blown breathalyzer—which would have ended his career were it not for someone in his own department that covered for him the night he drank a little bit too much and then hit that tree. Officer Wright's life was one big swing-and-a-miss. A lot of people strike out. People know when they strike out in life, know that the clock is running and that this game will end in defeat. Some bury their head in the sand and hope, while others are acutely aware of this failure and dwell on it—smacking themselves in the face every time they look in the mirror. Wright was looking in the mirror a lot more recently.

Wright pulls off the highway and onto the nearby suburb streets. It is dead quiet—the street lights the only things illuminating the way. Everyone is tucked in, asleep, waiting for the sun to come up. As he passes house after house he revels in the calm. The quiet. His stomach growls. He's hungry.

A black cat peers off the top of a garbage can—its eyes solid, stoic, reflecting the headlights of Wright's car. Wright stops his car as the cat continues to fix its gaze on him. The cat makes a quick move off the top of the cans and darts across the street, stopping only once to look back at Wright. He continues to traverse these quiet streets for the next few hours, only coming upon life sparingly. He pulls into a 24-hour diner on Wilmot Street, one of those old-fashioned diners that looked like it was delivered by a traveling circus—the base looking like it could be fork-lifted onto a stakebed and taken far away from this place. Rust stains the upper edges of the roof molding, streaks of brown running from top to bottom. The metal of the handrails are either unpolished or paint chipped, it's a worn home to those hungry at 3 a.m. Wright pulls into the third spot in the parking lot, eyeing an idling 90's Camaro toward the back—exhaust seeping loudly from the tailpipe. He grabs his jacket and as he exits the car, draping it over his shoulder. The weather has dropped a few degrees; it may rain soon.

The diner is empty, the only stragglers seem to be city folk, the local college was out of session. Wright accounts for eight people—the old man sipping soup in the corner booth; young lovers having their quarrels near the television; four young men, definitely drunk, who hushed their voices a few octaves when they saw Wright enter the diner. Finally, a young woman reading a book, not a speck of food on her plate touched.

Wright takes a seat at the counter on the right side of the restaurant, draping his coat over the back of his seat.

"Is there something I can get you, Officer Wright?"

Wright looks up to see Allyssa, his usual waitress. She's in her late 20's with dark hair that was always tied in a bun. She is pregnant, her belly growing a little bit every time Wright sees her, she must be about seven or eight months along by now.

"Coffee, just coffee," Wright replies.

Allyssa grabs a cup off the steam rack and places it down in front of Wright, filling it slowly.

"Tell me when to stop."

Wright keeps his eyes on the cup as its contents grew higher and higher.

"Stttttttttop," he spouts as Allyssa stops pouring. Wright takes the coffee and puts it to his mouth, closing his eyes as it travels down his throat, a supercharge to his mind.

"You have the best coffee," Wright mumbles.

"What?"

"You have the best coffee," Wright says again, this time clearly. Allyssa tips back the pot again, refilling his cup.

"You deserve it," she says.

Wright tips his cup to her and drinks once again. Allyssa walks out from behind the counter and toward the tables, asking each customer if they needed a refill.

Wright spins around in his chair, looking out the set of windows on the east wall of the diner. A speck of light was coming up on the horizon.

He watches Allyssa as she navigates the diner. Sliding across the tiled floor, spinning like a ballerina, refilling coffee cups without stopping. What was she doing here? Why wasn't she home? Why was she working the night shift, where all sort of obnoxious characters lurk? She should be home; she shouldn't be doing this.

It looks like the four guys are giving her gruff; Allyssa walks away with her head down. She returns to the counter, punching something into the register.

"You okay?"

Allyssa turns to look at Wright. She cocks her head, "Yea, I'm fine." Wright turns back around to look at the four men who, when seeing Wright fixing his gaze upon them, put their heads down and take to muttering quietly.

Once again turning back to the counter, he puts his coffee cup to his mouth. Allyssa finishes up at the register and prints out a receipt, slowly returning to the table of the four men.

Wright adds some whole milk and sugar to his coffee. He rubs his eyes. They feel heavy. This coffee isn't helping.

Two of the men get up from the table and make their way to the front door, exiting quietly and swiftly. Soon a third follows, putting on a baseball cap backwards and leveling his eyes at the ground. All that is left is the loud one, who finishes his coffee and reclines into the booth.

Wright looks back out the east windows and sees the three men get in a car and quickly peel out. Wright sees the fourth man rise from the booth, holding the check in his hand. He places it into the check holder, raising it toward Allyssa.

"Keep the change," he says, in a low gruff voice that was different from his loud tone of before.

Allyssa waves him thanks and goes back to tending to the old man a few tables away. She then makes her way over to the no longer loud section of the diner and opens the check holder...its empty.

"Fucker," Allyssa says, at first loud then trailing off to a hushed silence. Wright turns to see Allyssa looking out the window.

"What's wrong?" Wright asks, getting out of his chair and heading toward Allyssa.

"He ditched," she says, opening the check holder and turning it upside down. Wright bolts for the door, which causes Allyssa to yell out, "It's alright!"

Wright blows through the door into the cold night, his eyes search the world left and right, finally tracking the loud man, sprinting across the street.

"Stop!" Wright screams. The loud man looks back slightly and only increases his pace, dashing into the darkness.

Wright begins to run, puffs of his warm breath trailing him. He continues to yell toward the man, each plea a bit more strained. Wright keeps the boy in his sight though, seeing him turn down a neighborhood street.

Thank God I had that coffee, Wright thinks.

It's the only coal powering this locomotive. He begins to gain on the boy, who is quickly losing steam, his legs wobbling, his head down. He stops briefly, looking as if he was about hurl, he must be a smoker. Wright just hoped the boy's body crashed before his does. As Wright turns a corner he sees the boy about 50 feet ahead of him. Then he feels his engine seize, a quick pain in his gut. He's tired, he's sucking air, the temperature making each breath burn. But he's determined and the boy is within ten feet when he makes one final push. The boy turns around just as Wright is about to grab him, a shocked look in his eyes that this lumbering relic of the past was about to apprehend him. He cuts toward the street and Wright goes flying by, tripping on an uneven sidewalk, falling to the ground, sliding a few feet more. Wright looks up from the pavement to see the boy looking at him from five feet away.

"Give me the money," Wright says, "and you can go home." The boy looks back at Wright, standing emboldened, pitying this old man on the concrete. The car with the three boys from before pulls up behind the loud boy, the back passenger door opens.

"Fuck you, pig," the loud boy says back, climbing into the car, which screeches away before its back door is closed.

Wright rolls onto his back, looking at his elbow, blood dripping off of it like a leaky tap.

"I should have got that guy, fuck."

Wright gingerly climbs back to his feet, the knee torn in his pants, his back stiff. He begins to walk back to the diner, a pain in his knee worsening by the second. It was the longest walk, a walk of defeat. How could he go back in there and tell Allyssa he didn't get the money, that he didn't get the guy, that he failed?

Wright crosses the street and heads to the gas station, stopping at the ATM, he withdraws $60, placing it in his back pocket. A few minutes later, he stands outside the diner. Limping up the steps, he pauses for a second to compose himself. Wright swings open the door and heads toward the counter. Allyssa looks up and hurriedly runs toward Wright. As she approaches she sees the tear in his knee and bloody elbow. She gasps and expresses concern, which Wright quickly shoots down.

"What happened?" she asks, looking him over to see what kind of shape he was in. Wright pulls the $60 out of his back pocket and hands it to Allyssa.

"I caught up with him down the block and in exchange for not getting arrested, he gave me the money for the bill," Wright says.

Allyssa looks at the money and then says, "But this is more than the bill was."

"I must have scared him then; keep it as a tip, you need it more than he does," Wright says, continuing with his Clint Eastwood narrative.

"They'll never come here again, and if they do, you call me," Wright finishes, his voice dropping a few levels.

Allyssa gives Wright a hug, holding him for a second, saying, "Thank you" quietly as everyone in the diner watches.

"I gotta get going; I have to head back to the station before the end of my shift," Wright mumbles out.

Allyssa releases her hug and grabs Wright's hand, looking into his eyes. They both fall silent.

"It's my job," Wright says, grabbing his coat off his chair and turning toward the door. He gives Allyssa one last look and leaves, heading to his car.

Walking across the parking lot, he tries to feel better. Even if it was a lie, Allyssa was better for it.

Wright drives back down that quiet dawn road, the speck of light on the horizon now a full-blown beacon, a pinkish hue lighting up the sky. Wright sits at a stop light, reaching into the glove box for some gauze to clean his elbow, dabbing some alcohol on the wound. The newly green light shines on his face, causing him to press the gas while still eyeing his cut.

"Whoa!"

Wright stops and looks up quickly, seeing a man in front of his hood with his hands out.

"I'm sorry, officer," John Kenney says, a little shaken up. Wright sticks his head out the window, "You okay, son?"

"Yea, I'm sorry," John replies. Wright gives John a nod and continues on his way down the street. John shakes out his arms and continues crossing. He's sloppily dressed in a suit, his tie hanging loose, his shoes untied. He puts his foot up on a street bench and begins to tie each of them—loop, swoop and pull.

It's 6 a.m.; the morning light brings the birth of a new day. Coffee and bagel shops opening their doors for the morning rush, fresh baked bread sitting in brown boxes in front of doors next to wrapped morning editions. Street sweepers clean the roads before cars take residence in the daylight. John continues walking down this small town's sidewalks. Peering in windows to see workers prepping and drinking coffee to wake themselves up. John walks up to a flower shop, pressing up against the window to see if anyone is inside. The darkness reaches all the way to the back of the store.

John crosses the street and enters a coffee shop, getting a coffee with skim and two sugars, deciding at the register to get a blueberry muffin.

He returns to the flower shop to see not much has changed. He takes a seat on the bench outside and begins to drink his coffee and devour his muffin. This only distracts him briefly. Soon he sits forward on the bench, his foot tapping the sidewalk, maybe a side effect of the two sugars, maybe not.

John returns to the coffee shop and this time grabs a newspaper, deciding at the register to get another cup of coffee.

Back to the street bench he goes, the foot tapping recommences, this time it may have something to do with the sugars.

The town's clock reads 6:55 a.m. as John sees a man walking toward him, a paper under his arm, a hat on his head.

John gets off the bench as the man opens the front door to the flower shop and invites him in. John enters as the lights flick on, the fluorescents slowly beaming up to power, shining down upon the various flowers, plants and small baskets of budding bulbs.

"So what are you in the market for today, sir?" the florist asks, wrapping an apron around his waist.

"Some flowers," John responds.

"Good flowers or bad flowers?"

"What?" John replies.

"Are we getting flowers for something good or something bad?" the florist explains.

"Something good."

"Well that's a good way to start a new day," the florist says with a smile. After combing through some suggestions, John settles on an arrangement of roses. As the florist removes the thorns and wraps them up, John paces around the shop. He fixes his tie in the reflection of the flower case, first straightening, then retying it all together.

The florist finishes up and hands the flowers to John, who looks them over, nodding his head in approval.

"Thanks so much," John says as the florist punches the keys of the cash register.

"No problem; I hope they enjoy them," the florist replies. John hands over his credit card and is soon back to walking the sidewalks. He heads north toward the apartments on the hill. As he climbs the stairs to the courtyard, he starts to become spastic, his limbs shaking and his legs a bit weak. He enters the building and walks up two flights, his body now really jumpy. He walks to the door of 2B and stops for a moment. He closes his eyes, takes a deep breath and reaches into his pocket, pulling out a handful of keys. He opens the door slowly and closes it quietly, tiptoeing across the wood floors of this small apartment. He drops his keys on the coffee table and heads for the back bedroom, the morning light coming through the open door into the living room. As he nears the door, he sees the room lit a golden yellow, light bouncing all over the place. John walks up to the bed, getting down on one knee, looking at a woman with light brown hair. She is nestled into her pillow, blanket up to her chin. John tucks her hair behind her ear.

"Jenna," John says, quietly, just above a whisper. Jenna's body moves a bit, readjusting into the pillow.

"Jenna," he repeats, this time, with a bit more of a reaction.

"Go back to bed, we have time," Jenna mumbles without opening her eyes. John smiles and reaches into his pocket, pulling out a small blue box, opening it in his right hand.

"Jenna."

Her eyes opened, squinting, adjusting to the morning light.

"Hey, green eyes," John says. Jenna sees the flowers and the ring, a feeling slowly warming over her.

"Jenna, I want to wake you up for the next 65 years...if that would be okay with you," John says with a smile. Jenna sits up in her bed quickly.

"Will you marry me?"

Jenna's mouth agape, right hand on her heart, "Oh my God." John smiles back.

"Yes," Jenna gets through her smile. "Yes, yes, yes!" John puts the ring on Jenna's hand and then climbs into bed with her, kissing his bride-to-be.

"My god what time is it? I need to go back to bed," Jenna says with a laugh, looking over at the clock, "Jesus 7:30 a.m., I had another 45 minutes left."

"Alright, I'll come back in 45 minutes," John says as he climbs out of bed. Jenna pulls him back by his tie, "You're not going anywhere." John happily falls back into bed.

"I love you."

"I love you, too."

John gets laid, because if there is one time that a guy is definitely going get laid in his life, it's this time.

Later, as he lies in bed, Jenna bounds out of the bedroom, heading toward the living room, grabbing the house phone on her way. She settles into the sofa and flips open her phone book, dialing and dialing, sharing the news in seconds flat. She calls her father and her girlfriends, starts pondering dates. John listens from the bed, smiling as she does it. He no longer feels nervous or unsure of himself, he is completely and utterly devoted to this woman. He is 28. He's building something, hopefully lasting. But like everything today, who knows?

Jenna jumps in the shower to get ready for work and John gets out of bed, puts his suit from before back on and grabs his cell phone off the nightstand.

John sends out mass texts to people about the news. His friend Chris D'Ascoli wrote back, "Huge mistake." Others reply with a tame, "Congrats." He calls his mom; she couldn't find the words. His sisters congratulate him and then quickly get back to their own marriage and kids. Both of his sisters sounded like they were doing a few things while talking on the phone, one strapping in the car seat, the other buttering toast and making lunch for her daughter, Emma.

Jenna gets out of the shower and gets dressed quickly, having lost track of time while calling to tell others the news. She kisses John and runs out the front door. He brews some more coffee and takes a seat on the couch. Just like that, it's quiet again.

He putzes around the apartment for a few, puts the flowers he got Jenna in a vase, and sits them on the windowsill. His phone begins to ring, picking it up he hears his friend Matt McDonnell's voice. Matt was from way back—his running buddy for close to a decade now, his closest friend.

"So you did it?" Matt says on the other end of the phone.

"Yea, it went great actually. She didn't say no...so that's always a plus," John replies.

John walks back to the kitchen to pour the now brewed coffee, his third of the day. He looks out the window down into the courtyard. A father walks his son down the steps, adjusting the straps on his backpack.

"You at work?" Matt asks.

"No I'm going in late today, I don't have anything until ten," John replies, his eyes looking away from the father and son.

"Alright, give me a call later."

"Alright man, I'll talk to you later," John says as he hangs up the phone and drinks his coffee. He quickly recoils, and sets the coffee down on the kitchen counter. Enough coffee he thought, it's only nine in the morning.

Parking his car at work, John wonders how he should let the news flow. Tell everybody at once, or just let the information float out to anyone who asks. He wasn't tremendously close to any of these people but still, he should tell people, right?

He then remembers what his friend Richard Baratta told him years ago when he found out he was going to be a father.

"I can tell every person in here, but honestly nobody really gives a shit," Richard said that day.

He opens the glass double doors of the firm to see his co-workers working the phones, trying to sell ad time on this radio show or that television show. Men and women tell the voice on the other end of the phone why they should put their product in between the music or during primetime. John exchanges waves and good mornings as he makes his way to his office. Dropping his briefcase on the desk and his coat over his chair, John settles in for another day of hawking wares. As he picks up the phone to make his first call he hears a knock outside his office. Looking up, John sees Elliot Lee who wears a scowl.

"Peterson didn't come in again today," Elliot says. John puts his phone back down and rubs his chin.

"Did you call him?"

"Yea I called him and he didn't pick up; it's bullshit, John. He hasn't been doing anything for two weeks—now he's missing days," Elliot continues bitching, his voice rising as John gets up from his chair and closes the door. Elliot sits down, his arms crossed, scowl still present. John returns behind his desk.

"I'll call him," John says, trying to assuage Elliot.

"It's bullshit, John. It's fucking bullshit. He makes more than me, is here less and I still have to do all his work, I don't mean to be bitching your ear off bu—"

John puts his hand up, "I hear you, alright? Just go back to your office, I'm gonna call him."

Elliot huffs and puffs out of the John's office, closing the door behind him. John throws two middle fingers in the air and waves them about to no one in particular. He opens his rolodex and dials Peterson's number.

Answering machine. John thinks for a second; Peterson's missed three days in a row. Something's up. He hangs up the phone.

John looks down at his watch, 9:45 a.m. Grabbing his coat, John opens his office door and walks across to the receptionist.

"Hey Janette, I'm expecting a call at ten from this guy Roger Daldry, he's a rep out of North Carolina. I have to run out unexpectedly, when he calls in can you forward it to my cell phone?"

"Any other calls that you would like forwarded to your phone while you're out?" Janette says as she makes a notation on her desk blotter for the Daldry call.

"If Jenna calls you can forward her on through," John replies.

"How's she doing?"

John smiles, "She's good...we got engaged this morning."

Janette looks up from her blotter with a smile. John puts his finger to his mouth, as if to say, *keep it a secret.* Janette gets up and gives John a hug and a kiss, "All the best."

"Thanks Janette," John says, turning toward the glass double doors. He wonders if she really gives a shit.

In the car now, John takes the call from Daldry. He's looking to expand on his furniture empire out of North Carolina. He's fishing for quotes on what a campaign might cost—radio, television, the whole shebang. John knows he's fishing and doesn't want to dismiss Daldry completely, putting another call on the books for next week. Peterson's apartment looms up the road. The spire atop the apartment growing longer as John crosses each block. As he pulls up in front, John spots his car across the street with a ticket on its windshield. John takes out his cell phone and gives Peterson one more call before entering the building.

Answering machine.

John doesn't know what to do; he needs an answer as to why Peterson has been slowly disappearing over the last few weeks. He used to be tack sharp, now he coasts, drops work on Elliot—who put up with it for a while, but has been burned too many times for this to continue. John likes Peterson, thinks he's a good guy, but he can't afford for him to drag his division down. John goes back to his car, going so far as to open the driver side door, but he stops. He needs to know. John heads for the vestibule door.

Walking into the building with another resident, John checks the mailboxes.

Peterson—12B.

He reaches the 12th floor and walks down the hallway looking for 12B. An elderly woman exits her apartment with a parakeet, squawking in its cage as she walks toward the elevator. Down the hallway, John sees a woman storming toward him, shirts and pants on hangers over one arm and rolling a suitcase behind her. She is discombobulated, dropping her keys as she walks, causing her to contort her body in a way to avoid from dropping the closet's worth of clothes to the floor. John jogs over and grabs the keys off the floor, placing them back in her hand. The woman continues without a word.

John watches as she power walks toward the elevator, getting on the lift just as the lady with the parakeet enters.

As John gets closer to the end of the hallway, he sees 12B come into view, the same apartment the power walking garment hoarder just exited from. John proceeds with caution, slowly moving toward the door, which is open just a bit. Music leaks out into the hallway through the open door, getting louder as John approaches.

He knocks, but the sounds of Dylan's "Idiot Wind" overpower it. John cracks open the door and peeks inside. The apartment is a mess, clothes line the floor, segmented out—some folded, some in big piles. The drapes wide open, shining through the apartment a harsh white light on a disaster area.

"Hello?" John says loudly, trying to speak over Dylan. John moves a little further into the apartment, looking down a hallway, pictures taken down off their hooks, resting against the wall.

"Peterson?"

John continues his search, walking down the frame littered hallway, looking into half empty rooms. He reaches the end and a closed door. Opening it slowly,

John sees Peterson sitting by the windowsill in a bathrobe, a mug in his hand, looking down at the street.

"Peterson," John says. Peterson spins around fast, startled. John puts his hands up, waist high.

"What are you doing here?" Peterson says, getting up out of his chair and tying his bathrobe.

"I came here to make sure you were alright, you haven't been...at work...are you alright?"

Peterson takes a drink from his mug and returns to the windowsill, "I'm fine; you should get back to work."

John looks around the room, one pillow remains on the king size bed, the closet empty, except for a few dress shirts and suit jackets. Scuffed dress shoes litter the floor.

"What happened?"

Peterson shakes his head, putting his mug down.

"What do you think happened?"

John walks a few steps closer but decides against going any further.

"You know we...we try and keep the balls up in the air all the time, we try to balance things...to keep things fresh, to keep feeling in our lives. But eventually we just lose it all. We lose ambition or honesty; we become the things we always hated in our parents. The indifference swallows us whole. The big lie is in fact the balance; it's impossible. You're either chasing pussy or you're chasing money; you can't have both. You start chasing that money and the hours get longer, your life shorter. Things were much easier between us when there were fewer balls in the air. So I pull back on the job, miss a few days, call in sick, leave early for a 'doctors appointment,' try and fix things, but now I'm bad at two things...instead of one. I lost her and all the balls hit the floor," Peterson says.

"I'm sorry man," John offers, not sure how much of a help that is.

"Thanks, I appreciate it."

"Do you wanna go get breakfast or something? We don't have to talk about work or anything lik—"

"No, it's alright," Peterson interrupts. "I have some stuff I have to do here...like buy some clothes hangers. She took all of my clothes hangers," Peterson mumbles.

"Alright well, I'll get out of your way—If you need anything...uhh—give me a call," John says, starting to make his way to the hallway.

"John."

John turns back around to Peterson.

"Am I fired?"

"No, I'll see you when I see you," John says, tapping the wood panels of the door and pushing off down the hallway.

Peterson stays looking out the window, a view that looks right down on the main street in town.

It's busy, rush hour has passed; it's mostly soccer moms running errands. Peterson hears the front door close. He gets off his ass and heads toward the living room; he stumbles over one of the framed photos in the hallway. He looks down at it, something from a day in the past; it feels fake in a way. They should have known then, he thought. They should have taken it off the cliff and moved along. Peterson tosses the frame down the hallway, toward the bedroom, smashing it to pieces.

"Hey babe, make sure you wear shoes when you go to the bedroom, there's some broken glass down there...oh wait you're fucking gone, fuck you!"

Peterson continues to the living room, taking *Blood on the Tracks* off the record player, "...that's enough depressing shit for right now." He pulls out Fleetwood Mac's *Tusk,* putting on side two.

"What Makes You Think You're the One" begins to blare through the house speakers. Peterson turns the dial all the way to max. Running over to the windows, he opens them, he thinks about jumping, but this song is too good not to listen to. Lindsey Buckingham singing for every guy that has ever walked this fair earth.

Peterson begins to sing with the song, *"What makes you think I'm the one/Who'll be there when you're callin/What makes you think I'm the one/Who will catch you when you're fallin."*

Dancing around his living room, morphing his hurt into something else, crumbling to the floor, he continues, *"Everything you do has been done/And this won't last forever."*

Lying on the floor, with the wind blowing in through this window above his head, Peterson stares at a stark white ceiling. The song ends and the world is silent for a few seconds. No music, no honking from the cars on the street below, no squawks from Mrs. Feely's parakeet.

Just silence.

And then it comes on.

"Every night that goes between/I feel a little less."

Stevie Nicks tears a hole in the ceiling.

The first few bars of "Storms" wash over Peterson like a rising tide, his eyes closing, listening to Stevie singing for every woman who has ever walked this unfair earth.

Peterson opens his eyes and the ceiling may as well be blue, his eyes running, looking up through glassy pupils. Every fight, argument, disagreement— summed up in this tour de force by Ms. Nicks.

"So I try to say/Goodbye my friend/I'd like to leave you with something warm/But never have I been a blue calm sea."

"This house is empty," Peterson says into the air. The words float out the window with the breeze. Stevie makes her closing arguments as the bass winds down, seeping from the speakers into the floorboards.

"I loved you from the start/Save us.../And not all the prayers in the world -- could save us."

Peterson takes a football near his head and flings it at the record player, knocking it and *Tusk* to the floor, once again bringing silence to the world. It was hers anyway he thought.

Peterson gets up, wipes his eyes and heads for the kitchen. Grabbing a broom out of the closet, he sweeps up the broken glass near the bedroom. Then he begins to assess, walking around and seeing what's left in this place. What she left is almost as telling as what she took. The dark spots on the walls, the dust cleared areas of the bookshelf. It's as if a painting had just certain colors flushed out of it, leaving strange anomalies on the surface, the darkness fading toward the background.

Peterson places the record player up on the shelf and puts *Blood on the Tracks* and *Tusk* back in their sleeves. He drags the large metal garbage can from the kitchen into the living room, placing it dead center. He starts to comb the apartment, picking up things and throwing them into the can. Photos, old socks, yellowed letters. All things that made him feel empty, reminded him of her. He rehangs some pictures, makes his bed, putting the one remaining pillow dead center. He straightens his closet, finding some old cheap plastic hangers in the back, he hangs up all his shirts, arranges all his shoes. His hidden cigarettes above the stove go into the garbage, but not before taking one out and lighting it. He walks through the apartment with the cigarette dangling from his lip, perhaps his last fuck you to the old lady, the carcinogens seeping into the walls she wanted to paint taupe. The smoke flutters around his head, enveloping his dome in a haze. He thinks about flicking the lit cancer stick into the morning pages lying on the floor. He thinks better of it. He heard being burned alive was pretty painful. He instead puts it out under the water tap, letting it escape his fingers down the drain.

Peterson takes the trash down the hallway and dumps it down the garbage chute. He returns to the apartment and takes a moment to consider this reconstituted Monet, its worldview a little less cluttered, but no less clean. He realizes she took his favorite book. He feels angry for a moment, but then the moment passes. Everything looks in its right place.

Peterson takes a shower and a shave, flosses even. He puts on his father's watch and the finest pinstriped suit in his closet and returns to the living room. He grabs a piece of paper and a pen off the desk and sits down at the kitchen table. He begins to write.

Angel Sara with the Brown Eyes,

I'm sorry that I've disappointed you Over & Over, my selfishness

doomed us. Don't Think About Me, I'll Never Forget You.

Always look out for the Storms.

That's Enough For Me.

Sincerely,

-E

Peterson puts the pen down and straightens his tie. Walking over to the window, he walks out on The Ledge and plummets to his death.

Peterson died on the way down. He imploded before he ever hit the sidewalk. Soon police are on the scene, moving along the soccer moms Peterson was looking down on before. He died in his favorite suit, blood now staining the lapel.

Rashida James, a crime scene investigator, crosses the police line and picks up the sheet covering Peterson. She looks him over then drops the sheet back down.

"Any idea what happened here officer?" Rashida asks the man first on the scene. The officer flips through his pad, running his finger along the chicken scratch.

"People up on 12 said that Mr. Peterson here has had some marital troubles as of late and that his wife moved out this morning. We got in touch with the wife, she's upstairs, she's damn near catatonic. We called his place of business, he missed work today and a man by the name of John Kenney, a superior of his, came by to check on him. He seems to have missed a lot of work in the past two weeks."

"Any motive he would have to do this?" Rashida asks, looking up toward the window.

"Who?"

"Mr. Kenney."

"It doesn't seem that way, he was back at his office when this all went down, he's clean, it all checks out."

Rashida nods her head, "Alright, thank you officer." She takes one more look skyward and then pulls out a camera to take pictures of the scene.

Up on 12 now, Rashida looks at the note Peterson left. She peeks around the apartment. The bare shelves. She then moves toward the back bedroom where Peterson's wife Sara sits on the bed, staring out the window.

"Mrs. Peterson, I'm sorry for your loss," Rashida says from the doorframe. She waits for a response. Sara doesn't move. Rashida returns to the living room where some police officers are standing together.

"We should get someone to come and get her, a sister or mother or something," Rashida says, taking off her latex gloves.

"We tried, she doesn't have anyone," one officer replies.

Rashida looks puzzled, "What do you mean?"

"She has no family members—she's an only child, both of her parents have passed away, we're working on getting someone from her office or a friend of some type, but she's not saying anything...she's alone right now."

"Wow...well..." Rashida seems almost dumbfounded, "I guess just make her comfortable, she can stay here as long as she likes; this is pretty open and shut."

The officers agree and head out into the hallway. Rashida again walks to the back bedroom. Sara remains still on the edge of the made bed. Rashida sits down next to her.

"Hi...my name's Rashida and I just wanted you to know that you take as much time as you need here. Some officers are gonna stay with you and if you need anything don't hesitate to ask."

Rashida reaches into her pocket and pulls out a business card, placing it on the nightstand next to Sara.

"That's a colleague of mine who deals with traumatic loss, if you need to talk to someone or whatever...whatever you need...and once again, I'm very sorry for your loss," Rashida says. Rashida puts her hand on Sara's shoulder. Sara swallows and turns to Rashida, quietly murmuring, "Thank you."

"You're welcome."

Rashida stands up from the bed and leaves the room. She walks down the hallway slowly, trying to keep her eyes from glimpsing the photos on the walls. A certain detachment is needed in his world, a world that feels like you have a fatal touch, that death is always just a phone call away. Rashida retreats from the apartment and heads downstairs; that would probably be the last time she ever saw Mrs. Peterson. She says goodbye to the officers outside the apartment, enters the elevator and disappears from this world just as quickly as she entered.

Downstairs, Peterson's body is being loading into an ambulance. Rashida has one final talk with the coroner, making sure all the bases have been covered.

"I'll see you soon," Rashida says, slamming the ambulance door closed. As the ambulance pulls away from the apartment complex, the coroner watches in his side view mirror as Rashida disappears again.

It's not too long of a trek to Williamson General Hospital. A few side streets and then the highway.

"What are you doing tonight?" Carl, the man driving the ambulance asks. Cliff squints out the window, "I hope it doesn't rain…and nothing I'm exhausted—I worked a double today."

"You?" Cliff asks back.

"Going out and getting drunk," Carl replies with a smile. Cliff nods and laughs, "I miss those days."

As the ambulance makes it way off State Street toward Union, Cliff raises the volume on the radio. The two men begin to bob their heads to an old song by John Pepper, each singing the lyrics quietly.

This is the end of the way/for every day I stay/Hope you're on the way/That you'll be back by May.

"What happened to him?" Carl asks.

"Who? John Pepper? I don't know…I think he died. Actually I don't know…I get all those guys mixed up," Cliff replies.

The highway is sparse. Carl changes lanes. Small raindrops dot the windshield, even with the sun in full bloom. Cliff begins to nod off, this double shift was killer, a lot of ugliness the last few hours.

"Go to sleep, I'll wake you up when we get there," Carl says. Cliff obliges, falling asleep in the passenger seat.

Carl pulls into the loading bay behind the hospital; Cliff awakes to the sound of the ambulance reversing.

The men unload Peterson's body, shuffling through documentation for what's to happen with him next.

"Get out of here man, I got it from here," Carl says.

"You sure?" Cliff replies, putting down his clipboard.

"Yea he's not going anywhere," Carl replies, pointing to Peterson. Cliff pulls off his jacket and heads for the locker room. Soon he's changed, clocked out and through the doors of the morgue.

"I'll see you tomorrow," Cliff yells back to the working Carl.

"See you tomorrow," Carl calls back.

Cliff walks through the basement hallways of the hospital, cutting upstairs through the back stairwell. Now out on the main floor, he stops at the hospital commissary, grabbing a bagel and a coffee. Not minding where he's walking, he bumps into a man, spilling the man's coffee on the floor.

It's Mark, finally at the hospital after his long drive, trying to escape his father dying upstairs.

"I'm so sorry man," Cliff says, grabbing napkins and sopping up the coffee.

"It's alright," Mark replies.

"Let me buy you another one," Cliff says, throwing the soaking napkins into the trash.

"Thanks man, I've been driving all night, I need something to wake me up," Mark replies as they head to the counter.

Cliff pays for his bagel and the two coffees and nods at Mark, "Have a good day."

Mark gives him a wave and then pours some sugar into the cup, pouring and pouring until he snaps out of his haze. He walks out of the commissary and heads back upstairs.

The family lounge on the ICU floor is much bigger than every other lounge in the hospital for some reason. The nicest place to wait while your favorite gravely ill person dies. No one spends much time in this lounge; anyone on this floor who comes to visit sits in the patient's room. It seems strange to waste time bullshitting in a lounge when most of these people have so little time left.

The only thing this lounge is good for is sleeping, which Mark's mother Jane is currently doing. She's curled up in a ball in front of the windows, using her son Charlie's jacket as a blanket. This is the first sleep she's getting in days. Mark looks down the hallway and sees Charlie sitting in the room with their father. They still haven't talked since Mark arrived, only sharing a short glance and a nod. Mark walks into the lounge and sits next to his mother. He drinks his cup of coffee as she snores quietly.

Charlie's brain is fried. His thoughts are a jumble. This cold coffee from hours earlier isn't helping him. Charlie's eyes wander around his father's room.

I hate hospitals and everything they represent. I hate the fake plants and the mass produced furniture. Such an expensive place, that is ugly in every facet. I can't stand it. Why does he have to die here? Why not at home or somewhere else? Just not here. He always hated being here. To die in a place you hate, could there be anything worse?

The wheezing of his father's oxygen machine shook him out of his thoughts. This room is closing in fast.

Mark takes another sip. Hospitals always have the worst coffee; I guess it isn't a pressing priority.

He goes to the nurses' station and finagles a blanket for his mother, bringing it back to the visitors lounge and draping it over her.

Mark does two jumping jacks to wake himself up then returns to the hallway. He twists his neck back and forth. Looking back down the hallway Mark watches as Charlie exits their father's hospital room and walks to the ice machine. He takes a drink of water and then disappears into the bathroom.

Mark turns back around to look at his mother. She lies there quietly, somewhere far away. She deserves the tranquility, even if it's only for a moment. His gut churns, angry with himself that he hasn't seen her. He knows this is the end, perhaps the easiest part of this journey—that the ugliness has passed. All that is left is the casket being lowered into the earth. She fought the war for a long time. He is only coming in to bring it across the finish line. A cloud shifts and the afternoon sun beams down through the large windows in the lounge, bathing Jane in warm sunlight. She awakens, looking across the lounge at Mark. He waves.

Mark turns back toward his father's room and begins to walk. He enters the room and takes a seat in front of the window. It's quiet; it's never usually this quiet. His father is still. Mark gets up out of his chair and moves closer to his father, hearing the oxygen coursing in through the mask over his mouth. He gets closer, he hears nothing. His father isn't breathing.

Charlie enters the room with a plastic cup of water, standing in the doorway, looking at Mark. Mark slowly turns and drops his head.

"He's gone," Mark says, moving past Charlie and out of the room.

Charlie moves to his father's bedside, lowering his head in close to his fathers, just like Mark did. His head comes up and his body spins. He looks out through the windows of the room, seeing Mark approach the nurses' station— two nurses bolt out from behind the desk and sprint toward him. They bust through the door and head for the bed. Soon their diagnosis is the same as Mark's, James is gone.

Charlie crumbles into a nearby chair and begins to cry. Mark continues to walk down the hall, his pace moving into a gallop. He walks back into the visitors lounge and the sun was gone, his mother once again cloaked in the gray of a stubborn cloud. Jane sits up on of the couch as she sees Mark standing on the edge of the hallway.

She knows.

Jane gets up and walks over to Mark, wrapping him in a hug.

"I love you," she whispers into his ear. She lets go and begins the walk down the hallway. Mark sits down, leaning against the wall, and watches her walk. It seems like she walks for days. It becomes the never ending hallway.

She reaches James' room and hugs her crying son, Charlie, balled up, sobbing next to his father's bed.

It was so quiet.

Charlie watches as one of the nurses brings breakfast into an ailing man two doors down—the nurse slowly cranking his bed upward. The man awakens, looking up at the nurse and smiling. He turns on his television.

Jane closes her eyes and prays for James. She kisses Charlie on the forehead and leaves the room.

Walking to the nurses' station, she ties her hair with a scrunchie and wipes her eyes.

"What do I do now?" she asks the nurse.

Mark rises to his feet and heads toward the stairwell. He sprints down the stairs, swinging around the corners. He stops on the second floor, his body reeling into the stairwell wall. He begins to weep, far away from anyone's eyes, anyone's judgment. His sniffles and wails bounce off the cold gray concrete, echoing into the highest recesses of this prison of steel and brick.

The second floor door opens and Mark turns toward the wall, wiping his face and faking a cough. He feels someone lingering behind him. He wipes his eyes one more time and then turns.

He sees Marie, her eyes still moistened hours after Andrew's death, standing with her arms crossed. Her hair in a ponytail, those big eyes that stared at Andrew in the diner, lit up by a nearby light.

"Are you okay?" she asks.

"Yea...I'm fine," Mark replies.

Marie pauses for a second, but then decides to keep moving, descending the stairs to the bottom floor. She enters the lobby and takes a seat on one of the large couches near the receptionist. She unfurls her hair, pulling out the elastic band currently holding it up. Her hair falls over her face, hiding her eyes for the first time in a while. She looks down at her shoes, white Keds, a speck of blood sitting on the edge. She stares down at the speck, it's seemingly growing with every second, about to engulf her entire shoe. Marie closes her eyes and breathes. One deep breath and then two, her small frame expanding and deflating.

She's been here for a few hours, waiting on a person she's never met to arrive. She hasn't slept, doesn't feel very tired though. More zombie-like, her arms and legs moving by their own volition.

She thought about leaving, but she doesn't know where she would go. Go home and go to bed? That suddenly felt like a waste. Sleep was for the dead now. She remembers the day her grandfather died. Marie watched as her grandmother did everything short of standing on her head over the next five days—talking, crying, living, making bacon, reading the newspaper. Marie was amazed by the continuous motion, unable to compute how someone can keep going, how her grandmother never sat down. It feels like there was too much to do to sleep. Maybe you just can't sleep. You're afraid of what you might see in your dreams. Maybe you won't dream at all; that would be the worst. Just blank space, a black hole in your head.

"Are you Marie?"

Marie raises her head and looks skyward. A woman, clutching her pocket book is standing directly in front of her. Marie looks at the woman for a second, her brain catching up.

"Yes."

"I'm Andrew's mom," the woman says. Marie gets to her feet and gives her a hug, laying her head down on Andrew's mom's shoulder.

"I'm sorry it took me so long to get here," Andrew's mom says.

"It's okay, Mrs. Winters," Marie replies.

"Call me Mary."

"I'm sorry we had to meet like this," Marie says, stepping back from Mary. Mary sweeps Marie's hair behind her ear.

"Me too, sweetheart," Mary replies.

Mary and Marie stand in the hospital atrium, sun beginning to peek through the glass ceiling.

PART TWO:
225

CHAPTER TWO

"The purpose of today's meeting is to give you tips on how to get back to work. Most of you here today have been on long term unemployment...some for the better part of two years. It's ugly out there, I'm not gonna lie to you. Things have changed, priorities have changed, expectations have changed. I know all of that can sound very scary but hopefully after today, each and every one you will feel a little bit more confident, a little more inspired; hopefully some of you may even have a better outlook on your situation. So let's get to work."

The man in the pinstriped shirt and green tie takes a seat in front of the assembled mass, a small conference room, packed to the rafters with people, each and every one with a story, a reason why they were there, a reason why they lost their job, their life, a certain lifestyle.

Charlie sits in the back, between a guy texting his girlfriend and an older woman taking meticulous notes on the labor officer's tips on finding a job. Charlie shifts between the man's words, his tips and tricks for getting an interview and the dry erase board just above the man's head, some faint words not exactly erased. When he tires of trying to make out departed sentences, Charlie stares at the various inspirational posters lining the walls. He snaps back to attention when the unemployed guy in the turtleneck speaks in that holier-than-thou voice, indignant to his current position in life, blaming the government, foreigners and

43

the burgeoning (a hilarious joke) youth work force for taking his job, the job he worked at for 25 years, a plane he jumped out of with a golden parachute. Charlie quickly grows tired of this man's rants, his declarations of the downfall of America, all while sporting a Rolex on his wrist, oblivious to the other stories of the people in this room—like the woman who lost her job, her husband and her house. Charlie is pretty sure she isn't wearing a Rolex.

It's a strange room, but telling. There really is one of every kind—old, young, black, white, brown, yellow—all people deemed expendable by others in positions of power, people who vary as greatly as the douche in the turtleneck and the single mother kicking a can and searching for a quarter.

As the labor officer goes over how to perfect your resume, Charlie excuses himself, retreating to the toilet. Putting some paper towels under the door and propping open the window, Charlie lights up and blows weed smoke out into the courtyard. One person knocks, but gives up eventually. The bathroom is pretty clean for a government building. Usually they are graffitied to the hilt, every asshole's tag from floor to ceiling tile. This bathroom is different. Charlie wants to shake the custodian's hand. This is strong weed. Charlie's been to a couple of these meetings, mandatory check-ins for those on unemployment for more than 26 weeks. Every one of them is the same—a living horror painting, every face the same, every face different—the state of America written on the faces of the downtrodden and broke.

Feeling properly refreshed, Charlie returns to the conference room, seeing even more people now in attendance.

Sitting on his chair is a piece of paper detailing the "feelings" after job loss. Running his eyes down the paper Charlie sees words such as *shock, denial, relief, anger, depression, acceptance.*

"Thank God I smoked that weed," he thinks. Charlie slumps into his chair, beginning to re-read the posters on the wall.

Charlie now sits in a living room. His feet are crossed at the ankles, his hands folded at his stomach. The dull hum of the television is the only sound that is heard in the house.

The funeral was yesterday. A send off for a man that few would say was less than grand. The funeral home and church were packed wall-to-wall with people from yesterday and today—friends, family, co-workers, all individuals who were touched in some way by this man, a man who fell out of the public eye as sickness started to take his body. Many hadn't seen James in close to three years, when the hospital carousel started and never let him go. The pictures that decorated the funeral home showed a man at the peak of his powers physically, emotionally and publicly. The man in the casket was the shell of what remained. He fought until his last day, not wanting the sickness to beat him. But like everything, his body had an expiration date. At the funeral, people preached to Jane, Charlie and Mark that James wasn't gone, his body had died, but he hadn't. That he was in a better place. That's what they say. It sounds all well and good when the person in the casket isn't your father or ex-lover. Jane doesn't remember much of what she said to anyone the past few days. A flurry of people offering condolences, Mass cards, guilt money. Mark stayed close to his girlfriend, the one piece of serenity in an otherwise chaotic existence. She balanced him, calmed him, deflected the bullshit. She went over and kissed him when she thought he needed it, held his hand when he sat in front of the casket and whispered something in his ear to make him laugh—the topic of the funny, something or someplace that only they know. Charlie entertained people he had never met before, though they knew him. He listened to stories about his father, that one time here and there when James was the party, the one taking the pictures or the guy they played stickball with. He heard how much he looked like his father, something that people said to him as if no one in the history of the world had ever said it to him. Charlie was used to seeing that momentary spark in someone's eye and then the big smile, "Oh my God, you look so much like him." The visage of his dead father now in full view anytime he looked in the mirror. It was exhausting.

Charlie turns the television off and slumps into the chair. He can't hear a sound. He just waits. For something, anything—whether it is a fire engine, a screaming infant, a gunshot—to break the silence. But there's nothing, just silence. As his eyes traverse the living room landscape, he can't help but be overwhelmed with the reminders of his father.

He bought that table in '94. That painting was hung on the wall the day I was cut from the lacrosse team in senior year. That television made its way through the front door on that day my Mom was sick with the flu.

All inanimate things, but all things that still had the lingering touch of his father.

The doorbell rings. Charlie gets out of his chair, throws a T-shirt on and goes to answer the door. On the other side is a large man, holding a tray of food. Charlie accepts the sandwiches, hands the deliveryman a tip and places the eats next to the others that had come in previous days. They have enough meatball heroes to last them until next spring. Charlie hates meatballs.

He pauses momentarily, trying to decide if he's hungry, he hasn't been in days. He wasn't tired either, hasn't slept that much. Charlie grabs his car keys off the counter, his coat off the rack and heads out of the door.

On the road, in his barely-hanging-on Civic, Charlie flips through the radio, trying to avoid static from the decades-old receiver. Tacky pop hits and bombs in the Middle East are the highlights as he moves up and down the radio band. After minutes of finding nothing, he opts to turn it off completely. He watches a mother walk a young boy across the street, holding his hand as the boy skips. The young boy is able to get away from his mother, who quickly catches up and scolds him. The light turns green.

Charlie pulls into the second driveway of Tennessee Street—the house with the yellow shutters and blue doors. The driveway is littered with pinecones and dead leaves. The car lurches over all of them as he finds a spot near the backyard. Charlie hops over a bush and climbs down the stairs on the side of the house— stairs that lead to a small brown door with a broken light above it.

He knocks twice.

Charlie looks up at the house and then peeks in the small window adjacent. He reaches up above the door and feels along the siding, coming down with a key, he opens the door and enters.

Inside, it's dark, the flat screen television in the corner has Sportscenter on mute. Charlie maneuvers around some clothes on the floor, which could be either clean or dirty, maybe a bit of both.

"Joe?" Charlie asks into the darkness of the basement. His voice echoes. Walking some more, he comes upon the old couch and its current occupant, Joe.

"Joe," Charlie says, shaking Joe awake. Joe pushes off Charlie hand, "Give me ten more minutes, Mom, I'll take the trash out later." Charlie shakes him again.

Joe looks upwards to see Charlie.

"I thought you were my mom giving me shit," Joe says as he rises from his stupor.

"Rise and shine Joseph," Charlie says, stumbling over some magazines on the floor on his way to the window, opening it with flair, light streaming through the room, basking it in all its unkempt splendor.

"What time is it?"

"Two o'clock," Charlie replies, returning to the couch and sitting next to the now vertical Joe. Joe reaches for the end table and picks up the bong, checking for some bud; he lights and inhales. He passes it to Charlie who does the same.

Joe exhales and then gets up off the couch. He cracks his neck left and right, doing a few pushups for good measure.

"I would have cleaned up if I knew you were coming over," Joe says, who grabs the remote and takes it off mute.

"You literally say that every time I'm here; I've known you for six years and I've never seen the floor. It could be zebra shag carpeting and I wouldn't be the wiser."

"They say marijuana robs you of ambition," Joe replies with a laugh.

Charlie takes another rip of the bong and places it on the coffee table, leaning his head back to stare at the ceiling.

"You want something to eat?" Joe asks as he makes his way to his make shift kitchen. Charlie remains fixed on the ceiling, "Nah, I'm alright."

"You sure? I just went shopping, got some Hot Pockets," Joe says, almost pleading.

"No, I'm good."

Joe unwraps the Hot Pocket and throws it in the microwave. He grabs a drink out of the fridge and leans against the counter, looking out at Charlie, who is flipping through channels.

"Do you want to do anything today?" he asks. Charlie shakes his head no.

CHAPTER THREE

"Call me when you get home," Mark says as he kisses his girlfriend, Emily. She throws her pocket book onto the passenger seat and closes the door, looking back at Mark and smiling.

Mark watches as she pulls out and disappears at the corner. He stays a beat or two, looking at the neighborhood. Mrs. Shelley on the corner with the blond hair has aged a bit since he last saw her. She works on her garden, pulling weeds and growing tomatoes. Mr. Lee and his black labradoodle, running down the street at the same time every day, he keeps his head down, indulging in whatever is coursing through his headphones. Mr. Asner, sitting on his porch like some sort of neighborhood guard, even though a stiff wind and a wayward dog could knock him to the ground—all of these characters in a story that Mark has been written out of. The only differences from those past days are a few gray hairs on Mrs. Shelley's head.

Mark is a little shocked about the reaction he got at the funeral. He had left for a bit, gotten away from this place for reasons one or another. People from the past greeted him and asked him where he was, what he was up to, how they had seen that show he had a small role in. They spoke of it as if he performed it right in their living room, the vivid nature of the details like it was the only thing that had remembered...ever. He remembered most of their names, forgot others and faked it for those he couldn't quite remember.

It's strange being back here, back in this place. He had left for a reason, knowing that this would be the event that would make him shadow this front door once again, knowing that he would have to see his brother again and his mother crying. Mark knew she would be crying, either for his father passing or because she thought about everything all over again.

Mark looks at the house. It's in shambles. Charlie obviously stopped caring, came and went at his leisure, only stopping to help his mother with the groceries. Mark was still angry with him, but held it together for his mother. He doesn't want to disappoint her; he never did, that's why he had to get away. Get away from Mrs. Shelley and her blond hair; get away from Charlie and his spiral, knowing that sooner or later he would pull Mark into it.

Mark walks over to the garage and pulls out a broom. Returning to the front steps, he begins to sweep, brushing the dead leaves and branches and twigs toward the sidewalk. As he sweeps, he begins to see the granite beneath, the stains that had developed with the leaves sitting there for so long. He sweeps faster. As he finishes the walkway, he sees Mr. Lee doing his second lap of the neighborhood, this time looking up to acknowledge Mark. Mark waves back and sweeps the final bit of branch into the street.

Returning to the garage with the broom, Mark stops for a second to look at the tarp-covered mass residing inside. He lifts up one side, seeing his father's restored 70's Camaro, still as shiny as the last day he drove it. It had sat in this garage since the day James went into the hospital. No one dare touch it, let alone drive it, since. James would not have been happy. He was stern, in a word. He could be described by a few other words, but they are not exactly welcomed in a formal setting. He was a complicated man—that might be letting him off the

51

hook. He was a prick at times. He was the cliché asshole father from 80's movies. You know the one who loved the car more than his son. The one that was really hard on his son protagonist, acting as the outward hand of either incompetence or bewilderment, berating his son and his choices for 89 minutes of the film's running time before pulling the deux ex machina of showing he really cared about his son. James was a lot like that, but he was never "redeemed" by a rushed screenwriter or a studio head worried the character was unlikable. He was an asshole. Not outwardly; he smiled through his teeth at the locals, everyone knowing his name—the "Mayor of Williamson" with his perfect persona and well-coifed hair, but inside the walls of their home, Mark and Charlie grew up with a sad asshole. Those two had different memories then those relayed to them at the wake. He was a man of two faces. Mark didn't like either. He drops the tarp and goes into the house.

Inside his mother is on the phone. Mark walks into the kitchen and rubs his mother's shoulder; heading to the fridge, opening it to see nothing, save for milk and a single beer.

Mark picks up his car keys and heads for the front door.

The local supermarket is undergoing a renovation, turning it into one of those big chain supermarkets with automatic checkout lanes sans clerks that people will never understand how to operate. Mark walks up and down the aisles, throwing this and that into the cart. As he wanders, he flips through the store circular, putting "x's" next to items of interest, something his father did when Mark was just a boy sitting in the shopping cart. Mark pulls his ballcap down over his eyes, not wanting to draw attention or have to deal with a stop and chat from the mom of someone he played CYO basketball with. Mark felt talked out; he's said every word in the death book. He's said thank you 1,000 times. It's all gotten to be too much. He knew people cared; he doesn't need to keep hearing it.

As the cart fills, Mark finds this and that, something his mother liked or used to eat. It seems food turns into a big thing when someone passes away. Comfort food isn't bullshit. People think it fills some void and usually it does, between your waist and kidneys. That's when he sees it.

Pop-Tarts. Charlie loved Pop-Tarts. Mark looks at the display for Pop-Tarts for five minutes before deciding to move on without grabbing one. Charlie can buy his own fucking Pop-Tarts. He leans over the rails of the cart, pushing it with his forearms, making a left hand turn into the frozen food aisle.

Then he sees her. Regina. Regina was short—it feels like she was the same height in kindergarten as she is now. She has long blond hair; so long you might think it was longer than her, tied in a ponytail atop her head. Brown, square glasses on her nose, she is looking at a frozen turkey, one of those big Butterballs, getting in close to the label, as if the words on it were the size of fleas. She puts the turkey down and picks up a smaller one, this time with one hand, the other one sliding into her back pocket.

Do I stop? Do I say hello or should I run for the check out lane? Maybe she won't see me; maybe I can get out of here unscathed.

As he inches closer, he debates, when the answer presented itself. A young gent, not much older than Regina, slides up next to her and puts his arm around her, he too now looking down at the turkey.

Mark puts his head down and keeps walking.

As he loads the groceries into the back of his truck, Mark sees Regina walk out of the supermarket empty handed. Guess she decided against the turkey. Regina and the guy get into a beat up Mustang and tear out of the parking lot, nearly running over an old man that looks a lot like Mr. Asner. Mark closes the trunk to his car and goes home.

As he drops the groceries on the kitchen counter, Mark sees his mother is still on the phone. He listens to her conversation as he loads up the fridge. Who knows who was on the other line—his mother having to repeat the same shitty set of circumstances of the past five years over and over again. He wondered how she does it; he would have taken the phone off the hook by now or just started peppering the story with outlandish tales to see if the person was really paying attention. Especially now, when all those people who "heard" call, wanting to express their "condolences" even though they didn't give a shit any second before this one. Maybe grief is just making him bitter. Maybe.

The front door opens and Mark cranes his neck to see Charlie sneak in and run up the stairs. He hears the bedroom door close upstairs. Mark finishes unpacking the groceries.

Jane gets off the phone as Mark walks back in from taking out the garbage. As she walks into the living room, the phone begins to ring again.

"Don't pick it up, Mom," Mark says, to his power-walking mother, already closing in on the phone.

"It might be someone; I have to answer it," Jane replies, picking up the phone.

"Hello?"

Mark shakes his head and grabs a cup out of the cabinet, filling it with ice and tap water. Jane returns to the seat she left less than two minutes earlier, repeating the same shitty set of circumstances from the past five years.

CHAPTER FOUR

The lawyer's office is small. He's an old family friend, Mr. Garmin. He sits behind his manila folder-lined desk; flipping through the papers sitting on his blotter. Charlie and Jane sit in the two guest chairs in front of Garmin's desk. Mark leans against the doorframe.

Garmin is breathing heavily, sweat marking his brow. It's hot in the office—the air conditioner isn't working. Mark's eyes wander along the law books stacked on one of the shelves.

"I'm sorry, I'm just trying to get myself together," Garmin huffs out.

"It's alright, take your time," Jane replies. Charlie slumps into his seat. He looks like he would rather be anywhere else. Mark wishes that too, wanting to slap Charlie for being stoned as Willie Nelson for the reading of their father's will.

Garmin gets himself together and begins to flip through the will.

"This should be quick. As you know most of James' assets were wiped out in order to pay for his extended hospice stay, so there are only a few line items here that actually still apply," Garmin says, running his finger down the page.

"The primary residence, currently home to Jane and Charles, shall be given in full to my ex-wife Jane. She is now the prime signatory on the deed. Any other possessions, such as jewelry (except for any notations below), electronics and miscellaneous items shall also be given in full to Jane. My car, a '72 Camaro, shall be given to my son Charles. My collection of watches shall be given to my son Mark. All other property is to be dispersed at the discretion of my ex-wife Jane."

Mr. Garmin closes the will and reaches into a box sitting on the edge of his desk. He pulls out three envelopes, handing one to Jane, Charlie and Mark. Jane looks at the envelope for a brief second before putting it into her purse.

Charlie rips open his envelope, pulling out a single lined piece of paper. Opening it up, it reads—

"Don't fuck up the car."

Charlie shakes his head and shows it to his mother. Jane rolls her eyes, offering, "We should have buried him in that fucking car."

Charlie puts his father's final wishes back into its envelope. Mark opens his envelope to see an index card with an address written on it.

"225 N. Washington St. Butler, PA 16001"

"What the fuck is this?"

Passing the card to his mother, Jane looks at the address, trying to jog her mind. She shakes her head, handing it back to Mark.

"I don't know," she says.

"Was there anything else attached to this Mr. Garmin?" Mark asks, flipping over the index card, seeing nothing. Garmin looks back into the box and shakes his head.

As the three bereaved drive home, Charlie sticks his hand out of the passenger side window. Mark is falling asleep in the back seat—rubbing his eyes every few seconds trying to stay awake. Jane stays steady behind the wheel as she sits at the railroad crossing, waiting for the passing train to move through.

"I can't believe he gave me the car," Charlie says to no one in particular.

"Why do you say that?" Jane asks.

"I don't know, I figured...he loved that car more than anything in the world...I don't know," Charlie fades off.

"I'll give you the watches when we get home, Mark; I had them polished a few months ago...he loved those watches," Jane says, looking in the rear view mirror at Mark.

"Okay," Mark says, looking out at the barreling train.

Mark sits at the desk in his room, staring at the index card. He flips it, puts it up to the light, doing everything in his power to understand this simple 3x5 lined piece of paper. What's the illusion? What is this? It can't just be this; it has to be something more. Mark puts the card down.

"This is some mind game, some final 'fuck you' from beyond the grave. I'm gonna go there and I'm gonna find like a half brother or something else fucked up. Something that is gonna shatter my world and he's gonna be looking up—not down—up, just laughing, just completely fucking laughing at the final turd in the punchbowl," Mark says to himself, irritated at the very notion of this index card.

"The watches were good enough. Thanks Dad...I don't wear a watch but now I have 20 of them. I asked to wear one to senior prom but you said 'Fuck off, you'll probably scratch it, or lose it, get out of here. But wait...change the channel on the television; the remote's broken.'"

57

Mark screams at the card, his veins bulging out of his neck. He composes himself and gets up out of his chair, pacing around the room.

Jane pokes her head in the room.

"What's wrong? I heard screaming," she says. Mark waves her off.

"Nothing, I think it's just the dust in here; my allergies are killing me," Mark says, hoping to dissuade his mother from inquiring further.

"Let's go for a walk," Jane replies.

Jane and Mark walk under the late afternoon sun, little specks of sunlight shooting through the branches of trees above. Jane has a shawl draped over her shoulders, fending off the cool air the shade brings. Mark kicks small rocks along as he walks.

"You've been home almost a week and I feel like we haven't even had a full conversation," Jane says.

"I feel like I've talked to everyone else in the entire world...about the same thing 1,000 times," Mark replies.

"A couple of months ago, I read this book about death that said in the days and weeks afterward it's such a shock, such a rush, it's almost as if your body is running too fast to even realize what's going on...like your body is jumping out of a plane every hour," Jane says.

"I haven't really slept that much...but I haven't really thought about it either. Like I cried at the funeral, that's a given. But the wake? I just felt like I was interviewing for a job and the boss kept changing every three minutes. I felt like I needed to perform...or something...that me just being me wasn't enough."

"I hated the wake. You two just felt so far away…I'd look up and I wouldn't see you guys and I'd get this sinking feeling in my chest, like I was alone," Jane says.

"Alone…surrounded by all those people. Yea, I felt that too."

Jane pulls the shawl tighter, brushing her hair over her ear.

"Have you talked to Charlie at all?" Jane asks, looking down at the crooked sidewalk.

"Not really," Mark replies.

"I think you should," Jane says.

"We got nothing to talk about."

"I think he's very lonely. He never leaves his room anymore; he just sits in the dark listening to music," Jane continues.

"He needs to get a fucking job. He did it to himself. He had a great job, one that I got for him, and he pissed it away. He's a fucking loser…he's stoned constantly, he can't hold a job, it's embarrassing—the way he is," Mark replies, sparing no words.

"He's been through a lot," Jane replies.

"Yea and so have you and so have I…and so has every fucking person in the world that gets up in the morning, but we're not all fuck-ups like him."

Jane stays silent, knowing she's not going to win this argument.

"I'm sorry," Mark says.

"It's okay," Jane replies.

Jane and Mark cross the street. They walk into an open field, some park benches to the right, a baseball field farther out. Jane takes a seat at one of the park benches, Mark sits down across from her.

"You cut your hair," Jane says. Mark runs his hand from the back of his head to the front.

"You need to shave though," Jane continues. Mark laughs.

"I'm too lazy," Mark says, scratching up under his neck.

"You're so handsome; shave that crap off your face," Jane says.

The two sit in silence, feeling the breeze blow through the field, the sun low on the horizon, about to disappear.

"It's so nice," Jane says. The spring wind flies quietly, ruffling leaves blowing across the field, forming mini tornadoes at points. The grass is a light green, brown at parts, burnt out from the long winter. Jane closes her eyes and listens. Mark lies down on the bench, looking up at the tree above him. It's so quiet. So peaceful. They stayed there for a while.

Mark feels a pulling, one that points him toward the setting sun. He feels like he was levitating in this windswept habitat, hovering above the coming storm, the winds the sign of impending doom. So much left unsaid, too much shuttling through his mind, a truck stop on the road to ugliness. It would fester in him if he said nothing, if he lets the index card settle amongst the dust on his desk. If he never found out. As much as he doesn't want to know what was at the end of that road, he needs to, he has to open the box or the envelope or stare out into nothing there. His house is not in order. His mother is alone—he can't depend on his brother. Maybe he'll take Jane with him, leave Charlie with the house. Charlie would probably burn it down—maybe he can't take his mother. Maybe she is the calming force in this calamity of protons and electrons, the only thing holding this ship together. His mother's birthday is on Tuesday; he could get in the car and make it back by then. That's plenty of time. He sat up, looking to the left and seeing his mother, staring out into the field, her eyes glassy, her graying hair floating in the wind.

CHAPTER FIVE

"I'm leaving in the morning," Mark says. His mother turns from the sink, her hands covered in yellow rubber gloves, still scrubbing marinara sauce off a plate—their dinner from earlier.

"I'll be back by Monday," Mark continues. Jane puts the plate in the sink, it disappears into the suds.

"You don't have to chase it; it could be nothing," Jane says, sticking her hand back in the sink. "Whatever you find will just disappoint you."

"He gave me that card for a reason. Whether it's a punishment or a bank vault with his Rosebud in it, either way, I gotta know," Mark replies.

"Okay," Jane replies with a smile, returning to the dish-filled sink.

Upstairs, Mark packs some clothes into a gym bag. He juts around the room, grabbing things off shelves and from drawers. He hears the front door close, turning briefly to see Charlie fly up the stairs on the way to his room. Charlie gives a peek in on his way by, seeing his brother packing up.

"You leaving?"

Mark closes his desk drawer and looks up at Charlie.

"Just for a few days; I'll be back for Mom's birthday," Mark replies, throwing some pens and pencils from the desk into his bag.

"You're going to that address...lemme come with you," Charlie says, a plea at the end. Mark looks at his brother. Charlie sways in place, looking like he's about to jump out of his shoes, hoping he'll be picked for the kickball team.

"I don't think so," Mark replies.

"Why not?"

"Because I don't want to spend three days in a car with you," Mark says.

Charlie sinks his shoulders, a scowl marking his face.

"Fine...go fuck yourself," Charlie replies, retreating to his room, slamming the door as he does it. Soon his music nearly blasts said door off the hinges, "Notorious Thugs" by The Notorious B.I.G. reverbing in Mark's direction.

Mark closes his door, dulling the sounds coming from Charlie. His very loud sign of protest reaffirms Mark's picture of Charlie as a petulant child, ready to stomp his feet and scream at any second, always wanting to get his way.

Charlie opens his bedroom window and lights up a joint, blowing the smoke into the clear moon air.

The moon soon goes to bed and the sun rises on time, coming into Mark's back window, showing all of the dust floating in the air, inches above his bedroom's floor. Mark stumbles out of bed, takes a shower, kisses his mother goodbye and pulls out of the driveway.

A map sits on his passenger seat, his bag in the back and some food that his mother packed sits on the floor. Mark fills up at a gas station, grabbing a coffee and a scone for the road. Seen just off in the distance, cars are traveling past at light speed.

The index card sits taped to the dash, a red sharpie line on the map, charting Mark's course. It will probably take about a day to get there. He hasn't decided if he is going to do it in one shot. He probably shouldn't, but maybe he should. He is zoning already, the road merging and merging and merging, passing through towns, feeling like he's running in place.

Charlie awakes from his drug-induced haze; the sun is harsh, punching him about the head. He left the drapes open last night; he never does that. Man that weed was strong. It felt delicious, hitting the spot of self loathing just enough, satiating him for a few hours. He slept like a baby. Maybe he could still convince Mark to let him come with him.

Charlie scratches his balls, opens his bedroom door and sees his college degree hanging on the wall. He laughs. Turning down the hallway, Mark's door at the end of the hallway is closed. Good, he hasn't left yet.

Charlie rummages through the cabinets, pulling out some fruity pebbles, dumping them in a bowl with milk. He starts to formulate his plan to go with Mark. Maybe he'll just hide in the backseat. Talking isn't going to do it. Too much had happened for a simple conversation to fix this fucked car crash of a relationship. This morning feels like it is moving too fast.

Jane comes in the back door. Hanging her coat up, she comes over and kisses Charlie on the head.

"How are you, sweetie?" Jane asks, putting the kettle on the stove. Charlie drinks the milk out of the bowl, using his forearm to wipe his mouth. He returns to the kitchen, rinsing his bowl and putting it in the dishwasher.

"What are you doing today?" Jane asks, shuffling through the mail.

"I was gonna try and head out with Mark," Charlie replies. Jane looks up at Charlie.

Charlie darts out the front door, seeing Mark's car gone, he mutters a "fuck" under his breath. He opens the door to Mark's bedroom—empty. He can't believe he left. He thought maybe something would have gotten in Mark's head, maybe he would have taken pity on him. Well not pity...maybe pity—something that would have made him knock on Charlie's door before he left. Then again, he didn't knock the last time he left.

Charlie closes his bedroom door and returns to his seat by the window. He licks a rolling paper, drops some weed into it, rolls it up real tight. This is probably the thing he is best at. That's depressing somehow. He puts the joint to his lips and searches around the room for a lighter. The desk is empty, the one on the nightstand is bone dry. Looking under his bed and loafers, he comes up empty. Charlie returns to the window, putting the joint on the windowsill. He leans back into the felt of the chair, the sun hitting him right in the face. It feels warm.

Charlie packs a bag, prints out some directions, kisses his mother and heads for the garage. The garage smells like every other garage. Musty, the smell of old boxes in the corner stained with water damage. Charlie walks to the back of his father's Camaro and pulls off the tarp, rolling it up slowly, opening the trunk and placing it inside. He slowly unlocks the driver's side door, easing into the seat, treating everything with kid gloves. He's never driven this thing. Well that's not true. He took it out one night, never told anyone, rolling it out of the garage in neutral so no one would hear him until the engine roared upon ignition. He rolled it a half a block away before firing up the engine, peeling out down on Fenimore Road. Today is his first "official" time ever driving it, in case anyone asks. He puts the key in, and turns, filling the garage wall-to-wall with sound.

That sound was what he woke up to most Saturday mornings when his father would go on an early morning drive, that sound he heard when he peeled out that time on Fenimore Road. It was a beast this thing. It feels like Steve McQueen is about to walk into the garage, chase down a perp, pull the guy's ass out once he crashed and beat him to a pulp. Charlie understands why his father loved this car. He doesn't get why he did a lot of things, but he gets this one. Jane opens the garage door, walking up to the driver's side window.

"It sounds good," she says, peeking into the car.

"Yea, it feels good," Charlie replies, looking through the glove department. Charlie looks back up at his mother, extending her hand—money for the trip. He shakes his head, "No, I'm okay."

Jane smiles and puts the money back in her pocket.

"Well, call me if you need anything. I hope you can catch up to him, he left not too long ago," Jane says, looking out into the driveway.

"Be safe," she says, knocking on the doorframe. Charlie waves and slowly pulls out of the driveway. Jane follows him out into the street, grabbing the newspaper off the front lawn.

Mark changes lanes, merging onto the interstate. The road is sparse, a late morning work day drivescape. The middle lane is his friend, easy does it, cruising over the land, changing stations as he goes. He feels a small ringing in the chassis, as if the undercarriage had become his extended skeleton. He isn't worried; he's felt it before, a kink in the automobile that usually had to do with the changing of gears. This feels a little bit different though. The thought soon evaporates from his mind; static on the radio is the current topic of discussion between himself and the car.

Then a lurch—the ringing becomes a bumping, the bumping becomes a clanging. Mark feels a lacking, a loss of momentum.

"Fuck."

Heading off the nearest exit, Mark pulls into a nearby gas station and the car is put up on lifts. He thumbs through a magazine in the office. He's steaming. His head nearly as hot as this sun-lit window. He's hoping it's something small. Even if he's lost a night, he could check into that hotel nearby. He's not too far from home; he could get back if need be, but that opens up a whole other box of issues.

The minutes turn into hours, the two mechanics leaving at one point to go eat lunch, returning two hours later.

"What's the deal? Is it something that could be fixed?" Mark asks the returning mechanics, one still has a piece of lettuce sitting on his shirt.

"Oh, nobody told you? That engine is shot, it needs to be rebuilt," one mechanic says, returning behind his desk.

Mark looks up the ceiling, wanting to explode from the anger boiling from his toes to his throat.

"So how much is that?" Mark asks, biting his lip.

"About five grand...we can rebuild it, get you back on the road in a week," the other moneyman mechanic chimes in.

Mark rubs his chin and exits the office, loudly mumbling every expletive that he can formulate. He nearly trips on the curb, wandering out into the increasingly hot afternoon sun. He stops in his tracks, thinking of what his next move should be. He takes out his cell phone.

Jane turns off the vacuum and runs over to the ringing phone, picking it up mid-stride. "Hello?"

Charlie flies down the left lane, swerving into the center lane, thumbs running up and down the steering wheel. He turns up the radio, "Power" by Kanye West blowing out the old speakers, rumbling through the 70's steel. He lip-synchs, a gangster of this tin box, throwing his hand with each West punctuation. He's hoping to see Mark on the highway, humming along in the right lane, losing in the race to this finish line.

Charlie's phone rings, turning down Kanye, he answers, "Hello?"

Mark sits on the broken wooden bench outside the mechanic's office, leaning toward the ground—head still, hands in his lap, elbows on his knees. He looks out into the two-lane street beyond the gas station's jurisdiction. He sees the heat simmering off the asphalt; it's getting hotter by the second.

"So what are you gonna do man?" the mechanic says, poking his head out the window of his office. Mark gives him a half turn.

"My mom is picking me up...as embarrassing as that sounds," Mark says, balancing on the bench, trying to avoid falling through the splintered wood.

"Hold the car for a few days. I gotta think if it's even worth it to get a new engine...the thing's probably not even worth that much," Mark says turning back to street vision.

Then he sees it.

His father's Camaro—the dark green road warrior with the gold stripe from bumper to bumper. Mark shakes his head, thinking it to be a mirage. He stands up as the car pulls into the gas station, a tiny scrape of the street on the undercarriage. Mark flinches when he hears it.

The car stops in front of him, the rumbling of the idling engine sounds like a charging group of bulls on the horizon. Charlie kills the engine and gets out, standing behind the driver's side door, tapping his hand on the roof.

Mark takes a moment to look at his brother. This is his ride home, or to that address, somewhere. The thing he wanted to avoid, the only option at his disposal.

"I'll call you in a couple of days, I'll let you know what I wanna do with the car," Mark says, turning to the mechanic in the window. Mark grabs his bag from the curb, heading toward the passenger side door. Charlie lowers into the car again, firing up the engine. Mark tosses his bag into the back seat and reclines his seat. Charlie gives him a look, seeing his brother already drawing lines in the sand, standing off and claiming his own inches. Charlie pulls out of the gas station.

The first few miles are quiet. Charlie rarely looks off the road, driving slower than before, taking a steady pace. Mark remains reclined, his eyes closed, his body still, as if he was sleeping. Charlie can't tell if he is or not.

The radio is low, a quiet ambiance more than anything. Traffic develops around Route 84. Charlie eases off the gas, rolling to a stop, soon sitting in traffic as far as the eye can see. He lightly taps the steering wheel. He relaxes into his seat, his head hitting the head rest, seeing a group of girls in a Volkswagen Bug— girls in their teens, smoking cigarettes, heavy eyeliner.

I bet one of the girls' names is Ramona. A pop culture nurtured, crumpled pages of early Joan Jett biography, fuck men, I'm a woman hear me roar soaked abomination of punk groupies.

One of the girls looks off her Parliament just long enough to flip off Charlie, his eyes quickly sprinting to the forward, still not moving traffic. Mark remains still...maybe he's dead. Charlie doesn't want to say the first word.

Charlie gets out of the car and looks up over the traffic. He sees two guys throwing a football across the two-lane parking lot. He walks a few car lengths, hoping to see anything, any indication of what everyone was sitting behind.

He walks back to the car, giving another look to the goth girls rocking out to Fall Out Boy...he takes back the Joan Jett part. Joan Jett was fucking boss; these girls don't know Joan Jett.

Charlie gets in and closes his door. Back to the cone of silence.

"What's going on?" Mark says, not moving from his near catatonic pose. Charlie looks quickly down, then back forward.

"I don't know, there are cars for as far as I can see," Charlie replies. Mark sits up in his seat, pulling it out of recline.

"Where are we going?" Mark asks.

"The address," Charlie replies, trailing off as he says it.

"I told you I don't wanna go there with you," Mark replies.

"Then get the fuck out of the car," Charlie replies. Mark shakes his head, grabs his bag and leaves the car. He slams the passenger door.

"This fucker," Charlie says, turning off the car and getting out to follow.

"Where are you going?" Charlie yells after Mark, walking down the side of the road.

"What did you get into a fight with your boyfriend?" one of the goth girls says to a pursuing Charlie, who looks back but doesn't say anything.

Charlie catches up to Mark and walks in front of him.

"Where the fuck are you going?" Charlie asks.

"I'm not going with you; I'll head into town and rent a fucking Pinto as long as it means I'm not going with you," Mark replies.

"What's your fucking problem? You think you're so much better than everybody," Charlie replies, keeping pace with the fast walking Mark.

"No, I only know that about one person, you lazy piece of shit," Mark says.

"I'm a pothead, good one, you fucking mental case. You know what? Fine. Run off, little boy, just like you ran off on Mom and Dad," Charlie says. His words a body blow to Mark, who stops in his tracks. He gets right up in Charlie's face.

"Don't you fucking talk to me like that ever again because I will fucking punch you the fuck out," Mark says.

"Do it! That's what you've wanted to do for how long? Maybe I am the loser brother that you told everybody I was, the one that flushed all his potential away, the one that betrayed you...go ahead do it," Charlie says, goading Mark.

They stand chest to chest.

"Do it," Charlie repeats.

Mark steps back from Charlie, taking a seat on the highway side railing, dropping his bag onto the highway gravel.

Charlie takes aim on Mark.

"We've had our problems...we will never agree on one thing for the rest of eternity. And you know what? That's alright with me. But our dad is dead. Dead. He's never coming back. The last time we saw each other, some words were said and then you disappeared. Dad died and now here we are. We've made a life out of hating each other but now there are only three of us left. Me, you and Mom— that's it. You can keep being mad at me; we can fight until we're in the ground next to Dad—either way, I'm going to that address...with or without you. You're welcome to come along," Charlie says.

Mark pulls cigarettes out of his pocket, lighting one.

"It's up to you," Charlie says, turning and heading back to the car. Mark exhales, hanging his head and rubbing his eyes.

Charlie closes in on the car, shuffling through his keys.

"What did you kiss another guy?" the goth girl from before continues.

"Eat shit, Taylor Momsen," Charlie says, getting into the car and closing the door. Mark drops the cigarette to the floor, stomping it out with his boot. He looks toward the traffic. There must be someone sitting here who could get him back home. There's so much traffic up ahead.

He picks up his bag and heads the other way, back to his father's car. He kicks the small highway gravel, a wake up call for those sleeping behind the wheel that they're about to hit the railing. Mark kicks away, shuffling back to the Camaro. He opens the passenger side door and slinks into the car—landing on the seat quietly. He ruffles through his bag, pulling out his map. Placing it on the dash, he throws his bag onto the back seat. Charlie remains looking forward, rubbing his chin. Mark consults the map.

"Take the next exit, there might be a way we can get around all this traffic," Mark says, tracing his finger along the printed road. Charlie shifts into drive, pulling around the car in front of him, onto the shoulder. Rolling slowly past the parking lot that has developed, the car rumbles over the rocky terrain, each and every piece of uneven gravel lifting and dropping the car slowly. The Camaro gets off at Exit 47.

CHAPTER SIX

Darkness descends on the land. It's late now; the boys are exhausted from taking turns behind the wheel. The highway markers reflect in Mark's eyes. He looks over to see Charlie passed out, snoring something fierce, his temple resting against the window. The roads are pretty empty, a spare 18-wheeler here or there.

"Charlie," Mark says to his slumbering brother in the passenger seat. He repeats it, then repeats it again, unable to arouse him from his dream state. Mark punches Charlie in the arm, jolting him awake.

"Wake up," Mark says. Charlie stretches, his arms hitting the roof. He shakes his head viciously, loosening a few bolts.

"What's up, where are we?" Charlie asks.

"Scranton. You wanna call it a night? Do a straight shot tomorrow?" Mark asks.

"Sounds good to me," Charlie replies, sitting up in his seat.

The boys pull off the highway into downtown Scranton. It's quiet in town. School is out of session; the drunkards of the university are all home getting drunk somewhere else. Charlie dials some hotels as Mark navigates the streets. The Clarion on Meadow has a room...they head that way.

The room is small, two beds, both with hideous comforters. The window looks out over the parking lot, the Scranton airport within view.

Charlie drops his bag on the bed and bends over to pick up a cigarette butt.

"Did we pay extra for the roaches?" he asks, tossing the butt toward the garbage can near the television.

"You should feel right at home," Mark replies, heading into the bathroom. The door jams, the door and frame not aligned particularly well.

"I'm gonna take a shower; don't come in," Mark shouts from the bathroom. Turning on the shower, putting his hand under its head. He shakes off his hand after a few seconds.

"A cold shower, it seems."

Charlie shakes his head, not really giving a shit about Mark's shower predicament. He turns on the television; snow and rolling bars greet him. It was off just as quickly. So much for that.

Mark lets out a yelp as he gets into the shower; the ice cold water hits him like a sledgehammer.

Charlie scribbles a note on the hotel stationary, places it on Mark's bed and heads out the door.

Mark quickly gives up on the shower, opting instead for "bathing" in the sink. Using the faucet to wash his face and a damp washcloth for his armpits.

After showering like a two-dollar hooker, Mark leaves the bathroom. Seeing the empty room, he grabs Charlie's note.

"Went out drinking, be back later."

Mark crumples up the note, depositing it with the cigarette butt from earlier.

Charlie wanders the streets, peeking in bars as he passes them. He ends up at a dive bar on South Webster Avenue. Framed photos and firefighter ladder numbers mark the walls. The bar—splotchy—looking like ten million drinks had rested on it during its lifetime. The bartender is portly, staring up at the Penguins game on television. Charlie takes a seat and throws ten dollars on the bar top. The bartender places a beer on the bar top. The Pens game is tight; a vocal contingent sits in the booths on the opposite wall cheering every check into the boards.

Charlie finishes off that beer and soon another one. He hasn't been out to a bar much lately. He missed the ugly ambiance of it—a whole bunch of people joining together to get completely obliterated in one small amount of square footage—the smell of dirt and puke rising to the heavens, the griminess of the chairs, the broken toilet seats. All signs of ugly happenstance.

Mark, going stir crazy in the dank hotel room, grabs his coat and heads out.

A few drinks later, Charlie is buzzed. The Penguins let up a shorthanded goal, down 4-3 heading into the third period. Charlie looks up from his beer to see a girl at the end of the bar. She is twirling her hair in her fingers, typing away on her cell phone. The LCD light illuminating her eyes—a sharp blue—maybe that's just the color of the screen. Maybe Charlie is just drunk. He must be because he gets out of his seat and heads for the other end of the bar. Plopping down next to the girl, he smiles, "Hi."

The girl looks up from her text love affair to look back at Charlie.

"Hi," she replies, before returning to her phone.

"Do you want a drink?" Charlie asks, throwing up two fingers to flag down the bartender.

"Sure," the girl says, once again only giving a cursory look off the keyboard.

"Do you come here a lot?" Charlie asks. The girl puts down her phone as the bartender drops two beers in front of them. Her eyes *are* blue.

"Yea...and I've never seen you here before," the girl replies, leaning on the edge of the bar top.

"I'm from out of town—I'm Charlie by the way."

"Nice to meet you Charles," the girl says, "My name's Katrina."

"Katrina...I've never met one of those before," Charlie replies, beginning to go to town on his seventh, make that his eighth beer.

"Well not everyone can have a name like Charles; every third person has that name," Katrina replies, beginning to look around the bar.

"It was my father's middle name," Charlie replies, chugging down the remainder of his beer. He lets out a burp. He feels a little rough. The screams of the Penguin fans amplified in his ears.

"Wow, it is loud in here...shit," Charlie says, rubbing his temples.

"Why does that guy keep staring at you?" Katrina asks, pointing down the bar.

"Who?"

Turning around Charlie sees Mark sitting a few seats away. Charlie hisses, turning back to Katrina, "That's my wet blanket of a brother."

Mark stays where he is, watching the closing seconds of the Penguins game. Most of the bar patrons rise to their feet as Sidney Crosby goes racing down the ice with the puck, seconds running down in regulation. As he winds up for his slap shot, the air in the bar gets sucked out, an eerie quiet enveloping, a low hum of anticipation. As the shot floats through the air on the way to the net the noise begins to raise, "Aaa...aaaaa...aaaaaaaa....aaaaaaaaaaa...AHHHHHHH!!!"

The shot sails right, clanging off the glass behind the goalie, who skates to center ice as time expires. As loud as it was a few seconds ago, it is just as silent now. A few mumble, "fuck," sucking down whatever beer they have left.

Charlie, all that alcohol now hitting him, grows the brass balls to say, "I'm just gonna say this. I think we should get out of here and just have a night of amazing sex. Err—amazing for me, maybe not you, but—shit, I'm just kidding." He begins to laugh, a joke seemingly only funny to himself.

Katrina looks at him and grabs her coat off the back of her chair.

"No, no, wait, wait, just hold on...don't go," Charlie stumbles out of his mouth, putting his hand on Katrina's arm.

"Let go of my arm," Katrina says, pulling it away.

Mark looks on from down the bar, standing up ever so slightly.

"Is there a problem here?" a man overstuffed into a Penguins jersey asks.

"I'm fine," Katrina says to the man who wears a mean scowl.

"Yea, she's fine, fat boy," Charlie says, slapping the man on the shoulder. "Oh you're a Penguins fan? Too bad they fucking suck—Rangers!" he screams, throwing his hands above his head.

"Listen asshole, you can get the fuck out of here or I can pick your scrawny ass up and toss you out of here," the man with the scowl says.

Charlie looks down at the man and continues, "If my friend Jeff Singer was here right now he would only have one thing to say to you right now, 'RANGERS! RANGERS! RANGERS! CROSBY'S A PUSSY!'"

The Pens fan looks like he's about to explode.

"That's it asshol—"

Charlie takes a swing, hitting the Pens fan in the right ear. He recoils in pain, stumbling backwards holding the side of his head.

Another Penguins fan takes a swing at Charlie, grazing his forehead. Charlie falls back into the bar dazed and sees another friend of the overstuffed Penguins jersey coming right for him. He gets ready to swing when Mark tackles the incoming threat. Then a brawl starts. Fists thrown, Mark and Charlie getting hit and giving it back to the Penguins fans. Mark catches a punch to the nose, staining his white collared shirt with blood. Two bouncers come in and separate the men, grabbing Mark and Charlie and leading them to the door. Holding them by their shirt collars, the bouncers walk the two brothers to the nearby corner and dump them to the ground.

Charlie dusts himself off, preparing to stand up and return to the fight. Mark grabs him by the jacket and pulls him back down to the ground.

"Don't even think about it dipshit," Mark says, wiping blood from beneath his nose.

"Don't fucking touch me," Charlie replies.

"I'll touch you all I want because, like usual, I take the brunt of your fuck ups," Mark replies.

"Fuck you, I didn't ask you to get fucking involved," Charlie says, turning away from Mark and sitting on the curb.

"You're welcome," Mark says, sitting down next to Charlie. Charlie winces as he reaches into his jacket and pulls out his cigarettes, taking one out and lighting it. He puts the pack back into his jacket.

The two brothers sit in silence on the corner, looking down the tiny street lined with houses. Mark holds his shirt to his nose, trying to soak up whatever blood might still be running out.

Charlie reaches back into his jacket and pulls out his cigarettes again, opening the pack and holding it in Mark's direction. Mark looks down at the pack and then at Charlie, who is gazing out into the street. Mark with his free hand grabs a cigarette, putting it on his lips.

The men smoke their cigarettes, something before tonight that was always done apart, never done together.

"What were you thinking? That guy was like twice your size," Mark asks. Charlie shrugs his shoulders, rubbing his drunken eyes.

It's quiet again.

Charlie lets out a laugh.

"What?"

"Mom would probably be pissed off...the two of us sitting here, smoking cigarettes," Charlie replies, looking down at his cigarette.

"I don't think she would be," Mark says.

"The cancer...it'll kill ya," Charlie says, flicking his cigarette out into the street, it rolling down a sewer grate.

"Life...it'll kill ya," Mark replies, blowing smoke rings into the air.

"Dad smoked," Charlie says.

"Dad did a lot of things," Mark replies.

"Dad smoked cigarettes for how long? Twenty years? Thirty years?"

"Something like that, but that had nothing to do with him dying," Mark said.

"Yea but it couldn't have helped," Charlie replies. Mark shrugs his shoulders, returning to his cigarette.

"I heard him take his last breath," Charlie says, wincing as he adjusts himself on the sidewalk, pulling his jacket out from under him. Mark looks at Charlie, his face hanging, eyes unblinking.

"What?"

"Yea," Charlie replies, nodding his head.

"I was looking at him. I was fucking exhausted...I hadn't slept in days, I was in that chair...and I was just looking at him. He was quiet, the blanket on top of his chest going up and down slowly...his eyelids were flickering. It looked like his eyes were moving around in there...searching through the darkness, I didn't know if he just didn't want to open his eyes, or he couldn't...he really didn't do much in those last few days. So I'm watching the sheet go up and down, the oxygen tank wheezing over in the corner of the room, and I just felt so tired, I wanted to fall asleep, but I kept looking at him. Then the sheet just stopped moving. It went up, and down again, and it never went back up. It was quiet. His eyes weren't flickering anymore. He was so still...so at peace. He wasn't stretching his legs and hearing the cracks of his knees or pulling the sheet up to his chin, hearing the slight strain in his throat. The oxygen tank kept pumping...breathing for nothing. I felt this stinging in the back of my throat. I knew what it meant; I just didn't want to be the person who was gonna walk out into that hallway and say 'Hey everybody, my dad is dead.' I couldn't do that. That oxygen machine kept making noise. That slow wheezing sounded like it was getting louder, and louder, and louder. It felt like a plane was about to crash on my head. I felt like I was sinking in quicksand. So I got up and got a drink of water and I went into the bathroom and I was sitting in the stall, staring at the broken tile and the mismatched paint job on the door. I couldn't focus on anything...I just felt like I was bouncing off rubber walls. I was just hoping that you or Mom walked in there...and then you did."

Charlie takes a pause, looking down at the street.

"I tried to act surprised when I came back. But I already knew he was gone. I wasn't prepared for him to die. Even when he was like knocking at the door a few times, I would say, 'No way,' you know, 'he'll come back.' And every time he did...until then. I so wanted it to be a dream that I just couldn't seem wake up from—that it was some cruel joke that my mind was playing on me. Because for as much grief as he caused, and fuck, he caused a lot of grief, I didn't want him to leave yet."

Mark flips his cigarette away.

"And I knew what it meant...I knew what was coming. Every fucking person showing up to tell us how great he was and how they loved him and how he loved us and pretty much telling us what we should think of our father. Like, you know—as if we didn't know him, that we didn't fucking live with him for all those years, like we were some sort of alien that was just dropped into that funeral home with a nametag that read 'Son.' I knew all that was coming over the hill. I had so much that I wanted to say to him, to ask him about. Shit, not father to son, fucking man-to-man."

"Like what?" Mark asks.

"Like what he thought of his life, if he was happy with what he accomplished, you know. I know he thought I was a failure. He never said it, but I read it in his eyes. That I didn't live up to some fucking gold standard that he placed on everyone but himself. I wanted to ask him why he cheated on Mom and divorced her and then how much of fucking pansy he felt like when he got sick and that skank he was with dumped him and Mom took him back in. And I defended him...so much...I defended him to you, which led to you packing your shit and moving as far away as possible. I defended him out of some sort of son duty, as if no one should ever question his motives or actions or the fucked up things he did on any number of occasions. I felt so broken when you left, that the final thing that broke everything past the point of fixing wasn't even something we did to each other. Like I didn't punch you in the face or you didn't crash my car or anything like that. It was an argument about our father where neither of us was right. It all just imploded after that. You were gone. Mom was taking care of everyone, me included. I fell into the cycle of nothingness because I felt like I needed to be with him every day, even though it seemed like he didn't want to see me. I think in his eyes, you became the son who ran away and I became the son who made you do it. He died a middle aged bitter man, with his failure son as the only witness to his last shallow breath."

Mark's head hangs. He's never heard this many words from his brother. The fracture in that surface, the canyon that developed afterward, thoughts he also had when he left.

"But I miss him, because above it all, he was still my father. He still bought me a baseball glove when I was six and took me out of school early one day to go see *Star Wars* when Kristin broke my heart in fifth grade and...he's still my dad," Charlie finishes.

Mark stares down at the dark pavement, blinking slowly. Charlie grabs another cigarette. Lighting it, he exhales a big puff into the air. He rubs his eyes one final time and gets up off the curb.

"Let's go back to the hotel," he says, looking both ways as he crosses the street. Mark pushes himself up off the ground.

CHAPTER SEVEN

The boys check out of the hotel and hit a convenience store on their way out of Scranton. They are only four hours from their destination. Charlie gets behind the wheel while Mark eats his breakfast burrito in the passenger seat.

The first few minutes of the drive are quiet, the boys fading off to different places. Charlie on the road, Mark out of the window. A lot of monosyllabic questions and answers—a few 'yea' utterances peppering the dialogue. Traffic develops, the Camaro idles loudly.

"This sucks," Charlie says, looking out into the traffic of the interstate.

"It's rush hour traffic, it's alright," Mark replies. He sizes up his second breakfast burrito, adding some hot sauce to it.

"I'm sorry about last night," Charlie says.

"It's alright," Mark replies.

"I just sort of lost my shit," Charlie says, turning away from his brother to look out the window.

"It happens," Mark replies, biting into his burrito.

"What do you think it is—the address?" Charlie asks. Mark shakes his head, swallowing his burrito.

"I don't know," Mark replies.

The road opens up and the boys start to move again, gaining on the address and the secrets it holds. Maybe it's a letter, maybe it's a house. Maybe it's a huge empty lot with weeds growing from its concrete surface, broken beer bottles littering the edges, the hangout of kids on a Friday night. It feels mythical, this place. The idea of it may be grander than whatever the address could hold. The Ark of the Covenant might even be a let down. It represents a destination, maybe an answer to a question, maybe the missing puzzle piece of their father—a reason for every decision he ever made. Or maybe it's just an empty lot. Whatever it is, his two sons are barreling toward it, taking their first and maybe last road trip together—united for a common goal.

Mark thinks about what Charlie said last night. He listened, for the first time in a while. He thinks about their fight, the reasons for it. He thinks about his mother, the one who got stuck in the middle. He thinks about himself, the one who ran away, chased a career, maybe even a different life. The road feels open, strange with Charlie leading the way. His little brother, someone once thought to be lost at sea, someone who might still return to the choppy waters once they returned home. Mark doesn't know what this trip signifies. He might not know until the end. He might never know. Even after looking back at what they found. Maybe some of this good will could be shattered by what lays at the end—that the two of them will be worse off. Maybe they've been right all along to separate, travel the streets alone, trying to find a way of their own paths. Mark just doesn't know. Something feels different than it had before.

About 100 miles away, the boys switch positions, Mark getting behind the wheel, the last runner in this baton race. As the centimeters on the map get smaller and the mile markers loom larger, each of the men feel a tingle in their stomach—the anticipation of Christmas morning, the feeling of running down the stairs to see what's under the tree.

As the men exit the highway, the Camaro running a bit low on gas, the 'Welcome to Butler, PA' sign towers over the scenery. It's an old industrial town; they built things here—have done so for more than 100 years. The old factories that use to spit out cars and trains line the city. Some are old and crumbling, their facades washed out and gray. The boys look out the window at one of the original Ford dealerships, authorized by Henry Ford all those years ago. It is old America—a bit of apple pie, the exposed red brick of the storefronts—it looks like 80's Spielberg small town scenery. But there is a hint of sadness behind these walls and windows, a time machine of melancholy, implying that this place had seen more fruitful times. Charlie stares out the passenger window, looking for North Washington Street.

"It's close," he said.

As the Camaro makes a left at West Brady Street, they see North Washington just up ahead. Mark pulls slowly up to the street, waiting for the coming traffic to pass before making the right turn. As the Camaro makes the right onto North Washington, the boys' stomachs ache. Mark looks out his side window, 225 sitting off to the left. Mark pulls the car off to the side of the street and turns off the rumbling engine.

Charlie cranes his neck across the car, looking out Mark's window. The building is ordinary. Brick stacked on top of brick. A blue door—the only entrance on the entire building front. A rusted 225 above the doorframe.

"You ready?" Charlie asks, taking off his seatbelt and opening the door.

"Wait," Mark says. Charlie looks off the door handle.

"I'm sorry," Mark says.

"Before we go in there I want to say I'm sorry for leaving you and Mom. It was selfish and I'm sorry for that. I'm sorry we don't have a relationship anymore...and I'm sorry I wasn't there for you when you needed me to be. You're right, it is only the three of us now and...uh...I don't want us to be that way anymore. Okay?"

"Okay," Charlie replies.

"Whatever's in there is in there and I just wanted to say that I'm glad you're with me for this," Mark finishes.

"Alright."

Charlie and Mark exit the car. It's mid-afternoon, the sun beginning to fade behind the buildings, the block is draped in shade. Charlie unzippers his coat, Mark rings his hands. As they approach the door, Mark shuffles in his shoes. Mark nods for Charlie to open the door. His hand grabs the brass doorknob, turning it open.

Charlie moves slowly in, a small space lying behind the door. As the boys enter 225 North Washington they take in the room. Three walls, the wooden floors sparsely populated, the walls barren, save for some dark red paint. A flat counter sits toward the back, rows of lockers behind it; a set of swinging doors off to the side. The boys walk to the counter, a single bell sitting on top. Mark hits the bell—the clang runs through the room. The boys hear footsteps from behind the swinging doors, starting quietly then getting louder and louder until a thin man in his 60's walks through them. He has a worn face, salt and pepper hair marks his head. He's wearing a blue checked shirt, jeans and boots.

"Can I help you boys?" the man asked, stopping in front of them.

"Hi," Mark says, his eyes wandering behind the counter.

"We got this address...we don't really know why...from our father," Charlie says.

"Who's your father?" the man asks.

"James Murphy," Mark replied. The man nods his head; a slight smile comes across his face.

"I finally have some faces to put to the names," the man says. Mark and Charlie exchange a glance.

"Which one of you is Mark?" the man asks. Mark raises his hand.

"It's nice to meet you Mark, Charlie," the man says, extending his hand and shaking both of the boys' hands.

"He was a great man and if you guys are here, I'm assuming he's no longer with us," the man says.

"He died last week," Mark replies.

"That's a shame—I'm sorry for your loss."

"So...what are we doing here? What is this place?" Charlie asks. The man smiles, scratching the side of his face.

"Well I don't know what you're doing here. I do have something here for you two, but to be honest I don't know what it is. And before I give it to you, I need to see some IDs," the man says.

Charlie and Mark are surprised, "IDs? What is this, a bar?" Charlie asks.

"No, but I gave your old man my word that I wouldn't give it to you unless both of you were here together. That was his stipulation," the man continues.

"He said that?" Mark asks.

"Yep, he told me explicitly that if you two boys weren't here together that I shouldn't release it to either you, Mark, or to you, Charlie," the man says. Mark and Charlie take out their wallets and hand over their IDs. The man studies them, then places the IDs back down on the counter.

"You look like your dad, Charlie," the man adds.

He turns to the lockers behind him and places a key into one of the doors. Opening it, he pulls out a metal box. He turns back to the boys and places the box on the counter between them.

He hands each of them a key.

"Two keys to open, you gotta do it at the same time," the man says. Charlie and Mark take the keys and place them into the keyholes at each side of the box. On the count of three they turn, the top of the box opening ever so slightly. They pause for a second, looking at each other. Charlie nods his head. Mark puts his hand on the top of the box, slowly opening it. Inside is a shoebox, wrapped in brown paper. Mark takes the shoebox out and puts it down on the counter. The man grabs the metal box, closes it and returns it to the locker behind him.

Charlie and Mark look down on the box. It's wrapped ever so perfectly. They study the angles, run through all the possible things it could contain. Charlie goes to grab it, but reconsiders.

"Well it was nice meeting you boys," the man says, saluting the boys and walking back toward the swinging doors.

"Wait—that's it?" Mark asks. The man nods his head, "Yes sir, and once again, I'm sorry about your father, he was a great man." With that the man disappears behind the swinging doors.

Mark looks at Charlie. Mark picks up the box and heads for the front door as Charlie follows behind him.

Now on the interstate, the box sits on the dash. Charlie stares at it from the passenger seat, once again studying it.

It angers them with its simplicity. They were expecting fireworks, explosions, SWAT teams. This wasn't their father's bag. As they continue down the interstate, they throw out suggestions about what may line the inside of the box, what their father left—good or bad. After a while, they grow quiet. The sounds of the radio overcome their words. Mark searches the radio dial, stopping on an oldies rock station playing "Let it Loose" by The Rolling Stones. The two boys refrain to Jagger. Songs from John Pepper and Neil Young soon make their way through the speakers and the boys continue to let the words seep from the old speakers into the air, not blocking them with any interference.

"I'm not gonna open it," Mark says, looking at Charlie. Charlie remains fixed on the box. He bits his lip and then falls back into the passenger seat.

"Me neither," Charlie replies.

"So we're not gonna open it," Mark says.

"It could be empty," Charlie replies.

"It could be...it felt kind of heavy though," Mark says. Charlie takes the box off the dash and puts it on the back seat.

"Let's just go home," Mark says.

Charlie stays focused on the box.

"I'm hungry; can we get some food first?" Charlie asks, reclining his seat.

"Yea the first place I see we'll stop; I got some shit at the convenience store this morning," Mark says, fishing around the back seat with his free hand, keeping his eyes on the road ahead. He drops the black plastic bag into Charlie's lap, returning his hand to the wheel, changing lanes and accelerating.

Charlie searches through the bag, pulling out a box of strawberry Pop-Tarts, crinkling the wrapper as he opens one.

PART THREE:
THE WEDDING OF
JOHN KENNEY &
JENNA STEVENSON

CHAPTER EIGHT

This is the story of a few friends. One of these friends is getting married. John Kenney, the quiet punching bag of this group. His best man, his best friend, Matt McDonnell, is a quiet tornado of nostalgia. He revels in the past and speaks about it regularly—more so these days. Things may have gotten away from him a little bit, away from all of them actually. Jeff Singer just quit his job, a culmination of hating the way his father goes about business; he stormed out of the office after one exceptionally irritating day when every word out of his father's mouth was the verbal equivalent of taking a dump on his son's head. He's unemployed for the time being, his girlfriend supporting him throughout. Tom Bernabeo, unbeknownst to most of his friends, works for the CIA, jumping out of planes and killing despots. He's stayed out on the road for much of his adult life, taking job after job, a never-ending connecting flight. He hasn't been home in months. His roommate and CIA handler, Russell King, is quite the opposite, more inclined to be lying on a beach or the couch in their living room then out working. He's currently on the couch. Mike Pennisi, who lives with Russell and Tom, is finding his own growing pains after recently breaking up with a girl half a decade younger than himself. Chris Hall has moved into an apartment with his girlfriend, Erin, and is working on his fourth novel. The word marriage slowly being whispered in their general direction. Derek, Bob and Boyd—a debaucherous traveling circus of men—moved out to the west coast a few months ago, taking their brand of crazy with them. No one knows if they will be in attendance for the nuptials. Finally there's Chris D'Ascoli, a man who...well you'll just have to read about him yourself.

John Kenney and Jenna Stevenson will be getting married in two days.

CHAPTER NINE

"Fuck you!" Chris Hall screams into the living room abyss. "Hey! Christopher Hall, remember what we talked about? You need to tone down the language, okay? You're a big boy now, you can't talk like that," Erin says from the kitchen.

"First of all, only my mom calls me Christopher. And second, baby the Mets hurt me on a deeply, deeply personal level. They are the cause of all my health problems, all of my nervous ticks, all of my phobias. They are the abusive parent I never had."

"I can't settle between depressing or dramatic, so I'll just call you both," Erin replies as she closes the dishwasher and heads toward the living room.

Erin walks into the living room and sits down next to Chris, nuzzling into his neck as the Mets make a pitching change. They've been together for five years, slowly making that ascent toward 30. She has a job on the Upper East Side designing and planning events for yuppies and hipsters. She is the small town girl to his street running boy. The designing isn't something that she loves, but she has the skills to pay the bills. She dabbled in journalism, found it too slow. She assisted a film producer for a few months, found it too fast. The designing came out of nowhere and stuck. She's been at it for a couple of years now and really found her niche, picked up a few accolades along the way. While some of her friends are either unhappy in a relationship or unhappy in a marriage, she has struck just the right balance. Sure, Chris still hurls a remote control at the wall when Luis Castillo commits an error, but he's it. She settled for the designing job, but she didn't settle for him.

He stays up late, writing and drinking, paying the bills with his words. They rent an apartment in the West Village and she decorated it all modern and proper, a far cry from the place Chris shared with Chris D'Ascoli and Mike Pennisi previously. The only essence remaining from the dirty decadence of his drinking youth adorn the walls of his writing room. Autographed vodka bottles, framed photos, pages filled with memories. It's still a part of him, he still writes about it from time to time, but it is decidedly frowned upon. Viewed by some as a burned out man child reliving his so called glory days, the critics think his subjects should be evolving as he inches out of the station of twenty hood. His last novel was full of bombast, blue language and balls, and the critics hammered him.

An excerpt of one review:

"An unbelievably obnoxious experience. Mr. Hall thinks that a quick phrase that somehow involves a curse and mention of a bodily fluid or sex toy equals good writing. Well I'm here to tell him that it does not and I'm sure I speak for a lot of people when I say that. The ray of hope that Hall gave to us that he would write important literature is all but obliterated by this so called 'novel.' I put that word in quotes because this is nothing more than a man who wishes he was still the funny kid in the bar cracking dick and fart jokes strewn across some 275 odd pages. Grow up Mr. Hall, you're too good of a writer not to."

He was never a fan, so fuck him. Wait—he's not supposed to use that word anymore.

"What time should we leave tomorrow?" Chris asks Erin. She tussles her hair over her shoulder, closing her eyes as she replies, "I have a meeting with Richard's architect at nine...hopefully that'll be done by 11."

As the Mets bullpen gets out of the inning, Chris' cell phone rings. Getting up off the couch and stretching his limbs, he shuffles over to the kitchen counter, where his awaiting cell phone bounces and rings like a bell.

"Who is it?" Erin asks, now stretched out on the couch. Chris opens his cell phone and puts it to his ear.

"What's up, D'Ascoli?"

Chris D'Ascoli stands in his walk-in closet, shoes and clothes littering the floor. Rummaging through his shirts he asks, "This rehearsal dinner tomorrow, what am I supposed to wear to this thing?"

"Wear what you would wear to a wake for the rehearsal dinner and what you would wear to a funeral for the wedding," Chris replies.

"Very nice," Erin says sarcastically from the couch, throwing a pillow in his direction.

"Word. What time are you getting there?" D'Ascoli asks. Chris paces back into the living room and hops back on the couch. "Our flight is supposed to leave at three tomorrow; you bringing anybody?"

"Nah, I travel light—I'll pick up a bridesmaid or something. Call me tomorrow when you get there," D'Ascoli replies, throwing clothes onto his bed.

"Alright, I'll see you tomorrow," Chris says as he closes his phone.

"Wear what you would wear to a funeral, my God," Erin says in mocking contempt.

"I thought you'd like that. I'm only 12 percent kidding by the way," Chris replies.

"Only 12 percent? That's way lower than I thought it would be."

Chris looks down at Erin and kisses her, "I love you very much."

"Please don't ever ask me to marry you," Erin replies.

"Dually noted."

They fall asleep on the couch as the Mets drop a heartbreaker to the Phillies 3-2.

Chris wakes up the next morning to see that Erin has already left for work. Pulling himself out of bed, he walks to the kitchen to grab a Gatorade and then heads to his writing room. Putting Elliot Smith's "XO" on the turntable, he saddles up to his typewriter and begins to write some new prose. His new novel is about a guy who thinks he has cancer, but is too scared to go to a doctor to get it checked out. It's a comedy. The main character of the story's name is Bert; he rides around the city on the subway for hours at a time. Bert never goes up to street level, he just connects from train to train, watching a 1,000 faces a day pass in front of him. He probably doesn't have cancer, the story never reveals it. Bert is just a man chronically afraid of the unknown. Riding around the city, while the faces change every day, they form an unmistakable familiarity. People busying themselves with their daily routines, all while Bert's life is stationed in the same seat everyday.

"This is really fucking depressing," Chris says aloud. Getting up from his typewriter, Chris wanders around the apartment. He paces around the couch in the living room, moving it ever so slightly to line up with the love seat a few feet away. Now they are symmetrical. He is sure that he's not going insane.

Back now at the typewriter, Chris stares at the half-inked page. He slowly begins to pull out the depressing prose and puts a clean page into the feeder. His first new paragraph begins:

"So Michael Pennisi had this girlfriend, let's just call her Joanna. To say she was clinically insane might be an understatement, like saying that Goodfellas *is the best movie ever made would be an understatement. Alright, so I can give you the whole story of Joanna and Mike or I can just fast forward and tell you that the relationship ended with a stiletto heel, a flying lemon meringue pie and someone...and I say someone because this woman, shit, I mean this person scares me on a deeply personal level... screaming 'I will fuck you in the street, then I'll do it to your little doggy too,' like some sort of demented Wicked Witch of the West. She now resides in a place that has foam for walls and visiting hours between 5 and 6 p.m. on Tuesday. But only Tuesday; Tuesday is her good day. Any other day and she might go Sarah Connor in T2 on your ass and hold a syringe filled with drain cleaner to your neck. It is still Mike's most successful relationship to date."*

"That's kind of funny, right?" Chris asks the air. He pulls the Pennisi page out of the typewriter and holds it up next to the Bert story. Sizing them up, he lifts the Bert page and says, "Great *New York Times* review." He then lifts the Pennisi page, saying, "Not blowing my brains out."

He throws both pages down onto the desk and wanders back into the living room.

Across town, Erin rushes out of her office. Looking at her watch she mumbles, "Shit." Reaching into her bag she grabs her phone. She dials Chris and puts the phone to her ear. Chris' finger drumming is interrupted as the phone rings. Picking up the receiver he answers, "Dunder Mifflin, this is Jim."

"Hey."

"Hey, what's up? Are you on your way home?" Chris asks.

Erin is bumped into by a man crossing in front of her and her entire purse spills onto the street.

"Listen I'm not going to be able to make the flight. They delivered the wrong marble and everything is just fucked up here."

"Shit—do you want me to stay and we can fly out together in the morning?"

"No, no. I'll just catch a later flight, you should go," Erin breathlessly gets out as she is on her knees collecting the contents of her bag.

"Listen I gotta go, call me when you land."

"Alright, I love you," Chris replies.

Chris exhales and puts the phone down on the desk. He scratches the back of his neck and points his head toward the window. It's raining. He gets up from his desk and walks down the hallway to the bedroom.

A hundred miles away, Michael Pennisi is packing a suitcase, a beard gracing his face, big and full like the one his father Lou owned back in the late 70's. He's quickly rummaging through his drawers, throwing socks and underwear in the general direction of the suitcase.

"Let's go we gotta catch this plane!" Russell King screams from the living room. Russell King, in all of his majesty, is sitting cross legged in a reclining chair. "Time is money Pennisi, let's go."

"I don't like being rushed, Russ," Mike screams back.

"Well take all the time that you want, but in ten minutes I will be getting in that town car downstairs and I *will* be leaving you," Russell replies.

Mike puts a middle finger to the wall for Russell not to see. "We can't leave anyway; Tom's not here yet," Mike says.

Russell takes another look at his watch and then pulls out his cell phone. Dialing Tom's number, he puts the phone to his ear.

Across the country, Tom Bernabeo is currently placing a silencer on his gun. His phone begins to ring. Answering it he says, "Russ, I'm a little busy right now."

"Where are you?" Russell asks. Tom takes notice of a man walking along the sidewalk with a suitcase handcuffed to his arm.

"Before I answer that, did you replace the hacksaw that you lost in London that I lent you?" Tom asks.

"Yea it should be in your kit, why?" Russell replies.

"I'm gonna need it in his about ten minutes. I'm in the place you got that blow jay from that hooker with the tattoo of Homer Simpson on her arm," Tom replies. Russell's eyebrows raise north, "Where is that?"

"You mean to tell me that you've had blowjobs from multiple women with Homer Simpson tattoos, Russ? You are one messed up dude," Tom says as he gets out of his car and heads to the trunk.

"Are you gonna make it to Kenney's wedding this weekend?"

Tom grabs the hacksaw and places it on his shoulder like a baseball player striding to the plate with a bat.

"That's this weekend? Shit. Yea I guess so, send me all the details. I'll hop on a plane after I finish this job," Tom says, now moving toward the door that the man with the suitcase entered.

"Alright, I gotta go do this shit. I'll talk to you later, Russ," Tom says as he closes his trunk. Just as he is about to hang up the phone he has an epiphany, "Shit Russ, you still there?"

"Yea, what's up?"

Tom puts his bag down and heads back to the car, "Can you grab me a suit out of my closet?" Russell exhales loudly and gets out of the chair.

Pushing open Tom's bedroom door, Russell heads for his closet. "Which one do you want?"

"There should be one in the corner of the closet in a black garment bag, just open it and make sure everything's in there," Tom says. Russell takes the garment bag out of the closet and throws it on the bed. He unzips the bag to see a black suit inside. He further inspects, "Tom, there's blood on this suit."

Tom grimaces, "Shit, I totally forgot to get that dry cleaned. Leave that on the bed, it'll remind me to take care of that when I get home."

Russell returns to the closet, "So what are we doing here?" Tom ponders for a second, "There should be a suit, three hangers from the left, check that one."

Russell grabs the garment bag three hangers from the left and throws it on the bed next to the bloody suit. He once again unzips the bag and inspects.

"Is that one okay?" Tom asks as he paces around his car.

"Zero for two, Tom. This one has a bullet hole in it," Russell says as he has his thumb poking through the lapel.

"Fuck, alright leave that one there too," Tom exclaims.

"I'm gonna buy you some Post-its, so you can remember shit like this," Russell says as he heads back to the closet.

"Aww shit just pick one that doesn't have anything wrong with it," Tom says, "Send me the info, I'll talk to you later."

Russell grabs the last remaining garment bag and heads back out to the living room.

Tom makes his way back to the door, once again throwing the hacksaw over his shoulder. Leaning up against the door for a moment, Tom listens. He takes a deep breath and then kicks it down, showering the room with bullets.

Mike walks into the living room with a suitcase. "It's about fucking time," Russell says. Mike rolls his eyes and scratches his beard, "Listen Russ, I don't have any time for your shit."

"Shave that beard, you look like a pedophile." This time Mike flips Russell off to his face.

Russell gets out of the chair, grabs his suitcase and the garment bag with Tom's suit and makes his way to the front door.

"Let's go see one of our friends flush his life down the toilet," Russell says.

Mike follows behind Russell and turns out the lights in the apartment.

Back to the spy business, Tom is clearing each room—making sure no one's hiding, waiting to bust a cap in his ass. He's still looking for the suitcase man. As he canvases the blood strained walls of this uncoothed establishment, he hears a sound in the back bedroom. He begins to make his way up the hallway when the door swings open, which is quickly followed by bullets raining down on him.

Tom ducks into a nearby bedroom and grabs a piece of broken glass. He uses the reflection to look down the bullet battered hallway. He sees someone rustling about in the bedroom at the end of the corridor—he drops the glass and gets to his feet. Making a quick move into the hallway, Tom is met with a kick to the chest, sending him down to the floor. The opposition is covered head to toe in black, with a slender, lanky frame. More importantly, they've got the suitcase. Tom avoids a high kick that would have splattered his brains on the hallway floor. Sweeping the leg, Tom is now eye-to-eye with the combatant. Each blocks the other's punches as they are now in full hand-to-hand combat while sitting on the floor. Tom throws another punch, which is swiftly blocked. The other fighter grabs Tom's wrist and twists it 180 degrees. The pop of his wrist echoes through the hallway. Tom delivers a quick blow to the neck and pulls off the assailant's ski mask. It's a woman. They both stop and look, each having that feeling of recognizing one another.

Suddenly a bullet flies by both their heads, fired by suitcase man's security, arriving to a distress call. Tom quickly retreats for cover, while the woman grabs the suitcase and sprints down the hallway. Security continues firing as she runs through the bedroom door and jumps out the window. Tom rolls his eyes, "Of course I get the assignment against fucking Catwoman." Tom pulls a grenade off his belt and hurls it down the hallway in the direction of the private security. Rolling into the closet, Tom covers his ears as the living room and hallway explode.

John Kenney paces around a living room—the living room of his soon to be father-in-law. He cracks his neck and takes a deep breath. The house is quiet, a sound that he hasn't heard in the past few weeks and one he shouldn't expect to hear in the next few days. The living room is littered with flowers, gowns, gifts. All for him and his lady. He met her two years ago last September, on a rainy day if he do remember. It was some sort of get together, maybe Chris and Erin's party for their new apartment. Jenna Stevenson came to the party late, walking into that living room backlit with a wind machine—at least John saw her that way. Her black hair was in a ponytail, her skin olive, her eyes green. D'Ascoli hit on her first, but she wasn't having it. D'Ascoli's game tends to be very polarizing. Girls will either eat up it up or pledge to never speak to him again. Jenna was not the former. John saw her from the kitchen, saw D'Ascoli was hitting on her—a common occurrence—and decided to instead focus on his Miller Light. As the night wore on and D'Ascoli turned his attention away unwillingly, John and Jenna struck up a conversation about the New York Giants. Her father used to play D-Line for them, a very underrated aphrodisiac for men, the daughters of former professional athletes. Those girls seem to have a head on their shoulders that will tell you to fuck off and try to fight you if you get out of line. They don't believe in the bullshit that people spew and they have even less time for it. John was no bullshit, he spoke his mind and he said what he meant. There was no two-way talk, no qualifiers.

"Babe," a voice says from John's back. He turns to see Jenna striding toward him, her hair in a ponytail, much like how it looked the first time he saw her. She smiles from ear to ear. She wraps her arms around his neck and kisses him.

"We have a problem," she says.

"What?"

"My dad is here and he's angry with you," Jenna replies. John's face goes pale and his eyes start to dart about. Then he enters the room. Jenna's father, William, is a big man, with a presence that made you notice him when he was in the same area code as you, let alone the same room. His stature tall, his face worn, he peers down from the heavens seemingly upon all—all six foot, seven inches of him. William stands in the doorway and there is silence. The type of silence that might make anyone in William's path leave a Bugs Bunny like body cutout in a nearby wall.

"Hey, Mr. Stevenson," John mumbles through teeth. William glares back and then replies, "Hey, John, come here."

John's face shows six different emotions in three seconds as he begins to walk toward William. As John enters the shadow of William, he feels what many quarterbacks felt in their time facing this large man, a deep feeling that shit was about to end very badly for them. As John looks skyward at the man he watched pancake many grown men on a weekly basis in his youth, he is suddenly welcomed in an embrace. William's still large arms wrap themselves around John like a child holding a small doll. William then says, "I can snap your neck at any second, don't you forget that."

John lets out a nervous laugh, which is then seconded by Jenna who says, "Dad, please don't make him run away the day before the wedding."

"I'm doing no such thing baby, but if he ever did run away from my daughter on such an important day, I would hunt him down and make sure he would never walk right again."

Another round of nervous laughter enters the room as John looks like he is about either poop his drawers or have an eyeball pop out of his head. The house phone rings and William releases John from the embrace, "I'll get it."

William enters the kitchen to answer the phone and John turns and stumbles back to Jenna. "Yea. I don't know if he hates me...or...he hates me."

"Oh, he loves you. Don't let the whole 'I'll hunt you down and break your legs' act get to you," Jenna replies.

"Should I have asked his permission to marry you?"

"You didn't?" Jenna replies.

"No, shit should I have...shit he hates me...shit."

"Say shit one more time," Jenna says.

"Shit," John replies.

Jeff Singer stares out the large bay window onto the tarmac. Raindrops hit the window and scroll like matrix code. Jeff rubs the cold out of his brown eyes and exhales. He listens to the announcements over the loud speaker. A storm in the Midwest continues to ground his flight. Now he waits. He wanders over to a row of chairs and plops himself down into one. It's been a tough year for him, a series of the cards breaking the wrong way. He lost his job over a disagreement with the way his father runs his business. He walked away from his father that day, something that has alienated him from the rest of the brood. He has been searching for meaning, the reason to get up in the morning. While he scuffles, his girlfriend is the beacon on the horizon. Doing that doctor shit, saving people's lives, Maria is the rock. Well, Maria is Maria. She's always taken care of him and has never given it a second thought. She's always been the more responsible one—always the higher grades, the better credit score, the one who keeps Jeff moving forward. She is his guardian angel, in flesh and blood, literally removing him from bad situations. Whatever he was searching for, she was going to help him find it.

This is not lost on Jeff. He adores Maria. Worships the ground she walked on. He just can't shake the feeling of inadequacy, like he was a noose around the neck of someone who was doing so much more with her life than he was. As much as he never hopes that she would leave him, he could understand it if it ever came to that—that she deserved someone who could take care of her, not the other way around.

This is all existential at the moment. Currently this flight is foremost on his mind. As he flips through a magazine, he peers around the terminal, searching for Maria.

But she is out of sight, out of sight to everyone in fact. She's sitting in a bathroom stall, looking at a pregnancy test. She taps her foot as she eyes her watch. As each second passes, the tapping increases. She exhales deeply, watching the seconds tick down, each second slower than the last. As the timer dips under ten seconds, she closes her eyes and exhales. A loud fart from the stall next to her abruptly makes her open her eyes. Initially startled, she soon remembers. Then she saw it. That little blue positive sign. That little indicator, that little blue signal that things have changed. Another loud fart from the stall next to her makes her laugh...laughter that is soon met with a tear.

As she collects her bag and exits the bathroom stall, she is left wondering what to do with the pee stick currently in her hand. As she walks over to the sink, she sees a woman washing her hands.

"Can I ask you a question?"

The lady turns to Maria and nods her head.

"Do you know what you're supposed to do with pregnancy tests? Like do you keep them or throw them away or flush them? What do you do?"

The lady flashes a smile of her two teeth and responds, "I have my six positives framed on the wall."

"Wow six...you're a lucky lady."

"Yea, it's too bad those things don't tell you who the father is though," the lady devoid of teeth continues.

"Have a nice day," Maria replies, sticking the test back into the box and putting it into her bag. Maria exits the bathroom and spots Jeff sitting near the window. She strides over to him as if she was walking on air, excitement pouring out of her, all of her muscles clenched as if they were seizing up.

As she nears Jeff, he rises from his seat and walks over to the information desk. Maria sits down in Jeff's seat and watches as he begins to speak to the stewardess. After a few moments, Jeff turns and walks back toward Maria. They meet eyes and she smiles. Jeff sits down next to her.

"She said that we're probably gonna board any minute now," Jeff says. Maria continues to smile and nods her head. "You alright?" he asks. Maria nods again with her smile. "Are you having a stroke?" Maria shakes her head no, smile still very present. "Are you gassy?" Maria punches Jeff's shoulder. "Because if you're gassy you should just get it all out now, we're gonna be stuck in a box for a few hours. And also if you fart, everyone is gonna think it's me. People never think it's the girl sitting next to a dude who farts. They always think it's the guy's fault."

Maria's face still doesn't change.

"I love you too," Jeff says, as he picks up his magazine and begins to flip through the pages once more.

"Now boarding Flight 137 to Adulthood," the stewardess echoes over the loudspeaker.

CHAPTER TEN

"Can you crack my back?" Russell asks as he and Mike stand at the baggage turnstile. Mike puts down his backpack and wraps his arms around Russell, lifting him skyward. After hearing a few cracks, Mike drops Russell back down to his feet.

"Don't say I never did anything for you," Mike says.

"What's wrong with you?"

"Nothing's wrong with me."

"You've been pissy all week, you were giving me shit this morning, you complained the whole flight here, what it is?" Russell asks.

"Fuck you," Mike responds.

"Yea, there's nothing wrong with you."

"I just don't know what I'm doing here. I'd rather be home playing with my dick. I'm not gonna sleep with anyone this weekend. I'm gonna get too drunk at the wedding, pass out face down in my own vomit, wake up Sunday morning feeling like shit, get on a plane feeling like shit, go to bed Sunday night feeling like shit and then go to work Monday morning feeling like shit. That's a lot of shit packed into a small time frame," Mike replies.

"That is a lot of shit," Russell replies.

"Exactly. And I had to buy Kenney some $250 chafing dish or some shit, some waste of money thing that they're never gonna use and I'm never gonna get anything back in return because I'm not gonna get married, and if I ever did get married I wouldn't make someone buy some fucking $250 chafing dish."

"Why did you buy a $250 chafing dish?" Russell asks.

"Because by the time I went to the registry to buy them a gift it was the only thing left because no one in their right fucking mind should ever have to buy a $250 fucking chafing dish!" Mike says.

A woman nearby covers her children's ears. "Only grown ups say those words," Mike says in the direction of the children.

"Chafing dish?" Russell asks.

Mike rubs his eyes.

"So why don't you just return it and give them money?" Russell asks.

"Because I already bought the thing and if I returned it then I would have to go back to that store and if I go back to that store I'm going to be reminded that I bought a $250 chafing dish. Plus, I'll have to answer some plucky lady behind the counter's question about why I'm returning such a great item and I might have to commit a homicide at that exact moment. This is a run-out-the-clock situation. As soon as I can get rid of this thing, I am dropping it and hoping I never have to see it ever again."

"Alrighty then," Russell says as he grabs his suitcase off the baggage turnstile.

"What did you buy them?" Mike asks.

"I was gonna ask if I could put my name on yours." Mike grabs his bag and walks away from Russell without saying a word.

"Mike, you can't leave; we're sharing the same limo," Russell says as he hustles after Mike. Russell reaches into his pocket and pulls out his cell phone.

"Hello?"

Elsewhere in the terminal; Chris walks away from his gate.

"Hey, you here?"

"Yea, me and Pennisi are at baggage claim, where are you?" Chris spots Russell across the airport and starts walking in his direction.

They embrace in a hug.

"Where's Pennisi?" Chris asks.

"He's in a terrible mood, he's cursing in front of kids about chafing dishes," Russell replies. Mike stops pacing in the corner and comes back to where Russell and Chris are. Chris hugs Mike.

"What's this shit about chafing dishes," Chris asks. Mike's face turns bright red. "Actually, you know what, doesn't matter." Mike starts rubbing his ears and pacing again.

"What did you get them?" Russell asks Chris. "Me? I didn't get them anything. I was just gonna ask Mike to put my name on his."

Russell and Chris look at Mike as he begins to walk away again. "I'm just kidding Mike. What did you say the same thing to him?" Russell nods his head.

"And it really pissed him off?" Russell nods his head again.

"Mike, I love you—come back."

Russell and Chris follow Mike as he power walks away.

Back at the bridal compound, the doorbell rings. John bounds down the stairs and through the living room to the front door. Opening it he sees Matt McDonnell—his best man.

"Man, you already look different," Matt says as he lays eyes on the soon-to-be-married man.

"In what way?"

"You look shittier than usual," Matt replies. He steps into the house and gives John a big hug, "How you feelin, big dog?"

John smiles and picks up Matt's bag.

Jenna walks in from the kitchen to meet Matt, waving her arms excitedly. She gives Matt a big hug that nearly knocks him off his feet.

"Someone's excited," Matt says as he regains his balance.

"I'm so happy you're here, I'm so happy you're the best man, I'm...so happy!" Jenna says.

Matt looks at John, who wears a big grin.

"Are you staying here at the house?" Jenna asks. Matt shakes his head and laughs, "No, I got a room at the hotel. All the guys are gonna be there...so...it's gonna get fucking crazy."

"Oh okay that's cool," Jenna replies. "Is Daphne coming this weekend?"

"Actually, me and Daphne broke up a couple of weeks ago," Matt replies.

"Yea, I told you that," John says to Jenna.

"What happened? I was really looking forward to meeting her," Jenna says.

"Uhhh...well this is awkward..." Matt says as John and Jenna look at each other.

"She wanted to get married," Matt says.

John laughs, "Who does that?"

"What time is the rehearsal dinner?" Matt asks, moving along to something else quickly before it gets too awkward. Too late.

Jenna clears her throat and replies, "It's at seven," an answer that pierces the current unease in the doorway of this huge house.

The house phone rings and Jenna and John both say, "I'll get it."

Jenna walks toward the phone, "I'll get it; you keep talking to Matt. It's great to see you again, Matt."

"Good to see you, Jenna," Matt replies. As Jenna disappears into the other room, Matt and John look at each other.

"That was bad," John says. Matt laughs and punches John in the arm. A light bulb goes off above his head.

"Oh shit, I almost forgot. I got two tickets to John Pepper at Madison Square Garden next month."

"Really? Nice! Jenna loves him; she's gonna be so excited."

Matt's eyebrows raise, "Yea...maybe we can get her a T-shirt or something."

John realizes, "Oh—you mean me and you go to the concert—shit, I thought it was like a wedding present or something."

Matt just stands there.

"I got you a wedding present but—I got the tickets for me and you to go, because we've seen him like four times and—."

"Oh yea, yea, sure—it's just wedding shit, like everything is me and her..."

Matt nods his head. The unease has returned.

"Alright, it looks like you got a lot of shit to do here—and I gotta check into the hotel and everything. What time are you getting over there tonight?"

"Probably five-ish, I wanna hang out with everyone before we start... everything," John replies.

Matt picks up his bag and opens the front door, "Alright dude, I'll see you later."

Matt walks across the grass to the driveway, putting on his sunglasses as he does it. John closes the front door as Matt gets into his car and pulls away.

"Do you sleep naked?"

The female limo driver looks into the rear view mirror quickly, "Excuse me?"

"Do you sleep naked?" D'Ascoli repeats. The driver stops short. She turns around and looks right at D'Ascoli.

"If you ever ask me that question again I will rip your balls off and shove them down your fucking throat."

"So that's a 'yes' then," D'Ascoli replies. The driver begins to drive again, slowly raising the partition between the front seat and back.

"Honest question..." D'Ascoli mumbles. Chris sits there slack jawed.

"Try to be on your best behavior this weekend. I mean it's not just us—there's gonna be grandmas and grandpas. You know, third cousins, little kids," Chris states.

"I love little kids, I hope to have a few of my own some day," D'Ascoli replies.

"I hope their mother isn't the one who replies favorable to 'Do you sleep naked?' I weep for those children if that's the case."

"I'm an inspiration to you, Hall. I give you all of your good material; I am the star of all of your *good* novels. You're just mad that you can't say shit like, 'Do you sleep naked?' to someone other then a blank page. I got a deep bench of girls—I pull girls off the bench like a sixth man—and don't freak out this weekend when you see your life flash in front of your eyes. You're next on this whole crazy 'let's get married, split everything I have with someone else, flush all my hopes and dreams down the toilet' thing."

"I don't know what you're referring to," Chris replies. D'Ascoli reaches into the bar in the limo and pours himself a drink.

"You don't know what I'm referring to—that's bullshit, Hall!"

"Hey, I'm not a huge fan of marriage, you know this. Her parents got divorced when she was six; she hates fucking marriage too. I don't think it's gonna happen any time soon, if at all. We both have too much shit we want to do," Chris replies pointedly.

"*Every* woman is a fan of marriage; you're a smarter man than that Hall. Alright, I got a question for you. Last night when we were on the phone and you compared the rehearsal dinner and wedding to a wake and a funeral what did she say? I know she was in the room—what did she say?" D'Ascoli asks.

"It was a joke."

"Yea but she still said something didn't she—didn't she?" D'Ascoli continues prodding.

Chris looks away from D'Ascoli and out the window.

"BOOM!" D'Ascoli exclaims, waving his hands wildly, almost spilling his drink.

"I hope you don't like those first two books, Hall, because when she's through with you—it might as well have her name on the cover. It'll be your words, but it'll be her cash."

"I'm not talking to you for the rest of the weekend."

As the town car arrives into the cul-de-sac of the hotel, Jeff is finishing a cigarette. D'Ascoli sticks his head out the window, which causes a smile to come across Singer's face. D'Ascoli triumphantly pushes open the back door and steps out, raising his hands in the air.

"Go home," Jeff says, dropping his cigarette onto the ground. D'Ascoli, still with drink in hand, walks over to Singer and gives him a big hug.

"I'm really sorry about him, I apologize profusely," Chris says to the female driver as he grabs his bags out of the trunk.

"It's okay, I usually get a lot worse," the female driver replies, "I'm Rachel by the way."

"It's nice to meet you, Rachel. Either way, I'm sorry," Chris continues, "D'Ascoli come and get your bags."

"Carry my bags, Hall. Without me you'd have no material for your next book," D'Ascoli replies.

"Yea, I wanna see some compensation coming my way. I'm not the huge drug addict that you made me out to be in the last book," Singer chimes in.

"You're an author?" the female driver asks.

"Depends on which critic you ask," Chris replies.

"Anything I might have read?" she continues.

"Probably not. I've done some stuff...but no...you haven't heard of me. Believe me—my mom has barely heard of me."

"Hmm...an author. I've never dated an author," Rachel playfully responds.

"Me neither," Chris says with a laugh. Rachel reaches into her pocket and pulls out a card, handing it to Chris.

"Give me a call this weekend, maybe we can get a drink or something."

"You're very nice, but I have a girlfriend," Chris replies bashfully, handing the card back in Rachel's direction.

"Either way...keep it," Rachel says, flashing him a smile as she moves past him. She grabs D'Ascoli's bags and tosses them out of the trunk, landing with a thud on the pavement.

"I'm gonna fill out a comment card...you're lucky you're very hot," D'Ascoli replies to the transgression. Rachel opens her door and gives Chris one more look before ducking inside.

Chris walks over to Jeff, giving him a big hug.

"What's up, beautiful?" Jeff says as he and Chris release their embrace.

"You guys were awfully chatty," D'Ascoli says.

"She gave me her number," Chris replies, showing Jeff and D'Ascoli Rachel's card.

"Too bad your cock is in the cupboard above the stove," D'Ascoli replies. He rips the card out of Chris' hand.

"I'll put this to good use."

"Where's Maria?" Chris asks.

"She's upstairs; she said she's not feeling good. Where are Mike and Russell?" Jeff asks, reaching back into his cigarettes.

"Their car was a little bit behind ours; they should be getting here soon," Chris replies. D'Ascoli reaches into Jeff's pack of cigarettes and pulls out one for himself to go along with his almost finished glass of scotch. He reaches in for another one to put behind his ear and pulls out a little white piece of paper with it.

"What's this?"

Jeff grabs the piece of paper out of D'Ascoli's hand and opens it.

"Maria writes me little notes and puts them in places for me to find," Jeff replies as he opens the mash note. Inside it reads 'Pookie.'

"Pookie? I guess that's better than Jeffums like Kim used to call you," D'Ascoli says as he glances at the note.

"Man—Kim. That was a long time ago," Jeff says as he reflects on one of his previous affairs.

"Maybe she'll show up this weekend," D'Ascoli says.

"You think so? Man, I hope not…is Kenney still friends with her?" Jeff considers.

"I think anyone is fair game to show up. Jenna's dad is footing the bill and she invited a bunch of people," Chris chimes in.

The three men pause for a second, as the faces and names of the people they hope don't show up run through their minds.

"I wouldn't mind fucking Deena again," D'Ascoli says.

"Wasn't she in a mental institution for a while?" Jeff replies.

"Crazy girls are always superwomen in the sack," D'Ascoli says with a smirk.

Mike and Russell's town car pulls into the cul-de-sac. Mike's car door flies open before his chariot even stops.

"Oh boy he looks angry," Jeff observes. He shouts out, "Hey Carmine, how you doin?"

"Shit—Carmine? I haven't heard you call him that in years," D'Ascoli says with a laugh.

Mike flips off Jeff without even breaking stride toward the trunk. Opening the trunk, he grabs his bag, and walks toward the assembled boys.

"I need a cigarette on my lips, a beer in my mouth and a pussy on my dick," Mike says. Jeff hands him a cigarette.

"And by cigarette you mean cum, by beer you mean cock and by pussy you mean Kenney's hairy anus hole," D'Ascoli replies. Mike lights the cigarette and exhales into the air. He grabs D'Ascoli's scotch and finishes it.

"Man that chafing dish is really fucking up your whole existence isn't it," Chris says.

Jeff laughs, "You bought that piece of shit?"

"Someone mentions that fucking chafing dish one more time..."

"And what? That's right, you're not gonna do shit," D'Ascoli antagonizes. Mike picks up his bag and walks into the hotel lobby.

"He's an angry little fucker today isn't he?" Jeff says. Russell wanders over after tipping the driver.

"That was the worst car ride of my life. He is either gonna commit suicide this weekend or tackle a 12-year-old during the chicken dance," Russell says.

"I hope it's suicide," D'Ascoli says.

"I'd rather he do a Macho Man elbow off the bar onto a grandma," Jeff chimes in.

CHAPTER ELEVEN

The rehearsal dinner space has 15-20 long tables; each one covered with huge centerpieces that would surely dive into the plates of whoever had the misfortune of sitting in its general vicinity. The bride and groom table is even gaudier, raised above all the others; it has a huge floral arrangement with strange yellow florescent gels illuminating it from below. The florescent gels looked like a stoned kid in 2010 saw a lava lamp and said, 'I can improve this.' The impeccably shined gold chairs and almost reflective table clothes that line every table did nothing to downplay the decadence.

"There is a lot of yellow and gold, I feel like we're in a late 90's Puff Daddy video," John says aloud. Jenna has her head draped on his shoulder, her hand moving up and down his arm.

"My dad had a lot of *interesting* ideas for the setup of the rehearsal dinner."

"Like when he was in those bubble jackets floating in the air with Mase," John continues, "With those big bug-eyed goggles."

"Yea I think I got it the first time," Jenna replies with a snap.

"Are we sure we're in the right room? Like is Prince and the Revolution in town or something?"

"Do you have one more in you?"

"Maybe."

"Just let it out."

"Did we jump in a time machine and end up where MC Hammer partied when 'U Can't Touch This' went gold?" John finishes.

"Honey, you are so damn funny," Jenna replies sarcastically.

"Does everyone that attends tonight get a free pair of baggy skirt pants like Hammer's? Can I wear a yellow leather jacket with nothing underneath when I'm giving my toast?"

"I hate you so much," Jenna says as she wanders toward one of the tables.

"It would match the floral arrangements baby," he continues. Jenna continues to wander through the room, adjusting silverware and napkins.

"Are you just doing that nervous thing when you are so debilitated by anxiety that all your brain can produce is 80's and 90's pop minutia?" Jenna says.

"Just don't let a remake of the 'November Rain' video break out tomorrow. I hate rain and none of my friends look like Slash. Well maybe Billy if we gave him a pair of leather chaps and an Abe Lincoln hat," he replies.

"I love you my little man boy," Jenna says.

"I love you too, stay around a while," John replies.

Jenna smiles and walks back toward John. He grabs her hand and they walk toward the door of the banquet hall. John stops in his tracks.

"Wait I forgot something," he says.

"What?"

"Ring the bell, school's back in!" John screams as he Hammer shuffles out of the room.

Chris steps out onto the balcony of his two-bedroom suite. Holding his cell phone to his ear, he closes the glass door behind him. Chris looks out into the evergreen trees that surround the hotel. The phone continues to ring. Voicemail. *'Hey this is Erin, leave a message and I'll get back to you'*

"Hey, it's me. I'm just checking in...I hope your day is going better. Gimme a call whenever you get a chance. I checked into the room, it's pretty nice...alright. I'll talk to you later. I love you."

Chris hangs up the phone and turns to open the door. He is instead met with a view of Mike's bare ass pressed up against the glass. Mike farts, which makes a strange sound bouncing off the coated glass.

Chris opens the door to Mike laughing as he pulls his pants up.

"I don't know why I thought sharing a room with you would be a good idea," Chris says.

"Shut the fuck up, give me a hug," Mike replies.

"No, I don't want to get any of your fart on me, you're like a skunk." Chris hugs him anyway and then wanders over to the couch. Grabbing the remote, he puts his feet up on the glass table.

"I miss you man," Chris says.

"I miss you too," Mike replies as he relaxes into a recliner. These two men were roommates for a good part of their adult years. What once was, is now again.

"What's with this grizzly man beard?" Chris asks.

"It's called being a fucking man, you should try it sometime."

Mike starts to itch the beard, looking at his fingernails when he's done.

"You looking for something in there?" Chris says as he turns on the television.

"You doing okay?" Chris asks. Mike looks at him.

"I'm doing great," Mike replies.

"No, I mean are you doing okay for real, not are you doing okay for the dickheads that ask because they have nothing else to talk about."

"I guess I'm alright; my job sucks...trying to look around for a new one. Russell and Tom are never around, Tom more so than Russell. They're always out on the road; they leave on short notice for all this shit. So that's a little weird. It's kind of like I live by myself, which is good for jerking off but not great when you have nothing to do on a Tuesday night," Mike replies.

Chris nods, "How's Monica doing?"

"That shit is over; we had nothing we could talk about. We kind of just ate out a lot and fucked in uncomfortable places."

"What?" Chris says with a laugh.

"She lived like half an hour away from me and she doesn't have a car. So whenever we went out I would have to drive all the way across town to pick her up. Then we would go see a movie or get dinner or something and we couldn't go back to her parents' place."

"Wait what? Her parents' place? How old is this girl?"

"Twenty-five. She moved back in with her parents because her credit got all fucked up, another reason why she doesn't have a car...so yea, that sucked. We would do something and I didn't want to drive *all* the way back across town to have sex at the apartment and *then* have to drive her *all* the way back to her parents' place, so we ended up going to a high school parking lot and fucking in my back seat," Mike continues.

"Why didn't she just sleep at your place over night?"

"C'mon man, I need my rest. I don't have any time for that shit," Mike replies.

"What, was the sex terrible?" Chris replies.

"The sex was fine, but after a while my back would just fucking kill me and any sort of pleasure that I would get out of busting my nut would automatically be numbed by the pain in my lower back—I swear to God, we used to make fun of my dad all the time when he would complain about his back and legs hurting. Remember? It's the truth; shit just starts hurting after a while."

"So how did it end?" Chris asks.

"It was probably the ninth time that we were banging in the parking lot of the field I used to play little league at, when I realized I was having sex with a 25-year-old girl who still lived with her parents and had a worse credit score than

Antoine Walker. I think that might have been the tipping point into, 'What the fuck am I doing?'"

"That'll do it."

Matt paces around the hotel room with a drink in his hand, a white dress shirt folded over his shoulder. He is flipping through index cards, perusing the best man speech he is due to make.

There is a knock at the door.

Matt drops the cards on the living room table and heads for the door. As he opens it, he sees John.

"Put a shirt on," John says as he walks past Matt into the room.

"Don't be mad that I'm in better shape than you," Matt replies. John lies down on the couch in the living room. He flips his shoes off and closes his eyes.

"What's wrong with you?"

"I have a headache and I'm exhausted," John replies. Matt opens the fridge and pulls out a bottle of vodka. He pours John a drink.

"Have a drink...or ten," Matt says, placing the drink in front of John's face. He rises up from the couch and takes the cup, moving it to his mouth in one fluid motion. He braces for the kick back.

"You got anything stronger?" John asks.

"I think I saw some turpentine underneath the sink," Matt replies. John takes another drink and then lies down. Matt takes a seat across from John, grabbing his notes off the table, he again begins to read.

A few moments of silence pass.

"We could be on a plane in 45 minutes," Matt says. John laughs.

"Yea, where would we go?" he replies.

"Amsterdam...New York...we could go to that bar in L.A. where Russell got the blowjob from that hooker with the Homer Simpson tattoo," Matt says without looking up from his notes. "This speech isn't very good anyway," Matt throws the cards on the table.

"Yea I wasn't expecting much. You cheated off me in English Lit for two semesters," John says, sitting up and continuing with his drink.

"What's wrong with you?" Matt asks. John chuckles. He finishes his drink.

"Give me another and I'll tell you."

Matt grabs John's glass and walks over to the bar. His pours him another drink and then walks back toward the couch. He stops in his tracks and reaches back for the vodka bottle. He hands John the glass and puts the bottle down on the living room table.

"It'll save on travel," Matt says.

"That's why you're my best man."

John takes another drink. "I just have this feeling like I'm missing something." Matt looks at him quizzically.

"What do you mean?"

"I mean, everything seems to be in its right place and I'm like, 'what?'" John replies.

"Alright, are you drunk already or am I? Cause your speaking some sort of language that I do not have the cognitive ability to understand."

John cracks his neck. "Alright, for my whole life, there has always been something wrong. Like things go good for a little bit then my cat gets hit by a truck, or my computer crashes or my car gets totaled. The universe always corrects itself, everything good eventually gets smashed with a baseball bat. You know what I mean?" John says.

"No, but keep going."

"When I met Jenna, my life sucked—like *sucked*. I had a shitty job and my dad just died and...she came out of nowhere. She was the autocorrect. Since then everything has been great and I can't help shake this feeling that something bad is coming down the pike," John continues.

"Like what?"

"What if I'm a shitty husband...or I lose my job...or she leaves me...or she turns into an axe murderer like what happened to Mike Myers."

"Great movie," Matt replies.

"Very underrated."

"I don't think she's gonna leave you," Matt says.

"You don't even really know her that well though," John replies.

"That's true. But I know you," Matt replies.

"Jesus, I need to drink more," John says, pouring another drink.

"Another thing is like, what am I giving up? Don't get me wrong, I never had a great single life where I bedded women left and right like D'Ascoli. I was the guy who maybe, *maybe* hooked up with a girl once every couple of months. But now I'll have all these responsibilities to someone else and I can't go out drinking on

Tuesday after work because I have to go to the supermarket to pick up cough medicine or lettuce or Pepto Bismol because she's constipated. I can't just pick up on a whim and go to the city with you guys and do stupid shit. Like all of the stuff that isn't advertised in the marriage pamphlet where they tell you how everything is so great."

"Alright. One, you're getting married, not serving under Chairman Mao. She'll probably let you go out after work for a drink. Two, she'll have to buy Pepto Bismol for your constipated ass at least once, probably ten times. Three, all of us are never really under the same roof unless we're in a funeral home or a wedding chapel, it's not like all of us go out five nights a week with strippers and huff Leroy Jenkums in a church parking lot with crack heads. And finally, like you said, since she showed up, shit has been pretty good. You have to stop being a worrying little pussy," Matt replies.

"Do you believe that?"

"No, I'm just telling you what you want to hear," Matt replies.

"It's just fear of the unknown man; it all comes down to—I can't be stupid anymore," John says.

"How about we do something stupid then?" Matt replies.

John looks up from his drink, "What do you mean?"

"I mean today marks the last 24-hour period in which you can do something incredibly stupid and not get yelled at by your wife. You can get yelled at by your fiancée, sure, but a wife tongue lashing and a fiancée tongue lashing, according to my dad, are two entirely different things. Let's get some stupid in."

"What do you want to do?"

"Two questions. Do you know D'Ascoli's room number and have you taken a shit today?" Matt replies.

D'Ascoli sits at the hotel bar next to a brunette he is chatting up. Her name is either Stephanie or Ashley, he can't really remember. He stares into her blue eyes as she talks about politics, poetry and pool cleaning gear. D'Ascoli is only listening passively, he's mostly thinking of what this girl would look like naked.

As she continues her speeches and press releases, D'Ascoli puts his finger over her lips. She stops talking and peers down at his index finger.

"We're grownups, talking about grownup things, at a bar at five in the afternoon, on a Friday. Let's stop being grownups for a little while," he says, lifting his finger away from her lips.

"I'm thinking champagne, chocolate covered bon bons and whatever else you'd like off the menu," he continues. The bartender looks at D'Ascoli quizzically, thinking, *"What the fuck is this guy saying?"*

Stephanie (or Ashley) looks at him with fierce eyes and turns to the bartender, "I'd like to close out my tab."

D'Ascoli looks down the bar at an old man watching this whole thing. They give each other a nod.

"I'd like to close out my tab as well and this should be enough for both of them," D'Ascoli says, throwing a 100 dollar bill on the marble and grabbing Stephanie's (or Ashley's) hand and heading out of the bar.

Stephanie (or Ashley) takes off her heels as she and D'Ascoli walk across the lobby. They head for the front desk, currently occupied by a man in a headset. D'Ascoli taps the little bell for service and the man in the headset looks up.

"Hey man, I'm gonna need a bottle of champagne, an order of bon bons—"

"Chocolate covered," Stephanie (or Ashley) chimes in.

"Chocolate covered bon bons, some whipped cream, anything else?" D'Ascoli asks, turning to Stephanie (or Ashley). She thinks for a second.

"A chicken parm," she says. D'Ascoli nods his head.

"You know what? Make that two. I'll probably be hungry afterward. That is going to room 428," D'Ascoli finishes. Stephanie (or Ashley) pulls D'Ascoli by the tie away from the front desk.

"As soon as possible, chief," D'Ascoli bellows as he is pulled toward the elevator.

Jeff walks in from outside to see D'Ascoli heading toward the elevators. He follows suit to the lift.

"Look at you two lovebirds," Jeff says as he approaches. D'Ascoli pulls out his phone.

"Yea we're ordering in some room service, keep my seat warm at the rehearsal dinner tonight," D'Ascoli says as he pecks away at the keys on his cell phone.

Jeff's phone beeps, reaching into his pocket, he reads a message and then introduces himself to Stephanie (or Ashley).

"By the way I'm Jeff, what's your name?"

"It's Karen; it's very nice to meet you. Are you a friend of Christopher's?"

D'Ascoli makes a face and mouths "Karen?" He shrugs his shoulders.

"Oh yea, a long time, he's a good guy," Jeff says as the elevator door opens. D'Ascoli and Karen get on, followed by Jeff. Seconds after the doors close, D'Ascoli and Karen start making out.

"Don't mind me," Jeff says. Jeff looks over to see the two not paying attention. He starts to say things to no one.

"Man I wonder if the Rangers are gonna be any good this year."

Nothing.

"My pee has a green twinge to it...do you think I should get that checked out?"

Still nothing.

"D'Ascoli is hung like an infant," Jeff finishes.

"That's a lie," D'Ascoli replies.

The elevator stops on the fourth floor and D'Ascoli and Karen get out while making out. The door closes and Jeff continues on his way up to the sixth floor. As the doors open, Jeff is met by Matt and John. John is holding his ass.

"What the fuck are you doing, Kenney? Hiding your wedding ring up your bunghole?" Jeff asks as Matt and John enter the elevator.

"Have you seen D'Ascoli?" Matt asks.

"Yea he went back to his room with some hottie; they ordered room service or some shit," Jeff replies.

Matt screams, "Yes!" The elevator doors close and Jeff stands there stunned, "What the fuck is going on?"

In room 428, D'Ascoli and Karen are engaged in some heavy petting. "You taste like peaches," is overheard from the hallway. John waddles down the hallway with Matt not too far behind. They approach room 428 and hear D'Ascoli scream out something not fit for print.

A few minutes pass and John continues to hold his ass, "I can't hold it much longer captain, where is this room service?" As he says that, the elevator door clicks open and down the hallway comes a cart of D'Ascoli's food.

Matt starts to walk down the hallway, "Oh great! It's here; we are famished."

The delivery boy pushing the cart looks up, "Mr. D'Ascoli?"

Matt gets into character, "Yes, the one and only Chris D'Ascoli. I want to thank you for your quick service. I'm gonna take this food and eat it off of my lover over here," Matt says.

"It's no problem sir, just sign here," the delivery boy says, handing Matt the bill.

"You have done such a good job today that I want you to do two things," Matt continues. The delivery boy nods his head.

"One, I want you to add a $100 tip to this bill. It's yours; that's the small gratitude I can show to you for delivering this food so quickly for my lover and I."

The delivery boy looks at John who gives a wave and then quickly moves his hands back to his ass.

"And two, I have a friend up on the sixth floor in room 624, his name is Matt McDonnell. I want you to send him a bottle of champagne, just bill it to my room."

The delivery boy shakes his head again, "Definitely sir, thank you so much for the tip, it's gonna help me pay my student loans."

"No problem. You know what? Make it $200 and keep chasing the American dream son," Matt says.

The delivery boy is overjoyed, he turns and sprints toward the elevator, "I'm gonna go get that champagne sir, on the double."

"Thanks so much. Oh! One more thing! Do you know who does the payroll for this hotel? I sell payroll for a living and you must have 200, 300 people on staff here—"

"Honey, I'm really hungry let's go," John shouts out. Matt turns toward John and then back to the delivery boy.

"Forget it, have a nice day." The delivery boy boards the elevator and Matt takes the shiny silver cart and wheels it toward John.

Matt lifts the tops off the sterling silver containers, looking at what's inside, "Chicken parm and bons bons. Wow—that's a combo."

Stopping in front of John, who looks like he's about to blow, Matt takes the top off the chicken parm and says, "You ready?"

John nods, drops his pants and squats on top of the chicken parm.

A few moments pass and there is a knock at D'Ascoli's door.

"Room service!" a voice shouts out.

D'Ascoli breaks his flow and runs over to the door. He opens it to see the silver cart sitting in the hallway. He rubs his hands together and begins to peek inside each of the sterling silver containers.

"Champagne, bon bons, one chicken parm..." and then as he lifts the last one, "and the...WHAT THE FUCK!" D'Ascoli looks down on the chocolate doody covered chicken parm. D'Ascoli's eyes dart around the hallway to see Matt and John peeking out behind the corner and laughing hysterically.

D'Ascoli mouths, "You motherfuckers!" in the loudest one can whisper. Matt and John flip him the bird and then run toward the stairs.

D'Ascoli is beside himself.

"What's wrong, Christopher?" Karen says from the room. D'Ascoli scrambles.

"Nothing sweetie, I think they just put the chocolate covered bon bons on the same plate as your chicken parm," D'Ascoli says as he takes the contaminated chocolate frosted plate and puts it down on the ground.

D'Ascoli rolls the cart into the room.

"You can have mine, beautiful; I think I've lost my appetite."

D'Ascoli's hotel room door closes for a second. It swings back open and D'Ascoli takes his 'DO NOT DISTURB' sign and puts it over the poop parmigiana container sitting on the floor.

"That's about right," D'Ascoli says with a shrug.

John ascends the hotel stairs gingerly, hoping to duck in the first bathroom he sees to wipe himself—yes, that is as disgusting as it sounds. Matt bounds up the stairs in front of him. Reaching the sixth floor, Matt pulls open the door and almost runs into a mountain—William Stevenson.

"Hey, Mr. Stevenson," Matt mumbles out, like a kid who runs into a teacher when he is doing something wrong. John appears through the door and meets eyes with William. Fear surges through his veins. He's standing in front of his future father-in-law with poop nuggets in his drawers.

"John, I've been looking for you," William says. He soon puts his nose in the air.

"Do you guys smell something?"

John's eyes widen; he takes a step back. Matt turns around and looks at John, his eyes widening to a comic proportion.

"I stepped in some dog shit. I was outside, and this lady was walking her little, what do you call those things? One of those cross breed things, like a cockapoo or a beaglehuia or something. One of those little fuckers," Matt spits out.

"Yea, I read a story that those little dogs have surprisingly big digestive tracks," William replies.

"Oh yea, this was a *huge* shit, I don't know how I missed it," Matt continues, "I cleaned up my shoe but I guess—"

"Well just don't wear them tonight, obviously," William says.

"Of course sir, of course," Matt replies.

"So what's up?" John asks.

"I was wondering if I could talk to you about something," William replies.

"Yea sure, absolutely. Now?" John replies.

"Yea now would be great."

John and Matt both nod their heads.

"Can I just go to the bathroom first?" John asks.

"Sure."

John walks toward Matt's hotel room and quickly ducks inside. Matt closes the door behind him as John runs into the bathroom. John closes the door and after some rustling he utters, "Shit."

"What?" Matt says as he walks toward the bathroom door.

"I got some inside my pants. I need pants...gimme a pair of your pants," John says, poking his out of the door.

"What are you kidding me? My pants will never fit you, fat man in a little coat," Matt replies.

"Give me something! I'm not going to have a talk with the father of the girl I'm marrying in 18 hours with shit running down my leg!" John exclaims at Matt.

"Maybe you aren't cut out for this marriage thing," Matt replies.

"This was all your fucking idea. I'm fucked. You gotta find me something and quick; I can't have Hulk waiting out there too long," John shoots back.

Hulk knocks on the door. John makes hand motions toward the door for Matt to go to talk to him. Matt shakes his head 'no.' John picks up a roll of toilet paper and flings at Matt.

"Personally, I think you're gonna need that."

Matt walks over to the door and opens it to see William.

"Is he alright in there?" William asks.

"Yea he's fine, just some bad Chinese food...how about you go down to the bar and he'll meet you down there," Matt quickly thinks up. William looks at Matt with narrow eyes.

"Alright, tell him to hurry up. The rehearsal dinner starts in less than an hour," William says, turning and walking away.

"Will do, Mr. Stevenson! I'll see you soon." Matt yells down the hallway and then quickly closes the door. John walks out of the bathroom in a towel.

"C'mon man, I only got two of those," Matt says, pointing to the towel.

"Fuck you. I need new pants and I don't have enough time to go back to his house to get some. So what are we gonna do?"

Matt thinks.

"There's only one person who would have pants that might fit you."

D'Ascoli opens his door in a bathrobe.

"You owe me a chicken parm...and a boner," D'Ascoli says to Matt and John—still in a towel standing in front of his hotel door.

"I don't know what you're talking about," Matt replies.

"Why are you in a towel?" D'Ascoli asks, looking down at John's mismatched wardrobe, shirt and tie up top, checkered towel down below.

"I need a pair of pants," John replies.

"What happened to yours?" D'Ascoli asks.

"I spilled some red wine," John says with a straight face.

"Man, red wine on black pants. The only thing that I can think of that might ruin black pants would be something white...or brown," D'Ascoli says with a smirk.

"Are you gonna give me the fucking pants or what? I got less than an hour until this dinner and I still gotta meet with her father," John says impatiently. D'Ascoli reaches into his robe and pulls out his phone.

"Sure I'll give you pants, but, you have to record a new outgoing message for my voicemail that says, 'My name is John Kenney and I shit my pants on the day of my rehearsal dinner,'" D'Ascoli offers.

John exhales, "Fine." He tries to enter the room but D'Ascoli puts his hand out.

"No message, no pants," D'Ascoli says, extending his phone into John's face—who grabs the phone and records the message.

"Make sure you press the pound button or that shit won't save," D'Ascoli adds. John presses the pound key.

"I don't have any extra pants," D'Ascoli says as John walks into the room. John's head swivels quickly.

"WHAT?"

D'Ascoli laughs, "Nah, I'm just fucking with you...come on."

John enters the hotel restaurant and pans the space for William. He spots him sitting at the end of the bar, his large frame tucked into the corner of the establishment. John quickly walks over and pats William on the shoulder.

"Hey, you feeling better?" William asks.

"Yea much better," John responds as he takes a seat next to William.

"You want something to drink?" William asks. John shakes his head. William smiles and begins to stare at his future son-in-law.

John feels the unease setting in again. William continues to look at John and with each second it seems as if William is growing in size, like he is about to bust out of the roof of this bar. The silence makes John shift in his seat.

"Are you nervous?" William asks.

"About what?" John replies meekly.

"Getting married! It's a big deal, life changing some say," William continues. "Or are you just nervous in general? Because every time I see you it looks like you smelled a bad fart."

A smile creeps across John's face.

"Actually, no...I'm not nervous, I'm actually pretty happy."

"Why are you happy?"

"I'm happy because of your daughter; she's the only good thing in my life and I'm only nervous around you because I wouldn't wanna fuck that one good thing up. I was talking to Matt before, and I realized that since she's come into my life...everything's been great. I don't think it's merely coincidental. I don't know how you feel about me, because frankly we don't know each other all that well, but I am head over heels in love with your daughter," John says.

William smiles, "I think you have something to ask me."

"Can I please marry your daughter?" John asks.

"I'd ask you why you wanna marry my daughter, but I think you just said it," William replies.

William and John shake hands.

"Better late than never," John says. William gives John a big slap on his back.

"Don't fuck over my daughter or I will break your legs...slowly."

"And there goes the Kodak moment," John replies.

"Go to the rehearsal hall, I'll be over in a second," William says as he finishes his drink. John reaches into his pocket and pulls out a $20.

"Drink's on me," he says, placing the $20 on the marble bar.

"It's the least you can do. I've paid for everything else this weekend," William says with a laugh.

John pats William on the back and walks away from the bar.

Rain hits the car hood as Russell King sits in the backseat of a town car. He peers down at his watch and taps his foot, anxious that Tom still hasn't gotten to the car and the rehearsal dinner is due to begin shortly. Looking out the backseat window, he sees Tom running with a jacket over his head. Tom rips open the door and dives into the backseat.

"Alright man, we got him. Punch it Chewie—the dinner starts in 25 minutes," Russell says to the driver peering in the rear view mirror. Tom shakes his head, spraying rain droplets around the car.

He pushes the button for the glass divider, it slowly closing off the back seat of the car. As it seals, Tom makes himself a drink.

"How bad it is?" Russell asks.

"I didn't get the suitcase…and I think I have a broken wrist," Tom replies, raising his bandaged wrist.

"What was in the case?" Russell asks.

Tom shakes his head, "I have no idea. They just sent me in to extract."

"Alright, Langley will track it down and we'll go get it next week," Russell says, rubbing his eyebrow. Tom wears a look of uncertainty.

"What?"

"I don't think we're gonna have another shot at this thing; this girl was a pro," Tom replies.

"A girl, huh?" Russell says with a laugh. Tom flips off Russell and continues with his drink.

"Wow, a girl kicked your ass," Russell continues.

"Can we just drop this? I have a headache," Tom replies. Russell nods his head and looks out the window. The two men relax in the car.

"Wow, a girl kicked your ass."

"Fuck you, Russ."

"I can't believe I forgot about this," Tom says.

"What?"

"The wedding. One of my best friends is getting married and I need you to remind 24 hours before," Tom continues.

"You work too much man. You gotta take a vacation or something; you haven't been home in weeks."

Tom nods his head, "I do need a vacation, don't I?"

"You do; you miss too much stuff trying to be fucking Captain America. I got out of that; I'm sitting at a desk now, not fighting superwomen who affect my masturbation habits," Russell says. "We're not 21 anymore."

The two stare out their respective windows and watch the scenery. Tom rubs his eyes—he's tired, he hasn't slept in a while. He's coming upon another stop on a never-ending tour. Russell is right, he doesn't come home anymore; his home is his carry-on bag. The job he's always wanted, and is very good at, is sapping his life. Maybe it's not worth it anymore. Maybe he should ease up on the gas pedal, stop dodging bullets everyday. Being a spy is a trying racket. But then again, maybe seeing his friends will recharge him. Make him feel whole again, even if just for the weekend. He's been sloppy at work lately, lost just a little bit of zeal for it all.

CHAPTER TWELVE

Beth sits outside the hotel smoking a cigarette—the flame of the butt the only thing keeping her fingers warm. The atmosphere must have dropped a few degrees due to the rain. She's here for the wedding; she doesn't really know why she was here though. Maybe she is one of those cursory invites. Like a seat filler. Someone much more important couldn't come and she is the alternate. Beth is a very negative thinker. There is something about being here though. Any wedding actually, it acts as an alarm for people and their life clocks. They tell each and every person that isn't married that someone else is doing it, and maybe even raise the question of why your not. Some people are fine with this question. Some aren't. Some stress as if they are the ones getting married. They think as if they are wasting their time, that they should be married by now, that they should have a kid right now. Some people react to this crisis of faith by banging the nearest groomsman or bridesmaid. Others drink the tap dry, stumble out to the car and then puke on the bride's aunt. Humans have a weird way of dealing with things.

Beth continues smoking. Maybe she should get in the car and get out of here. Go somewhere warmer—a place where the cigarette in her hand wasn't the warmest thing within 100 miles.

"Beth?" a voice says. Beth looks off her cigarette to see a woman, a friend from yesteryear. Beth looks at the woman for a second and can't place her. Her brain flips through the rolodex of her memories until she lands on that face. It's Caroline.

"Caroline," Beth replies as she flicks away her cigarette and gets up off the bench. She walks over and embraces Caroline in a hug.

"It's so good to see you," Caroline says. Years had separated them now. They use to be close, but years let their respective ships float further and further away from one another. They commiserate about their lives and where they are now. They fall back into that old rhythm like jazz partners who reunite after years of playing their saxophones with others. They bring up old memories and those stories. Beth feels a little bit warmer. They both wonder aloud who will be at the wedding.

"What are you doing now?" Caroline asks. Beth smiles and runs down her CV. "I went to graduate school to become a teacher. Graduated, then found out I hated kids."

Caroline laughs at the discovery.

"After that I wandered around for a little bit. I went to Europe for a few months, tried some lives on but none of them really fit all that snugly. I came back and lived with my parents for a while, then I kind of lucked into this job for a commodities firm," Beth continues, "I drifted for a while and, to be honest, I'm glad I did."

"I wish I had explored a little bit more," Caroline replies.

"What do you mean?" Beth asks, unsure of Caroline's words.

"I got divorced last year."

Beth's eyes explode to the margins, "From Gary?! You guys were like...I don't know...I don't have any positive marriages in my life that I could point to. Wow, why?"

"I have some space from it now and to be honest I don't think we were wrong for each other. We had great sex, we both had careers, but the mixture wasn't right. Maybe it was too soon? Too much too soon? I don't know. We both cheated on each other. It felt like we were still in college when we got married. We never had that moment after college where we could be complete morons, just fuck up left and right, get fired from jobs for being too drunk the night before and wandering into work with the bar toilet paper still attached to our shoe. We wanted to do those things but having a ring on your finger doesn't allow you to do that," she replies. Beth and Caroline both fall silent.

"It's really good to see you," Beth says to nothing in particular.

"Yea, it's good to see you. I wish I could say the same for the rest of these slobs," Caroline replies.

"I'm sure it'll be good to see Mike though," Beth says, part question, part statement. Caroline smiles.

"Yea it'll be good to see Mike."

"I wonder if that dickhead D'Ascoli is here," Beth says.

D'Ascoli knocks on Mike and Chris' room door.

"Let's go! I'm hungry," he says as he drums on the door. "Come on, stop jerking each other off."

"Come back in five minutes," Mike says from behind the door.

Chris opens the door to see D'Ascoli standing there with a drink in his hand.

"Drinking already?"

"I'm gonna have to be shitfaced to get through this rehearsal dinner with every aunt and uncle getting up and saying some bullshit speech, babbling on and o—"

"Kind of like what you're doing right now," Mike says as he walks out into the hallway past D'Ascoli.

"People actually like hearing what I have to say, Michael," D'Ascoli replies.

"Well I'm not one of them so shut the fuck up."

"Shave that shit off your face you squirrel looking fuck," D'Ascoli antagonizes.

"I swear you get funnier by the year, Christopher. I don't know how you do it."

Mike hits the elevator button.

John paces around the rehearsal dinner hall. He sees the guests filing in, taking seats at their gold spaceship tables. He reads the lips of some who question quietly, "What the fuck?" and he snickers to himself. Jenna's father shakes hands with all those entering; most people shake off the pain as they proceed to their tables.

Jenna strides over to John.

"Why did you change your pants?" she asks.

"What are you talking about?" he replies.

"They're different. What did you shit your pants?" Jenna continues.

"I don't know what you're talking about—these are totally the same pants that I was wearing before," John says as he wanders away to the front door.

"Where are you going? They don't sell Depends at the hotel gift shop," Jenna says.

John turns as he walks and blows Jenna a kiss. As he nears the door, Russell and Tom enter.

"Always late," John says to Tom, "What's up with the arm?"

"Boating accident," Tom replies quickly, as he moves past John to the tables.

"I didn't know you had a boat."

Tom comes to a stop.

"I don't."

John looks at Russell, who shrugs his shoulders. Tom stops walking and turns back toward John, he gives him a big hug.

"I've missed you John, congratulations," Tom says. John is surprised. Tom releases his hug and continues on to the tables.

"That's the first hug I've ever gotten from him," John says perplexed.

"It's a weird weekend, Kenney, just accept it," Russell replies.

Mike, Chris and D'Ascoli sit at a table toward the back of the hall. D'Ascoli continues to sip on his drink.

"No landmines yet," Mike says quietly, continuing to canvas the rehearsal hall.

"What do you mean?" Chris replies.

"I mean like no one so far that I need to avoid, no one where an awkward conversation might arise."

"You're awfully quiet," Chris says to D'Ascoli.

"I'm laying odds in my head of who I'm gonna be able to sleep with tonight. I'm thinking even on Melissa."

"She's got a boyfriend now," Mike replies.

"Really? She's got a boyfriend? I better take it off the board then, because now it's definitely gonna happen," D'Ascoli says, finishing his drink as he does it.

Then it happens. As D'Ascoli continues figuring if he needs to lay points, they walk into the room. Caroline and Beth. The long lost loves of the two boys sitting next to the odds-making idiot.

"Holy shit," Mike and Chris say in unison. Mike turns in his chair to face the wall. Chris continues staring. This was odd.

"Wow Pennisi, looks like your weekend just got a little worse—Hall, yours a little better," D'Ascoli says to the opposite facing men.

"You wanna go talk to them?" Chris asks Mike who is staring at the floorboards.

"Fuck no!" Mike replies, "That girl ripped my fucking heart out, pissed on me, then took a big dump on my dog's head."

D'Ascoli picks up Chris' phone from the table.

"If I know the universe's way, and I clearly do because look how fucking good looking I am, your phone will start ringing in five...four...three."

All of the boys' eyes widen. "Two...one...," D'Ascoli counts down.

Then...ringing. D'Ascoli's eyes widen.

"Holy shit, we're fucked," Mike says. Chris reaches for his phone and grabs it from D'Ascoli's hand. He looks at it.

He sees D'Ascoli's number.

"I totally got you," D'Ascoli says as he raises his phone from his lap. Chris cancels the call and puts his phone down on the table.

"I hope something awful happens to you this weekend, worse than herpes," Mike says to D'Ascoli.

Chris phone again rings, the three of them look down at it. D'Ascoli smiles.

"It's Erin," Chris says, as he grabs the phone and gets up from his seat. D'Ascoli pumps his hand in the air.

Chris opens the phone, "Hey, where are you?"

Erin sits crunched up in an airport terminal, peering out onto the dark tarmac, flurries bouncing off the large bay windows. "It's snowing here and my flight is cancelled, so I'm on standby for a fucking 11 p.m."

Chris runs his hands over his mouth, "What are they saying? Do you think you're gonna be able to get on it?"

"They don't know. I just figured I would let you know. How's it going over there?" Chris looks across the room to see Beth and Caroline.

"It'll be better when you get here," Chris replies.

"Baby you ready? We gotta get going," Jeff calls out from the bedroom. He makes his way across the room and toward the bathroom. Inside, Maria is blow drying her hair. She pauses for a second and turns off the blow dryer. Her eyes stop moving, her mouth pinches a bit and she throws up. Hunched over the toilet, she turns the blow dryer on again so Jeff won't hear her. Jeff nears the door, and hearing the blow dryer, enters. He comes upon Maria throwing up.

"Oh my God, are you alright?" he says, moving toward Maria and grabbing her hair. He gets down on his knees and gets close to her, rubbing the back of her neck. Maria gives another dry heave and then raises her head. She wipes her mouth with a towel and turns to look at Jeff.

"Is it something you ate? We don't have to go to this; we can just stay here and watch a movie or something...," Jeff stammers out.

"It's not food poisoning," Maria replies. Jeff leans back.

Inside the dining hall, the dinner begins, speeches are made, tears are shed and as they begin to eat, people begin to think. It gets very quiet, as each and every person gets introspective about where they are sitting. Idle chit chat, the 'where have you been,' 'what have you been up to' rule this area because frankly no one really knows what to say.

D'Ascoli scarfs down his filet mignon as Mike tries to avoid being noticed.

Tom reaches into his pocket and pulls out his vibrating cell phone—it's work...the third time they've called since he's sat down. He cancels the call. He thinks about how his quest for a career has left him as the quiet guy at the wedding who doesn't have anyone to do the electric slide with. He's outgrown his job; it's not that fun anymore. He's missed too much, taken too many phone calls.

A spitball hits him right in the forehead. Scanning the room like he's looking for a sniper, he sees Matt taking a straw off his lips and then subtlety flipping him off. Tom laughs and mouths, "I'm gonna kill you."

Jeff sits on a bathroom floor with the only girl he has ever loved and thinks about just how much has changed. Most of all he thinks about how he would have to change. How the antics of old won't pass the mustard anymore—that Maria can't take care of two kids. As he strokes her almost dry hair, he sits on this cold hotel room floor, the walls pinching in just a bit.

Matt looks up at John, who is beaming like a pageant winner, as he is told by every Aunt Louisa and Uncle Bill how this is the best time of his life and how perfect he and Jenna are together. John cracks the facade a few times, mockingly blowing his brains out as he catches eyes with Matt. Matt feels weird. His best friend was moving just a little further away. John being the first person to get married is about to blow a hole in this ship that these men have been traveling on. Everyone is being nostalgic about the past—for a time that was gone before it even came. Maybe it's better that way.

As the speeches continue, Chris gets up and heads toward the large doors of the dining hall and out into the lobby. Wandering around for the bathroom, he keeps his gaze hazy, eyes darting for the little white rigid man on the sign.

Then she appears.

"Long time, no see," Beth says.

CHAPTER THIRTEEN

"What do you want to do today?" Beth says, dressed in Chris' white sweatshirt and Carolina shorts. Her hair was up in a ponytail, wrapped messily and hanging just off her right shoulder. Chris squirms into his pillow, slowly cracking his eyes, then his window shades open. There is snow for days outside, with more hitting the ground every second.

"It looks like we're all stuck here," Chris replies, his face back to hitting the pillow.

Beth rolls across the bed and straddles Chris' back, starting to poke him in the ribs. He resists quietly, with every poke and tickle rising him from his stupor, finally with him turning the tables on Beth, rolling her onto her back and replying in kind.

"You're way more ticklish than me," Chris says, Beth giggles and then gives him a titty twister, causing him to fall off the bed, landing with a thud on the floor.

"The pain in my shoulder will distract me from the pain in my nipple," Chris says, lying on the cold wooden floor.

Beth gets up and throws on some slippers, opening the bedroom door shortly thereafter. Chris' door opens right near the front door of the house, where the cool air from the winter wonderland beyond the porch creeps through every crack and crease of this decades-old party den. Its shingles are a dull white, stained with rust and vomiting from windows, the wooden porch battered with broken panels and spray paint. Some remnants of broken eggs remain stuck to the front door, reminders of a girl who was no longer fond of Russell. The front porch light is broken, blinking ever so often, sending out Morse code to ships passing by that they party here.

Beth throws on a winter hat and opens the front door—snow slowly blowing into the house. She walks out onto the porch and sees cars spinning their wheels and the Indian owner of the gas station digging out his sidewalk. It was a regular winter in these parts, the cold of the Hudson and clouds of the northeast always dropping large amounts of white stuff on its citizens' heads. Chris joins her on the deck and holds her around her waist, his head resting on her shoulder.

"I'm gonna go see if anyone else is up," Chris mumbles, pulling himself inside while Beth watches the streets and snow and the perfect couple they make to kids in school hoping for a day off.

Chris walks around the corner, into the living room and sees Jeff passed out on the couch, his mouth agape wide enough to throw in a bowling ball. Entourage reruns on the television. Jeff's right hand grips the remote, his left hand down his pants. Day-old Taco Bell and pizza boxes line the floor and coffee table. Chris walks over and grabs the remote, turning off the television and putting a blanket over Jeff, who awakens.

"What time is it?" Jeff asks.

"10:45 a.m.," Chris replies.

"I'm not going to class, fuck it," Jeff says, closing his eyes and pulling the new blanket over his chin.

"Why are you sleeping on the couch?"

"I had a dilemma; pass out here on this comfy couch, or get up and walk five feet to my bed… I made the right decision. Give me my laptop; I gotta email my cheese dick professor a bullshit excuse for missing class."

"There's about a foot of snow outside," Chris says.

Jeff's eyes pop open and he bounds out of the living room toward the front door. Coming upon the vision of snow, he throws his hands in the air.

"Hey whore, get off my porch," Jeff says to Beth as he walks through the front door and reaches his hand out to feel the snow coming down. He runs back inside.

"Anyone else up?" Jeff asks.

Before Chris answers, Jeff begins to pound on Russell's door, "Russ, wake up you pansy ass bitch it's a snow day!" He continues to bang loudly and then decides to just plow into the room where he jumps from the foot of the bed and lands hard on Russell. Russell lets out a loud grimace, pushing Jeff off him and on to the floor. The girl lying next to Russell jumps out of her skin seeing a raving Jeff screaming from Russell's floor.

"Nice to meet you," Jeff says to the brunette with the makeup running down her face.

Jeff bounds out of the room and toward the stairs, screaming, "Russ, you could do better."

Chris watches dust fall from the ceiling as Jeff lumbers around upstairs, going into everyone's rooms and waking them up.

It all began with Matt. He pulls a keg off the back porch that he bought the night before, the weather Nostradamus that he is.

Soon Russell's brunette and Matt's blonde are making pancakes and bacon in the kitchen. The scent makes its way through the house, stinging the nostrils of everyone. Mike and D'Ascoli argue and play Madden upstairs, ending with Mike throwing his controller into the couch as D'Ascoli holds his arms above his head triumphantly. Bob and Boyd return from campus after spending the night with a junior and freshman, respectively. Bob goes to bed, Boyd to the bathroom. Singer chases John through the house, flinging snowballs in his wake. Tom was "home" for the weekend, when he was in fact overseas. Derek runs through the snow in his boxers with a shirt wrapped around his head. Other luminaries of the community come in and out throughout the day, boys and girls wandering the streets as if it were Halloween, looking for alcohol and a puff or two from the bong. They show up at the front door without a second thought.

When the sun went down, Caroline came over, Mike retreating to his bedroom where he and Caroline fucked and then fought and then fucked some more. D'Ascoli continues to play video games like Mike was still there. Jeff soon joined Derek in running through the snow, smashed off the now empty keg, screaming like a drunken dog at the passing cars. Marie brings him inside and makes him chicken soup, hoping to fend off the oncoming pneumonia.

It's a fever dream, never one to stop.

As the hours pass, the snow falls and falls, never allowing a clear road. It was almost as if it was never going to stop—that this was the end of days, everyone to drown in snow. Chris and Mike sit on the porch and smoke cigars in the moonlight, the smoke combining with each exhale of warm breath, making it look like the men are breathing fire.

"How's it going?" Chris asks, choking a little bit on the smoke.

"Usual shit man, it just snowed more today," Mike replies.

Mike closes his eyes and exhales, blowing smoke rings that snowflakes hurdle through on their way to the ground. The snow has reached up the first two steps of the porch, slowly but surely making its way closer to the front door, threatening to seal off this beer and vodka-soaked brick and mortar...everyone would probably be too drunk to notice.

"We're toxic...we fight too much," Mike says. He shakes his head and takes another drag.

"I'll go upstairs and she'll yell at me because she'll taste this on my breath, then she'll throw something and call me a piece of shit," he continues.

Chris brushes some snow off his shoe. Rather than volley back, he let Mike vent.

"The extremes are too much...we're not even keeled like you two."

"I'm bored sometimes though. At least you can step out of your body and laugh when she's ranting—Beth never seems to be all that passionate. We're playful and shit, but it's too easy, she's too easy on me," Chris replies.

"You wanna trade?" Mike asks.

"Sure," Chris replies.

The boys puff on their cigars.

"This will be gone soon," Chris says, throwing his cigar into the garbage can almost full with snow. Mike takes another drag and reflects, rubbing his eyes.

"Maybe not, you know. Maybe one of us can hit the lotto and we can live here forever. Or you can sell some of those typewriter pages and buy this house. We can always live here, though maybe we could upgrade things a bit, get a Jacuzzi in the living room; maybe just kick Kenney out and put it in there. It doesn't have to end."

"I was talking about the snow," Chris replies, "But I get what you're saying." A car begins to skid down the street.

"I'd love to invest my money in a unique fixer-fixer-upper-upper in this neck of the woods, with the gas station across the street probably poisoning our water and wood floors that have been warped from the pee and beer of every malcontent in this area code, not to mention the dead carcasses of animals taking shelter in our basement. Other than that it's a slam dunk," Chris continues.

Mike laughs.

"But maybe you're right," Chris replies.

"Nothing matters before you turn 25," Mike finishes.

The morning soon arrives and not much has changed. The snow continues to pile skyward—school once again cancelled, alcohol once again flowing. Everything feels right. These people would never want to leave this house, snow or otherwise. They would be okay dying in this kingdom, choking on their vomit or dying of old age. It is the only thing that makes sense to them, makes them feel alright, that feeling, that feeling of being solitary, yet full. Broke enough to eat pasta four nights a week and go to happy hour just to eat free wings. Fucking anonymously and running out with their underwear in their hands or staying in bed all day—all the things that felt right in this world—this world of no judgment or bedtime or religion other than the hours between 10 p.m. and 4 a.m.

Soon the snow would stop falling, be plowed to the right, seep into the granite. Some more might fall, but not enough to stop the travel to and from campus. Spring would come and, with it, green grass. Girls in tight sweaters run into phone booths and come out with short shorts and wife beaters, tightly rolled joints tucked into jean pockets and forties in brown paper bags, cigarette butt fortresses ten feet in diameter outside bars. Sparks falling off eyes in the glint of the moon light down by the Hudson, lovers and their partners in crime laying together under it, maybe a little drunk, maybe a little high, getting ready to run at the nearest sign of campus security.

There is no substitute, no barbiturate, no feeling that compares to these days and foolishly they/we threw them away. Everyone thought these days would last forever, that there was never anything else but this. Now they're gone, those days and those people. We're lesser because of it.

Chris gets up and steps away from his typewriter.

CHAPTER FOURTEEN

"Well that was fucking brutal," D'Ascoli says, walking through the hotel lobby—reaching into his coat pocket for cigarettes. Russell and Tom follow closely behind.

The three head out a side door and walk into the garden. D'Ascoli takes a seat on the nearest bench and lights up.

Tom grabs a cigarette, while Russell taps away on his phone.

"Text from Bob. His flight with Boyd and Derek got cancelled, they're driving" Russell mumbles out.

"Good luck with that," Tom says as he lights.

"What now? Is there somewhere we can go and get drunk? The watered down drinks here aren't doing it for me," D'Ascoli says in between puffs.

"I saw a few bars in town on the way from the airport," Tom replies. D'Ascoli looks up to the sky then he puts his hand out.

"I think it's raining."

Russell follows suit, "No it's snowing." D'Ascoli starts to laugh, first quietly, then a bit manically.

"What's so funny?" Tom asks.

"It's gonna snow on Kenney's wedding day, that poor silly bastard."

Tom's phone begins to ring again—he quickly cancels the call. Russell peers over and looks at Tom, "Not answering?"

"They get enough of my time man," Tom replies, putting his cell phone back in his pocket.

"I love you...maybe I haven't said that enough. Have I said that enough?" Jeff stumbles out of his mouth. Maria kisses him.

The two sit on their bed, Maria in a bathrobe, Jeff holding a ginger ale. Maria grabs the ginger ale and takes a gulp. Jeff lies down next to Maria, his legs outstretched over the edge of the bed.

"So have you started to freak out yet? Or should I start the countdown?" Maria asks. Jeff laughs and then puts the pillow over his face, screaming as loud as he can within seconds. Maria giggles.

"At least we're communicating."

There's a knock at the door. Maria begins to get up but Jeff springs past her and tells her to stay still. Looking through the door's peephole, he unlocks, then opens.

On the other side of the door stands Mike, who is looking up and down the halls like he just stole something.

"What's wrong, Carmine?" Jeff says in mocking contempt. Mike moves quickly from the hallway inside the room, motioning wildly for Jeff to close the door.

Jeff begins to close the door, but then sticks his head out and screams, "Who ever is looking for Mike he's in room 1137."

Mike's eyes bulge out of his head as Jeff closes the door.

"What's wrong with you?" Jeff asks.

"She's here."

"Who's here?" Jeff replies.

"*She* is here."

Jeff's eyebrows explode, "Oh shit, really?"

Maria looks at these two men speaking in code and can only say one thing, "Who's here?"

Mike turns to her and says, "The worst woman of all time." Maria looks at Jeff who mouths, "Caroline." Maria nods her head.

"Did you see her?" Jeff asks as he walks back over to the bed.

"I had sex with her," Mike replies. Jeff's head nearly tears from his spine from the double take.

"Shut up, no you didn't!" Maria says.

"I thought she was married?" Jeff ponders.

"I was tired of sitting with D'Ascoli, listening to one of Kenney's cousins talk and talk about some fucking basketball team they played on together 20 years ago, so I decided to get the fuck out of there."

Downstairs, 15 minutes earlier, Mike, minus his buffer in Chris, gets up from his dining table and heads for the exit. He eyes Caroline in his periphery and is sure to not look directly at her. As Mike makes his way to the exit, his arm is grabbed by Adam—a kid you wouldn't want to talk to even if he held the secret to the female orgasm.

"I hate that cheesedick," Jeff says.

"Yea, me too. Let's just say that if I ever see him again, there's gonna be a misunderstanding... I'm fucking him up on site," Mike replies, channeling the late, great Bernie Mac.

"So this asshole starts talking me, you know, about something I don't even know...some bullshit and I'm so distracted by him talking to me that BOOM she's right there."

Mike is able to wrestle free of Adam's douchefield when he sees Caroline walking directly toward him.

"You should have stiff armed her...just leveled her with a hit stick and kept on moving," Jeff says.

Mike runs through a fantasy of throwing a stiff arm to end all stiff arms directly to Caroline's face, sending her flying backwards like she just got hit by Thor's hammer. Then he comes back and kicks Adam in the balls.

"I should've done that," Mike says, pulling a small bottle of vodka out of the mini fridge, opening the top with a, "I don't care what it costs, I'll pay for it."

"Alright, just get to the sex," Maria says.

"I don't even remember how it happened—she must have used some sort of whore temptress magic on me or something because the next thing I know we're talking in like a nook, what do you call it, not a vestibule," Mike stumbles for the word.

"An alcove," Jeff chimes in.

"Exactly, an alcove, the one where the ATM is, and she just pulls down my pants and humps me up against an ATM machine, just going to town on my tiny weinus," Mike continues.

"What?" Maria ponders.

"Weiner, penis, weinus, come on—try and keep up," Jeff says. Maria is sorry she even asked.

"But then she just stopped."

Maria and Jeff look at Mike surprised.

"She stopped and leaned in....slowly...and whispered," Mike lowers his voice, "Tell me you want me to suck your cock."

Jeff bursts out laughing, "WHAT!"

"I know. Have you ever heard anything as fucking insane as that? Tell me you want me to suck your cock. Holy shit...I thought I was in a porno for a second—like that there was a camera in the ceiling or something. I've watched a lot of porn, believe me—sorry Maria, but...shit."

Jeff goes to the bathroom and you can hear his laughs through the closed door. Mike takes another swig from the vodka bottle.

Jeff runs water over his face and then returns, patting a towel on his face.

"Holy shit. I think I can go home now, nothing's gonna top that shit. Where is she?"

"I don't know... she finished, I'm trying to be respectful here Maria, kissed me on the cheek, told me to shave my beard and then just walked away...leaving me with my pants around my ankles," Mike continues.

"What did you do?" Maria asks, almost immediately regretting it.

"I pulled my pants up, took $60 out of the ATM and came up here. I'm looking for Hall; he fucking disappeared."

"He's probably in his room writing or something," Maria says, getting up and grabbing the remote off the desk.

"Maybe. What's going on with you guys?" Mike asks.

"Let's change the subject."

Chris looks across the table at Beth. He smirks. Beth peers back, almost studying him like a painting.

"You look tired; you have bags under your eyes. You always get those when the writing isn't going well," Beth says. Chris laughs to himself.

"It's not going well is it?" she continues.

"How would you know?"

"Believe me. I saw you many a morning and those bags were always there when you wrote five words, all of them being, 'I. Can't. Think. Of. Anything.'" Beth continues.

"When is it my turn to critique your physical appearance?"

"I'm just saying if you need something to write about, I can give you something to write about," Beth continues on, slowly inching up in her chair, getting closer and closer to the table. Chris remains reclined in his chair, his right leg crossed over his left.

The bar starts to fill in as the time nears 9 p.m.; Chris spots some of John's extended family seated a few tables away. He doesn't see any of his friends though, which at this particular moment is troubling.

"I have a girlfriend," Chris replies, emptying the silence since Beth's strange last comment. Beth stays unwavering.

"How's that going for you?" Beth asks.

"It's going great, she's never cheated on me," Chris replies, now leaning toward the table—this is a shot across Beth's bow.

"Wow, that was once and we had gotten into a huge fight 20 minutes before and you told me that you didn't want to talk to me ever again," Beth fires back.

"I'm a writer—I speak in grand platitudes, even if I was breaking up with you," Chris replies back.

Beth nods her head and smirks.

"Are you gonna punch me in the face or something? Just let me know, I wanna be able to get my hands up...don't wanna have a black eye tomorrow," Chris says.

"No, I'm not gonna punch you in the face."

Chris wipes his brow.

"Can we just get along, even if it's just for 72 hours?" Beth asks.

"Who says we're not getting along? I have no problem with you, I have no ill will, nothing like that; it's good to see you," Chris replies as he gets the attention of a waiter.

"Can I get a Corona? Do you want anything?" Chris says, asking Beth. She shakes her head no. The waiter makes his way to the bar.

"I read your first book a couple of months ago," Beth says. Chris looks surprised.

"Really? Wow...any good?"

"No, it's pretty terrible," Beth says with a laugh.

"The first one has a certain raggedy charm to it, but the second one is better," Chris replies.

"Yea, but the second one isn't about me."

"That's true, that's why it's better," Chris replies with a smile.

"Ohhhhhhh, what a witty dickhead you are," Beth says back with a sting.

"Hey, you dated me so it reflects just as poorly on you," Chris punctuates as the waiter brings him his Corona. He drops the lime into the bottle and takes a sip.

"Good to see it's still your favorite drink," Beth offers.

"Some things never change."

Chris' phone vibrates, sending a hum through the table.

"I'm sorry to cut short this cute screwball comedy routine we got going here, but Mike needs me, I gotta go," Chris says.

"The real love of your life calls and you go running," Beth says.

"I'm sorry, he gives better head," Chris says, getting up out of his seat and reaching into his pocket. He pulls out some money and throws it on the table.

"See you later?" Chris asks.

Beth nods and waves. Chris walks out of the bar and into the hotel's lobby, disappearing as he heads toward the elevators.

Beth reaches across the table and starts to drink Chris' unfinished Corona.

John and Jenna walk hand-and-hand down the hallway. John reaches into his pocket and pulls out his hotel room key.

"I think it went well," Jenna says.

"Easy for you to say. Your grandma didn't show pictures of you naked in a tub when you were five years old. Knowing Hall, he'll make a T-shirt of it and wear it to the wedding."

"You were hung like an infant," Jenna continues, opening the door to John's suite.

"I was an infant," John says quickly.

"You still are."

Jenna flips on the lights and throws her sweater on the couch in the living room. She soon follows, landing and stretching.

"I'm exhausted, are you exhausted? If I have to shake one more hand or hear one more speech I'm gonna snap."

John goes into the bathroom and turns on the shower. He stops to look in the mirror, popping a small zit on his face. He cranes his neck and looks for more—none to be found.

He returns to the living room and joins Jenna on the couch, picking up her legs and sitting, returning her legs to his lap. John dips his head back and closes his eyes.

Jenna and John revel in the silence.

Then the phone rings. They try to ignore it, but Jenna begins to move.

"Don't even think about it," John says, still slumped into the couch. Jenna swings her legs off the couch and John grabs blindly to try and keep her down.

"Let it ring," John continues. Jenna wanders over to the phone and answers it sleepily.

"Hello? Oh my God! ... What are you doing here? ... Yes, yes of course, come up! John, what's the room number up here?"

"I'm heading downstairs, I gotta find some aspirin—you want anything?" Tom asks Russell, who is preparing to shotgun a beer in the bathroom.

"No, but hurry up we gotta go out soon."

Tom waves him off and exits the room—Russell shotguns the beer and lets out a primal scream.

"Ahhhhhhhhhhhhhhhhhh."

Russell shakes his limbs lose, shadowboxing in the mirror. Russell's hotel phone begins to ring.

Russell runs in and answers, "Hello?"

"WHAT THE FUCK IS GOING ON OVER THERE?" the voice screams through the phone.

"Who the hell is this?" Russell replies, popping open another beer.

"King! This is MacArthur. Why the fuck aren't you or Bernabeo answering your phones?"

"Good evening sir, I wasn't expecting you to call," Russell says to his boss, quietly freaking out.

"I'll ask you again—why aren't you answering your phones."

"Well I'm off for the weekend and Bernabeo is...dead. He's dead sir," Russell replies.

"This is no time for jokes, Colonel; we have a situation and we need you to handle it," MacArthur continues.

"Sir, listen I know I'm your number one guy, but I can't handle every single—"

MacArthur cuts off Russell, screaming into the phone, "I don't want to hear about your vacation days King! We have a situation in the hotel that you're currently in. The case that Bernabeo was unable to extract is in the hotel. How I don't know; maybe they tracked you."

"Where is it?" Russell asks, reaching into his bag and pulling out a bullet clip.

"The lobby. Where's Bernabeo?"

"He's downstairs getting some Tylenol," Russell replies, immediately regretting saying it.

"Find him—they may have come back to finish him off," MacArthur finishes, "Call me when it's done."

Russell hangs up the phone and loads his gun. He picks up the phone again but remembers Tom turned his cell off. He rushes out the door, heading for the stairs.

Tom looks through the painkillers in the hotel gift shop, reading the ingredients on the back.

"You got anything stronger than this?" Tom asks the clerk stocking the shelves. The clerk looks at him with shifty eyes.

"You a cop?"

"No, I'm not a cop," Tom replies.

"Alright, because if I ask you, you can't lie—"

"Forget it, I don't want whatever hillbilly heroin you're selling," Tom says, grabbing Tylenol off the stand and throwing it on the counter.

"You're the hillbilly..." the clerk trails off.

Tom walks out of the gift shop, spotting a blonde near the front desk.

"Damn."

Tom continues leering as he opens the Tylenol, taking two with a bottle of water. The blonde turns around...it's the agent who beat him to the case before. He quickly ducks back into the gift shop, peeking out from behind a magazine rack.

The blonde walks over to the elevator, the case in her left hand. As she gets onto the elevator, Tom makes a move across the lobby.

The doors close.

Tom watches the numbers above the elevator click up, up and up, finally settling on the tenth floor.

Tom dashes for the stairs, opening the door and colliding with Russell.

"Shit," Russell screams, stumbling backwards, "You hit me right in the face."

"Sorry I fucked up your face, Russ," Tom says, closing the stairwell door.

"The case is here; MacArthur's been trying to get a hold of you," Russell says, holding the right side of his face.

"I just saw her get on the elevator, she's up on ten," Tom replies.

"Before we go up, come here," Russell says, waiving Tom over. Tom moves in and Russell slaps Tom right across the face.

"Oww! Fuck Russ!"

"Now we're even," Russell says, bounding back up the stairs.

Tom and Russell peek out of the tenth floor stairwell door. Tom pulls out a tracking device, emitting beeps as to the location of the case. Russell motions and the two men make their way into the hallway. Each one sticking close to a wall, Tom looks down at the tracker, monitoring as they move past each room.

The beeps begin to pick up pace as Russell and Tom close in on the end of the hallway, with room 1014 directly in front of them.

"Stick behind as backup, if she sees you it's all over," Russell says to Tom, who pins himself against a wall as Russell approaches room 1014.

Russell holds his gun behind his back as he makes his move, he's about to knock when the door opens. Russell jumps, only to see John coming with an ice bucket.

"Russ, what are you doing up here?" John asks. Russell is surprised.

"Kenney, whose room is this?"

"It's mine," he responds.

"Who's in there?" Russell asks, tucking his gun behind his back, into his waistband.

"Me, Jenna and Jenna's friend Amanda; I think you've met her before," John replies, opening the room with the ice machine. Russell follows John and waves off Tom, who goes running down the hallway.

"I don't remember an Amanda," Russell says.

"Well come in and meet her…she's pretty hot."

"Look who I found wandering around in the hallway," John says, opening his hotel room. Russell enters and scans the room. Jenna sits on the couch, turning around to say hello.

"So where's this Amanda," Russell asks, not seeing her in the room.

"Right behind you," Amanda says, appearing from almost out of nowhere. Russell turns quickly, looking up at the tall blonde by the name of Amanda.

"Wow, you are sneaky, I didn't even see you there," Russell replies, extending his hand—Amanda shakes.

"Not sneaky, just quick. I'm Amanda, are you the famous Russell King?" Amanda asks.

"Russell King yes, famous no," Russell replies. Amanda looks right at Russell and smiles, whispering, "Not here."

"Jenna I'm gonna get going; I gotta drop some stuff off at my room, I'll see you later," Amanda says, not taking her eyes off Russell.

"See you later beautiful," Jenna says, waving from the couch. Amanda opens the door, picking up the briefcase near the door.

"Kenney, I'll see you later," Russell says, following Amanda out of the room.

Now in the hallway, Russell pulls his gun, sticking it into the back of Amanda. She laughs.

"Not so rough, Russell, I barely know you," she punctuates.

"Listen, you're not gonna throw me with some sexy spy routine, I'm taking the case and that's it, okay?"

"If you say so," Amanda replies, beginning to walk down the hallway, Russell's gun following closely.

"How did you know me?" Russell asks.

"You? I saw you before you got up this morning. I must say though, I am a fan of your work, when you're doing it and not sitting on the couch playing XBOX."

"Well the new Call of Duty just came out, so I've been a little busy," Russell replies.

"And where is your partner, the man who never sleeps? Tom? Are you out there?" Amanda asks down the hallway.

Tom peeks out from behind a pillar.

"I'm sorry about your wrist," Amanda says to Tom, who is making his way toward Amanda and Russell.

"What are you doing here?" Tom asks.

"I'm here for the wedding, just like you two," Amanda replies.

The three get on the elevator and head downstairs. As they reach the basement, they navigate through the kitchen, exiting out the back door—leading out to the woods, the darkness disappearing into the edges of the trees.

Snow blankets the ground, out past the sight line, huge flakes flying and hitting the trees and grass.

"Snow on a wedding day, that's a shame," Amanda says, walking with her back to Russell. She walks a few more steps while Tom and Russell stand back.

"Alright, you're gonna give us the case, get on a plane and get out of here," Russell says, pointing his gun at Amanda.

"I'm afraid I can't do that," Amanda replies.

"Why is that?" Tom asks, now also pointing his gun at Amanda.

"Because I bought a wedding gift and I would like to give it to the happy couple myself. Also, my plane ticket is non-refundable."

"You're hilarious, but we're taking the case," Tom says.

"Come and take it," Amanda says, putting the case on the floor.

"I'm not gonna hit a girl," Tom replies.

"Is that why I kicked your ass this morning?" Amanda replies. Russell snickers. Tom looks at Russell.

"Alright, Russ—hold my gun," Tom says, handing over his gun and walking up to Amanda, who takes off her long coat and folds it over the briefcase.

What follows can only be described as an ass kicking, a swirl of arms, legs and blonde hair, a quicker and stronger Amanda soon sitting on Tom's chest, looking up at Russell.

"You wanna try?" she asks Russell.

"I have a gun," Russell says, looking down again, "Actually two guns," training both guns on Amanda. Amanda pulls a gun out of her boot, pointing it at Russell.

"Funny...me too."

"I still have two guns," Russell replies. Amanda pulls a gun out of her other boot.

"Anything else you're hiding over there?"

"Wouldn't you like to know," Amanda replies. Two guns to two guns, with Tom still lying on the ground underneath Amanda.

"So what are we gonna do? Stare into each others eyes for the rest of the night?" Amanda asks, who looks down to see Tommy now also pointing a gun at her.

"I got two guns too," Tom says, flipping Amanda off him to the ground, her guns flying away. Tom quickly gets to his feet, training his gun on Amanda who gets to her feet and begins to dash off into the woods with the case. Tom fires off a shot wide, hitting a tree a few feet from Amanda. She stops running, turning back to look at Russell and Tom.

Amanda walks back and picks her jacket off the ground, putting it back on.

"Alright, we have quite the predicament," Amanda says.

"What's that?" Russell asks.

"I certainly don't wanna ruin Jenna's and John's weekend so I propose a truce. No fighting, no gunfights, nothing. We become perfect friends until Monday morning then we decide who takes the case," Amanda offers.

"How are we gonna do that?" Tom asks.

"It's a long weekend, we'll figure something out. Until then, I'll give the case to the hotel, they can hold it until Monday, so it's fair to everybody," Amanda says.

"I don't like you," Tom says. Amanda smiles.

"It's too bad because I think you're cute," Amanda replies.

"Now I don't like you either," Russell offers.

Chris opens his hotel room door, hearing the sink running in the bathroom. He takes off his jacket and flings it across the room, "Pennisi?"

Opening the bathroom door, Chris sees Mike hunched over the sink shaving off his huge workman's like beard.

"Wow look at you..."

Mike looks up, half of his face shaved, the other covered in shaving cream.

"I fucked Caroline," Mike says, continuing to shave, "Actually, I should say she fucked me." Chris nearly coughs up a lung.

"What? What year is it? Did I step into a time machine?"

"Where were you? I was looking all over for you," Mike asks, working on his neck.

"I had a drink with Beth," Chris replies. Mike stops shaving and looks at Chris. Mike fills a Dixie cup with water and throws it in Chris' face.

"Are you fucking kidding me? I thought you would have a little self-control where I didn't...Jesus. Fucking Beth, that bitch. I never liked her. I don't know why, but I don't like her," Mike says, back to the shaving.

"So let me guess, this is a Caroline request, this whole shaving thing?"

"C'mon, I'm a man; I do what the fuck I want to do, I don't listen to her," Mike says. Chris nods his head.

"Sure."

There's a knock at the door. Chris walks over and opens it to see Matt and D'Ascoli.

"Let's go, we're going out," Matt says, walking past Chris into the room, "Pennisi, get some pants on that you won't mind throwing up on later."

"That's all my pants," Mike says from the bathroom.

"You're shaving your beard?" a surprised D'Ascoli says, walking into the bathroom and spraying shaving cream all over the mirror. Mike pushes D'Ascoli out of the bathroom as D'Ascoli giggles away.

"You still look like shit Mike," D'Ascoli says, heading for the door.

"He had sex with Caroline," Chris says to D'Ascoli.

"Good for you Pennisi, do you have a wart on your cock yet?" D'Ascoli says—a fall away insult as he exits Chris and Mike's room and runs down the hallway screaming.

"Five minutes. Be downstairs," Matt says, closing the door and following D'Ascoli.

Within ten minutes, a whole crew of no good doers congregate in the lobby. Jeff helps Maria with her coat as she catches up with Caroline and Beth. D'Ascoli hits on the girl doing the late shift behind the desk. John and Matt stand in the corner, talking about something away from the prying ears of others, looking like they were the ones getting married the next day. Tommy licks his wounds, again, while Russell dances around to a beat in his own head.

"Where's Hall?" Russell asks.

"D'Ascoli, call up Hall, tell him to get his ass down here," Russell yells across the lobby. Wendy, the hotel desk clerk currently at the receiving end of D'Ascoli's advances, dials Chris' number and hands the phone to D'Ascoli.

Upstairs, Chris is on the phone with Erin as Mike puts on aftershave. He slaps it on his face and screams.

"No, I'm alright, Pennisi is screaming," Chris says to Erin. The room phone begins to ring. Chris motions to Mike to pick it up. Mike jumps over the couch and grabs the phone.

"Hello? ... No, fuck off dickhead." Mike hangs up the phone, "They're waiting for us downstairs."

D'Ascoli shouts across the lobby, "They'll be right down."

"Alright baby, I love you," Chris says, hanging up the phone. Chris puts the phone to his head and cringes.

"She can't get in tonight; all the flights are cancelled until tomorrow."

Mike looks at Chris and smiles.

"I hate where this is going."

"Yea, me too," Chris replies.

Downstairs, three lost men wander in from the cold, snow flakes sitting on their jackets and heads, barely dressed women on their arms.

Derek, Boyd and Bob have arrived. After driving the last eight hours in the snow—determined to get to the wedding after their flight was cancelled.

"Holy shit, look at these three," Tom says from the couch. Russell and Tom each give them a hug. Jeff, D'Ascoli, John and Matt soon follow. For the first time in a long while, all of the friends are under the same roof.

"Who are these three?" Jeff asks Derek, who leans in and whispers, "Totally hookers."

Bob gives Jeff a thumbs up.

"The filthiest you've ever seen," Boyd adds. Jeff has to turn away from laughing in one of the lady of the night's faces.

Jeff walks over to Maria, who is wearing a smile.

"You won't believe this—"

"Hookers? No I think everyone can see that," Maria says with a laugh. Chris and Mike turn the corner, barely getting a glimpse of the three men when Mike says, "hookers." The assorted mob exits the hotel automatic doors and disappears into the night.

Walking into town feels like the old days—navigating the quiet streets, screaming into the night, pushing, fighting, peeing on private properties. John and Jenna walk up front and kissed, illiciting jeers. D'Ascoli flings snowballs at Mike, who walks ahead of Caroline, ignoring her. Derek's hooker's heel broke—so he gives her a piggy back ride.

They find a small bar in town named DeSimones, a pub with a bouncer that looks more like Bruce Banner than the Incredible Hulk. Inside, the walls are papered with dollar bills, each one with a different inscription or scribble. Yellow bar lights line the tables. The girls move to the back of the bar, sitting down at a round table near the kitchen.

Some of the boys head for the bar. John takes a seat with Matt and Mike. A few rounds deep, they get to talking.

"So when are you gonna call all this off?" Mike asks, sucking down a beer. John laughs and shakes his head, refusing to answer the question. Mike puts his middle finger right in front of John's face.

"I asked him before," Matt continues, "We could be on a plane in two hours."

"How are we gonna get there? Fucking dog sled? You see how much snow is out there?" John says, drinking his beer, a bit pissed off.

"What's your problem?" Mike asks.

"Why do I need to hear this bullshit 12 hours before my wedding?" John replies. Matt is a bit taken aback.

"Because if we didn't ask you these things, no one fucking would. I saw that fucking dinner, those assholes who'll be pushing daises in less than 20 years and the fake smiles and bullshit speeches they spout make you think shit is peachy...it doesn't work that way," Mike says.

"Well that's your opinion," John replies.

"Listen to me, don't listen to me, I don't give a fuck. I got to where you're at, I gave that bitch over there a ring and guess what? It ruined my fucking life—and we didn't even get this close," Mike continues.

"Don't compare you and Caroline to me and Jenna—it's completely different." Mike shakes his head.

"Hey man, if you're happy, I'm happy, but you need to hear this shit before you do it, you can't bury your fucking head in the sand and think that somehow your relationship is gonna be different than anyone else's," Mike finishes. John gets up and walks away.

"He's a fucking baby," Mike says, drinking his beer. They both watch as John walks to the bathroom. Matt gets up and follows.

John walks into one of the stalls and slams the door. Matt comes through the door, dodging a guy who's spraying water from the faucet everywhere.

"Kenney?"

"Give me a fucking second man," John says from behind the lopsided stall door. Matt goes up to the urinals and breaks the seal. John walks out and heads to the sink, washing his hands and grabbing a paper towel.

"He's just trying to talk to you...making sure you didn't make the same mistake he did," Matt says, face to the wall. John throws his paper towel in the garbage.

"I know that, but for fuck sake I don't want to hear it. He took a shot at this and he picked the wrong girl—that's it, it has nothing to do with us. I don't want to hear how all marriage is shit. My parents were together for 25 years and sure they fought, whose fucking parents don't fight. I've seen it—believe me. But when my dad was dying in that bed, looking up and knowing he was dying, the person sitting on the edge of the bed was my mother. Call me a sap, call me a dipshit, I don't know a lot, but I know that."

Matt flushes the toilet.

"Alright," Matt says.

"Alright."

"Alright," Matt repeats.

The bar is beginning to fill, people looking for something to do while the snow is falling, readying themselves for a snowed-in Saturday morning. D'Ascoli stands on a small stage toward the back of the bar, a mic in his hand, flipping through a karaoke book.

"What should I sing?" he shouts to Russell.

"Backstreet Boys," Boyd shouts from the bar. D'Ascoli looks back at the DJ and flips through the book again.

"You got any LFO?" D'Ascoli asks.

Bobby and Boyd look on as their hookers are involved in some heavy petting, making out and licking each other's faces. Derek picks his cell phone up off the table.

"I'm gonna send this to my mom," he says, snapping the photo.

Outside, Jeff leans against the bar's aluminum siding and smokes a cigarette. Chris opens the door and dances over to Jeff. Grabbing cigarettes out of his jacket pocket, Chris lights up, toasting Jeff. Jeff looks down at his cigarette before putting it in his mouth.

"It's the last play at Shea," Jeff says, raising his cigarette.

"Quitter," Chris replies.

"Maria's pregnant," Jeff replies, with a smile. Chris turns to him wide eyed, then taps his beer bottle with Jeff, a quiet moment in a weekend without a lot of them.

"Thanks man."

"That's awesome, when did you find out?" Chris says, taking another drag.

"Today," Jeff replies—halfway through his last cigarette, "Don't tell anybody." Chris smiles and pours out a little bit of his drink.

"I'm pouring this out for you—Compton style," Chris says.

He gives Jeff a hug.

"Yea I figured I should start small, stop smoking, then maybe build to something else important. What—I don't know," Jeff says.

"Maybe raising a kid," Chris replies. Jeff nods his head. The snow continues to fall on this silent night.

"Man, this is quite the weekend," Chris says. Singer exhales then flicks his cigarette into the street.

"Wow, you're not even gonna finish it," Chris says. Jeff cracks his knuckles.

"Me from ten years ago would call myself a pussy right now...and you know what? I'm alright with that."

Jeff slaps Chris on the ass and returns inside, "I'll see you later." Chris leans back into the wall, watching a police car roll by the bar slowly. Chris hears D'Ascoli singing "Girl on TV" horribly off key as the door closes. He misses Erin. The side door to the bar slowly opens. John and Jenna creep out.

"Kenney!" Chris screams. John stumbles, nearly knocking over a garbage can. Jenna puts a finger to her lips.

"Where are you guys going?" Chris asks.

"We're sneaking out of here...don't tell anybody," Jenna says, lightly running with John away from the bar.

Tom peers across the bar to see Amanda sitting alone, sipping on a beer. He gets off his bar stool but then sits back down. He reconsiders and heads over to where Amanda is sitting.

"Is this seat taken?" Tom asks, standing behind Amanda. She looks back and smirks. Tom settles into the bar chair next to her. Amanda looks ahead, ignoring Tom to a degree.

"I'm surprised to see you here," Tom says. Amanda flips her hair over her ear and looks at Tom.

"Jenna invited me...I don't know where she went though...and my therapist says I need to start doing more normal things outside of work, like talking to other people."

Tom nods his head and laughs to himself.

"Well you seem to really be working on it, sitting here by yourself."

Amanda rolls her eyes, "I was sitting over there," pointing to the table with Beth, Caroline and a few other girls, "but all they kept talking about were boys they've had crushes on for ten years, it was pathetic. Felt like I was in a bad Kate Hudson movie. So it was either slowly pluck off every fake eyelash from their pretty little faces or sit here by myself. I chose the corner seat and this sombrero," Amanda says, pointing to the sombrero adorning the wall.

They both sit in silence, nodding at their drinks.

"I gotta say, you've got some good moves. I mean that little jab you threw when we were in the hallway this morning..." Tom trails off, quietly praising Amanda.

"Thank you," Amanda offers, still apprehensive of talking to Tom.

"I just thought you should know," Tom says, returning to his beer and looking across the bar.

Mike, now sitting with an assembled audience of Russell, Matt, Maria and Jeff, continues his dissertation on the bane of his existence. He's a little drunk.

"Love! Like it ever fucking existed. It's a prayer and a song sold to us by movies and television shows and corporations. It's bullshit. It's just a way for you to get married and then buy a house you can't afford and drive a foreign car. It's bullshit. Don't even get me started on kids—that's just the transition from buying shit that I don't need, to buying shit that they don't need. The whole thing is a crock of shit. It's bullshit," Mike explains.

Russell laughs, "I think you're trying to say that it's bullshit." Mike nods his head, finishing his red bull and vodka.

"It is... and you should take me seriously because I've been to that land, well almost, and let me tell you, you don't want to be there. It's no man's land, literally—no man should go to it," Mike continues.

"So you're done with relationships?" Maria asks. Mike holds up his hand, showing it to everyone at the table.

"Five fingers, one palm, equals happiness," Mike says.

"So you're gonna jerk off for the rest of your life?" Matt gets out through a laugh.

"Hey, I know how to pleasure myself better than anyone; I've been doing it the longest. If they were giving out Olympic medals for pleasuring Mike, there would only be one person on that podium. Why should I go for something that will only please me some of the time and all the other times will just give me a headache?"

"I've gotten headaches from jerking off," Russell adds.

"Yea, on snow days," Matt says.

"I'm gonna have a headache tonight," Russell says.

"I have a headache right now," Maria adds. All the boys' heads spin to look at Maria. She puts her hands in the air and looks ashamed at the boys, "From D'Ascoli's singing...you sickos."

"I'm suspending my dick from all extracurricular activities," Matt says, looking down at his beer bottle.

"I'm sure you could pick up some disease-free lady here tonight, Matthew. I mean look at those girls over there...they look like they're going to prom next week," Maria says, pointing to four girls who definitely snuck into the bar.

"Is it bad that we're in a bar that is serving high school kids? Like are we those weird old people?" Russell asks, seriously pondering the question.

"It's only weird if D'Ascoli doesn't hit on one of them. And we're in the clear because I think I saw him singing a BB Mack song to one of them before," Maria says.

"Don't you miss sleeping with someone though?" Jeff asks, "Like, I can't sleep right when she's not there."

"I can't sleep either way. At least I have two pillows and no dead arm in the morning," Mike replies.

"You're making a lot of good points, Pennisi," Jeff says, which prompts a punch to the arm from Maria. Jeff kisses Maria on the forehead.

Derek runs through the bar and up on stage to join D'Ascoli in a duet. Jeff and Maria soon say their goodbyes, one of the few times Jeff hadn't closed out the bar in the presence of his friends.

"They recruited me right out of high school; I've been on the road ever since," Amanda says to the enraptured Tom.

"Me too."

"And it's never felt weird, you know? I've moved around the world, seen some cool shit, seen some bad shit and I feel like I'm making a difference, as crazy as that sounds," Amanda continues.

"I'm sort of going through this crisis, which is maybe why I wasn't all that impressive this morning," Tom says. Amanda sarcastically nods her head, smiling at Tom.

"Shut up. And I've just been thinking about everything I've missed. There's been a dozen of these weddings or birthdays or bar mitzvahs that I wasn't at because I was in Morocco or China or South Africa, and I'm starting to question whether it's worth it. Don't you ever think that you'd be happier if your job wasn't everything? That you could go into this bar and just sit here and have a beer, not look at the exits or whether the bartender is left handed or right handed? Just stop analyzing, stop thinking—just living, simply...talking to your friends about nothing."

Amanda begins to think, "Well..."

"What?"

"But isn't life to be experienced? Doing what you're put on this earth to do at the highest level possible? Going places few people ever go? Frankly, doing things that few will ever do. I look at it like this. There are about dozen people in this world that can do what I do...you included. We are insanely good at our jobs. Why should we give that up and be something regular, something ordinary? I went through the same thing you went through. I met someone and I thought about pulling back, being a girlfriend...but the pull was too much. Maybe I was bored, or maybe this job is just too good to deny. You wouldn't be on the road so much if you didn't love it," Amanda says.

"What happened to the guy?" Tom asks.

"I had him killed; it was messy," Amanda replies with a smirk.

Back at the hotel John pulls his shoes off, tossing them into the corner. Jenna comes out of the bathroom, drying her hands with a towel.

"Don't go yet," John says, falling backwards into his bed.

"It's bad luck to see the bride the night before," Jenna replies.

"Baby, it's 2:30 in the morning; we're getting married in ten hours. I think we're past the point of no return," John says.

Jenna tosses the towel onto the bench at the base of the bed and joins John. She lies next to the sprawled out body of her soon-to-be-husband, propping her head up with her right arm.

"I just don't want you to walk out that door and think that you're making a huge mistake," John says, eyes closed.

"I thought about that before, but I'm just gonna grit my teeth and bare it for the next 50 years and if not I'll just poison your food one day—go find some hot, young stud to spend all your money with," Jenna replies.

"Who says romance is dead?"

"Everyone," Jenna replies, "Doesn't mean we have to believe them."

John smiles.

"Oh! I found a song for you," Jenna says, bounding off the bed and running over to John's laptop. John opens his eyes and rolls onto his side, watching Jenna typing away at the keys.

Jenna gets up and heads back over to bed, the voice of Annie Clark quietly whispering through the hotel room. Jenna begins to lip synch to St. Vincent's "Marry Me."

"Marry me, John/ Marry me, John/ I'll be so good to you."

John and Jenna fall asleep together in bed.

Chris lights another cigarette. He's enjoying the snow; not being able to hear D'Ascoli singing is also a consideration for staying outside. The front door swings open. Chris looks and sees Beth wander out.

"Look who's hiding outside," she says, walking over to Chris.

"Just watching the snow fall," Chris replies, taking a drag of his cigarette. Beth puts her hand out and dips her nose at Chris. Chris exhales and pulls out his pack of cigarettes, opening the top. Beth looks through the box, pulling one out and grabbing Chris' lighter from his hand.

"I didn't know you smoked," Chris says. Beth lights her cigarette and inhales deeply.

"You haven't seen me in five years; I'm sure there's a lot you don't know about me," she shoots back. Chris nods his head, returning to his cigarette.

"I'm feeling a hint of nostalgia, I gotta be honest," Beth says.

"Yea? What for?"

"Everything—you, Caroline and Michael not talking, D'Ascoli's general way of life," Beth says.

"What's so nostalgic about me?" Chris asks, bouncing off the brick wall slowly.

"Well you look the same—I swear, people have changed their hair or gained weight or gained a lot of weight...but you look exactly the same. That same dork who was memorizing his fake ID zip code on line outside the bar."

"07753," Chris says quickly.

"You've never stepped foot in Neptune, New Jersey," Beth replies.

"That's a lie! I lived there for 21 years, my fake ID says so...I'm glad I'm the same."

They both take a few drags, the snow now reaching the tops of their shoes.

"You sound different," Chris says.

"I sound different? Like how?" Beth asks.

"I don't know, your voice sounds different. Maybe I just haven't heard it in a while, but it sounds different, more annoying to be honest," Chris replies. Beth punches him.

"Ow, I'm just trying to be honest."

"Well then I take back everything I said, you're balding and ugly and your face is sagging," Beth says back with a laugh.

"Alright, I can live with that," he replies. Chris kicks some snow toward the street.

"How are you? We never got around to talking about that during our Sorkin-esque tête à tête amoureux from before," Chris asks.

Beth takes a few moments, "Honest answer or fake answer?"

"Fake answer, we have no room for honesty here," Chris replies.

"Alright fake answer...I feel very unsure of my position, like where I'm at," Beth says.

"How so?"

"I have a good job...actually a great job, who am I kidding...but I don't have the confidence to keep moving. I feel very tentative because for the longest time it was, 'You have all the time in the world! Look how young you are!' Then it became, 'Get your shit together girl, you're too old to be so flaky.' That's my issue—jumping into the ocean with both feet. I've dated some guys, but when I'm really into it, they are just looking for someone to call at 2 a.m. and when I want to just find a piece of ass, the guy wants to start picking out centerpieces."

"You should give him the name of the guy who did the ones at the rehearsal dinner," Chris replies.

"Ugh, I didn't have the heart to tell her how butt-ugly those things were."

"Well you should be confident, honestly...no bullshit. You just gotta get out of your own head. The relationship thing I don't know, nobody's got that freakin answer," Chris says. "Just breathe and you'll realize that everything isn't so bad, everything passes eventually—even the worst shit dissipates after a while."

"You just said freakin," Beth says. Chris smiles.

"Yea, I'm trying to say 'fuck' less...Erin is trying to get me to say 'fuck' less," Chris replies. Beth nods her head.

"How are you?" Beth asks, "Like for real, not your stock answer." Chris squints his eyes.

"I'm really fucking great and I miss my girlfriend," Chris replies.

"You just said fuck."

196

"Yea I know but she's not here," Chris replies.

"What a softy you are, mellowing in your old age...I was expecting some writerly passion, some angst, some ugliness just waiting to bubble to the surface," Beth says with a smirk.

"Oh believe me there's plenty of that, but looking around this weekend I feel pretty good. Last year was terrible—just awful. My dad died and I lost my way a bit, but little by little I dug my way out of the hole...got above water. That's when I thought, this life is full of bad shit and I've been punched in the mouth more times than I wanna count, but there's always that moment that brings you back... and the pain doesn't hurt as much anymore. I'm just chasing those moments."

"Just when I thought I could hate you," Beth says, turning and returning to her cigarette.

"Why? What did I do?"

"You were such a dick before! My God, I wanted to throw a drink in your face," Beth gets out, exasperated at Chris and his ignorance.

"How are you supposed to talk to an ex?" Chris says, shrugging his shoulders, "Then you go and bring up the whole writing the first book about you, Jesus, what am I supposed to say to that?"

Beth smiles and moves closer to Chris.

"But you did write it for me, about me, about the two of us...I'm the girl," Beth says, continuing with the prodding.

Chris shakes his head and lights a new cigarette, "You're driving me to smoke. You see this—I was gonna quit before you came out here."

"Bullshit, you've been out here for an hour; c'mon out with it," Beth says, beginning to poke Chris in the ribs.

"Fuck, alright enough with the poking...I need a drink. Who told you that by the way?"

Beth shifts her weight from right to left, looking like a boxer who's choosing what side of the body to batter next.

"I have my sources," Beth says, poking Chris in his ribs again. Chris laughs and moves away.

"Wow, you laughed!" Beth says. Chris picks up a snowball and throws it at Beth. Beth dodges and then makes her own snowball, winging it toward Chris, skimming the right side of his head.

"Shit, you almost got me," Chris says, running his hand through his hair. He settles back into the bar's wall.

"I can't believe this snow," Chris says, closing his eyes and exhaling into the air. Beth picks up a handful of snow and dumps it on Chris' head. Chris slowly shakes his head, "I can't... believe...you just did that." Beth starts laughing loudly, gasping for air.

Chris bends over and shakes the snow off his head, looking at his now wet cigarette.

"And you put out my cigarette! God, you're the worst," Chris says, flipping the cigarette into the street. Beth joins him back on the wall. She looks up at Chris and then puffs away on her cigarette.

"If this was a few years ago we'd totally be getting a cab to go and hump each other's brains out," Beth says. Chris shrugs his shoulder.

"But it's not."

"I know. It's a shame," Beth replies.

"Alright…I wrote the first book to impress you…and yes…the girl was *partially* based on you," Chris painfully spits out. Beth looks down at the ground and smiles.

Chris reaches into his jacket once more, lighting up the last cigarette he has.

"I just gotta ask…do you love her?" Beth says.

"Yes," Chris replies.

"Then why aren't you married yet?" Beth asks. Chris rubs his eyes.

"I don't really know…but maybe it doesn't matter. Because I hope this doesn't make you hate me, but this entire weekend I was looking forward to seeing everybody, to fall back into something comfortable—have those good feelings from college kind of wash over me. You know as great as it has been to hear D'Ascoli sing karaoke badly again or hang with Singer or see Boyd and Bob and Derek with hookers—I mean Jesus, those guys are my heroes. Even talking to you, someone who for the longest time I cared the world about, during all that, all those conversations and moments, all I was thinking of was her and how she wasn't here and I how I missed her. I don't think getting married would change that feeling; in fact it might just ruin it. So that's it."

"Okay," Beth replies.

"You used to be one of the rotten ones, and I liked you for that," Beth adds. Chris nods his head and smiles.

"I really wanted to have sex this weekend," Beth says.

"So what's stopping you?" Chris asks.

"Your girlfriend! I'm getting cooter blocked from 1,000 miles away," Beth replies.

"Go inside and flash D'Ascoli while he's singing. You'll be inside a bathroom stall in ten seconds flat," Chris says.

"Wrong Chris," Beth replies with a smile.

"You're the worst; you dumped me!" Chris replies. Beth gives Chris a titty twister—hard. Chris screams in pain.

"No you dumped me—and that's for you going and getting all grown up and falling in love and being sure of yourself and...fuck you," Beth says, returning to her cigarette.

"Alright let's make out," Chris says sarcastically.

Chris and Beth smoked cigarettes until their socks were wet.

Inside, the bartender rings the last call bell. Those still sober enough to hear perk their skulls up and head for the bar for one last beer. D'Ascoli gets back on the karaoke stage and grabs the mic.

"This is my favorite karaoke song of all time... and it goes out to Emily," D'Ascoli says squinting toward the back tables, "What? Oh she's sleeping? Alright, fuck her—she was boring anyway..."

With that, D'Ascoli launches into the greatest karaoke version of "Total Eclipse of the Heart" of all time. Firing on all cylinders, hitting the high notes, dropping to one knee, pumping his fist slowly—poetry in motion, as much poetry as blindly drunken karaoke at 4 a.m. can be. As the bass line drops out, D'Ascoli throws his tie into the assembled, also blindly drunken, crowd. Women cheer, men jeer, Emily awakens from her alcohol poisoning to a surreal spinning room with a bigheaded man blowing off the roof with a power ballad.

"This is my house now, fuck a Bonnie Tyler," D'Ascoli screams into the mic, evoking either Prince or B-Rabbit. The crowd cheers and D'Ascoli flips the mic to the DJ, crowd surfing out to the street.

Back in the real world, Russell and Tom carry a sleeping D'Ascoli over their shoulders. D'Ascoli mumbles the lyrics to "Total Eclipse of the Heart" as he looks down at the ground.

"Russ! I didn't get to sing 'Total Eclipse of the Heart' tonight! We gotta go back," D'Ascoli stumbles out of his mouth.

"Go back to sleep D'Ascoli," Tom says.

"I'm gonna write 'dickhead' in the biggest possible letters on this fucker's forehead when we get back to the hotel," Mike says.

As the drunkards reach the hotel, covered in the still falling snow, they stumble to their various rooms. Russell and Mike drop D'Ascoli into his bed, Russell putting a garbage can next to him. D'Ascoli knocks it over saying, "I ain't a bitch like Pennisi; I can handle my liquor like a man." With a laugh and a burp, D'Ascoli passes out. Russell hands Mike a Sharpie and watches as Mike does what he said he was going to do.

Tom says goodnight to Amanda, watching her from the elevator as she walks toward her room. He hopes for her to look back, but she doesn't. The elevator doors close as she enters her room.

Chris lingers in the lobby, talking to Bob. Derek and Boyd had headed upstairs minutes earlier with their paid-in-full ladies.

"What's the deal with the hookers?" Chris asks. Bob shrugs his shoulders and laughs.

"Boyd's out of his mind. He said we needed dates for the wedding. He paid for 24 hours of company...they gave him a fucking discount," Bob replies.

"Did he have a coupon or something?"

"More like the hooker equivalent of a frequent flyer card," Bob says.

Chris laughs.

"He's just trying to hold on to that feeling...he's drifting for as long as he possibly can," Bob says, "Plus I think he was hoping he wouldn't have to see Annie this weekend. Is she coming?"

"No, I don't think so," Chris replies.

"Good...seeing her just crushes him," Bob says.

"Yea, I've been seeing a lot of that recently."

Mike and Russell close D'Ascoli's hotel room door.

"Make sure I'm up in the morning; I'll head over to the church with you," Mike says, backing up toward the elevator.

"Alright...where are you going right now?" Russell replies, following Mike to the elevator.

"I think you know, Russ."

Russell shakes his head and pushes the up elevator button.

"What?" Mike says, repressing the button.

"I think you know what," Russell replies. Mike looks down at his shoes.

"Just stop man—stop being so miserable. There's nothing up there anymore. She's not gonna make you 20 again...or fix whatever's wrong with you. Just stop doing it to yourself," Russell says.

"Everything's fucked up...things were better when she was around, as fucking crazy as that sounds."

"That has nothing to do with her. We were 20; we partied five nights a week, and our biggest obligation was going to class for two hours a day...and we couldn't even do that. You've been drowning, man, having sex with her isn't gonna help that—shit, she'll put her hand on your head and push you down further," Russell says, putting his hand on Mike's shoulder. "Don't give up on this shit yet, the game ain't over...no matter how much you think it is."

The elevator doors open.

Bob and Chris wander around the hotel gift shop, grabbing bags of chips and water. The lobby is quiet; it's about 4:30 a.m. after all. Boarding the elevator, Bob worries about what he's about to see when he opens the door to the room he's sharing with Boyd and Derek. As the doors open to the fourth floor, Chris and Bob hear screams coming from said room. Bob sighs.

"If they whip out cameras and start filming, give me a call," Chris says to the departing Bob. Chris leans against elevator walls, enjoying his bag of chips.

Getting off the elevator, Chris sees Mike exiting the stairwell. Chris grabs a bag out of his back pocket and flips it to Mike.

"I just drew shit on D'Ascoli's face," Mike says, opening his bag of chips.

"That's awesome," Chris replies, opening the room door.

Mike turns on the television.

"Jesus, we gotta go to bed, turn that shit off," Chris says, hanging his suit jacket in the closet.

"I'm gonna see what's on Pay Per View," Mike replies, lounging into the couch.

Chris jumps over the couch and joins him. Mike flips through the movies.

"I was just talking to her—"

"You went up there?" Chris interjects.

"Yea...I was talking to her and it sounded like a conversation that I've had 1,000 times. It summed up my whole fucking life. I get stuck in these holes and I can't get out, so I just say 'fuck it' and build a house in the hole. Then it rains and the house floods and I wonder why it happened."

"You are getting really deep," Chris says.

"I think I'm stealing from one of your books right now," Mike replies. "But honestly, I've known that girl in one way or another for a decade. Ten years of my life I've known her and I knew the first day we weren't right for each other and yet here I am, ten years later being humped against an ATM machine, which I'll admit was pretty great."

"Yea, that is pretty awesome; totally stealing it for my next book."

"But...it's awful, and I feel shitty all over again. Back then it was just a passing diversion—I didn't know any better; I didn't care. Now I just get angry at myself that I'm in the same place I was ten years ago—nothing has changed."

"Well I wouldn't say that," Chris replies, "You just have to stop settling. I do it too, we settle because it's easier. I should marry Erin tomorrow; fuck Kenney, because she's the girl I want to be with, but I haven't…because of one fucked up thing or another in my head. It's easier to do nothing, but maybe that isn't good enough anymore."

The boys are quiet. Mike rubs his now bare chin.

"I'm tired of wasting away, letting everything that happened yesterday slather everything that happens today in shit. Every relationship since her has lived in the ugly glow of that fucked pairing…and it's not like I'm bashing her—it's not her fault, it's my fault. I have to take responsibility for the fact that I haven't moved on. She was the first girl I've ever loved and because of that she occupies a small part of my brain…that will never go away and she's just as fucking screwed up as I am. She's just trying to find a way to live and cope with all this bullshit in our heads. We just have to stop crashing into each other and fucking those thoughts away. I have to find a life…as big as that sounds. I have to get a better job, and a car, and a fucking *New York Times* subscription because if I'm still the guy at the bar yelling my head off about how much love sucks at your wedding or Russ' wedding—whoever gets married next—because I'm still in the drowning house at the bottom of that hole, I'll have to stop coming up for air," Mike says.

"Well let's start tomorrow," Chris says.

"The good thing is that at least nothing matters before 30 anyway," Mike replies.

"I thought you said 25?"

"No, I think I said 30."

Mike scrolls through the list of movies, eating potato chips as he does it, "What time are you picking up Erin tomorrow?"

"Her flight lands during the ceremony. I'm gonna go and pick her up after, then head back to the reception."

"The hotel's got 'The Big Lebowski' on Pay Per View," Mike says shocked.

"Why haven't you pressed play yet?"

Chris puts his right hand up, Mike slaps it.

"I love you man."

"Shut the fuck up, Donny," Mike replies.

CHAPTER FIFTEEN

The ceremony was beautiful, and well attended, even with the snow. You should have been there. Everyone was there, well except D'Ascoli—he was too busy scrubbing 'dickhead' off his forehead. The wedding was as understated as the rehearsal dinner was gaudy. It was quieter as well, because most of those in attendance were over the age of 50 and as you get older, you tend to speak lower. Everyone else was extremely hung over. John looked so happy. I don't think I've ever seen that kid smile so much in all the time I've known him...and you know what? He deserves it. Also Derek, Boyd and Bob showed up with their hookers...who surprisingly clean up really well. One of the girls and Boyd disappeared from the church at one point...to do what, I don't really know.

"I don't really want to know."

CHAPTER SIXTEEN

Chris opens the town car door, holding it as Erin lifts her dress to avoid the snow on the sidewalk. The all-night snowfall is now slush, after a brighter-than-usual early morning sun melted it all away. Chris grabs Erin's right hand as the two move swiftly into the wedding reception hall where people are just starting on their appetizers. They weave through the maze of guests, exchanging 'hello's' as they attempt to find their table. Seeing a standing Mike waving toward them, Chris and Erin find the lighthouse to their port.

Weddings are whirlwinds. There's a lot of eating and talking and seeing long lost faces and second cousins—1,000 different eyeballs, all seeing different things.

Everyone was there, even more people then before—blips from the past popping up everywhere. The resident wino of the group, Celeste, got drunk on all the red wine the open bar could provide. Soon she and D'Ascoli were talking, Celeste expounding on the ludicrous nature of a cash bar at a wedding. It was right around the time she was saying, "People who don't have enough money to have an open bar at their wedding just shouldn't be getting married, I'm sorry," when D'Ascoli was wondering just how many more cabernets it would take for him to close.

"What are you doing later?" he asked. She peeked up from her wine glass.

"I don't know," she replied with a smile.

"I do."

The answer was two cabernets. They disappeared shortly thereafter.

Amanda sits alone at the bridesmaids' table, buttering a roll. Tom slinks over to her, sliding into the seat next to her.

"Hi," he says, barely above a whisper.

"I'm holding a knife; never sneak up on me like that," Amanda replies.

"Sorry," Tom replies. Amanda goes back to buttering her roll.

"So what's up?"

Tom clears his throat, "I'm lonely and you're lovely."

Amanda looks at Tom, smiling for the first time, "Where did you steal that from?"

"Nowhere, totally made it up, just right now," Tom replies.

"Well, thank you."

"Listen I'm not good at this sort of thing...I can't talk to women. I've had like, one girlfriend, and we never really ever broke up. One day we left a party and neither one of us ever called each other again. It's weird I know, but...what I'm trying to say is...I don't want anything other then to spend the next two courses of meals with you. And then tomorrow I'll forget to set an alarm and you can take the briefcase and run away with it because, if it's alright with you, I wanna chase you...if that's okay," Tom says.

"Okay," Amanda says, sliding her buttered roll on a plate in front of Tom. Tom picks it up and is about to eat it, stopping and saying, "It's not poisoned is it?"

"No, but that would be a good trick right?" Amanda replies with a smile.

The events started to swirl again.

Bobby sees Crifo, Purvik and Stricker, old members of the running crew, sneaking around with fake mustaches on. They crashed, because Jenna hates the three of them and told John to not invite them to the wedding.

All the guys couldn't believe how hot Tara still was.

Then a few glasses are tapped and Matt finds himself standing in front of that rogues gallery of friends and family. John looks up at Matt, who really does seem nervous, as he shuffles through his index cards. Matt clears his throat and drops the cards down on to the table.

"It wasn't very good anyway," Matt says, which garnered a few chuckles.

"I've known John for a very long time...everyone here has, well except for Boyd's date—but that's not important. When I first met John he was a shut-in. I mean the guy stayed in his dorm room and played NBA Jam with Russ until 3 a.m. on a nightly basis and...somehow never got any better. He really is the worst video game player of those who devote their entire lives to them and don't even get me started on World of Warcraft...Jesus. He'd come out of his bedroom after one of those benders looking like a crack head. I'm sorry I just said crack head in a best man speech."

Matt takes a breath.

"But his most enduring quality is his soul. He's got soul; he's a truly genuine person in a world where there isn't many of them left. I could name the countless things that he's done for me over the years, or for anyone in this room for that matter, but honestly, they are better left unsaid. He's the best of us...and it's no shock that John's the first one of our friends that a girl has deemed passable enough to marry. I mean we are a rotten group of individuals and I'm happy that we haven't rubbed off on John too much. I was talking to John yesterday and I was telling him that if he wanted to a hop on a plane and blow this whole thing off, we could be in the air within 45 minutes. He declined, clearly...if I had D'Ascoli with me I probably could have persuaded him, but he looked at me and he told me how much he loved Jenna. How she was the best thing in his life. That she was the angel that appeared in the wake of a terrible time and brought him out of a valley of despair. That she made him a better person...that she was someone who made the dark past fuzzy, and the future on the horizon that much brighter. I was raised in a generation that trumped cynicism over romance, and the words 'true love' were as ugly as the Katherine Heigl romantic comedy they came from. But for the first time, I looked at a man saying that he utterly loved the woman he was with, and I completely believed him. There was no double speak or rolling of the eyes. He loves her... and for someone to love another individual that way, that love must be reciprocated just as brightly. I have to be honest, I'm still not completely sold on 'love.' But seeing these two people, two people I have the highest regard for and two people who...complement each other so well, I think I speak for a lot of us when I say that I'm going to give love a second look. Here's to Jenna and John."

And John and Jenna dance their first dance while Matt looks on happily, and as Jeff holds Maria's stomach, and as Boyd humps a hooker the third stall from the right while he's thinking about Annie, and as Amanda joins Tom on the dance floor, and as Derek and Bob find out their girls' real names, and as Mike sits, not drunk, he takes a picture of John and Jenna, and as D'Ascoli gets it on with a hot blonde from college he's always had a crush on, and as Chris whispers into Erin's ear, Russell looks out over it all—the quiet leader of this band apart.

PART FOUR: JOHN PEPPER

CHAPTER SEVENTEEN

"How long will you be staying with us sir?" the bellhop with the crooked hat asks. The question might as well have been posed to the revolving door the bellhop is moving toward, for the intended recipient of it has bulky headphones over his ears and aviators over his eyes.

John quickly pulls off his headphones—getting that feeling in his gut that he is missing something by having his ears blasted by "Rocks Off" from The Rolling Stones.

"I'm sorry did you say something?" John replies to the bellhop with the crooked hat.

"Oh nothing; I just asked how long will you be staying with us, sir?" the bellhop sheepishly repeats.

"What's your name?" John asks the bellhop, who is now holding open the front door so John can come in.

"It's Clark sir."

John extends his hand and shakes Clark's.

"It's nice to meet you, Clark, and to answer your question—I don't know. I'll be sure to keep you in the loop though," John replies.

John enters the lobby of a high-rise hotel in mid-town Manhattan. Its vastness is only equaled by its decadence and bankruptcy. It looks like every hip hotel in the world—trashy, bullshit art graces the walls. Fabulously beautiful people litter the furniture as if they are waiting for a director to yell "Action!" on the next take of a shampoo commercial. John is met by a scrambling group of people, who run up to him with their hands full.

"Mr. Pepper, how was your flight?" the short man with the bald spot and the horn rimmed glasses asks John. He's some executive from the record company, speaking a mile a minute about something. John would put on his headphones again, if he wasn't so fascinated by the fact that someone who he's never met before cared so much for his wellbeing. The woman to the man's left hands John an itinerary of events that he is to attend in the coming week. John quickly looks at the list as the short man with the bald spot continues to speak, his words forming a gelatinous blob of noise.

"How does that all look to you, Mr. Pepper?" the short man concludes with a flourish.

"Looks great," John replies, "Thank you for taking care of me."

"No problem at all, Mr. Pepper. If you need anything, there is a phone number on the itinerary. You can call that number at any time, day or night," the woman says. She next reaches into her bag, pulling out two room keys.

"You are already checked in, room 1137. Anything you need, room service, laundry, anything, just charge it to the room and the company will take care of it," she finishes.

"Thank you, I appreciate it," John replies humbly. Shaking hands with the record company representatives, John picks up his backpack and heads over to the elevator. Clark the bellhop, pressing the button to summon the elevator, waits with the rest of the John's bags. The elevator doors slide open and John and Clark enter. Pressing the button for the 11th floor, John leans against the back wall of the lift.

Silence rules the elevator as it climbs the floors to John's place of residence for the next however many days.

He closes his eyes as the elevator continues its ascent.

"I'm a really big fan of yours," Clark says, breaking the silence.

John opens his eyes to look at Clark, a smile crossing his face. "Thanks man, I appreciate it."

"Really, no bullshit, *All In Together Now* was the soundtrack to my teenage years," Clark continues. "I haven't listened to a lot of the newer stuff, but man *All In Together Now* is fucking sublime."

"You wouldn't be the only one," John says with smirk.

"I'm sorry, I didn't mean to be a dick," Clark quickly says to recover.

"No, no it's okay. Honesty is a commodity traded less and less lately," John replies.

"What are you in town for?"

"I got an album coming out and I'm doing a show at the Garden" John replies, stretching his arms.

"No shit! When's it coming out?" Clark quickly asks. John lets loose a little laugh and replies, "Today."

"Oh...that's uh, awesome man. Good luck with that," Clark replies as he turns to look back toward the door.

John reaches into his backpack and pulls out a CD, handing it to Clark.

"It's no *All In Together Now*, but it's free," John says as he hands Clark his new album. Clark accepts the CD, saying, "Thanks, I'll give it a listen."

The elevator stops on the 11th floor, its doors part. Clark steps off the elevator and leads John and a cart full of his bags down the hallway. Reaching room 1137, John opens the doors and enters. Clark places all of the bags in the living room as John roams the apartment. Dropping his bag on the bed, John returns to the living room. Handing Clark a tip, he bids him farewell and locks the door after his departure.

John heads over to the fridge and scans the choices for consumption. Settling on vodka, John walks into the living room and settles into the couch.

CHAPTER EIGHTEEN

John peers up at the clock above the flat screen television adorning his wall. He stretches his neck to the left and right as he climbs to his feet. He stumbles a bit, stubbing his toe on the living room table. Letting out a grunt and a grimace; he shuffles over to his bedroom.

Opening the luggage that hasn't moved since Clark brought it up from the lobby, John pulls out a jacket and a baseball hat. Putting them on, he heads to the door, his gait slowed by the stubbed toe and his swagger influenced by the free record company vodka.

Exiting his hotel room, he sees a young couple kissing a few doors down. With the girl grinding into his crotch and kissing his neck, the man looks over at John and nods happily. John closes his door and heads to the elevator.

As the couple down the hall makes a porno with no camera and the elevator sits motionless on the seventh floor, John sways back and forth, rubbing his eyes. Looking over at the garbage can that sits next to the elevator door, John sees the CD that he gave to Clark. Sitting on top of a McDonalds fast food bag and a torn open box of condoms, probably both belonging to the humping couple a few doors down, the CD seems almost part of a mosaic of commercial porn. Its photoshopped cover of John, portraying a man he hasn't looked like in years, with flames shooting into the sky and a harem of women off to one side. A cover that the record company thought would appeal to both John's older fans, i.e. people who liked him when he made music that mattered, and a new group of cash rich, easily impressionable fools who have never spun a record or experienced the smell of lighter fluid as it floated through the air at a sold out concert. A focused grouped cover to a focused grouped album. John would rescue it from the trash if he didn't already feel it belonged there.

The elevator door opens and John enters.

Hitting the revolving doors of the hotel, John bundles his jacket and pulls his ball cap down over his eyebrows. Hiding not due to a fear of recognition and adulation, but recognition and embarrassment. Walking down one of the most populated streets in the world, John looks down at the sidewalk. He sees the cracks, some that run from storefront to street and others the size of the edge of a quarter. The signs of decay, wear without upkeep and just general time passage. None of these little cracks could ever split open by themselves and shallow the street and its inhabitants whole, but if the cracks ever had a meeting and decided to fuck shit up, their combined power could eat us alive.

Entering Bryant Park as dusk settled on the high glass windows of sky rises, John wandered over and sat at one of the tables. Pulling a small notebook out of his back pocket, he scribbles what could best be described as things. Words, stick figures, detailed mosaics. A jumble of ideas, beliefs, thoughts. This particular book is nearing the end, its previous 100 or so pages filled likewise with a jumble of crap indecipherable to anyone but John. He pulls his cap above his eyebrows and leans back into the wooden chair.

"Are you John Pepper?" a voice asks. John shakes back to reality. Looking up he sees a guy, around 50, standing in front of him, shaking like a leaf. The guy looks excited. He repeats his question. John pulls his cap back down low and nods his head.

The guy freaks out.

"Holy shit, I can't believe it's you!" the man squeals. John wants to go hide in a bush right now.

"Alright, alright," John says quietly, peering around to see if anyone is noticing this guy having a conniption. He sees one or two people turning and whispering to the people they're with.

"I'm totally going next week to the concert, I've seen you like…I don't even know…ten times, 12 times. I'm sure I put your kids through college with how much stuff I've bought with your name on it," the zealous fan continues.

"Well I appreciate that, thank you," John replies. The zealous man nods his head quickly.

"John Fucking Pepper, John Fucking Pepper, everybody!" he screams. Now a lot of people turn and look. With that, John gets out of his seat and shakes the man's hand.

"Thanks man, have a good night," John says, beginning to walk away. The fan doesn't let go of the handshake, holding John in place.

"Hey man, you wanna go get a drink or something? I'll totally buy," he says.

"That's nice of you but uh…I'm an alcoholic so," John replies.

"Shit I forgot, how about a burger?" the fan continues.

"No man, I'm good, have a good night," John says, finally able to extricate himself from the man's handshake. John darts toward the steps, down onto 42nd Street, quickly hailing a cab.

On the way back to the hotel, John looks up every couple of seconds to see the cab driver catching glances. Pulling up to the hotel monolith John tips a little bit more, as if to say thanks to the cab driver for not regaling him in conversation. He ducks in the revolving door and makes his way toward the elevator. He sees them in sight.

"Mr. Pepper," the voice says. John turns to the hotel clerk who is holding out a piece of paper.

"A message for you sir," the hotel employee says, passing the note to John.

"From who?"

"A Mrs. Longfield," the bellhop replies. John looks down at the note—a phone number its only message.

"Did she say anything?" John asks.

"No sir."

John nods and heads for the elevator.

John opens his hotel room door and tosses the message into the garbage. Opening the fridge in the kitchen, John thumbs through the mini liquors on tap. He grabs a scotch, scoops some ice and pours. It goes down clean. It's good scotch, not great, but good scotch. He grabs the scotch and heads for his bedroom. Sitting on the edge of the plush bed, he sinks into the sheets. It's like quicksand, John feels as if he's about to drown. He finishes his glass of scotch, placing it on the end table. He eyes the telephone.

It's one of those faux rotary phones, a rotary phone for someone who's never used a rotary phone before. It doesn't quite work right. John takes a moment, looking skyward, trying to dial from memory. He coughs, moving away from the receiver.

It rings and rings.

Answering machine.

"Hey, it's Melissa and Chad. We're not home, so please leave a message and we'll get back to you as soon as possible."

John hangs up the phone. He rubs his fingers into his palm and picks up the receiver again. He reconsiders, putting the phone down and laying down into the quicksand bed. Maybe it'll swallow him.

He lies down for a few moments.

I wish I had more scotch. I shouldn't have another one though. I'll feel like shit in the morning. But I already feel like shit in the morning. The ceiling is off white. Actually the whole room is. The sheets are even off white. It doesn't look real, this place.

John gets out of bed and heads to the desk across the bedroom. He picks up the list of obligations for tomorrow.

6:45 A.M.- Pick up

7:00 A.M.- H/MU

8:30 A.M.-9:15 A.M.- Today Show

9:15 A.M.-9:45 A.M.- Breakfast

10:00 A.M.-12:00 P.M.- Radio interviews

12:00 P.M.- 1 P.M.- Lunch

John drops the piece of paper without finishing. He returns to the kitchen, pouring that second scotch. No ice this time.

John stares out into the cityscape. The clock is winding down. A light is on in the building across from John's window. He watches the window, shadows of two people on the wall, a yellow bedroom lamp giving them their light. Soon the light goes off, the shadows disappearing with it. John loses focus on the window, the loss of the illumination fading into the rest of the dark façade.

He sits on the edge of his window, looking out into the city from his suite— the world moving on and on. What's he doing here? He should have gotten out of this thing a long time ago. It holds nothing for him anymore.

This chair feels nice though. He's drunk now.

I shouldn't have had those two scotches. I can't drink like I used to. Two scotches used to be lunch, fuel before a show. I should drink some coffee. I don't want to throw up on Meredith Vieira. Coffee makes me shit though. I don't want to shit my pants in front of Meredith Vieira. I'm so weak now. I've never met Meredith Vieira before. What song should I play tomorrow morning? They'll probably want something from the new album. All those songs fucking suck. Maybe I just won't play. Maybe I'll just say my throat hurts, laryngitis or something, that's worked before. Maybe I'll make the lie bigger, say I have pneumonia or something—then I won't have to go at all. That would be terribly yellow of me. I'm so weak now.

John rearranges the furniture in the hotel room, turning the entire room 180 degrees. It's 5 a.m. now. John returns to his chair in front of the window. A tiny speak of light lights up the horizon, morning is close.

I can't do this shit.

John walks into his bedroom and grabs his itinerary. Looking down the page he sees the number of the short guy with the bald spot. Dialing the man's number, John roughs up his voice. Picking up on the first ring, the bald man sounds calm.

"John, I was just about to call you," he says. John coughs.

"Little fucking world amirite?" John says, punctuating the lingo with another cough.

"You alright John?"

"That's actually the reason I'm calling you *(cough)* I've been up all night just throwing up and *(cough)* my throat is on fire, hold on *(cough, cough)*. I don't think I can *(cough, weeze)* excuse me, I don't think I can do all that stuff today, I wouldn't want to hurl all over Meredith Vieira you know what I'm saying? *(cough)*" John replies.

"I'm sorry to hear that John, I'll send a doctor over right away, just get in bed and rest," the bald man replies, sounding positively cheery.

"I gotta say I'm surprised *(cough)*, most of the time I'm told to go up on stage even if I have a *(cough)* hatchet in my head, you seem pretty al*(cough)*right with this," John says.

"Well that's the reason I was going to call you, the people from the *Today Show* called a few hours...well they wanted to bump you. They've been trying to book this Disney kid to play the plaza for weeks and they finally got him..." John almost drops the phone.

"I ripped the guy a new asshole but they love this kid and the little tweens love him...I don't know...but with this it makes us look better," the bald man says.

"Yea I guess, who is it? Bieber or something?" John asks, forgetting to cough.

"The kids are over Bieber, this new kid makes Justin Bieber look like Axl Rose. It's ridiculous, I can't keep track of all these little mouseketeer fuckers running around. Listen it's fine; just get in bed and the doctor will be over in an hour," the bald man finishes.

"Wow even Bieber's done? (*cough*, he remembered) Well that makes me feel even less relevant," John says.

"Kid's name is T.J. Carter—don't worry about him—I'll reschedule everything else, just get in bed, you got a big week," the bald man says.

John nods...then remembers to cough. *(cough)*

"Alright, I'll talk to you later," John says, hanging up the phone. The definition of rock bottom is being redefined by the second.

John sits back down in front of the window. The sun blooming. A cop car goes screaming by down below. The city is waking up.

I bet Meredith Vieira is on the way to work. Forget Meredith Vieira, never gonna meet her now. Whatever—she's probably not even a fan.

The front desk calls; the doctor is on his way up. John tussles his hair (not much needed to be done), throws on the hotel robe and jumps into bed. This does nothing; he still needs to open the door. But he's method; he'll wait until he hears the knock of the door.

Knock, knock.

John slowly moves from the bed, a few loud coughs on the way to the door. The doctor comes in; he's a nice guy, takes the vitals, stethoscope, tongue compressor, the whole deal.

"Well you look alright to me...maybe it's a stomach bug," the doctor says. John coughs.

"Yea, maybe," John replies. The doctor looks at him.

"Just get plenty of bed rest, drink a lot of fluids," the doctor starts to list.

"I think I threw out my back when I was throwing up before... is there any way I can get something for the pain?" John asks, suddenly having a coughing fit, then grimacing from his back pain. The doctor looks at him. He reaches for his pen and then pauses.

"Threw your back out, huh?"

John nods. The doctor pulls a prescription pad out of his bag.

"I'll write you a prescription for some Vicodin, about a week," the doc says, ripping the prescription out of his book and placing it in John's hand.

"You can't drink on it," the doc continues. John nods his head. The doctor looks back at John. The scotch glass sits on the end table.

"Don't overdo it...and get healthy man," the doctor says, picking up his bag and heading for the door. John follows. The doctor leaves without saying goodbye. John stands in the living room, a bed sheet draped over him. He heads over to his television, turning on the *Today Show*.

Man, Meredith Vieira looks good.

"The moment you've all been waiting for—T.J. Carter!" the man with the microphone screams.

T.J. Carter comes bounding on stage to the shrieks of every pre-pubescent girl in the greater Manhattan area.

"Why aren't these kids in school?" John mumbles aloud, bitterly biting into some room service breakfast that he had sent up. Launching into his radio hit, T.J. Carter runs up and down the stage, slapping hands, singing to the girls in the front row, general teen heartthrob behavior.

John turns off the television. He drops his toast onto the tray on the end table. *I hope the hotel isn't mad I rearranged all this furniture.*

John gets to his feet, takes a shower, grabs his prescription and heads out the door. Getting out of the elevator, not wanting to be seen by the concierge, he heads toward the restaurant, through the kitchen and out onto a side street. He's added a scarf to his hat disguise today, easily navigating the streets. John ducks into the nearest pharmacy, about two blocks from the hotel.

There's a line at the pharmacy. John flips through an *US Weekly*. T.J. Carter is on the cover; supposedly he's having trouble with his teen actress girlfriend. John doesn't recognize many of the people in this rag. Reality TV stars and one-hit wonders from years back marking the bleeding pages. He returns the smut to the newsstand and looks down at the blindingly white store floor tile.

"Next!" the girl behind the counter screams. John flinches at the sound of her voice. He gets to the counter and hands the girl the prescription, she looks it over then passes to another man. She looks at John for a second; he is doing his best not to make eye contact.

"Excuse me Mr. Pepper," the girl says. John slowly raises his head.

"Can I see some ID please?"

John nods his head, reaching into his pocket, pulling out his license. The girl looks over the ID, bending it then handing it back to John.

"It'll be ready in an hour," she says. John grabs his ID and heads away from the pharmacy. He turns back to look at the girl, who smiles at him.

"Next," she says quieter than before.

John putzes around the shampoo aisle. This free hotel stuff isn't going to cut it. John takes off his hat and runs his hand through his hair. It's stringy, a little greasy. He quickly puts the hat back on his head. He slowly wanders up the aisle, looking at all the different bottles. He stops, pulling a red bottle off the shelves. It says that it's supposed to help with "volume."

Why are there so many options? Why can't there just be one? Though I guess "volume" will help with my hair. I don't want an afro though, I don't think I'd look good in one of those, but maybe volume means a perm. I haven't had a perm since the 80's. Never mention that outloud. I've never had a perm. Good boy. You just convinced yourself. Now you're not actually lying.

John suddenly feels uneasy about this bottle, putting it back up on the shelf. He takes one step back.

This aisle looks like the Great Wall, why is there this much shampoo? Every one of these bottles is five deep on the shelf. Do people wash their hair this much? Jesus, I don't think I've even used a tenth of all the shampoo in this aisle in my lifetime. Maybe that's why I'm losing it. But still, who buys all this shampoo? Does shampoo go bad?

John leaves the shampoo aisle empty handed.

He'd return to the magazine aisle, but it's close to a group of people. He chose the pharmacy waiting chairs instead. John looks down at the hands folded in his lap. His knuckles were hairy.

Maybe I should shave that. Man, my fingers are fucked up—the fingers falling victim to years of jamming.

His left index finger can't touch his middle, a product of a firecracker going off in his hand when he was a kid. He can't play the guitar for too long, these fingers begin to hurt. Then his back hurts (for real this time), slumping in the chair, maybe due to age, maybe anger at not being able to play as long as he used to.

This is the loneliest waiting room.

Maybe it's his fault. He was too cool for school for too long. Everyone got tired. Now he only gets his daughters answering machine when he calls. Maybe people just see a fading star, a supernova about to collapse in on itself. That's bullshit! This might be the last go around—the last tour through the public consciousness. Maybe the record company will crunch the numbers and deem it no longer worth it to push the ramblings of a man 20 years past his time. Maybe the people are just tired. Maybe he's tired.

"Mr. Pepper!"

That voice again. John looks up to see the pharmacy girl leaning over the counter, staring right at him.

"Yea?" John replies, clearing the lump out of his throat. The pharmacy girl motions for him to come over. John saunters over to the counter, the pharmacy girl tracking him, he looks at her, she has nice eyes.

228

"I'm sorry, but we don't have enough stock to fill your prescription," the pharmacy girl says.

"Oh, okay," John replies.

"I can give you what we have and then we can deliver the rest when it becomes available? Probably this afternoon," the pharmacy girl says, scribbling on a pad in front of her.

"I can't believe New York City is out of Vicodin," John says.

"Believe me, it's not," the pharmacy girl replies quickly. John laughs and nods.

"Oh, I believe you."

The pharmacy girl spins around the pad and moves her pen down the list, "So we need just your name, address, phone number."

John begins to fill in the listed areas, scribbling with his hairy knuckled fingers.

"Do you guys have any stuff for waxing," John asks, his head down. The pharmacy girl laughs.

"Doing some man-scaping are you?"

John looks up from the pad, his nose wrinkled, "What the hell is man-scaping?"

"Never mind," she replies. John finishes up his scribbling, spinning the pad back around to the pharmacy girl. Her eyes are huge. They're deep and full, they stretch out from her nose, almost reaching her temples, round like jawbreakers.

"Have a nice day," she says.

John vanishes back to the hotel room, taking his Henry Hill like route through the back of the hotel and into the elevator. In his room now, he grabs the scotch and the partial Vicodin prescription and marries them. Drinking them down at room temperature, easing into the leather love seat. This love seat just became infinitely more comfortable. The smooth layers of leather, leather not pleather, a lush feeling on the back of John's exposed arms. His mind slows. The voices inside breathe a little bit easier. He feels his gut churning like cream instead of butter. The edges blur. He forgets about T.J. Carter. He falls asleep.

He's back in his hotel room—many years ago. When, he doesn't know. The room is full. And loud. Fuck, is it loud. A man with a mullet and a mustache pounds a beer and then flings the empty across the room, tearing a hole in the nicely framed art décor of this suite. A girl whispers something in his earlobe. John rings his finger in there, thinking it was water trapped in there from the laps he did in the hotel pool earlier. Only turning did he realize that it was a woman. She soon evacuates to men willing to pay attention to her. People converse with each other, their eyes wandering to the corners, seeing exactly what John is up to. He is the gravity of the room, sitting there with a scotch in his right hand and cigarette in his left. He feels them push in on him. Somewhat relishing the fact that he is the whale in this aquarium visit—that all of those eyeing him right now will never be in this position again—that they're only visitors, students who will be behind their desks when school is back in session tomorrow morning. John liked the changing faces, it reminded him who he was. He was John Fucking Pepper, the Rock God, the pussy magnet, a platinum record with two legs. He liked the attention. Constantly up on stage, the man under the floodlight. A fight breaks out with the mustache and mullet guy toward the front of the room. It's short-lived; the man's mullet only making it so much easier for the bouncer to grab a hold and toss him through the hotel room door.

The memory flips. Soon he's lying on his back, staring at the cracked ceiling, a groupie with large breasts riding him hard. He thinks he's having sex; he's too drunk to know for sure. He blinks and she's pulling her dress down and grabbing her shoes, looking back only briefly at the rock star that she just fucked. John rolls over and rubs his eyes. It's 4 a.m. and the party is still going on outside his door. He hears knocking, faint, quickening its pace somewhere above his head.

Then it goes dark. John feels a breeze on his face. A cooling breeze, a breeze felt in the Hamptons in '74, sitting on that beach. The knocking gets louder, becoming a jackhammer in his mind. Boom. Booom. Booooom. Boom.

John's eyes pop open, the scotch glass in his hand, the afternoon sun shining just out from behind the skyscraper across the street. The door rings out with a knock. John coughs and gets to his feet. Putting the scotch glass on the kitchen counter, he buttons his shirt and opens the door—to see no one. John peeks out into doorframe, seeing a woman walking down the hallway back toward the elevator.

"Hi," John yells out, the girl stopping and turning back. It's the pharmacy girl. She spins around, her eyes a bit fiercer than the last time that John saw them.

"I'm sorry," John says to the pharmacy girl, who trudges back down the hallway toward him.

"I thought you were dead, I was about to go get security," the pharmacy girl says, extending her arm with the prescription. "You gotta sign."

"Well thank you for that," John says sarcastically, then thinking twice about her reasoning, "Why did you think I was dead?"

"I don't know...you look like you're getting up there in years," the pharmacy girl replies, looking down at the slip that John is signing. John laughs.

"I thought you would have said because of who I am, my career has a high percentage of suicides," John replies, handing over the signed slip.

"Why, who are you? You own Dr. Pepper or something?" the pharmacy girl says, putting the slip in her back pocket. John stays staring at her, his mouth a bit crooked, unsure of how to reply.

"Yes, a lot of suicides in the cola wars, lost five men last week," John replies to a barely registered response from the pharmacy girl. She gives a half smirk and begins to walk back to the elevator.

"Have a nice day," she says over her shoulder, trudging back toward the elevator and pressing the button.

"What are you doing right now?" John yells down the hallway, "Do you want to go get a drink?"

The pharmacy girl turns back toward John.

"I have to go back to work," she replies, returning her view to the elevator. John stays staring at the girl, tapping away on her cell phone as she waits for the elevator. She's beautiful, her wit an added bonus to those big eyes. If he had to guess, she probably hated him. The elevator doors open and the girl boards, disappearing from John's still blurry, sleepy eyes.

As John returns to bed he thinks about the pharmacy girl. There was something. Something he couldn't compute. He gets out of bed and grabs the prescription delivery off the kitchen counter. Opening the bottle, John takes out two pills, places them on the counter, closes the top, grabs the pharmacy bag and heads out the door.

Now back in the pharmacy, he waits on a shorter line than before. Looking behind the counter he sees the pharmacy girl running around filling orders. As he gets to the front of the line, she sees him and lets out a sigh.

"Yes, Mr. Pepper," she says. John walks forward, putting the pill bottle down on the counter.

"You shorted me two pills and I don't want to get you in trouble or anything...the real reason I'm here is because I want to ask if you wanted to get drinks sometime this week?" John spits out with smile.

The pharmacy girl looks down with a scowl.

"Okay...one, I didn't short you two pills. That bottle, like every bottle is checked by three people and believe it or not," the pharmacy girl drops her voice, "they all got the same number. And two, while I find your invitation for drinks as flattering as the ones from every other middle aged man who comes in here and hits on me, no, I'm sorry I won't be able to join you for drinks," the pharmacy girl replies with a shit-eating grin. John looks grim, the tongue lashing he just received hitting him deep, only managing an "Okay," as he picks up his pill bottle and heads for the exit.

"Have a nice day," the pharmacy girl says.

Back in his hotel room, John paces the carpet back and forth, raising the hair on his arm.

I should kill myself. It would really make that pharmacy girl feel like shit.

John doesn't know what to do. A girl hadn't rejected him in a while, he hasn't tried in a while to be honest, but even a rejection was met with less resistance than the pharmacy girl's scorched earth. Adding this to the T.J. Carter pancaking this morning, John Pepper was getting his ass kicked by young people today.

The phone rings. John stays stationary, debating whether or not to pick it up. After the third ring, he drudges over to the phone and picks up.

"Hello?"

It was the label, they had business to discuss, weren't so much asking him as telling him. They would be over in a half an hour. John puts down the receiver and scolds himself for picking up; he could have run this sickness out for a few more days like a kid who didn't want to go back to school. As he straightens up and hides his booze and pills, John combs his hair and practices his greeting in the mirror. He wasn't nervous though, that was what the Vicodin was for.

CHAPTER NINETEEN

The head of the record company was short; he should have been called 'the foot.' That sentence kept rattling around in John's head as he nodded and answered positively to their questions and concerns. They were sitting in the living room of John's suite, John sitting by the window, draped in a comforter, still playing the part of the sick kid home from school.

"So we have a problem, John...and this is gonna be hard to say to you because you've been such a big part of this company for so many years," the record exec says. John's eyes widen, not sure of what was coming next. In his head he starts to fill in the blanks of what this guy was really saying.

"We have an image problem because you're not *(the record isn't selling)*...I'm trying to find the right word...you're not on the tip of everyone's tongue *(no one gives a fuck; this CD is going to be either in a bargain bin or a landfill in days)*...the Garden show might have to be moved into the theater downstairs because we are not selling as many tickets as we thought we would *(actually pretty straight forward for this snake oil salesman)*."

John nods his head, "So...what do you want me to do?"

The record exec looks to the two yes men on either side of them, talking as if they hadn't already figured out not just the words but the amount of syllables they were about to use.

"We need you to get out there and remind people who John Pepper is."

"People don't know me anymore I guess?"

"No...it's not that John, uh, it's more they haven't heard from you in a while," the record company foot carefully says.

John nods his head, the final cherry on the top of this shit sundae of a day. The record exec gets up and pats John on the shoulder, "You wer—are one of the biggest rock and roll icons of our time; you just got get out there and remind everyone."

John nods. The execs grab their coats and bags and exit the hotel room, one of them giving John a two finger gun salute, a gesture at that moment that John wished was real. Minutes pass when John grabs a glass and hurls it across the living room, it bouncing into a couch and landing quietly on the floor, looking no worse for wear. John rips the comforter off and goes into the bathroom. Throwing some water onto his face, he wakes himself up. He gets dressed in a ripped T-shirt, some old jeans and black boots—Superman stepping into the phone booth and putting on his rock outfit. He looks into the mirror once more, slaps himself and walks toward his hotel door.

Opening it, he sees the pharmacy girl. He takes a step back. The pharmacy girl looks up from the piece of paper in her hand.

"Can I help you?" John asks, wearing the scowl seen before on the pharmacy girl.

"I was writing you a note...of apology...I was a bitch before and I'm sorry," the pharmacy girl replies.

"It happens...and I'm creep so...no harm no foul," John replies. They exchange a head nod and the pharmacy girl hands over the note. John looks down at it.

"Sorry I was a bitch. It's been a tough d—"

"It's very to the point," John says, looking up from the note and throwing it on the table by the door.

"That's me, what's the sense in dancing around the truth, you know?" the pharmacy girl replies. John extends his hand, "I'm John."

"I'm Jill," the pharmacy girl replies, shaking John's hand. They share another uneven nod, both of them unsure of what else to say to each other.

"I'm gonna get out of here...again I'm sorry," Jill says, giving John a wave, then making her way down the hallway. John holds the door open for a moment, wondering if he should wait until Jill is gone. He instead turns off the light in his hotel room and closes the door, making his way to the elevator.

"This elevator is slow as shit," Jill says, staying looking at the elevator, swaying back and forth on the balls of her feet. John nods his head slowly.

"You still alive back there old man?" Jill says to the quiet John, leaning against the hallway wall. John snickers.

"Am I that old?"

"I've seen older, not many, but yea," Jill says with a smile, now turning to look at John still leaning against the wall.

"I think you owe me a drink now," John says.

In the bar downstairs, John twirls the scotch in his glass, staring into his drink hypnotically, following it around and around. Jill drops the lime into her Corona, taking a big drink out of the nectar from south of the border. She looks at John's blank stare.

"You drink it," she says, pointing at the glass. John breaks his hypnosis, looking back at Jill, "Oh believe me...I know."

John takes a swig, biting the aftertaste. Jill looks around the empty bar, only a few people marking the walls and tables of the establishment.

"So what do you do?" Jill asks. John looks up from his scotch, dipping his head back, looking up at the ceiling.

"Really? You don't know who I am?" John replies, a bit frustrated to even use the words. Jill shakes her head no and John's head hits the bar.

"Kids these days have no respect for the past...who are you?" John asks back, a twinge of anger in his voice. Jill smiles.

"Me? Oh I am a 25-year-old college graduate who walked off the commencement stage into the worst job market in 50 years with $100,000 in debt and a worthless piece of paper. Among other things, I will live at or below the poverty line for the next half a decade at a career I didn't study in school or ever want to do in my entire life. That's who I am...there's a whole bunch of us like me just wandering the streets. I also enjoy walks on the beach," Jill replies with a smile, "I have a question for you. Do you get fancy hot towels in your expensive hotel room or does that sort of stuff cost extra Mr. Sorry I Don't Know Who You are?"

"They come with the room..." John mumbles out, his head still on the bar top. Jill nods and drinks from her Corona.

"It must be so hard to be you," Jill says. John looks up.

"You wanna know who I am? I am one of the top 25 rock and roll recording artists of all time; I've sold more than 30 million records, I've toured 100 countries, I've banged supermodels and been on magazine covers," John replies.

Jill takes a moment, looking over John, "So?"

"So...." John ponders himself, finishing off his scotch and asking for another.

"So why are you alone in a hotel, drinking by yourself, looking like an old man who borrowed some clothes from his grandkid to go to a Halloween party? Are you aspiring to be the biggest fucking cliché in the world or *are* you just the biggest fucking cliché in the world?" Jill asks. John starts on another scotch.

"Alright I'll try and speak as *real* as you do...is that what you kids call it...'real?' I am a rock star who is past his expiration date...tossed out with yesterday's trash so the T.J. Carter's of the world can soon lead a teen revolt of culture and storm the White House and enslave all of mankind. Is that enough downtrodden to excuse my big hotel room?" John replies, continuing his scotch.

"Almost...but why do it at all? If you've been so successful why not just go home? You must have 'fuck you' money," Jill asks.

"Here's the cliché part...I don't have much money...I lost it...evaporated into the air...and various money pits. I don't have a home; well I shouldn't say that, I have a home...just don't like it very much. I don't have a wife...I got a kid, she doesn't like me much...cliché number two. It's hard to be a father when you're living out of a suitcase for the better part of your adult life."

"Okay," Jill says, easing up on the gas.

"It's one thing to feel like you've never been noticed. It's another thing to have been noticed and then forgotten about...used up...thrown away," John says, taking a deep breath, "You're too young to be jaded; don't be jaded."

John returns staring to his scotch, the only thing he had been honest with lately, now this girl. Who was she? Why was she here? John looks at this girl who had her youth, the ability to do something. Maybe not; maybe she was just a pretty girl, a pretty girl who was told she could be President one day. The crushing blow of inflated expectations is perhaps the worst pain one can feel. You don't feel much disappointment when you never expect anything. You don't really live much either, though. Her eyes betrayed her. There is anger there, floating just below the surface, past those pretty pupils.

"So why are you bitter?" John asks.

"I just feel like I was lied to. Not in a bad way, not maliciously, but I just feel like our parents and teachers lied to us. We can't do *anything* we set our mind to. It's just not possible and I don't know where they got the idea that we could—or why they felt the need to tell us so. There aren't enough opportunities, not enough jobs with advancement, no successful marriages. We were spoiled too much. Doesn't the brand of bullshit that we were sold and fed at the dinner table and preached to in classrooms all those years ring hollow? Most of us will be failures. Flat out failures. We won't be in the history books or make a positive influence on anyone in this world, let alone ourselves. We will be the generation of jerkoffs, the ones who fell below the bar, and the ones who didn't keep pushing forward. Our entire history is full of failure, laziness, and utter disregard for succeeding. We'll have the stink of Iraq and Afghanistan hang on over us for the rest of our days. I'll die and we'll still be fighting there for another 35 years afterward. We'll be paying more and more while prices keep going up and up without recourse, all while swimming in debt for the rest of our natural lives. Our kids will be even bigger brats than us because we have been so fucked up and damaged by our fucked up and damaged parental figures that our brats will run the streets wild trying to pick up whatever the new thing that Steve Jobs shits out every holiday season. *Blade Runner* will really happen. *Wall-E* too. There doesn't seem to be any end to it. No single person who will stand up and change our minds, convince us again that we can do something with this life. We're too numb to change now. Too tired of the lies and the bottomless pit of self-loathing. We're ciphers. No longer human beings. Just cliché spouting, pop culture referencing, super douches who blast others on the Internet anonymously; say racist things behind closed doors; and program the television, Blu-Ray, air conditioner, alarm clock, toaster oven and window shades all on one remote so we don't have to move the morning after an all-night drinking binge where we tried to convince one another that there was change around the corner. But there isn't. Obama sold us on that once and look how that turned out—another brand of bullshit that we bought in bulk like we were shopping at Costco. It's a shame really. Maybe we really did have the potential to do something great. Not be the fuck ups that we turned into. Who knows how this is all going to turn out. I'm sick of trying to predict it. All I know is that when Mark Zuckerberg is our Alexander the Great, we are destined to be shit out of luck. Look at me, I'm bitching about a golden age that never came. I'm as much a part of the problem as anyone else, because, frankly, I'm a proud member of this fucked up generation. I just feel like my time has come and gone already and I didn't even know the game had started yet."

John looks at Jill.

That shallow pain in her eyes now swims on her eyelids. She looks relieved to get it out, as if that bitter haiku has been sitting in her gut waiting for someone to hear it. She drinks her Corona, a small smile after every gulp.

"Well it's been fun, I'm gonna go home, eat some cereal for dinner and pass out," Jill says, spinning off the bar stool and grabbing her coat.

"Maybe I'll see you around?"

Jill puts on her coat, pulling her hair out from below the collar, "Yea, I'll see you around."

John looks toward the bottles behind the bar, motioning for the bartender.

"Hey John," Jill says. John turns back to Jill.

"Give it one last ride," she says. John smiles as Jill walks out of the bar.

Back upstairs, John sits a little drunk...alright, a lot drunk. He sits next to the phone, his head leaning back, his eyes closed, his mouth slowly moving. He's trying to remember that number again. He should write it down. It almost acts as a test. He remembers it, dialing and hearing it ring. It's late, a sober John would know better than to call at this hour.

"Hey, it's Melissa and Chad. We're not home, so please leave a message and we'll get back to you as soon as possible."

John hangs up the phone and slumps over into his bed.

CHAPTER TWENTY

The lights on the call switchboard aren't blinking. John keeps his eyes trained on them, glancing up every few seconds to make the DJ think he's not staring at the switchboard lights. The DJ is yammering on, talking about John like he wasn't sitting five feet in front of him. The man lists John's CV, going all the way back to the first album. Some things were wrong though, maybe the DJ did his research on Wikipedia, or maybe his intern did. It sounded like a eulogy in all honesty. This is the first interview of the day. John just looked back down at the switchboard again.

"So what happened yesterday with the *Today Show*?" the DJ asks—a man with oily hair and a weasel face. He peers across the phone switchboard at John, who wears a smirk, the first rock star mask he was putting on today.

"What do you mean?" John replies, playing dumb.

"You were supposed to perform on the *Today Show* yesterday and then the show comes on and T.J. Carter had replaced you, what's up with that man? How does a rock star of your stature, of your legend, allow a teenybopper to replace him?"

"He didn't replace me," John replies somewhat cryptically.

"Then what happened?"

"Oh, I don't think I should say," John replies playfully.

"Oh, come on! What are you not telling us?" the DJ replies, being whipped into a frenzy, playing morning zoo sounds, cannons, screams.

"Alright, you're getting the exclusive here," John says, pausing for dramatic effect. He looks out through the glass pane into the control room, one of the record company stooges giving him a thumbs up.

"So I got into town two nights ago and I was preparing for a quiet evening, you know maybe do a few pushups, drink some tea to warm up my voice," John says, casting the bait.

"Drinking tea! Oh John, don't tell us these things," the DJ says in disgust.

"Can you let me finish? So I'm about to get into a bed and curl up with a nice Grisham novel when my room phone rings. So I'm thinking maybe it's the concierge telling me what time they were gonna ring me for wake up...you know, who knows."

The DJ stares across the studio at John.

"It's not the concierge," John replies with a smile.

"Who!? Who was it!?" The DJ is foaming at the mouth.

"I can't say...I wouldn't want to embarrass her, she's a big movie star. I wouldn't want to be talking out of school," John continues with the bait.

"You're killing me; you can't leave me hanging like this."

"Alright so I pick up the phone, she's an old friend of mine. Actually I shouldn't say that; she's a *young* friend of mine and she was just sorta seeing what I was doing for the night and I told her, 'You know baby, I gotta get my rest, I'm a little bit older now I can't turn up the volume like I used to.' So she laughed and said, 'Oh I'll make you turn up the volume.'"

The DJ is having a conniption. John looks through the glass pane again, the stooge is nodding like a bobblehead.

"So we finish talking on the phone and within 15 minutes she's at my hotel room door with some party favors and a few girlfriends, you know, so we'd have enough people to play Monopoly or something," John continues.

"Monopoly! This guy—unbelievable," the DJ replies.

"Unfortunately we ended up not playing Monopoly...a real bummer because it's my favorite board game. Come to think of it, I had sex on top of a Monopoly board once...I had to pay the hooker $200 to pass the blow...can I say that on air?"

"No, I don't think so John," the DJ replies.

"So I was upset; I've had a nice history with board games...so instead there was some music and dancing and some heavy petting and we all just got naked and...well do I need to say anything else?"

"Yes! Yes you do!"

John looks down at the switchboard; three lights are blinking...and now a fourth.

"So we partied and partied and inevitably when you party naked you kind of lose track of time...some more people came over. You know the room phone

245

starts to ring for my wake up call but I'm playing naked, drunken Twister with three models and a movie star and frankly I just ignore it...then the record label calls...I don't hear it, you know shit happen—"

"Whoa! John you cannot say that word on the air," the DJ blurts out.

"What, shit? Oh shit, I said it again," John says with a laugh, peering down to see the switchboard lit up like the skyline atop the city.

"The FCC will have our heads on a platter!" the DJ exclaims.

"Oh fuck them, I'll pay the fines."

"Whoa! John Pepper is in rare form this morning...our switchboard is exploding with people wanting to talk to you, John. Would you like to take a couple of calls?" the DJ asks, putting through the first call before John can answer.

The stooge throws up two thumbs and a shit-eating grin. John grimaces a little bit.

Throughout the rest of the day, John tore through radio, print and television interviews, telling the tales of the rock star everyone believed him to be. It even made John laugh, some of the stuff he was coming up with. He felt like he was the main subject, not the footnote. In his stomach, he felt a pain. He started thinking about the daughter that wasn't picking up his phone calls, and whether what he was about to do over the next few days would give her reason to never pick up again.

John collapses onto his bed later that night, exhausted from whoring and lying. He spun some webs today, hoping he wouldn't get caught up in them.

The phone rings. Picking it up he hears a squeal on the other end, one of the record company stooges congratulating him on the day, as if he actually did something of note. John moves the receiver away from his ear, flinching at the octave this guy is talking in. Through the nails on the chalkboard, John hears, "sold 5,000 tickets," which snaps him back to attention.

"Wait—what? We sold 5,000 tickets today?"

"Fuck yea, we—actually *you* sold 5,000 tickets today…getting up there and making everyone wish they were you. We're back baby! A few more days of this type of attention and you are gonna sell out the Garden. Fucking Madison Square Garden," the stooge replies. As he continues onto other things, John fades from attention, instead thinking about selling out Madison Square Garden, something that gives him a buzz in his stomach. He forgets about the whoring, accepting the crassness for the end result, momentarily blinded. Soon the stooge stops talking, the phone is put back on the hook and John falls back into the bed. He feels old. He doesn't want to reach down to take off his shoes. He thinks about making a drink. That might keep him up. He wants to sleep. Soon he's downstairs in the bar. Every few minutes he looks up, hoping Jill would walk in. Each time he's disappointed. A few drinks later he's feeling sleepy; he stumbles into the elevator and upstairs. He passes out on the living room couch.

CHAPTER TWENTY ONE

Day four of press was going much like the first three had. John saying outlandish things, hoping to bring the light back his way—each interviewer thanking John afterward for the great copy. He was riding a wave, putting himself back on the tips of people's tongues—his antics becoming the story, fueling the entertainment media for the past few days. Suddenly everyone wanted to talk to him. He might have been enjoying it a little bit too much.

Then John stepped into Harold Kemp's studio. Harold Kemp had developed a reputation as a bad boy of the media elite. Fistfights with guests after prying too far into their lives, outrageous sex acts live on air, numerous fines. He was no Howard Stern, but he was trying his hardest to imitate The King of All Media, succeeding at only being a pale imitation.

Kemp's studio was big, his staff even bigger. Camera's lined the studio for Kemp's radio show, simulcasting the radio program on television and the Internet. John didn't like Kemp much. In fact, he had outright disdain for him. John had a run-in with him at a party once. Later, he had heard some unflattering things said about him by Kemp on his radio show after John's drunk driving charge a few years back. John had blocked that out, instead intending to use Kemp as a mark, get everything out of him that he could and move on.

So as he strode into Kemp's studio, shaking hands with Harold himself, he wore a smile. Another mask, another lie, but shaking this guy's hand just reminded John how much he loathed him.

"How are you doing, John? It's been a long time," Kemp says, patting John on the shoulder.

"I've been good, how are you?"

"I've been great; show's getting higher ratings than ever...it's really great to see you. We should go get dinner before you leave New York," Kemp says, shoving a big smile in John's face. John's blood begins to boil at this wolf in sheep's clothing, this fake hack, this buffoon sucking at the entertainment teat.

"Yea maybe," John replies, taking a seat on the couch across from Kemp, who goes behind his microphone and puts his headphones on.

"Back in ten seconds," the executive producer intercoms into the studio.

"John Pepper, ladies and gentlemen, the rock star people can't get enough of. It's an honor to have you here in the studio today, John," Kemp says into the microphone, reverbing through radios around the world.

"Thanks for having me," John replied.

"I have to be honest, and I'm sure I'm not the only one to be thinking this—I hadn't thought about you in years. I mean you disappeared, fell off the map. You had that drunk driving charge, you sort of fell into oblivion and now after a week of outlandish behavior—you got into a fight with a paparazzo outside of Jay-Z's 40/40 Club the other night, which is all over TMZ, you're cursing on radio shows and CNN, now I'm reading you went on a date with Lindsay Lohan the other night (*I was in bed*)...I mean Jesus, you're everywhere, you're stroking the flames left and right. Who do you think you are—me?"

John laughs, adjusting the headphones on his head, "It's been a busy week."

"Don't give me that shit, where have you been?" Kemp asks.

"I've been around, you know, living the life, no complaints," John replies.

"You seem awfully quiet today John, are you hung over or something?"

"Nah I don't get hung over. I just got every fucking chucklehead like yourself asking me the same dumb questions," John replies with a sting. Kemp reels from the response, a gasp coming from Kemp's employees standing in the room.

"Wow, chucklehead? I've never been called a chucklehead before," Kemp says, somewhat stunned.

"Well there's a first time for everything," John says, taking out a cigarette and lighting it in the studio.

"John Pepper is smoking a cigarette in my studio. John, I know you haven't been to New York City in a while but Mayor Bloomberg has banned smoking inside," Kemp says with a laugh.

"Yea? Well he's a fucking idiot and so are you," John replies, the cigarette dangling from his lip. Kemp laughs.

"Man you are out of control; I love it," Kemp continues, "If you want to see this madman in concert he is playing Madison Square Garden on Friday night."

"Get your tickets now, they are selling like hotcakes...even though I don't know what a hotcake is or why they sell so fast," John interjects.

"So I feel like you've been everywhere this week and have said everything that could be said, I don't know if I could come up with a question that hasn't been asked of you already," Kemp says. John shakes his head, tapping his cigarette into a soda bottle sitting on the table next to him.

"Some fucking journalist you are. The fucking Jay Leno of radio over here, how many more things are you gonna steal from Howard Stern? You hack," John says with a smile, flipping Kemp the bird.

"I've never stolen anything from Howard," Kemp replies sheepishly.

"Whatever helps you sleep at night. But that's alright you don't have a question, because I actually have an idea," John replies.

"What's that?"

"I was wondering if I could borrow a camera for about 15 minutes," John says, pointing around the studio to the two men with cameras on their shoulders, taping the interview.

"What for?"

"On my way over here, I actually saw T.J. Carter's tour bus parked a few blocks up...I wanted to go take a piss right on the door of the tour bus," John replies, dropping the finished cigarette into the soda bottle.

"Shut up! You are not gonna pee on that kid's tour bus," Kemp replies.

"Believe me, I saw it like two blocks up, he's rehearsing for his tour. I asked my label and they confirmed it."

"Is there a way we can do that, guys? Give him a microphone or something and we can keep the interview going while he goes up there? Yea? Alright," Kemp says, talking to his producers in the control room.

John gets out of his chair, takes off his headphones and heads out of the studio. A producer in the control room hands John a microphone and an earpiece to hear Kemp when he leaves the studio.

Now down on the street, John speaks into the microphone to Kemp who is back in the studio watching this all unfold. John slaps hands with people on the street, starting a "John Pepper" chant in his wake. Crossing the street he gets up on top of a stopped cab, doing a dance on the hood. The cab driver motions out the window at John to get off his car, screaming expletives in a foreign language. People on the street who see the cameras and John begin to follow, joining the people chanting John's name.

"This is my favorite city in the world," John says into the microphone.

"So what do you have planned for the rest of the day, John?" Kemp asks, looking through the monitor at John as he crosses another block, closing in on T.J. Carter's tour bus.

"I think Chris Brown is in town too, maybe I can go leave a flaming bag of dog shit outside his tour bus...other than that, no plans," John replies. As he turns the corner, John spots Carter's tour bus—a big, light blue monstrosity—the pop star's already ubiquitous face painted on the side. It had streaks of white running down the side, the words "Anything is possible," Carter's catchphrase, painted over the windows.

"Man I wish I had a tour bus like this," John says into the microphone, approaching the bus. John walks up to the tour bus door and turns to the people who have followed him in his walk over from the studio. Teenage kids chant John's name, John putting his hands in the air, trying to quiet them down.

"Alright, alright, who wants me to piss on this little brat's bus?"

The crowd roars, John nods his head and pumps his fist, turning around to the bus, pulling down his zipper and giving the tour bus door a golden shower. Using his free hand he puts a cigarette to his lips and asks for a light. A girl runs up and lights his cigarette.

"Thank you, darling," John says, blowing puffs of smoke into the air while he continues peeing, "Don't smoke cigarettes kids; it's bad for you."

The crowd roars with approval. John pulls up his zipper and turns back around to the chanting crowd.

"I'd slap all your hands but I got piss on mine," John says, a gross statement that elicits even more cheers.

"John Pepper just peed on T.J. Carter's tour bus and he has a chanting crowd of people up on 44th Street," Kemp says to his radio audience. "We are almost completely out of time John, do you have anything else to say?"

"Yea only one, Harold Kemp blows goats, I have proof," John says into Kemp's camera. John turns back to the crowd and starts a 'Harold Kemp Sucks' chant.

"Fucking dickhead," Kemp mumbles under his breathe as he goes to commercial. John continues to lead the assembled mass in a chant.

CHAPTER TWENTY TWO

"Supposedly I just joined Twitter and have like 50,000 followers in a few hours," John says, putting his hand over the cell phone. "Well that's great...yea come up with something good, alright I'll talk to you later."

Jill sits across from John, watching the man on the back pages hear just how popular he is again.

John drops his cell phone on the table. "Have you noticed that no one says goodbye anymore, it's crazy."

"You seem to be putting a lot of thought into your tweets, really speaking directly to your people, 'Come up with something good!' I hope people rise up and kill all the celebrities," Jill says.

"Well I'd be fine because I'm not a celebrity, I'm a rock star."

John shifts in his seat. He wears a smile.

"You're as happy as a pig in shit aren't you? Mr. Rock Star back in the news. You think you're all important? Where are all the groupies?" Jill says, craning her neck around the empty restaurant.

"You're my only groupie and I'm pretty sure you hate me," John replies, spinning his drink on the table.

"That is correct," Jill replies.

John pulls down on his ballcap. It's late afternoon. The sunlight dimming outside, casting shadows on the floors of this chain restaurant. No one seems to be looking their way. The waiter has a momentary, "Where do I know this guy from?" moment, but otherwise hasn't said a word.

"So what about your daughter? Have you heard from her?"

John clears his throat.

"You don't want to talk about it?" Jill asks. John shrugs his shoulders.

"No, I don't want to talk about that."

"Why?"

"Because this is a happy day and that just makes me feel like shit," John replies, more willing to commit hari-kari then continue with this line of questioning.

"Okay," Jill says dismissively, sucking on her straw, looking up at John with big puppy eyes.

"Just give me one thing," Jill says.

"What?"

"What's her name?"

John smiles, "Melissa; we named her after my mother."

"It hurts to talk about...knowing that you didn't treat someone that you love very much the right way. I was a terrible father and I wouldn't want to talk to me either, but only now when everything is fucked beyond repair is the time I wanna reach out," John says.

"Why now?"

"I think I know I'm near the end—not music wise—life wise. Like how many good years do I have left? My body hurts, my mind is weak, I've torn through this life without looking down and now I see I don't have much. I have great memories...I do have those...but those will go sooner or later, some are going now. She's the thing I failed at. I was never a good father. My career sucks now, but when it was good, wow, it was good. Nothing was impossible. But now I'm a *Trivial Pursuit* answer, a 'Where Are They Now?' column, a joke...a joke," John says, his eyes fading toward the window.

"A joke with 50,000 Twitter followers," Jill says.

"Don't let go of your people. People are important. They may annoy the shit out of you sometimes but man...people make everything okay. When the right person is standing in front of you at the right time and they look at you and you feel okay in your gut and your heart—that's it, that's the only thing that matters," John finishes.

"Then why are you sitting here? Go, go see her. Go knock on her door, sit on her porch," Jill pleads. John shakes his head, waving off Jill.

"Because she won't answer. The phone is easy, it just rings and rings—there's no risk of being hurt. Even if she picked up the phone and told me to fuck myself, it's still a separation. But if I go up there, drive to her house, knock on her door and she answers. If she looks me right in the eye and then slams the door in my face, I don't think I can handle that. That's why it was always so easy to keep

257

working, to never go home. It meant I wouldn't have to see her disappointed face, as selfish as that sounds. I wouldn't have to kiss my daughter goodbye and see her disappointed eyes looking at me as I left. I always thought about myself instead of her."

"Why don't you finally go home then?"

"I don't have one," John says, a catch in his throat as he says it. "Why do you talk to me? I mean seriously. I hope you're taking notes, jotting down all the things not to do with your life."

Jill laughs. She spins her straw in her drink.

"You're so scared. You're like a scared little boy," she says.

"What do you know?" John replies, a sting to his words. Jill looks up from her drink.

"Obviously nothing," she replies, looking back down at her straw.

She's just trying to help.

"Let's get out of here; I feel like going to record some music," John says, slinking out of his booth and dropping a few dollars as tip.

Jill looks through a large window into the studio. John sits behind the piano, his legs crossed, softly tapping the keys. He scribbles on a notebook next to the piano. He's alone.

Jill turns to look at the technicians, who adjust and calibrate the soundboard. Behind them sit record executives, some on their cell phones, others flipping through paperwork. Others just idly sitting, staring through the glass, looking at John.

A few moments pass. John uncrosses his legs and begins to play the piano, his loud play producing thumps against the walls, sounding like an elephant banging against its cage. John's falsetto begins to creep through the notes, sneaking in between the thumps, a rough twang, his voice sounding like it was left out in the sun and shriveled. He sounded terrible. Jill looks away from John, back to the techs that scramble with the board, trying to play with John's voice, make him sound less like the crypt keeper. The execs continue their idle chatter, their cell phone conversations, their star gazing. Not one of them is paying attention, each one of them somewhere else. John continues hammering on the piano, the results rough and sloppy. He makes mistakes left and right. He seems distracted. He winds down on the piano, his body arched over the box of wood, looking like a hunchback.

"This is terrible," Jill mutters to herself. John finishes. His head bowed and eyes closed, listening to the echo of the piano keys. He leans back on the piano stool looking up through the window to the sound room. All of the record execs throw John thumbs up. John returns in kind, nodding and smiling.

Jill is dumbfounded. She questions if she's standing in a bad spot for sound, unsure if everyone in the room heard the same thing. John leaves the studio and comes into the sound booth, shaking hands with all of the execs who applaud his new "music."

"We're gonna start mixing right away, have it out as a single by next week, maybe you can play it at the concert on Friday?" one of the suited execs says.

"Yea maybe," John says, noncommittal. Maybe he knows he sucks too.

The car ride back to John's hotel is quiet. Jill stares out the window, wondering if she should tell John how bad he sounded. That this circus was getting out of hand. That he was a joke. That those execs looked at him like the golden pork chop of the moment, the musical Charlie Sheen, the joke everyone laughed with at until something funnier came along. This would blow over—the heat, the Twitter followers, the story. John would soon be that ghost again. The town car pulls up in front of John's hotel.

"See you later?" John asks Jill, who nods her head. John opens his door and walks out into the paparazzi light bulbs, shielding his eyes as he moves toward the revolving door of the lobby.

"We're going to Brooklyn next," Jill says to the driver.

"Where have you been?" Jill's roommate, Erica asks. Erica walks through the living room drying her hair with a towel. Jill types on her laptop on the couch. A web search of Melissa Pepper turns up only a few pages of results. Jill clicks away, trying to put together the puzzle of who this woman is, where she might be.

Soon Jill is printing out an address, grabbing her coat and heading down the street to the subway.

CHAPTER TWENTY THREE

"I need to go somewhere," Jill says from the doorway as John shuffles through the magazines on the kitchen counter.

"Alright, I'm not your father, you don't need my permission," John replies, picking up a copy of *Rolling Stone* and flipping through its pages. Jill is silent for a minute, watching John flip through the magazine, stopping every few pages to skim an article. John feels her standing there, he looks up.

"Is there something else?"

Jill nods her head.

"What?"

"I want you to come with me," Jill replies.

"Why?"

"Because I need you to come with me." John closes the *Rolling Stone* and gets to his feet. "Right now?"

"Yea, so that way you can be back by the label party tonight," Jill replies.

"Okay."

On the highway, John flips through the radio station dial, commenting on each song, telling Jill how he would have done it differently, how he would have made the song better. Jill looks down at her directions every few minutes, checking to make sure that she is still on the right course.

"Is this your car?" John asks, looking around the car from the passenger seat.

"No, it's my roommate's; she let me borrow it for the afternoon." John nods, drumming his fingers on the window frame.

"It's very nice."

"Please, it's a piece of shit," Jill says with a laugh.

John begins to wonder where they're going. Jill is quiet. Small talk at a minimum, eyes focused on the road. After a few minutes of idle radio jockey verbal diarrhea, one of John's songs begins to play. It's slow—a steady building bass backing John's words. John smiles.

"I haven't heard this song in...God...15 years," John says, flexing his fingers in his lap. It feels strange, to hear this song, here and now. A time capsule to another time, unearthed at an opportune time—a younger version of the man in the passenger seat speaking through the galaxy, bringing John back to a better time.

"I wrote this for my daughter...and I'm hearing it right now for a reason," John says, turning to look at Jill, "We're going to see my daughter aren't we?"

Jill stays fixed on the road.

"Why are you doing this?" John asks.

Jill continues on the road, looking over her shoulder as she merges into the left lane.

"Jill, you're starting to scare me," John continues, speaking to the mute Jill. The song ends, John's sweet lullaby to his daughter falling to static. The DJ comes back on.

"That was an oldie from John Pepper, you may have been hearing from him the past few days. I mean—the guy has completely lost it...or has he? Is this some huge ruse to get people talking about him again? Either way it's working."

John turns off the radio. "These fucking people."

"He's right though," Jill says.

"What do you mean?"

"Do you think that song you recorded today was good?" Jill asks, pulling up to a red light. John looks at her, his eyes narrow, startled, unsure if he's more angry or hurt.

"What?"

"You have an opportunity to actually come back, to prove that you *are* good, that you're not some fucking media creation like that teeny bopper whose bus you peed on and you're taking the path of least resistance," Jill says, looking at John for the first time since they left the hotel. "Sure that song will come out and it might do well, but is that all you're capable of? You're not gonna be the most outrageous person in the world next week, you know that right? Some TV star is gonna throw a fit and go into rehab or some starlet is gonna crash a car or leak a tape of her blowing a guy and you're gonna be old news, just like you were last week and what will you have to show from it?"

"A lot of fucking money, that's what," John replies sternly.

"Is that what it's all about? Money? I'm sorry—*a lot of fucking money?* I thought I was talking to *Mr. I Was One of the 25 Greatest Rockers of All Time and Nobody Knows Me.* You seemed a lot more mindful of your legacy last week."

"That's not fair," John replies.

"Why? Because I'm the only one who will say it to you?"

"Hey, I don't shit on you like this, *Ms. Working in a Pharmacy and Being Miserable About Everything.* I've been successful. I've been on top. What have you done? Huh? Answer me that," John says.

The light turns green.

"I haven't done anything and believe me that sucks, but I'm also not a miserable old drunk fuck like you," Jill shoots back.

The car behind them begins to beep.

"Well guess what? You will be. Because you're too scared to try anything. You like being able to blame all of your problems on the bad economy or the old people who have all the money. You'll be miserable in that job for the rest of your life because you like being depressed. You're more like me than you want to admit," John says, snapping open the door, getting out and slamming it shut.

The car beeps again.

"Fuck you!" Jill screams at the beeping car. John goes walking along the suburban sidewalk. He takes cigarettes out of his coat. Searching through his pockets he can't find a lighter. He flings the cigarettes into the street.

Jill pulls off to the side of the road. She turns off the engine and watches John walk down the side of the road, sunglasses over his eyes, his jacket collar up. She breathes. Closing her eyes, she bows her head.

John walks. He's filled with regret. He doesn't know where he is. He sits down on the sidewalk, taking his glasses off and rubbing his eyes. He looks down at his hands. His hairy hands—his wrinkled, hairy hands.

I should shave them before the concert. Fuck the concert.

John looks down the road toward Jill. He sees her head on the steering wheel. The cars flying by him in this suburban town called nowhere. The wind picks up, blowing the dust and dirt down the roadside, into John's face. He turns away from the breeze, away from what was just behind him, toward the little town.

I'm a fucking asshole. Why did I do that?

Jill opens her eyes. Looking up through the windshield, she sees John sitting on the sidewalk. His legs stretched out, looking like a little boy waiting for his mother to pick him up from soccer practice. She wants to drive away. To never see John Pepper's face again. She wants to go back home and get in bed and put on a movie or read a book or spin a record. But that's what she's always done. Retreat. Walk away from people like John. Walk away from things that were too scary, too real, too right. He's as right as he is an asshole. She just couldn't bring herself to go get him. To open that passenger door and let him back in.

John finds the lighter on the inside of his jacket. It's useless now, his pack of cigarettes sit in the middle of the road, run over by a passing car. John looks back down that road, his eyes into the wind, back toward that woman in the car. Here he was again, sitting in the road by himself, an apology away from something. He gets to his feet and dusts off his jeans.

Jill looks at John, that figure on the horizon, lit by the glare of the sun, standing by himself, looking for someone to save him. Jill wipes her eyes and puts the car in drive, rolling up the road to John. Stopping next to him, she unlocks the passenger door. John pauses, looking back down that road toward the town. John gets in the car.

Easing into the passenger seat, John's knees crack. John's age echoes through the car.

"I'm sorry."

"So am I."

"Why did you do this? Why did you bring me up here?" John asks.

Jill considers for a second, rubbing her chin. "I wish someone had put my dad in a car and driven him back to me. But it never happened. He left one morning and never came back. He might still be out there somewhere or maybe not. Then I thought about you and how he was just like you. He couldn't get in the car. He couldn't come back by himself."

"Sometimes it's just better to stay gone; comebacks are always disappointing. It's never the same," John replies.

Jill looks down at John's hands. They're trembling, John trying to hold them together.

"She's better off without me. The last time we spoke I told her that I would leave her a ticket at the box office for every show I ever did for the rest of my life. That if she ever wanted to come, there would always be a seat for her. Before I go up on stage, my roadie shows me a one or zero, letting me know if that ticket was picked up. A one if it was still sitting there, a zero if the box office was empty.

It's never been a zero. I wish I had that feeling of seeing him show me a zero. But it's never come. That's the pain I carry. That I'm the zero," John says.

Jill grabs John's trembling hands, steadying them. John's hands begin to slow.

"Let's go home," John says. Jill uses her free hand to put the car into drive, turning out on to the road.

Johnny Cash's "On The Evening Train" begins to play on the radio.

John is asleep in the passenger seat as Jill drives through the New York City streets. A calm drizzle dots the windshield. Jill opens her window and hangs her arm over the door, the rain cooling off this hot day. As she approaches the hotel, Jill sees paparazzi camped outside the entrance. She drives past, circling to the side door of the hotel. Jill sits parked as John sleeps. She looks out of the window of this dying day in the Big Apple. People leaving work and heading home, taxis barking and subways rumbling beneath their heels. She feels the rain on her arm.

"John."

John slowly wakes up, looking around.

"We're here," Jill says. John rubs his eyes and unbuckles his seatbelt.

"Are you coming to this party tonight?" John asks.

"I don't think so," Jill replies.

"Okay...what about the concert, are you coming to that?"

"I don't know."

John nods his head slowly. "Well, I'll leave you a ticket at the box office."

"Okay," Jill replies.

John kisses Jill on the cheek.

"Don't end up like me...it's not fun. Okay? Promise me that," John says, the tremble returning to his hands. Jill nods; she feels her eyes getting heavy. She looks out her open window.

"Bye," John says. John opens the door and steps out into the street.

"Don't be a joke," Jill says. John sticks his head back in the car.

"Don't be a joke," Jill repeats.

"I'll try not too," John replies with a smile.

"Bye," Jill says.

"Bye."

John walks away from the car, ducking in the side kitchen entrance to the hotel, shaking a busboy's hand. Jill watches until John disappears from view through the rain-dotted window.

John walks into his hotel room, spying a large box sitting on the living room table. He heads into the kitchen; opening the fridge he pulls out his bottle of scotch, placing it on the counter. He leaves it, heading toward the large box.

Opening the card it reads,

"Good Luck Friday Night.

Love, Everybody at Top 5 Records"

John drops the card on the table and flips open the box top—inside, an acoustic guitar. John pulls the guitar out and sits down on the couch. He strums the strings, then adjusts the wayward tuning. John begins to play. He never makes it to the party that night.

CHAPTER TWENTY FOUR

The journalist shifts in his seat flipping through a note pad, scribbling words with his cheap pen, a second cheap pen behind his ear. John cracks his knuckles, relaxing in the folding chair in the corner of the dressing room. He looks at the reporter. The sweat accumulating on his forehead, the quickening of the flipping of pages.

"It'll just be a few more moments...I'm just trying to find my first question," the reporter trails off, the sweat from his forehead now rolling down into his eyes, fogging up his glasses. He snaps to attention, ready for his first question. John puts out his cigarette in the ashtray on the end table, rubbing his hands together, readying himself. The reporter clears his throat.

"What is art?"

John snickers, rolling his head a little.

"That's your first question?" John asks.

The reporter shrugs his shoulders.

"That's a hard question to answer because...any answer that I give will be pretentious because the word 'art' automatically puts whatever it is you're talking about above a guy getting in his car and going to work in the morning. That guy works way harder than I do and gets paid a shit load less. In short—art is bullshit. You know? It's nothing—a guy can be a maestro with a calculator or a ginsu knife or a fucking guitar, but every one of those people has something that drives them to do those things. Howard Hughes was an artist; he thought up crazy shit that no one believed he could do and he did it. He built Hercules, but he also pissed in milk bottles in his later years. My mom was an artist, she worked for the church for 35 years and raised me and my brother by herself and never got a fucking award or a million dollar bonus check for her artistry. She was just a person that was extremely good at living a life. She influenced me in more ways than any piece of poetry or a chord or song could ever do. The word art should be thrown out the fucking window, taken away by the breeze, get caught in a sewer somewhere. It should be replaced by what you dedicate your life too," John replies. The reporter looks across the coffee table at John, a look in his eye that betrays his mind.

"But like I said, any answer will be pretentious, so here's pretentious..." John steadies his mind, saying, "Art isn't made in palaces or lofts or fucking recording studios built on the moon—it's made in the dirt, coming out of the ugliness, the wake of the destruction of life. It's every person alive who ever wanted to say something, reaching into their gut and pulling out the malnourished, neglected stepchild that eats away at your insides until you have to tear it from your body or otherwise succumb to it swallowing you whole. It's Joan Jett on the floor of some scummy house in the Valley mumbling to herself. Coming up with words that echo through the rest of existence, bouncing off of every person that has ever felt alone. It's Dave Chappelle disappearing into the night, leaving all that bullshit behind. It's Kerouac hitting the road, writing every detail and then not wanting to change even the smallest ugly occurrence to make it safe. People today—these people got it all wrong, thinking they could go and be rock stars and gods to millions of people, being worshipped every second of every day being told that even their stinkiest shit was golden. It doesn't work that way. That shit will leave you and you will be stranded on the side of the road with no legs and no thumb to stick into the air to hitchhike home. It will leave. Then what do you have? You have a lonely man in a penthouse looking down at what he used to have. Ranting to a magazine about the way things used to be. Down in that ditch, looking up at that blue sky from the brown of the earth. I found myself on the side of the road and I dragged myself home. Through the muck and the dirt, discovering the gut that I had on the way back. And when I finally got back? I wrote a song and I wrote it real fucking well because that's what I do, that's my job. So maybe that's art or maybe it's what my mom did in her 'career.' You can pick one."

The reporter scribbles away. John looks around the room, at the stark white concrete walls.

"Okay...you are from a generation that indulged in the excesses and blazed a path, you lit guitars and hotel rooms on fire, you spoke about politics and then made noise when the wrong path was being plowed...what do you think of musicians that are coming up today? Do you think they will have the same cultural impact that you and your contemporaries had?" the reporter spits out, readying his pen just as he finishes the last word.

John breathes, grabbing another cigarette and lighting it.

"Forget about the musicians, what about you?"

The reporter looks back up at John, peering over the rims of his glasses, "What do you mean?"

"Well do you think that you, yourself are living up—no living up is not the right word. Do you think that you're doing the best possible job that you could do? And I'm not talking about breaking stories or your writing style or anything like that. Do you put your head down at night and feel confident in what you did that day...like what you're doing is worth it...and it's not about being heard by a lot of people. I've been heard by a lot of people and, believe me, it does nothing to help me get to bed at night because I've lived a life where I haven't been the best person. Do you think that you're maxing out, that you feel that you're making an impact or doing something important?"

The reporter stays still.

"I was talking to this girl, a friend of mine, the other day, and she's in her 20's and she's educated and she's smart and she felt so worthless...so adrift and I'm not talking about the usual 20's depression bullshit, I'm talking about a girl in this world who feels like she can't win. That she won't be successful...you kids these days are just too afraid to speak up. Here's a smart, gorgeous woman who has been beaten down already...and she's fucking 25! Cynicism has become a cancer. The people that I grew up with didn't believe in that shit. Maybe we were just too stupid, we didn't want to accept the words of those up above us. If we wanted something, if we didn't like the way the tide was turning, we changed that shit. We went out and changed it. We didn't ask permission. We didn't accept the word 'no.' We didn't ask our fucking parents if we could. We just did. You guys don't do enough 'did.' We made a lot of mistakes, but man when you got that feeling in your gut, that locomotive at your back and everything in front of you is what you always wanted...there's nothing better. I had that feeling. I lost it, but I had it for a short time. She hasn't had it yet. I told her this and she got mad at me. Like I was casting judgment on her. But I get it...I felt it...I still feel it. Life is so fucking hard...there's your pull quote...life is fucking hard and you can be knocked off course so easily. The current beneath your hull shifts and you end up in a place and you don't know how to get home," John says, the ash on the end of his cigarette long, a few seconds from dropping off the end. The reporter keeps writing notes.

274

"You're in your late 50's now...some might say that this might be the last go-around. The last couple of years haven't been great, you lost your band mate, your star has kind of faded from view, only reignited again after this last week of press offerings. What do you want people to remember you for?"

John drops the cigarette into the ashtray, stroking the small growth of hair on his chin.

"That's a good question and honestly...I don't know. I don't know, and frankly don't care if people remember me. I've had some good times, made a little bit of money, gained some notoriety, sold out the Garden tonight...that's nice. But that may have more to do with my antics this week then anything else. I think...I think ultimately sooner or later I'll be forgotten and my records will crowd basements and attics, my resume and life story tucked up on the top shelf of the library or in the annex gaining dust by the second."

John pauses.

"...and I think this goes for everyone...it's the life you live and what you leave behind that people remember you by. You forget some days, the big events of yesterday morph in your mind, becoming new things entirely. But the tactile things, the things you share, friend-to-friend, person-to-person, father to son or daughter—that's what remains. I used to write about the girl I couldn't get, now I write for the daughter that doesn't want to see me and the granddaughter that I've never met. That they might put on one of my records one day and find something that they enjoy...something...even if it's just for a second. That though I lived a shitty life, that I left something here that was meaningful, that warrants me even existing. That's the stuff you start realizing when you get older—a legacy. I'm not terribly proud of mine, but what are you gonna do? Maybe I'll just serve as a cautionary tale to those who never make it home to bed at night.

Never sleep alone and if you do—make sure that there's at least one person that's only a phone call away."

"Alright, here's my last question," the reporter says, taking a breath before going forward.

"What have you learned?"

CHAPTER TWENTY FIVE

The roadie dips his head in, "25 minutes," he says, his head leaving just as quickly. The reporters gone; John sits alone in his dressing room. He wraps his fingers in bandages, armoring up for battle. His foot taps slowly on the carpet. A dull murmur of concertgoers can be heard off in the distance, the cattle being herded before the slaughter. John quietly prays, his lips moving barely, partially mouthing what he's saying to whoever he sees fit to pray to. His eyes closed, his head dipped, his teeth grinding, biting the inside of his mouth, a nervous tick he picked up. The songs run through his head.

He paces. The opening act has started. He hears the drums. They echo in his ear. Bouncing up to his brain. He stands still, his toes wiggling in his boots. A knock comes from outside. The knock of impending doom. John grabs the door handle and swings it open. Taking the walk through the bowels of the Garden, passing the framed photos on the wall. He keeps his head down, his eyes following the backs of the stage manager's legs—his compass toward the stage. When the legs stop moving, John stops moving. His head bowed as if he was still praying.

He sways from side to side; the crowd is on the other side of this thin curtain, rubbing their feet into the ground, each and every one of those people waiting for the man to take the stage, to take away their breath or their faith. The roadie puts an index card into John's hand. John leaves it down, his eyes still closed, trying to see with his eardrums, imagining what lays just a few feet in front of him. John opens his eyes, the curtain in front of him nearly as dark as the scene behind his eyelids. He lifts his arm, the index card with it. In the middle of the lined 3x5 is a zero. A circle. John folds the index card and places it into his back pocket.

"I'm ready," John says. The stage manager radios ahead, the lights go out, the sound of the crowd goes up. John parts the curtain, striding out onto that dark stage, wandering into the abyss of his life. The only place he has control. The only place that felt right. But a solitary place, a place of his own making, an island. The backing band, no more than window dressing. The stage is dark. The crowd grows louder by the second, John's silhouetted figure almost being able to be made out through the darkness. John opens his mouth and the lights come up.

John let loose over the next few hours, running through the years. He tore up his vocal chords, straining on a song or two. He felt present though, that this was the only place he could be. The pain in his back pulsed at points, slowing him a bit. He regained himself and continued on, hitting the guitar as hard as he had in years. The crowd carried him at parts, knowing full well that he couldn't fly as high as he once could. As they got louder, his ears numbed, the rush of energy coming at him like an arrow fired by a precise hunter. As the minutes turned into hours and the hours turned to the end of days, John got the sign from the stage manager that he was about to go overtime. He nodded his head and reached down to the ground, picking up a towel to wipe the sweat off his brow. He paused for the first time after three hours and looked out over that collection of faces—each and every one of them fixated on him. The whites of their eyes reflecting like mirrors in on himself. He cleared his throat and thanked everyone for coming. He turned to the band and said, "We got one more?" They nodded and the lights dimmed, the lone spotlight in the end zone focusing its gaze upon John, who sat upon the stool at the front of the stage like a broken down old puppet, his strings worn and weak, hanging off his shoulders, scraping the floor. He closed the show with a cover of Neil Young's "Out on the Weekend."

Think I'll pack it in/

And buy a pick-up/

Take it down to L.A./

Find a place to call my own/

And try to fix up/

Start a brand new day/

And as the pretty young girls danced to the harmonica and the old men sang from down below, John breathed deep—that vision of humanity fading off into darkness at the back of the Garden. As he took his bow, he closed his eyes once more, his vision once again by eardrum. The vivid dancing of life and death right in front of him, John opened up for one more look. That last hit of opium, that last rush of energy. The lights went out and John Pepper disappeared off that stage.

CHAPTER TWENTY SIX

Jill looks through the magazine rack. The wall of periodicals goes from floor to ceiling, everything from fashion to hardcore porno. Her eyes scroll the covers, facades of decadence, not one visage unaffected by the long touch of vanity. Even *Newsweek* airbrushes their cover subjects—fucking *Newsweek*. She gets on her toes and reaches for the top row, pulling down a magazine, placing it on the counter, handing over her five bucks and walking out into the sidewalks of Brooklyn. The sky was high. It was bright and hot. It was a Saturday in the summertime. Jill meets up with some friends, grabs some food and some beers and goes to Prospect Park. Spreading out a blanket, the group becomes a shade of paint in the collage that is bike riders, children running in circles and hipsters throwing Frisbees. As the sun becomes less harsh and a cool sweeps across the grass of the park, Jill dives into her oversized bag and pulls out the magazine. She opens to John's profile, a five pager that lead with a photo of John shrouded in darkness. The words printed sounded much like the ones she had heard before, John beating his chest, reminding everyone who he used to be. He has a way of humbly bragging like no other. As the prose dwindled, Jill read into John's last words.

"He looked tired, but maybe this man is who he says he is—a man who smiled at the fading belief in his religion and reignited believers with a week of bravado and visions of the past. As my time ran out, I asked him one final question. A question most people ask themselves when they've accomplished just about all that they can, 'What have you learned?'

"Pepper looked at me and smiled, perhaps dropping the façade, or even more likely, putting on a new face and said, 'What I've learned is that there is no right way to live a life. I've constantly made mistakes. I've loved, I've hated, I've been hated. I've woken up with one viewpoint for the day and went to sleep with one entirely different. I've failed over and over—and I'm fine with that. I've lived. I got out there. Do I wish my batting average was better? Sure. But ultimately, I'm still sitting here, kicking. So many people lost before their time, taken before they wrote their symphony. But I made it through by the skin of my nuts and what little hair I have left on my head. That's not to say that I haven't been close. I've died 100 times. I died when I lost my dad. When I lost a daughter. When I destroyed a lover. When I destroyed a friend. But those deaths signified mile markers for me. They propelled me forward, to climb the next mountain or dig the next grave. To go home again...or to hit the road...for when 'home' changes into something you can't make peace with. There is always the road. It can always take you somewhere. Maybe I just need to keep searching that road. In the downpour or the sunshine. See what's out there. Maybe one day the road will end with a mansion or a motor home...or maybe it'll just end, a highway never finished. I'm willing to take that chance to find out. To live on that thin line between heaven and hell. All of us are searching for something. Some find it, some die trying. I don't know which one I am.'"

PART FIVE:
THE PALE BOY
IN THE MIRROR

CHAPTER TWENTY SEVEN

"It blew a hole in me," the man in the plaid shirt says—sweat marking his forehead, his eyes staring at the ground. Marie flinches at the words. The man is as still as a statue. He's been staring at the ground for a while now, recounting a story that he's told before. Some here have heard it; he's said that recounting the event makes him feel better in some strange way. That trying to piece together the puzzle makes the act seem less senseless, less devastating. Week after week, drawing a picture, playing with the colors, thinking of ways it could have gone differently. He has talked about his wife, though very briefly, the one who stopped showing up with him after a few weeks. Her absence grew larger, then fell to the background when everyone just assumed the act of getting together and talking just wasn't her style. He showed up one day without his wedding ring. He soon talked about moving into a new apartment. It wasn't hard to piece everything together.

Marie stays staring at the man, wondering why he does it to himself, why he relives it, why he needs to bring the pain to the surface each and every Tuesday at 7 p.m.

It has been two months since Andrew was killed in that diner on that rainy night. She hasn't said much beyond her name since coming here. She instead opts for the numbing in her rear end from the hard plastic school chair, the recounting of tales from those well versed in loss. The man begins to cry again, at the spot in the story when he always cried, the point where the gate latch opened—the gate latch he never got around to fixing. Marie shifts in her seat. The woman who lost her husband to a drunk driver consoles the man, rubbing the back of his neck. He begins to sob louder. She doesn't know if coming here was helping, if all of this death around her is preventing her from moving on. A box of stuff from Andrew's apartment in the city still sits in her hallway, a thin layer of dust developing on top. She thought about throwing it out, going so far as to pick it up and walk it out to the garbage room. She thought better of it, returning it to the hallway and leaving it there. She hasn't touched it since.

She loved him for the longest time. She shared some great memories with him, memories that used to be framed on her dresser. Images that transported her back to another time, much like the videotapes of her trip to the Bahamas with him, or that road trip to Boston, or the summer they spent at the shore house. They reside in a second box in the hallway. A box that was packed the morning she decided she was going to end things with him. Tired of his actions, the ugliness that had developed in him since his father's death, the way the man in those images had morphed into someone else entirely. At first she knew it was grief manifesting itself, overcoming Andrew in a way he had no control over. But as the weeks wore on and the man continued to collapse in on himself like a dying star, Marie tried to heal him. As she pleaded with him, she told him that he wasn't letting her in, she told him not to throw everything away—he did just that. He yelled and he screamed, he told her that she had no idea what he was going through. He told her that she wasn't supportive, that she was out for herself. He packed a bag and left the apartment they shared. At first heading to his mother's, then moving into a small apartment in New York City, Andrew made only sporadic attempts to talk to her. A text message here, a written letter there. It went on for weeks. Marie hoping that whatever he was going through, he could pull himself out of it. But as the distance expanded and the small contact grew even briefer, Marie decided that she couldn't let Andrew pull her into that abyss with him. She called him, told him that she wanted to meet up at the diner on Grey Street at midnight. He gave one word responses, but promised that he would show. Before Marie went off to work, she packed up everything related to Andrew and put it in the trunk of her car.

She headed over to the diner after her shift ended at 11 p.m., making her way across the empty town streets, the rain just starting to drop onto her windshield. Taking a seat in one of the booths on the opposite wall, Marie ordered a cup of coffee. She waited, staring at the door, her eyes sometimes wandering but returning every time the little bell above the door rang out, each time bringing forth someone other than Andrew. It happened over and over, becoming this foreboding sound of disappointment. It became a bug in her mind, causing a slight recoil every time she heard it.

Andrew arrived three hours late. Marie went through many stages in those three hours, worry—*Maybe something happened,* regret—*I should have just done this in my apartment...or his, somewhere private,* anger—*I can't believe he did this to me.*

Anger stayed the most prevailing emotion, each cup of coffee and tick of the clock raising Marie's ire. She thought about leaving and never taking another call from him—completely cut him out of her life, forget he ever existed. She decided otherwise; she wanted him to know how much he hurt her, how much damage he had done. Let him know just what a piece of shit he was for treating her this way, for throwing away everything as if it meant nothing. When he finally darkened that doorway at 3 a.m. he shuffled into the diner, his face sagging, his mouth mute. He said nothing. Did nothing. Just sat there. The words flew out of her, so well rehearsed over those last three hours, each and every one the exact feeling in her soul. He just sat there. Then it all happened. Wrestling that man to the ground, defending her, like the old Andrew had just appeared from the past.

The gunshot.

It was so loud, like a building collapsing on top of them, the echo going on for years. The sound that replaced the bell above the diner door as the only twang in her mind. Him on the floor, blood dampening his clothes, his eyes clear, looking up from the floor of that diner.

"I'm sorry."

The words destroyed the environment. Why did he say them? Did he think that he was close to death? Did he know? Or was it just stored up from before, down deep, past his ego, his pain? He was gone 15 minutes later. Taking that box out of her trunk the next day and carrying it upstairs to her apartment felt like a Herculean effort. It was disorienting, those things she was feeling. The shift of the tide in those few moments haunted her. Which man was he? If he was never on that floor, would he have ever said those things? Then turning introspective, *I should have just emptied my pockets...told him to sit down and shut up...I should have done it at home, we should have never been here.*

"Our time is up for today. I'll see you all next week," the leader of group says, getting out of his seat and shaking the hands of those in attendance. Marie grabs her bag and leaves without talking to the others.

Her apartment is neat. Marie is always neat. Always together, always composed. She makes herself dinner. She flips around the channels for a little while; nothing's on. She lies down in bed and stares at the ceiling for hours. She hasn't slept much lately, nodding off only briefly, awaking just as quickly, body exhausted, mind racing. She makes herself tea and looks out the window. The phone has stopped ringing, the condolences have stopped coming, the questions no longer answered. Most have moved on from Andrew, but Marie hasn't. She nods off in the chair in front of the window.

The light hits on the bridge of her nose. Her eyes open slowly, looking out into space, just a glimmer of light peeking through the clouds overpowering the sky. She has a pain in her neck, probably due to her crooked sleeping posture. She straightens herself in the chair, rubbing her eyes and letting loose a yawn. It looked like it was going to rain.

In her car now, she drives slowly. The car behind her beeps...and beeps. Marie pulls over to the side of the road, sitting there for a few moments, watching as rush hour blows past her. She didn't know what she was doing. Sitting here—in this place. She called in sick to work and headed back home. Getting under the covers felt sublime—the covers cloaking her, the warmth making her less cold. She didn't want to leave this place.

She flipped through the television channels. She thought that maybe daytime television was bad on purpose, that maybe it acted as a deterrent to people wanting to be unemployed. If they showed *Mad Men* or *Community* in the middle of the day nobody would go to work—the ugliness of paternity tests and years-old soap sets instead triggered a gag reflex.

Now she knew.

She knew where he escaped too, at least a version of it.

The phone would ring over the next few days. Marie ignored it. She felt like going to work one day. She got up early, took a shower, put on some make up and got back in her car. She walked into the office as if she hadn't missed any days. She did her work, took her hour lunch break and got back in her car— heading back to her shelter, her broken castle. She fell back asleep in front of the window some nights, waking up and deciding whether to go to work. Some days it was yes, others no. The 'no' days consisted of watching the traffic ebb and flow out her window, her old self stuck in traffic then disappears, only to appear the same time later, stuck in the same traffic. On another 'no' day, Marie pulled all the furniture out of her bedroom and painted the walls a fresh coat of blue. In the morning she woke up in a navy blue room and that night she fell asleep in a baby blue one.

After returning home from work the next day, there's a message on her answering machine from Mary, Andrew's mother.

"Hey Marie, it's Mary...Andrew's mom. I'm just calling to check in on you...haven't talked in a while. Maybe we can get together, get lunch or something. Give me a call whenever you get a chance. Bye, sweetie."

Marie deletes the message and heads to take a shower. She sits on the floor after a long day of work. She thinks about Mary. Maybe she should go see her. She knows better than any of those people in that group. She knew Andrew. She knew him, she saw the same things Marie saw. She gets out of the shower and picks up the phone.

CHAPTER TWENTY EIGHT

Seventy-two hours later, Marie is sitting across from Mary. She's in her late 50's, her hair graying, tiny crinkles around her eyes. Those eyes are kind; they're the same color as Andrew's. It feels strange looking at them. The first few minutes of dinner, Mary and Marie each talk around everything. Faint allusions, the weather, the Yankee game. All of these things the two of them hope would be an entrance into the conversation they would get around to sooner or later.

"So how are you doing?" Mary asks. Marie smiles and continues to eat her salad, using it as a diversion to think of the right words. She wipes the sides of her mouth with a napkin.

"I'm doing okay," Marie replies.

"I'm not."

"Good, I'm not either," Marie replies.

They're on level ground and they begin to talk. About how Andrew took his father's death. How it enveloped him. It blinded him. He loved his father, never had the hiccups with him that some sons have growing up.

"It's almost like he didn't want to be around anymore...he lost all ambition in a way, like everything was for naught. I tried to talk to him and he said he needed space to think, to try to make sense of what happened and I gave it to him and he ran to the city. He got that little apartment and never left. He would leave me messages late at night talking about how he couldn't sleep," Mary continues. Marie listens, hearing the echo of her own pain, her own reaction, her own life.

Then Marie begins to recount Andrew's descent. The quiet sobbing from behind the closed bedroom doors. The distant look at dinner. The naps that turned into comas. Andrew wasting away, allowing his father's death to become his own. Wishing in some way that he had been the one to go. Taking everything beyond him.

"I remember when he got the call that he passed away. He just collapsed into the chair and I was like, 'What's wrong? What's wrong?' and he looked at me and his eyes were blank like everything had left him at that moment. His face was ghastly white. The day of the funeral he said he needed to go alone...that he didn't want me to see him like that. To meet his family for the first time on the day of his father's funeral," Marie said.

"And then we met for the first time—" Mary replies.

"The day he died," Marie finishes. The bus boy refills their water glasses.

"He didn't come," Mary replies, a lump in her throat as she says it. This was the first time her face sank as she spoke, the sunny facade dropping.

"He came back a few hours later and said he went to the baseball field near our house and sat in his car. He listened to Pink Floyd and stared out at the field he played Little League on. He said that he felt ill when he was driving toward the church and couldn't go any further," Marie says.

The two women go back to eating their salads, exhausting themselves for the time being. It feels heavy in the restaurant. The two feel something between them. They saw how it was; maybe they were the only ones who saw how it was. None of this was spoken or even thought about at Andrew's funeral. The cover story was his heroism at the diner that night. The tornado that had developed inside Andrew in the weeks prior only beat down the doors of the two women sitting at this table. No one else saw the man broken; maybe it was better that way. As the empty salad plates leave the table and the entrée's were served, Marie feels ready to talk again.

"I want to be honest with you, but I also don't want to disrespect your son because I know how much you loved him...but I'm in a weird place. I was so mad at him. I hated him...honestly, I hated him. He was so terrible to me for that period and I just don't know why. I don't know what I did...or what I didn't do...and...I don't know if he loved me. I don't know how to feel, you know; going from yelling at him to him maybe saving my life. I can't reconcile that, the two Andrews there that night. I miss him obviously, but I can't forget that time," Marie explains, staring at her interlocked hands, the tips of her thumbs rubbing against each other.

"You shouldn't...because that happened. He was terrible. Believe me; he was nasty to me too at times. He was broken and he was trying anything to figure any way to—I don't even know...you can feel any way that you want. You don't have to feel guilty that you were mad at him," Mary replies.

"Did he ever talk about me? You seemed to be the only person he talked to for any extended period of time."

"He talked about you all the time," Mary said. Marie looks up at Mary's eyes again, being taken somewhere else.

"I'd call him every day…sometimes he wouldn't answer for days and then sometimes he always picked up and you were the only thing he ever talked about. He loved you very much and, well I think he proved that…that night," Mary said. Marie has to look away, steering her eyes to the tables around the restaurant, wrestling with her eyes, trying to escape this feeling in her throat.

"He was never a man of *words*, he always stood up when he needed to though…he never shared," Mary says.

"I'm sorry," Mary continues. Those words ringing with an Andrew like tone. Mary grabs Marie's hand. She leans across the table, speaking just above a whisper.

"He just got lost, sweetie, it wasn't your fault…don't blame yourself for anything," Mary says.

A small child in the back corner is wailing as his mother tries to feed him. The mirrors on each wall of the restaurant reflect everything to infinity, looking as if these black paper matted tables go on for ages. It's as if you could look deep into the reflection and see someone you've never seen before, sitting to your right and left.

"I brought you something," Mary says, fishing into her pocket book, pulling out a small notebook. Mary put it on the table in front of Marie.

"You have it," Marie says almost in disbelief, staring down at the notebook, one that Andrew had written in for the past year or so. "When I cleaned out his apartment…I couldn't find it; I thought he threw it away or something."

"No, you gave it to him and he kept it with him all the time. The last time I saw him he left it at my house and we had made plans to meet up so I could give it to him again, but…I want you to have it," Mary says. Marie starts shaking her head.

"I'm serious, I want you to have it...you could do whatever you want with it, burn it, throw it off a bridge, whatever you want to do. I just thought that you should have it and now that I know you're confused with everything, maybe it'll have something," Mary says.

"Something," Marie whispers.

"Yea."

"Have you read it?" Marie asks, picking up the notebook, its edges scuffed.

"No...I couldn't do it...I thought about it but no—it's yours," Mary replies.

"Thank you," Marie replies.

"It's my pleasure."

Marie puts the notebook on the chair next to her, running her hand over the cover.

"Can I ask you a question?" Marie asks, continuing to look at the notebook.

"Does it get easier?"

Mary shakes her head, looking away from Marie toward the door.

"Sometimes...you have days where you'll think about it less, but it never ever goes away. Then there are times where it hits you right in the chest like a huge wave in the ocean—you feel dizzy just thinking about it...and then it all comes back and you miss them all over again." Mary turns back to Marie, her eyes closed.

"And then I lost my son," Mary says, the words slipping off her lips, as if she couldn't believe she was saying them.

"And then the pain just becomes a dull hum...an itching at the back of your throat. You never think that you could lose that much all at once...but the pain reminds you of them. It hurts for a while."

Marie looks at Mary, the cracks of her strong facade showing. The steely veneer built up by constant incoming fire losing some of its backing. It's as if she hasn't really thought about all of this until that very moment.

"But I think that's good. I think it means something because it's all just time really. We're all just on a running clock and the game stops sometimes and that pain you get, that wave that hits you reminds you that you're still here, that you can still do things...and you may not be able to do it with them, but they're with you. Breathing helps...prayer too. Sometimes when I pray for him, about him, I go to bed and I see him—in my dreams. He's standing there and he's smiling and...now I'm just getting gushy," Mary finishes, "You'll find a way to make the pain subside...even if it's just temporary."

"I'm not really religious," Marie replies.

"It's alright, neither am I," Mary says with a laugh. "Come on, let's eat, you look too skinny," Mary says as she picks up her fork. Mary and Marie go back to eating and don't speak more than a few words for the rest of their meals.

Mary and Marie stand outside the restaurant.

"This was a good time; we should do this more often," Mary says, throwing her bag over her arm.

"Thank you," Marie replies.

"For what?"

"Everything—lunch, talking to me, thank you," Marie said. Mary hugs Marie.

"I'll talk to you soon."

Mary turns and walks across the parking lot to her car. Marie puts Andrew's notebook in her bag.

CHAPTER TWENTY NINE

Marie flips through the newspaper, all the while eyeing Andrew's notebook. It sits on the end of her coffee table, a place it has resided since she got home. She refocuses on the newspaper; her eyes gravitating back to the book every few sentences. It holds weight, maybe answers, maybe nothing. Would it make her feel better? Or worse? What if he didn't mention her at all? That would be the cruelest crime, the utter invisibility in his writing. Maybe it would haunt her, never knowing. This is her last chance to understand what he was going through. It feels horribly creepy though. The words he wrote privately, tucked away.

Marie gets up from the kitchen table and walks toward the book. Picking it up, she runs her fingers along the edges of the pages. She goes into her bedroom; opening a drawer, she sticks the notebook in, closing it shut. She leaves the room and turns off the light. She grabs her keys and heads out for a walk.

Later, she lies down in bed, preparing herself for another night of ceiling gazing.

The shifting trees on the sidewalk cast shadows on the ceiling, the lamp post guiding it's light behind them, showing off their dancing talents to Marie's open eyes, the blue of the moon giving them their backdrop. The dresser looks like it is about to fall through the floor—disappearing forever. Marie takes her eyes off the dancing branches, throws her covers to the ground and opens the dresser.

PART SIX:
ANDREW'S NOTEBOOK

CHAPTER THIRTY

Andrew's unsteady handwriting marks the pages. Some scratches, some bends in the dead trees, some notations. His mind sprawled down in cursive. Some of the words are illegible, perhaps the product of a 3 a.m. scrawl, the spark of something in the soul.

Doubt continues to cloud Marie's mind. Maybe this isn't right. Maybe she should go throw it in the ocean, let it wash up somewhere else. She begins to read.

Drop into the void

With your friend Boyd

Tell a story with your eyes

Always order french fries

I miss your thighs

They were the perfect size

We got lost in the lies

You fell for the disguise

You always ate toast with rye

Loved to hear Biggie rap bout Bed Stuy

All these other brothers can't deny

You hated pecan in your pie

Keep reading your horoscope

Tell me I'm a big dope

Tell me to go, I'll say nope

I'd rather stay and watch some Leslie Knope

I wish you were there when I met the Pope

His breath stank, I wanted to give him Scope

Never understood how his assistant could cope

I guess its religion that gives people hope

They pray after they use their car to kill antelope

They'll never look at religion through a microscope

Never was much to push the envelope

My favorite thing is to walk the tightrope

rhyming is a tired trope.

the church is gonna hang me with a rope.

november 14th

So there's this girl. Brown hair, brown eyes—her mouth a small oblong opening of anxiety. She was a worrier. This girl. She was partial to the table in the back corner of the restaurant. She sat there frequently, spreading her belongings as if it were an annex to her apartment. Some days she read fiction, some days she made out with a new guy, some days an old guy. She rarely came in on Fridays. No one knew where she disappeared to on Fridays. She was the silent magnet of the restaurant. Even the regulars who had seen her sitting in that familiar place six days a week couldn't help but wander their gaze in her direction. She never once returned the favor. It's almost as if he thought she was alone in this place. That the countless men and women who traversed these tables and chairs never even existed.

Maybe they didn't, maybe she didn't exist. Just some angel who did her good work on Friday and saved some souls. Met her quota, then came back to this temporary existence to recharge. Maybe she just liked to sleep in on Fridays. I wish I had more to tell you, but no one has the nerve to actually speak to her.

amy awe.

november 20th

"Where did you go?"

He looked up from his cup and into her irises. He got lost all over again. He looked toward the window, again lost. Looking for the correct phrasing. It was absent or strange. Wasn't epic or miniscule. He looked back at her, done with racking his brain with trying to sound smart.

"I got lost, wandering around for a little bit. Saw some ugly things, saw some stuff that made me grow. I tried to become something else. Maybe try to be better. Try to not be such a loser. Maybe leave something more behind than just a big stump of granite in the grass with a name engraved on it. I bought some Neil Young vinyl and just traveled across the world. Met a girl, thought about settling down with her before I found out she was already married. I just picked up my guitar and moved along to the next town. It was carefree in all honesty, being beholden to nothing. Death still lurks, but you can escape his reach when you're that lost. He seems to only want to cause maximum impact, a lonely drifter on the road is small potatoes to him. He'd rather take away a father in a horrific way."

She continued to gaze in his direction as he stammered on some more. Telling her of the life he had created, this life that rejuvenated his mojo pin. Reset the button, remixed the ether.

He paused his thought and stopped wandering the restaurants real estate. This is just another stop on the journey. This isn't the end to me wandering. In a few days I'll take off again and go to some other town, some other place where no one knows my name.

She stayed fixed on him and again he looked back. He took out his wallet, placed ten dollars and exited the restaurant. She didn't know when he would be back.

long trip.

november 25th

We left our love on the outer banks.

Took a taxi home and told the driver thanks.

Took in a movie, it starred Tom Hanks.

301

Looked out into the street from our window, it was full of tanks.

I wrote you a letter in verse.

I first read it to my nurse.

I tried some new words, not one single curse.

When you weren't looking I stuck it in your purse.

We went to the movies on a Tuesday.

It was some indie we read about in Newsday.

Went to a concert after, the band's name was Refusday.

The drummer corrected our spelling, it was really Refusdai.

It ended up being a horrible date I fear.

One of the days when we knew the end was near.

The car had crashed, we couldn't steer.

I'm so sorry my dear.

same thing.

november 30th

Oh girl, oh girl. You drive me ever so loco. With your long legs and even longer hair. You came to me in a dream last night, told me all yours. Took you to a nice Japanese spot, ate some teriyaki, you had the eel. We used to wait to speak; now it comes in full verse. I really love you babe, my shit is stuck in reverse.

Let's go get married, give my mom and dad a grandkid. I'll introduce you to my folks, they'll fucking love you the most. Astral Weeks was on the record player the first time I saw you. You were the coolest thing in the room and I like that record a lot.

You made me feel born again, life not religion. You stepped right down and restarted my gut. Gave me the kick start to do this. For Love or Squalor you'll always be the one. So for that I say to you, I Love You.

monologue for Marie.

december 2nd

DEATH AND OTHER THINGS

Marie closes the book, throwing it across the room. After reading through some fiction, she finally saw a trace of the past. The day she first felt the cracks. Andrew didn't mention that this was the day his father was told to go the hospital for a follow up—

ground zero of this torrid downfall. The book sits on the floor, the moonlight sneaking through the blinds, drawing lines on its cover.

She reluctantly gets back up. Knowing full well what was about to happen. Seeing the words form the feelings, reliving Andrew's descent.

We broke up in early May or late September

A frosty day if I do remember

She spoke in different tongues

Where she used to breathe into my lungs

She moved out to the west coast

Looking for a place to be warm the most

I asked her to stay

She said she'll listen to Maggie May

"I loved you wrong," she said

"We never ever left the bed"

I took a job as a clerk

In a town where liars love to lurk

Met a girl

Her name is Pearl

Now I run at dusk

Get that ole manly musk

Tired of the run around

Now I stare at the Kennedy compound

Now I sit in these arms

303

I eat a lot of chicken parms

Italian she is

Her middle name is Liz

My dad got sick overnight

The only thing in his eyes was fright

His doctor's name is Dwight

Will he save him? I think he might

I'll run and run and run

Have calves stronger than an athletic nun

But she'll still be over there

In all honesty we were quite a pair.

rashida.

december 4th

Hello? Is there anyone out there?

Hello? Really? No one?

Things have gotten messy. There is a beached whale in the streets. The clouds are on fire and the buildings are seeping into the bedrock. I stare out into the blacktop and see nothing but white. Where am I? What's going on? Where has everyone gone?

The only thing to keep me warm is this brown fedora and some Scott Pilgrim comics. The streets have become almost predatory by nature, nothing to do with the beached whale. Instead it is the unbearable darkness behind every corner, the light that has all but vanished. I'm stuck in the world without rules.

What? Is there somebody out there?

fondree.

december 8th

He made up for lost time. Thinking about last year is vile. Tired of working for the man and his one dime. Easy was never much his style. He don't care, he don't care, he don't care, he don't care.

Ran home looking for his pops. Got held up trying to buy some milk. Hopped on the express, there was hardly any stops. He couldn't quit staring at the girl with the scarf made of silk. He don't care, he don't care, he don't care, he don't care.

Made it home to his father, held him in his arms. Wish he could've held on longer. Ran into the kitchen whipped up some chicken parms. Was still searching for his mother, couldn't bare not seeing her any longer.

He's alright, he's alright, he's alright, he's alright.

He kissed his father on the head, put him to bed. He was late to work, back to the express he would go. What he would do to stay here instead. Watch another episode of the Simpsons, listen to Homer do D'OH!

He's alright, he's alright, he's alright, he's alright. Yea?

comforting sounds.

december 9th

I'm out of ideas for tonight.

I was discussing the idea of being happy with someone today. It was an enlightening conversation because I don't really or ever have understood what exactly it means to be happy. Most people say that it's about being content. Well I think that's bullshit. If you are content that means you're static, content is another thing that I don't understand. It's such an ugly word to me. If you are content and think it's a good thing, you should throw yourself off a bridge and get busy living.

If happy is content, then content is not moving forward, not changing, not living, you're busy dying, anything not moving forward is dying, just ask a shark. Any walk without meaning, without purpose, without reason is pointless. Life is too short to walk aimlessly. Happiness is death.

Anyone can be happy, what's the point of that? Dylan said that and he nailed it.

Cold day in January. Dirty snow blackens the streets. The wind howls, knocking day old newspapers along the sidewalks. A woman is bundled up to her eyes, a scarf covering her face. The streets are empty, people are sitting by their lit fires, reading a novel by some 18th century man of reason. The sun never came out today. It's these days when you feel alive, a certain closeness develops inside *those warm walls. You only venture out because you want to be able to say that you did. Inside stay the friends and lovers, staying warm with liquor, making proclamations of love, eating coffee and scones.*

On the other side of this youth is years old bonds relishing the abundance of same. The rituals of old movies on VHS and yellowed books of yesterday sitting on the shelves of this musty apartment. A two handed animal of unmistakable wisdom, you see two people who don't need the word 'love' to quantify what exists between them. A companionship, a gamesmanship, a back and forth that has dulled on fresh but lives on a heart of life. While these two parties partake in different tasks on these cold days, they share a bond. While some search these cold streets for answers, the ones behind these warm doors have already found it. They once searched too. Soon the coffee and scones will turn into tea and honey and the VHSs to DVDs, but the people won't. We all replace those above us, the tree of life sprouts new branches every morning. So search those streets until you've find the right door, or wander the wilderness eternally, just find some place warm.

me and tia (11/41).

december 22nd

I keep diving into the ocean. Looking for those quiet moments. The soft murmuring of the ivory keys. The creak of the stairs behind closed doors. I hear these noises below, softly floating above my head. I look across the living room and see ghosts. Hear Franklin the Turtle hitting his head against the glass of his prison. Maybe one day he'll break out and die on the hot sidewalk, the sun above him cooking him into the cement. It will be a horrible way for him to go, but maybe he'll be free. Free to find his own prison, lock himself in. Maybe he was worse off in a better life. Maybe the prison is now better for him.

The rain hits the windshield. The woman on the corner covers her baby from the drops. I drive down the middle of the street, my car smacking the mirrors of those parked to my right. I keep moving, trying to outpace the rain. Losing a battle as the gas needle ticks slowly down, the energy seeping away, escaping into nothingness. Maybe this car is a temporary prison, escorting me in between life terms. My last window out into the free world. The last chance to breathe the fresh, wet air. Maybe I'll tire of that life sentence, pick away at the wall in my cell. Dig a tunnel so deep I'll see hell beneath me and heaven above. Maybe I'll jump down rather than turn back. Maybe I'll just stay perched on that ledge, leering up above, seeing the overwhelming light. Maybe.

maybe.

december 23rd

Let down the curtain.

Let me into the show.

Let me believe that you love.

My flight to Kansas is in the morning.

I'm selling some 401Ks to farmers.

Would you like to come?

We could drive down quiet roads.

We could go to sleep without the sounds of drunkards outside our windows.

drunk on a Tuesday morning.

december 25th

People here and there. Reading words from Fred Astaire. I'll go out running with my headphones on. Keep sprinting till I see my son. I've reached the edge of the coast. That's where I missed him the most. Tried and Tried and Tried. Only to find that the connection was fried. Kerouac went on the road. Ran away from the press and people's load. Never ever did what he was told.

I was a dreamer, shared the street with the geese. The only person who ever looked up to me was my niece. Her boyfriend's name was Reese. Always carried candy bars, he was offered me a piece. Had this great apartment in Nice, at least until he couldn't pay the lease.

People go and write this shit, record execs go and make it a radio hit. That's why all the good poets end up face down in a pit, the only thing they have for a pillow is their ball mitt. It's a silly thing, this whole creating thing, I do hate it quite a bit.

So I'll keep running till I find that sun, keep the shuffle on till it hits Big Pun. Keep writing the words people want the most, words I'll never find until I hit the coast. I miss my son the most.

musio monument.

january 1st

Sorry that I've been away. I've been searching for something that can't be found by blind men. It's something that hugs our heart and pulls at our arms. It's odd in all honesty.

I got in the car and drove for a few hours. I had to stop at this little gas station in North Dakota to get some gas and take a leak. I turned around and turned around and turned around and saw that no one was beside me. Saw that I was alone.

It is dispiriting in a way, to be that alone. To be so open to pain, to longing, to a stray cat. I could head to the border, maybe make a new life, write my novels under a stage name.

Then I thought about going to find that kid I put up for adoption all those years ago. See if he grew up to look like me. Whether he got the bad hip that I didn't get from my father.

I turned around again and looked down the dusty road. It looked so fucking inviting. It had no prejudice or preconceived notions. It just was, just that blanket that warmed you after running in the rain.

I thought about my mother, the only one who stayed through everything. She never ran when the going went foul or yelled at me for my mouth.

She always just stayed. She always stayed.

I'm gonna go see her.

cyprus avenue.

january 11th

Jennifer walked down the cold, brisk and all together to windy street. The storefronts were littered with 'FOR RENT' signs, showing how dilapidated said area was. Jennifer was in town for the night and searching for something to eat. Nothing had quite hit her fancy yet.

The wind blew another hearty gust right into her face, Jennifer flinched, it's cold.

As Jennifer rounded the corner she came upon a homeless man. He must have been in his 60's, his white beard told of being born in the 40's. He was propped up against the wall, a foam shred of bedding acting as his pillow. His shoes looked brand new, save for the hole in the big toe of the right one. He looked peaceful, almost saintly. His eyes reminded Jennifer of her grandfather, with the slight wrinkle of his left eye that looked like it belonged to a much younger man. Jennifer continued walked as to not awake the man.

A few blocks away Jennifer heads into a Spanish restaurant, after combing the menu for a few minutes she grabs her bag and departs, still in search of what exactly she wanted.

table #11 is free.

january 13th

"Honestly, honesty is a tired sport. It's ripping and cold and unbelievable. Every man and woman is out for themselves."

The man then jumped to his death.

The witness to the suicide of Eli Jones heard his final manifesto, his final liturgy, his final will and testament. It's deep business, this suicide thing; it's only for the serious. No flakey people decide to commit suicide, they'd change their mind too much. No room for that shit in suicide.

As the officers and reporters debriefed the witnesses they all said the same thing. Eli Jones did not stutter or stammer or stumble. He spoke those words as if you were asking him his name. Complete and utter conviction.

One witness who stood the closest to Mr. Jones said that his last words were, "I'll try anything once," a statement that I'm sure a lot of us could utter at any one moment. Or wish we had the balls to.

train hopper.

january 14th

I'm tired of burning down the house. Letting nature have at the remains, let the trees grow in. I wanna build something, something lasting. Erect a building, put my name on it. People may say that this mindset is narcissistic. I think it's just about doing something big. Doing something you're proud of, leaving something behind to be admired.

They don't need to remember me, but remember the work. Drink in the words, form an opinion about them. Let the things that are left behind spark discourse, create ideas, speculation. That's what I want to leave behind, kids might be nice, they might hate me though, a building can never hate you.

I can't write full sentences anymo—

bring me down.

january 15th

One of my all time favorite quotes—

"I'm having sex with my mind. It's intimate this sex. My mind is a very giving lover. Writing is the most intimate thing, outside of sex, that I do. It is my id, my evil mind, my impure heart. It envelops me from time to come, the writing. But ultimately it is my release. The vessel I purge all of my fuckups into. It allows me to keep moving, while addressing my fears, my mistakes, my ideas. It's all very protesty, this writing thing. It says that you think you deserve to be read. I don't feel that way. If people read the stuff and have a reaction to it, great. Good or bad. But it's for me. It's the only reason I'm still breathing. I wanna be able to do it till the day I die, and if not, then I'll just die."

-john pepper

tasting my brain.

january 24th

I don't have a single emotion to tell you about. I am a broken vessel underwater, on the way to the UK. I called up Richie, he was angry about something. He said that I hadn't called in weeks. I replied, "That's why I'm calling now." He hung up after that. He was never much of a talker, that Richie.

There is something eerily similar in the emotions that you feel when both falling unexpectedly and meeting a girl you really like. At the starting gun for both there is this tremendous euphoria, everything is hanging in mid air. All of the thoughts and possibilities, all of the ways that this is going to end horribly.

With the falling you can hang for a varied amount of time, depending on how fast your life is going, how high you are etc. the length of the relationship representing the time before you hit the concrete varies upon fate, tolerance of one another, sometimes blind luck.

That blind luck allows some to die on the way down. Some have heart attacks, get cancer, get hit by a bus, all things that allow those lucky few to depart without ever feeling the pavement hit their cheek. The sting of defeat in love. Others hit the ground and walk away with scrapes, others have their brain fluid leaking into the sewer.

I was your puppet. You ripped out my seams. Stitched me some new threads, turned me into Frankenstein. Scrubbed a smile on my face. Strung me back up and lifted my legs. I wore that new smile you gave me, wore it like a champion. Don't. Just don't. Don't turn me into that person ever again. Just don't.

three arcanes.

february 5th

I've been dreaming a lot lately. Which is strange because for a few months there was nothing of the sort. I had a dream that I was in the projects with Woody Harrelson and we were cashing out a whole bunch of stolen bonds—like two million bucks in bonds. The whole dream was us getting out of the projects with the bag of cash. I ended up getting my hand sliced open by a gangbanger. As I looked down at my bleeding hand I awoke from the dream, to the pain in my real flesh and blood. A real stinging in the palm on my hand, which with a few shakes soon dissipated. It is odd though. What is the line between dream and reality? Where does the mind decide that one is real and one is not? I don't trust my mind. The way to believe that reality is reality and the dream is otherworldly is that reality always stays the same. The dreams bounce all over the place. They take me places, sometimes with Woody Harrelson, places I've never been before in this conscious existence. Maybe I have been there and I have not yet realized it yet. Maybe I've just watched the Inception trailer one too many times.

sheppard.

february 10th

The beat. The heartbeat. The mind beats. I reach for the tissues. The bottle, the spider. He looks up, he doesn't see me. He just hears the scuttling by the window edge. He feels trapped. He feels empty. He's hungry. He doesn't feel sick as much. He knows he's dying. Knows this is the end. Knows that he won't see another round of Jeopardy! Knows that the end isn't near, it's here. He calls out for Sylvia. Sylvia! He exclaims. His son cries. So do I. Then it all ends. The breath stops. The eyes close. The arms still. I exhale. He's gone.

hospice.

february 13th

Through the words, she saw Andrew in her mind—the days when he was writing these sentences. The dreams he would have about his father. The images of a man who had never been touched by death, wondering if it was about to bust through the door. The days his demeanor turned from loving to moody—his walks up the road to clear his head when bad news came about his father. But then.

They said he's gonna be okay today. That it was a false alarm. That it's not his turn to go yet. As the doctor spilled the beans I saw my father's eyes light up, the weight literally falling off his eyes. The glint back, the worry gone, my father of all those years looking back at me how he used to. In charge, in control, unsinkable. I felt safe again. That I wouldn't have to deal with this just yet, that I still had time to armor up, that I still was able to call him on the phone and ask advice. He's gonna leave me one day, but just not today.

311

good.

march 10th

These pages are soaked with salt water.

This car parts the street much too fast.

The lightning bug buzz.

They're everywhere.

The guys next door are doing coke on the front porch.

It's almost summer time.

The time of the late great Francis.

The ghost of the past.

His essence sings in the atmosphere.

It seems crazy to think it's summer time.

I'll sit on the porch.

Get drunk on this shit.

Continue to write for him.

Try something fresh.

Dance in the waves.

Chill on the surf.

Tire of the experts predicting doomsday.

I'll write it instead.

It'll be gone soon.

no date given.

I'm gonna move to New Mexico, learn some cowboy songs. Get some hair on my chest, listen to some Johnny Mathis on vinyl. People aren't ready for this shit. There are no more artists that speak about something. No ideas or thoughts or opinions, just 808's and melodies. Allen Ginsberg is no longer in the ether. We are left with frauds and pill pushers and bullshit artists. It's time for someone to speak up, to show some fucking sack. Someone needs to pervade the status quo, shake up those pigs in Washington to something fresh and new. I'm gonna go get on the train and get people excited again.

the dagger.

march 26th

Nothing has been resolved so far, it still floats in stasis. He came out to Los Angeles yelling his head off about something doing with Margie. Margie was his ex-lady, a mean cuss Margie was. She walked all over him at the most opportune moments, but in all defense—he was a shitty dude. He beat her, called her names, all the shit that should get your ass relationship marshaled.

So as he was screaming I wasn't really paying attention. Whatever his problem was, it was caused by him somehow, someway. His fuckup had finally come back to him. We meet these people all the time, the ones who shit on others and then are dumbfounded when the same is done to them.

It is impossible to understand why the world turns the way it does—that this incredible moving object does so without us ever feeling it. That this moment is deep, silent and yet overt. It's like the crumbling of a relationship, it starts small in your gut and in the air above your head. Never on the face. You'll grin and bear it and try to change things, try to stop the unfelt rotation. Things will continue to unravel until the core stops, blowing debris everywhere. Then the rotation knocks you skyward, hurtling you toward the burning surface of the sun.

So as he continues to yell and smash that stool I bought with Mary at a tag sale in '74, I scrolled through the text, the subtext, the reflex, the next. As I came upon the obits I saw that a man had fallen out of a plane and died on his way back down. The man had fallen back to earth, fallen off his high perch, landed on his head when he hit. His parachute never deployed. That happens more than we realize.

moon landing.

march 30th

Then the crash happened.

He's gone.

Gone to that place where people go.

The pain gone for him, no longer stuck in that glass castle.

Now he flies, runs and jumps.

Maybe enjoys some good wine.

I have nothing else.

untitled.

april 7ᵗʰ- 10ᵗʰ

'What the fuck?' I screamed into the night.

She turned back to look at me almost as a lark. She had no intention of coming back. As she kept walking off into the distance, I kicked a rock with all my might...and ended up breaking my toe. That day sucked.

Another shitty day was when my cat died. I came home from school and my mom told me that my Uncle Edwin ran Archie over when he was trying to leave the driveway. Edwin was late for his AA meeting and didn't bother to look behind. I wish she had told me before I walked through the driveway on my way back from school, all that was left of Archie was a red blotch on the bottom of my shoes.

But the thing that I've learned is that you can't live in the past. Well you could, but you'd need some plutonium and a flux capacitor. Living in the past is dangerous, to your health, your mind and your bravado. Didn't everything feel so much better back then? Better coke, better pussy, better movies. All this shit matters and yet we're so eager to dismiss it. The past is dead and so are we, but we just don't know it yet. Fuck, I can't believe Uncle Edwin ran over Archie.

fever dream.

april 12ᵗʰ

Someone please give me a reason not to stick my hand into the fire. Please give me a reason not to find the nearest tallest building and jump. The people and things that kept my mind off everything are now gone. Now all that's left are the pictures of him, the dreams where he talks to me, the urn on the dining room table. I feel so fucking lost, so fucking empty. I am every depressed cliché stacked on top of each other.

I wrote the other day that all I'm going to do is write for him. Things that he would have liked, but I have nothing left in me, everything that I had in me april 3ʳᵈ is gone. I am vacant.

314

The greatest pain is the long goodbye. I'm not at peace and I wonder when that will change. I haven't done anything this week but catch a foul ball. I don't even have enough energy to hate God right now.

I'm waiting on a dream that will never come true.

no dude.

april 13th

I wrote a letter to my father last night. I went to the ocean and threw it in, hopefully it'll reach him some day. Hopefully there won't be too many grammatical errors. I hope he's sitting in a comfy chair when he reads it, maybe sipping a glass of wine.

It's a mad world you left Dad. It's emptier without you here. The Mets are good this year, I have a feeling you might have something to do with that.

I went to a beach on a Sunday night and stood in the surf. I looked out into that big dark ocean sky and saw you. You were right there on the edge. Almost out of sight, yet still in view. You had that suit on that you wore on the cruise. You wore wayfarers and your hair was cropped short. You had the beginnings of a mustache, like the one you grew when I was in third grade.

We didn't say much to each other, though you did drop one little pearl of substance. As the water reached my ankles I continued into the waves, each one hitting a little higher. As I kept walking, you kept getting closer. I swam out as far as I could. As I floated in that ocean I glimpsed your eyes again, those big brown eyes. The eyes that looked down at me when I was a kid, those ones that looked up at me from a hospital bed. It felt so strange in this warm water, this baptism by surf. I awoke from my trance to shouting from the boardwalk. A little kid was screaming for his father, we had something in common. As I swam back to the coast, I saw you fade. Someday to return to my vision. Let's not make it too long. I don't live close enough to the beach.

3 a.m. surf.

april 22nd

Leave, leave, leave. Leave for something else.

Leave for all the shit that you wanted.

Free yourself, forget about me.

I hope that you feel better below.

Let the earth roads lead the way to forgiveness.

Forget all that you've done.

Run until you reach the bottom. Kick the habit of life, let it envelop you. Let go, let go of this all. Breathe in the past. Then exhale just as quickly. You've reached the end, now just pull back the hammer.

We had sex in that bathroom, that night. We made no more promises that night, or this night. So go do all the things I held you back from. Become a big movie star if you have the stomach for it. Do all the coke in Holland and bang all the bitches in Bristol. I'm gonna go to the south of France and chill out for a bit.

it's too late.

april 23rd

Where to begin...

I woke up yesterday and the sky was black. Crows stood at my back. I walked down that empty road, felt the gravel on my toes. Sulfur burned all the hair in my nose. I stared at your face, saw the dents and scrapes and culminations of interest rates. You were tired, you were broke, you wish you had gone on a few more dates. You said something, I couldn't make it out. I just kept looking at your pout.

I said I'm sorry, apologized for saying the things I did. I'm sorry for being jealous of Sid. I wanted to keep talking but you told me to shut my lid.

I took one more look around. Saw the scorched earth that you were leaving behind. Taking in the last few moments of this life, wish I could hit rewind. You spoke some damning words, then poof, I no longer existed. Gone from this engulfed place, I'm glad you never resisted.

It was dark, you were gone, now I breathe, see a glimmer far off, preach the good word, curse the gods, kiss the girls, kill mc's, baffle critics, speak in pauses—write back to you.

thanksgiving.

may 15th

I broke up with Marie last night. As I left she told me that she never wants to see me ever again, a proclamation that has been made before, she of all her tragedy. The constant victim that one, the one I loved. She will now go and cry up in Rye, tell everyone how bad I was to her, she of all her tragedy. She'll go talk to her new boyfriend and express what a piece of shit that I am, he will hate me by the transitive property. A property that I felt a lot, when I had Marie in my life, she of all her tragedy.

The good times quelled, gone to another universe. She'll stay up there in Rye, never ever leave. Marry some good guy, have a few kids, constantly complain about the only job she has ever wanted. Maybe she'll write a book about me one day, tell the world all the lurid details. Tell everyone how shitty I was to her. It'll be a bestseller, make her money to put toward her kids college fund. Said kid will read it and wonder what could have been. He'll look up my kid one day and meet what could have been his brother in another galaxy.

Maybe I'll see her again one day—that dark hair with strands of gray through it. Maybe on the street or in a café or on a plane. We'll exchange awkward hello's and talk about our lives since then. We might make cursory overtures about our relationship status', but ultimately it won't matter. For here was the girl that I couldn't live without, she of all her tragedy, but also the one I could never get it together with, she of all her tragedy.

So when I see her all these years from now I think I would only have four words to say to her, sorry and fuck you.

goodbye monopoly.

may 24th

I'd rather stash this energy on the page, let it marinate for you folks to enjoy. Losing it to drugs and booze is something that needs to be indulged at times. The page has been the parking spot the most lately.

She left yesterday and honestly I feel nothing about it. Don't get me wrong I thought about it today and every day before that, but the pain is gone. I don't know if the pain is gone due to time or whatever I'm doping myself up with now a days. Either way, she's gone. It seems to be those in between days—the days that exist in the phantom zone of pain and then hangover. They form this odd combo of relief and underlined thought—thoughts about the things that don't really bother you, but more about the smokescreens. The smokescreens are present right now, they tend to silence the gunshots.

I printed out her dear john letter and put it on my wall.

the broken vows club.

may 24th

Mothers come from right and left, trying to see if they can make me sweat. People write reviews based on my thoughts, tell me all that shit is for naught. I'll

317

keep writing to my girl out west, out of all them I miss her the best. I'll try and be strong, provide for my family. Maybe I'll go and surprise you and go big, maybe bigger. She never did really turn out the light.

I'm tired, I'm weak, the overall feeling is bleak. I'm gonna go listen to some Radiohead and maybe make my bed. I called home today, talked to my brother for a minute or two. He spoke of things in tongues. The line got disconnecting, never was all that affecting.

I'm tired, I'm broke, I never did call that waitress. She was from Columbia, spoke a mean mouth. She made my eggs with just a little bit of salt, poured me a mean malt. I asked her to explain what her name meant, the malt had been mean to my memory.

I traveled out to the shore, put my blood on the tracks, putting together all that the music lacked. Had an argument with the landlord, mistakenly called him an overlord. I don't think I'll ever be pure, but I don't really want all that much more.

red cup.

may 27th

What's the best way to get back at an ex? Would it be to fuck her best friend? Maybe I could kick her brother's ass. On second thought that kid looks like he works out. Maybe I could put a flaming bag of shit on her car hood, or in her mailbox, or maybe her porch. Can't do the porch, then her dad will kick my ass. Maybe I could write her a strongly worded letter. Really strongly worded. I could use those big words I learned in SAT class and finally have a practical application for them.

You got any suggestions? Any pearls of wisdom? Any sort of retaliation that worked well for you? When I was with her she made me feel like I wanted to end wars, now I just want to go Jack Bauer 'closed casket' on somebody's ass. Not her, but someone. I love her too much. Love always mutates to something ugly, it never stays right. Never keeps its sheen. A golden turd is still a piece of shit. I love her. She broke me.

from the broken hearted club.

may 30th

Scream for peace. Scream for pain. Scream for these things all the same. He thinks his mom is out on a date. He sits in his room and plays the piano. Slapping the ivory keys with an accuracy like Smalls, he plays to drown out the screaming upstairs. It happens around 7 p.m. every night, that must be the time that the husband gets home from work .The boy puts on the Mets, they're losing 7-0.

Oliver Perez is terrible. Just really awful. He hasn't heard from his ex in a few days. He called her, but she never picked up. A return call never came, that was four days ago. Now he's got the cocaine blues, had them for a year or two. They come whenever the timing is good, usually the summer, that is the time he feels them the most. They last for a few weeks at a time, making him itch his eyes and scream. I think I'm feeling them right now.He just broke the fourth wall, fuck. Now everyone knows his secret, they know where he lies. He's gonna go before he gives up too much.

conversations with.

may 31ˢᵗ

Then there is nothing. Marie flips through the book, empty page after empty page. Each page a single notation on the bottom with the date, almost as to say he was still alive this day. The lost period. The long weekend. Andrew at his worst. So bad he couldn't even state it. He would be sitting in that diner some two weeks later. Marie closes the book, choosing to forego the remaining pages, no longer wanting to stare at the car wreck. The book drops out of her hands.

CHAPTER THIRTY ONE

Marie has an early appointment this morning. She drags her ass out of bed and heads for the bathroom. The water pressure sucks, drowning her head in cold water. It wakes her up at least. She gets dressed quickly, grabbing her bag and power walking toward the front door. Marie rifles through her bag looking for keys. Coming up with nothing, she quickly moves through the apartment, searching tabletops and seat cushions. She walks into the bedroom, spotting her keys on the dresser. Next to it is Andrew's notebook. She grabs both and throws them in her bag. Remembering that it's due to rain later, Marie grabs her hooded green jacket and heads out the door.

It's cold on the street—unusually brisk for this time of year. Days were starting to shorten, fall coming fast, the leaves escaping into drainpipes and garbage trucks. Marie has lost track of time. The summer was gone.

"Fuck, it's almost September," Marie grumbles to herself. The crosswalk signal changes, Marie walking across the intersection, feeling the wind cut through her, chilling her to her bones. She looks into the coffee shop on the corner, looking to take shelter from the coming storm. Peeking through the window she sees morning commuters and caffeine addicts looking for their morning fix, packed like sardines into the hip establishment. Marie opts for the side of the building, standing behind the brick and mortar, the wind rubbing right up against the building in front of her—the sound of it whistling on down the block as loud as the passing cabs and people. It feels warmer on the corner of this building. Marie dips her hands into her jacket pockets and looks out into the street, watching it all go down. Her head fades down to her shoes, looking at her shoes sitting on the concrete. The cracks of this old cement break out to every corner—1,000 little reminders of the years. It felt so lonely on this corner.

Marie reaches into her bag and pulls out his notebook. She flips through the pages, her eyes canvasing the blank pine. She flips and flips and flips until she finds a scrawl deep toward the back of the parchment.

I heard you today. Over the car horns and yelling children.

I heard you.

I heard you say to stop being sad.

To stop laying in bed, to stop sulking.

I heard you say that you didn't teach me to act that way.

To feel sorry for myself.

I heard you say that you were doing great now.

That now, you get to see me every minute of the day.

I heard you say 'take your vitamins' like some sort of spiritual Hulk Hogan.

So I'm gonna do that.

I'm gonna listen for as long as you want to talk.

I've turned off my Internet, the phone is next.

I'm here to listen, to learn one or two more lessons.

I can feel you on my fingers and arms, in my heart and mind and soul.

I hear you.

Just keep talking, just keep talking.

Never be too far away.

I wish I could just talk to you one more time. Just one more quick word. I wish you could teach me one more thing. I'm lost without you. I think I've really fucked it up this time. I've been too bad for too long and to too many people. I'm sorry. I'm gonna try to be better. Try to make it up to Mom. Try to make it up to Marie. I just don't know if I'll ever be able to. Help me.

I love you, I'll only do things to make you proud.

None of us got enough time with you, but your spirit is immortal and it's sitting right next to me.

skinny man.

june 15th

Marie flips through the rest of the pages to see nothing—his last words on his last day.

It starts to rain.

PART SEVEN: RUNAWAY

CHAPTER THIRTY TWO

Andrew wakes up to a horrible pain in his chest. The sun batters the apartment, the product of no shades on the windows. He rises from his stupor, rolling onto his side. This pain is otherworldly in its persistence. He rubs his eyes open, looking around the room, he doesn't know where he is—an empty apartment aside from the bed he was laying on. He looks down, he slept in his clothes it seems, his shoes still tied tight. He pulls at his ripped white T-shirt, murmuring, "Fuck." Must have been a crazy night. Andrew rolls out of bed and grabs his blue jacket draped over the radiator. Putting it on, he makes sure he has everything and then heads out of this place, wherever he is.

The sky is even brighter outside, burning Andrew's eyes as he appears through the building's front door. It smells on the street. It must be the days-old garbage baking in the barbeque of the morning. Andrew pats his pocket looking for sunglasses. Nothing. He walks out from under the awning and squints down at the ground. Even the sidewalk granite seems lunar in its glare. He feels the heat through his shoes, cooking the rubber of his Chucks. If he stayed in any one place, he would probably melt into the sidewalk. He starts to move.

As Andrew begins to walk, the pain in his chest subsides. He can't believe his shirt ripped, he really likes this one, as plain as it is. His stomach growls, he should have finished that sandwich last night. The sun is burning the back of his neck, the tip of his nose. Fuck, it's hot.

Ducking into a local convenience shop, Andrew grabs a bagel and a Gatorade and brings them to the counter. He reaches into his pockets but pulls out nothing, no cash or debit card to be found. Must have left his card at the bar last night. He departs without the food.

The streets were surprisingly empty for this time of day, wait what time is it? Andrew looks at his watch, it reads 3:37 a.m. He shakes it, then puts it to his ear. Broken.

"That can't be right."

The pain returns to his chest, this time causing him to fall to one knee. Andrew thinks he's having a heart attack, he looks around for help, but no one is near. He closes his eyes and breathes, the pain once again fading from prominence. Andrew lies down on the sidewalk, staring up at the sky. On this New York City morning there is not a cloud to be seen, just one big bright sun. Even though he could feel the heat at his back, lying down on this sidewalk makes Andrew feel better.

Andrew walks into a local hospital to get checked out, see what is wrong with his ticker. The emergency room is empty, not one broken arm or concussion or car accident. Andrew rubs his thumbs, looking around at the machines in observation room two.

That looks expensive. What's taking so long? No one's here. Shit—no one's here. Maybe everybody's off today. Is it a holiday? I don't think so. The pain's not that bad anymore; maybe I should get out of here. I don't have insurance; well I do but it's shitty...every insurance policy is shitty. Let me rephrase—mine is the shittiest.

The curtain flies open.

"It's so weird, I've never had this pain before and I woke up this morning and it was shooting through my whole body," Andrew explains to the attending.

"What did you do last night?" she asks.

Andrew thinks for a second, "To be honest, I don't really remember. I think I went out...I woke up in some strange apartment this morning."

The attending looks at Andrew funny.

The emergency room physicians run a battery of tests, all coming up empty, except for one. Andrew hears this through the curtain, playing dumb when the doctor finally comes in. The doctor runs through the results of the tests, Andrew zones out.

Just give me an answer, asshole. I heard you through the curtain. It's a curtain, dipshit, not a bank vault. It's because I have shitty insurance. Right? You found something...but I can't pay for it. So you're gonna kick me out and then I'm gonna drop dead on the toilet next week...like Elvis. I can't believe Elvis died on the toilet.

"Alright, it's nice meeting you," the doctor says, turning and dropping the chart on the edge of the bed.

Soon he's gone, no answer given, giving way to a nice nurse with a smile as bright as that sun Andrew was just staring into.

Then the words, 'lump' and 'found' are uttered. Andrew stands at attention.

"What time will you guys know...like when...will you know whether or not...well," Andrew stammers out of his mouth.

The nurse with the well intentioned smile looks back at Andrew and responds, "Well we're gonna send in the follow up tests right now and then we'll see what happens."

"So like 5...6...6:30 p.m....," Andrew replies, rubbing his toes into the cold hospital tile as if he was digging into a batter's box.

"I wouldn't have that information, but I assure you that when I know, you'll know as soon as possible."

Andrew nods his head and applies a fake smile to his mug. He turns around and begins to walk toward the elevator of the hospital. As he shuffles his scuffed shoes against the stark white tile that makes up this interesting floor design, he rubs his eyes. That one lump has now completely enraptured his thoughts. That one lump that may have lived with him for a long time and never notified its landlord when it moved in. That one lump was a squatter. Andrew just hopes this squatter wasn't quietly drenching the basement with kerosene while his girlfriend forgot to turn off her straightener. Man those things are dangerous.

Fuck. I don't wanna die on the toilet.

As Andrew descends the floors, he peeks out of the elevator. ICU, cancer ward, burn ward, prenatal ICU, prenatal burn ward, shit this place is depressing. Andrew has made it his mission to avoid hospitals. Ever since his father came into this place with a small infection and never made it back out. Andrew usually wouldn't consider going to a hospital unless his head was severed so badly that he would be walking around with it in his arms like the Headless Horseman. These places spook him; they feel like the hand of death is reaching out and grabbing as many victims as it could. But now he had to break that vow, because of that fucking lump.

Now he waits, which may be the largest sin of hospitals, the waiting. The unknown of what's next. The next prognosis, the next set back, the next piece of bad news. Good news always comes quickly; doctor's can seemingly tell in ten seconds that you'll be fine. The bad news is the one that always takes the longest to come back around. It doesn't help that Andrew is a professional shithead basket case.

As Andrew gets off the elevator, he squints his eyes to adjust to the lobby lights. The lights are so bright here, there must be a reason for that. Maybe hospitals have brighter lights to make it seem less depressing? Less foreboding? Make it more heavenly? Surely it's not any of the above.

Andrew walks past an Asian family, the youngest carrying a "Get Well Soon" balloon. The young boy wears a smile, he must be no older then four or five. His eyes bounce around this bright lobby as if it were this cool new place he's never been. Drinking in every detail, his head on a swivel, he tries to absorb every bit of this new place, a place that he has no idea is so rotten behind its brightly lit entrance. Andrew looks at the rest of the family. As the age rises, the happiness seems less so. The middle child wears somewhat of a scowl, banging his Nintendo DS against his leg, either mad at the game or trying the trick of making the batteries last longer. The oldest child, a girl, looks tired, weak even. You can see all of the stress her mother has faced has worn on the girl. The oldest sibling always gets the blowback, the quiet moments when the parent breaks down and can't hide it. The younger ones usually don't feel the terrible sense of dread in the house, but the oldest always do. The youngest are always blissfully unaware; maybe it's better that way. The mother looks as if she has been hit by Thor's hammer. Her body slumped, her eye's bloodshot, her hair a mess. She staggers like a boxer that is heading out for another round of getting the shit kicked out of him—and being unable to do anything to change that fact. It's a terrible common moment of places such as these.

Andrew walks through the automatic doors and out onto the sidewalk, a sidewalk still unusually sparse for this time of day. He pokes through his jacket and finds a smushed pack of cigarettes. He bums a light off a bum and begins to walk—thinking of what, if anything, he could do to kill err---spend his time doing while waiting for this nurse's phone call.

Andrew wanders the sidewalks, passing through changes in status, wealth, culture and nationality. Seeing the dregs and high echelon of New York in only so many steps, Andrew walks through this churning machine.

His legs finally tire and he falls into a chair in Bryant Park. He people watches families, poets, dogs, each covering some sort of real estate in his airspace. It's quiet, yet brimming through the tall trees. Andrew sees a mother pushing a newborn in a carriage, only stopping to pull a hat down over the child's eyes. Nearby, an elderly man struts with his cane, a woman of equal age and frailty on his arm. They hold the spark of a much younger couple, some of whom they pass. While this couple, who has lived to see wars and depression and political unrest, enjoy the beauty of this New York day, their younger, former selves doodle in notebooks or make out on the steps. There seems to be no better signifier of the circle of life then the park at this very moment. The trees that line it seemingly form a barrier from the outside world. The car honks, the unbridled racism and salty language, all scrubbed from this utopia. All of it couldn't be more depressing to Andrew.

Here he is, completely alone. No one to tell that he may be dying or already dead by the time that test comes back. Not even a fake friend who could feign sorrow or worry. All the happiness that envelopes this park simply reminds him how alone he really is. He would never again be part of that young couple making out on the steps, and if news later was grim, he would never be a part of that elderly couple. Andrew closes his eyes and runs things through his mind. His mind is playing tricks, showing him the past, the image of the tumor growing inside his body. He really can't trust his brain; in fact no one should. He opens his eyes and nothing has changed, no one has saved him or kissed him or held him. He's still that weird guy sitting by himself, leering into the windows of other people's lives. That window feels so thick, so unbreakable.

Andrew gets to his feet and walks away. Exiting the park, he takes a turn and glances back one more time, letting the image of this vibrant park stick in his mind for just a few seconds. The way the trees move with the wind, the shade those same trees give to people looking for a respite from the hot summer sun. Then he turns and begins to walk again. He is never going to come back to this park.

Down 42nd Street, its sidewalk teems with people. Shoulder to shoulder, sidewalk to storefront, an overwhelming amount of human per square foot. He comes upon Grand Central Station, an epicenter of humanity if there ever was one. He moves quickly through the doors and into the station, dodging the newspaper men—when his phone starts vibrating in his pocket. Stopping dead in his walk, Andrew reaches into his pocket and gets bumped into by three or four people making there way through the door behind him. They throw him a scowl and keep moving on their way. As he fumbles around his pocket, all the thoughts of that prognosis bounce in his head. The reaper may be on the other end of the line. Looking at the caller ID, he sees an unknown number. He opens the phone and puts it to his ear, sticking his index finger in the other.

The voice on the other end is soft, quiet and has no chance of being heard in the noise of this hall. Andrew quickly retreats outside which, while not much better, gives the noise some more room to inhabit.

"Hello?" Andrew says into the receiver. The voice on the other end responds, "Is this Scott?" Andrew's shoulders slump, "No, this isn't Scott...His number is 8940, mine is 8904. Okay, goodbye."

Andrew hangs up the phone and puts it back into his pocket. This Scott guy is popular. Andrew gets one or two calls a week due to Scott's friends' dyslexia.

Andrew heads back into Grand Central and makes his way to the ticket window, but soon remembers he has no cash. He shuffles out of the line like he has somewhere to go. He instead retreats to the downstairs food court, to people watch. Each and every person going somewhere, just passing through this place, except Andrew. He's stuck here. Andrew bums a cup of water off one of the workers at the pizza stand. He returns to his seat, savoring the water, until there is not one drop left.

He falls asleep sitting up in his chair, holding his empty paper cup.

Andrew wakes up a short time later, his chest thumping, his tumor an eternal alarm clock. He passed out, just a blankness upon waking. He didn't dream about anything, doesn't know how long he had been out. Everything looks the same, people still moving, still boarding trains, buying overpriced gum. He stretches his arms, rubs a cramp out of his neck, these chairs are so damn uncomfortable.

A hundred dollar bill sits in his empty paper cup.

"Holy shit."

Andrew gets up and looks around, looking for someone playing a trick on him. Nothing.

"I should do this more often."

Andrew goes back upstairs and buys a train ticket, heading to track 25.

It's one of those new trains. Andrew doesn't care much for it. The seats on the older model trains were broken in, with thousands of asses of all sizes

DEATH AND OTHER THINGS

mushing the pleather into a fine comfort. Andrew appreciates older things, they remind him of the past. Everything new brings some string to it, some new wrinkle. Things were easier back then. These new seats lost the plether and went with some synthetic kind of plastic. Andrew shifts in his seat. He cranes his neck up over the rows to see a woman taking her seat toward the front of the car.

Her hair is a black, reminding him of someone, but he's not quite sure of whom. A scarf lines her neck—an oddity, considering the day. Small-boxed eyeglass frames lay on her nose, a book under her left arm. She's too good looking to talk to. Andrew goes back to looking out the window onto the platform. The window's scratched, with the numbers 137 and 42 etched into the corners of the frame. Numbers that remind him of his youth.

There was always something about trains that Andrew liked. Maybe it was the community of the whole thing. Maybe it was that no matter what, Andrew knew where he would eventually end up. The track was always finished, no detours or half built bridges. They were always remarkably on time, rarely any delays. No suspense really—steady, calm, no surprises. Maybe that's why these new seats bother him.

Andrew runs his fingers along the scratches. He thinks about where to get off this train once it stops moving. Maybe get off in the Bronx, go check out his parents' old neighborhood. Maybe see his grandparents, he hasn't seen them in a while. He wonders if they even still have the house there. The train closes its doors and begins to pull out of the station. Andrew slumps into his very uncomfortable seat and presses his forehead against the window, feeling the vibrations of the train against his skin. The ping of the automated voice narrating his departure, telling him where he is going.

Out of the corner of his eye, Andrew sees a man running down the platform after the train. Turning his head, Andrew spots a disheveled man wearing a

333

pinstriped suit, carrying a suitcase with sweat pouring down his face. The man's race is a losing one as the train picks up speed, soon turning the sprinting man into a speck on the horizon.

CHAPTER THIRTY THREE

Getting off the train in White Plains, Andrew shuffles down the steps to the street. White Plains was a strange town, a mix of urban and rural, business high-rises, malls and small bodegas. The sky has turned a dull gray, clouds blocking the sun. The atmosphere lends itself to impending rain. This is one of the last stops on the Harlem line before reaching Connecticut. Andrew has nothing in Connecticut, he has nothing much here, but definitely nothing in Connecticut. Like the New York ones before this train ride, Andrew begins to wander these White Plains streets.

He gazes upward at some of the buildings—they look tired. They look like they need rejuvenation, as if they are tired, old runway models. They used to be the cream of the crop, servicing companies that felt New York City was too big for them, but also that anything north of here was the boonies. Now they lay empty, floors and floors on the grid showing nothing between the glass and mortar. Urban decay, unstable markets and the virtual distrust in the private sector lead to the absence of these monoliths of business.

Andrew enters one of the taller buildings, its ledger reading 2 North Lexington Avenue. As he passes the double glass doors, Andrew sees an empty, wide open lobby. The only sign of the ferns that once lined the windows are the brown rings that remain on the lobby floor. The waterfall pond, which once

335

allowed for people to throw coins for good luck, is bone dry—brown rust starting to envelop it.

Andrew continues through the lobby, past the couches and old leather chairs that used to hold potential new job applicants and deliverymen waiting for payment. Moving toward the security desk, Andrew spots a 'Back in 5 Minutes' sign. Its paper yellow and dogged, it looks like it had survived since Draper was hocking ads—its calligraphy a relic of a time when business was proper and customary.

Andrew takes a seat in one of the old leather chairs and decides to wait until the guard comes back. He doesn't want to get popped for trespassing in a building. Looking down at his watch, the time read 3:37 a.m.

"I gotta get this thing fixed."

When Andrew closes his eyes, he can hear the old sounds bouncing off the walls of this once fluid building. The sounds of people coming and going from lunch, meetings, appointments. The sounds remain trapped in these walls like a seashell found at the beach. No matter how far removed from those times, it holds these old sounds in its epidermis.

Still no sign of the guard. Andrew rises to his feet and walks over to the ledger. Peering down the list, he sees some familiar names.

C.A.T.H. CO PORATI N 2ND F OOR

MERSON, STRICKER, LEB WITZ AND ASSOCIATES 3RD FLOOR

B.B.D.O. 4TH FL R

PLAIN JANE 7TH FLOO

BOVI E LTD. 8TH FLOOR

DEATH AND OTHER THINGS

PATTY, DU K, KEARY 10TH LOOR

Some of the rubber white letters had fallen away or changed colors based on their age. The glass case containing the ledger has a small crack in the right corner, maybe due to a frustrated fist, or a missing key.

Andrew turns and walks toward the elevators. The little 'UP' button still lighting up like it once did. The large gold doors part and Andrew boards the vessel skywards. Pushing the button for the seventh floor, the doors close. Andrew rests on the banister along the back wall, cracking his neck as he moves it to the left. As this old elevator makes its way up the floors with a slow draw, Andrew's eyes wander around the hanging box. Water damaged ceiling tiles, a busted light for the third floor sign above the doors, a large brownish stain in the back right corner. This building has aged like a bad wine, all of its one-time promise broken in different ways.

Just before the elevator reaches its destination, the door jams, allowing a few inches of vision out onto the floor. Andrew gets between the doors and pushes them open. Pulling himself up and sneaking out of the door before it closes on him, he enters the elevator lobby of Plain Jane.

The walls of Plain Jane are a dull yellow. The glass door separating the elevator lobby and the front desk is propped open with a brick. As Andrew begins to navigate the halls, he comes upon empty office after empty office. Some of them still have furniture, others just have a phone sitting in the middle of the room. Cobwebs have begun to form in the corners of the ceilings. Rolling chairs lay on their sides as if the running of the bulls came through.

Picking one chair up and setting it right, Andrew crosses the bullpen of cubicles and ventures over to the other side of the floor. Stopping in front of the third door from the right, Andrew wipes a layer of dust off the door plaque. It reads 'MOLLY BANK'

Molly was Andrew's first boss. When he met her, she was a kind woman in her 50's, blond hair with a varying amount of gray strands weaved through depending on the last time she had dyed it. She had kind eyes and a better heart. She had lost her husband a year into their marriage. Cancer got him—six weeks later he was dead. After that, she could have lived a less than ordinary life, yet she picked herself up. She started this company, a small line of specialty handbags. It started in her living room, grew to a small store in Scarsdale, then to this office, where they shipped her handbags all over the country. She named the company after her mother, who moved in with her after her husband, Molly's father, passed away.

She hired Andrew on a Tuesday. He sat in those chairs downstairs, top button buttoned, solid black tie, hand sweat crinkling the corners of his resume. She was a people person, could read them in ten seconds. She sat down with Andrew and gave him the job within five minutes. Andrew was eighteen, right out of high school, unsure of what he wanted to do with his life. He had seen the ad in the *Journal News* and figured that by working at a handbag company he could meet a lot of girls. He wasn't wrong. He met a lot of them in his time at Plain Jane, dated a few of them too.

Andrew wonders how Molly was. He had lost touch with her in recent years, an occurrence that happened to a lot of people in Andrew's life. He continues to roam the halls, finding that what he had already seen was not much different than what lay ahead of him. She must be in her late 60's by now. Not knowing the way this business left this building, by choice or by bankruptcy, Andrew wonders if she's still making handbags. They brought her so much joy, the creation of something that hadn't existed five minutes previously. Molly was the American initiative. She was of the time when America built things, something that America was really, and still could be if pressed, good at. Now America is stocks and IRAs and CDs. The emphasis has moved away from building shit, to now putting our money into something that we don't really understand but are told is the greatest thing in the world—that we can make money by literally doing *nothing*. An idea that has gained traction in the malaise generations that have followed Molly's. America used to be a nation of builders, now we are a nation of followers and consumers. We consume and consume and consume until our glutinous asses can consume no longer. We used to innovate and reshape and build everything bigger and stronger. Now we import everything and send nothing of value back. America's biggest exports are now summer action films, Michael Bay, our American Steel. It's a vomit. Thinking of all these things, Andrew hypothesizes that this boutique probably left the building unwillingly.

Andrew returns to Molly's office and slides the door plaque out of its holder. Putting it into his back pocket, Andrew makes his way back to the elevator. Pushing the 'DOWN' button, the doors creak open slowly and then outright stop.

Rather than risk plummeting to his death, Andrew opts for the stairs. Like he used to do on Friday afternoons, he navigates those stairs quickly, down and out of the building in less than five minutes. As he passes through the glass front doors again, he peers around at the foliage of the block. The tree leaves are the only things alive on this block. Andrew feels like the black widow, anything in his atmosphere dying in his wake. He wishes that the sidewalk would crack open and swallow everything up.

He begins to walk again. Soon he comes upon an old movie theater. The box office window has a crack that spans from top to bottom, a strip of clear duct tape the only thing holding everything together. The girl in the ticket window looks bored, this theater is long past its prime, long past the time when young couples would come and make out on Friday nights during a horror movie. By the looks of it, this establishment is now frequented by freaks and geeks—weird dudes with a hard on for 70's fetish cinema and floors that were sticky for reasons other then spilled soda. Andrew went on a date here once, it was some splatter flick, couldn't remember which one.

He buys a ticket from the bored girl in the box office window and enters the lobby. Its walls were stark, stained wall-to-wall carpets that haven't been cleaned in years, the place smells of body odor and stale popcorn. Andrew continues toward the theaters, passing concessions stands twirling grilled hotdogs that are brown and shriveled. This place is so dead inside, deafeningly quiet, aside from the occasional exploitation screaming that slunk out of the theater door. A gawky teenager stands at the ticket collection box, tapping away on his cell phone, probably telling the person on the other end of the line how much his job sucks, or maybe how awesome it is to get paid to stand in a living horror painting. This place is as much of a set as the ones on the screen. It is aged to perfection; a killer gunfight could occur in this theater lobby. The kid takes Andrew's ticket, tears it and mumbles, "Theater Two," peeking up from his cell phone only slightly.

Theater Two was surprisingly less repulsive than the rest of the establishment. Taking a seat in the seventh row, Andrew props his legs up on the seat in front of him. He watches ads for a local liquor store and supermarket flicker up on the screen. A few minutes pass when a man in a trench coat enters the theater and sits two rows in front and two seats away from Andrew. The trench coated man does not move from his seat for the next hour and a half as Andrew experiences the whole bloody 35 millimeter affair. As the credits begin to roll, after the huge Mexican stand off to end the picture, the trench coated man rises to his feet and exits the theater. Andrew follows suit and staggers out to the lobby, worn out from the overload of gloriously bad cinema. However bad it was, it feels comforting to him, the shared experience of witnessing something with others, even if it was a creepy trench coated guy. Movies and their theaters are the only true community experiences left. It took his mind off of...oh shit—

Andrew grabs his phone out of his pocket to see his received call log still empty, no call from the hospital. This slow waiting game was starting to get worse than whatever news would come through the line. Andrew looks back into that dank theater, the end credits still rolling, and returns to his seat. He sits down and folds his hands in his lap. The gawky ticket taker comes into the theater to give a cursory look for trash. Headphones on, his head rocks back and forth to a soundtrack that is not in sync with the current loud heavy metal playing over the theater speakers. It makes this place even stranger. After darting in and out of rows quickly, stopping only briefly to indulge in an apparent guitar solo, the teen leaves quietly, back out to the lobby.

The credits stop and Andrew thinks about a double feature. The horror of the call that he's expecting would fit in with whatever the screen was displaying at any given moment. Then he thinks about finding the highest bridge, or going to that hardware store on the corner and buying some cement to tie around his ankles. What better way to fight the disease then to not let it kill you at all? Andrew wasn't a tremendously spiritual man, apparent by the fact that when people usually dread something, they head to church, not the nearest grindhouse theater. Finally he thinks about his dad, that maybe he could see him again, if there was in fact an afterlife. The only person who ever truly cared, the person who kept his head above water, the loss that sent him into the tailspin. Since his father's death he has been a shell, lying in a crater of what was once a successful life. Now he sits in a movie theater with cum on the floor at three o'clock in the afternoon.

Then he thinks about how he would fuck it up. Instead of offing himself, he would end up paralyzed or turn into a vegetable and, in all of its irony, end up back in that hospital he so loathed. It's the defeatist attitude in him.

The supermarket ads pop back up again.

CHAPTER THIRTY FOUR

Andrew flips through the phone book, thumbing pages, looking for a name. The sky has grayed a bit more. Early afternoon has crept up over the horizon. As he moves his finger slowly down the page, he sees the name he was searching for—'MOLLY BANK.' Andrew tears the page out of the book, folds it twice and places it in his back pocket. He exits the phone booth and flags down a cab.

"Can you take me here?" Andrew asks, handing the phone book page through the glass.

The man behind the wheel studies the paper, crinkles his nose and passes the page back to Andrew. Andrew settles into the back seat, dropping his head back and closing his eyes. The cab takes a left at the intersection of Wright and Pilgrim. As it speeds down this expansive, empty avenue, rain hits the car hood. Andrew opens the eyes in his reclined head and sees the rain hitting the back window—a few inches from his retinas. The rain gets heavier; streaming down the window, its motion resembling a waterfall going sky high from Andrew's perspective. He steadies his gaze on the water wonder, the water tapering and widening on different parts of the window. The cab hits a pothole and Andrew is jarred back to reality. He tries to regain his previous perspective, but it is gone just as quickly as it had arrived. Andrew soon dozes off.

That yellow cab idles in front its destination. Andrew's knocked out. The cab driver lets the gas go and then jams on the breaks quickly—hoping to awake the sleeping dreamer in the back seat. Andrew awakens, rubbing his eyes and looking up, seeing the cab driver staring through him from the rear view mirror. Puddles sit on the sidewalks after that quick storm.

The house is much the same color as 'PLAIN JANE' was. A dim yellow covers the sidings. The window has a broken pane, the grass a bit unkempt—nothing that a cut in the near future couldn't remedy. Andrew closes the cab door and approaches the closed white fence. Jiggering with the broken lock, he pushes open the small fence door. It looks a little ragged at the edges, this whole thing. Molly always favored neatness and completeness. Andrew's gut starts to churn. As he climbs the porch stairs he catches some glimpses into the house. The dining room table, a plate still sitting at its head, a couch in the next room over—all its pillows in a row. A clash.

Andrew knocks on the door. Moments pass. No noises creep from the home's floorboards. This time, Andrew rings the doorbell. Again, no response. He goes up to the window nearest him and peers in—there's no one home. Maybe she's off food shopping or at work or at church, there are 1,000 places she could be. Andrew pulls the metal nameplate out of his pocket and puts it down in front of the door.

Andrew hears a voice from behind. "Can I help you?" it says. Andrew looks out upon a woman in her mid-50's standing at the edge of the fence.

"Who are you looking for?" she continues. Andrew does a double take and then walks down the stairs.

"I'm looking for something—err someone, Molly Bank, does she still live here?" Andrew replies. The woman looks back at Andrew for a second and runs her hands through her hair.

343

"Are you a bill collector?" the woman asks. Andrew shakes his head from side to side.

"You a member of her family?" the woman asks. Andrew shakes his head and replies, "No."

"Well I'm sorry to be the one to tell you this, but Molly passed away last week," the woman says, once again running her hands through her hair. Andrew's eyes drop.

"Shit," is all that Andrew could muster.

"Her daughters have been around the past few days...are you a friend of theirs?" Andrew turns and takes a look back at the house. "No, I didn't even know she had daughters."

Andrew turns again to look at the woman. She has kind eyes. There are a few seconds of silence between them before he asks, "I hate to be morbid, but how did Molly die?"

"Drunk driver. She was coming home from dinner...a drunk guy ran a light and hit her," the woman replies. Andrew nods his head, bobblehead like, trying to comprehend the information.

"Drunk driver," he mumbles to himself, letting it soak into his brain.

"Do you want me to give the girls a call, let them know that you're here?" Andrew turns again and looks at the nameplate leaning against the door. It becomes strangely hypnotizing.

"Do you want me to call the girls?" the woman repeats. Andrew finally breaks his gaze and turns back around. He looks at the woman and smiles.

"No, that's alright...they got enough going on. Please send along my sympathy," Andrew says, zippering his jacket up to his neck.

Andrew walks toward the sidewalk and opens the fence door, under the watchful gaze of the lady who likes playing with her hair.

"I will—who should I say it's from?" she asks. Andrew closes the gate and looks up at the woman.

"Nobody, they won't know me."

Andrew waves to the woman and begins walking down the sidewalk. Jamming his hands in his pockets, he wanders the streets of this little neighborhood. He always wanted to live in one of these houses, maybe have a family, take a kid to soccer practice. It feels so close to him, that it should have been him. He feels a stinging the back of his neck. He's achy, almost as if his body is shutting down. He feels empty inside. He feels worthless, in all honesty. A ship lost at sea with a drunken captain behind the wheel.

He's fucked up so badly; Andrew feels he's reached the point of no return— he's past the point of saving. Who cares enough to save someone who has disappointed everyone so many times, alienated, betrayed, let loved ones float away?

If his dad was around, maybe he wouldn't be this way. He would have kicked his ass, told him to stop being such a baby.

It begins to drizzle.

After wandering for an hour, Andrew collapses into a park bench, his legs exhausted; he hasn't walked this much in a long time. Andrew looks out into the street, a two-way with stores lining one side and this pretty park on the other. Across the street from Andrew stands a diner and an office building. He thinks briefly about heading into the diner for some lunch, deciding against it. He was never one for diner food.

Maybe he'll start a new life here—go into that office building and get a job, any job, be a janitor even. Didn't really matter much; he just has to shake this feeling of inadequacy. He needs to stop being such a whiner; God he whined a lot.

He stares out into that street—the dust and dirt hopping with every passing car. He stands up his eyes craning upwards toward those trees above his head, rustling in the breeze, rain falling off the leaves. The drops increase, starting like a leaky faucet, soon a shower, then a reservoir. It's pouring. Andrew stays still, letting the rain soak him, down to skin. His hair in his eyes, his ripped shirt soaked through. He just stands there. He didn't have anywhere to seek shelter, these flimsy trees his only umbrella.

"I'm gonna fly out of here, get on a spaceship and zoom away. I'm done making these mistakes, these errors of belief. If this lump is going do to its worst, I'm not gonna go out like some bum in the street. A panhandler at Grand Central, passed out in a chair. I know I'm dead, just not yet... not until I do some things first. If it doesn't work out, there's always the road. I'll keep going until I find a new home."

Andrew takes his cell phone out his of pocket and leaves it on the bench. He didn't want to know anymore. He doesn't need to know.

He sticks his arm out, feeling the wind in his fingers. The pain has dulled a bit, wasn't as biting in his chest.

A cabbie stops and Andrew climbs in.

"Take me home."

Andrew looks out the window as the cabbie drives past the state line, his radio tuned to latter day punk, "Monkey Gone to Heaven" by Frank Black, making the pulses of both men jump and dive. The rain comes and goes, beating the windshield with anger at moments. Andrew stays looking out the window.

Miles rang up on the odometer. He drives for days. The rain stops, the sun blooming on the zephyr.

He could get lost in this trip, this passing of colors, the age of the road felt with every uneven slope, every pothole. The cabdriver never turns around, staying fixed on the upcoming road. Andrew can't see the man's eyes, his ballcap pulled down low on his forehead.

The cab slows; rolling soon to a stop.

Then he sees her, his mother, sitting at a small table, sipping on an iced coffee—outside a catering bistro in a snooty neighborhood. She started here a few years back, made a pretty good living. She rose from the ashes while Andrew stayed burning slowly.

Andrew hands over the remaining money in his pocket to the cab driver, gives him a little bit more for tip and exits the cab. He stands and watches his mother, flipping through a magazine, as the cab pulls away behind him. She looks so good.

She always protected him, gave him the means to grow, and he did nothing but destroy her. Leave her at her most pressing time. She had just buried her husband, Andrew's father, when he left, for some reason that he can't even remember. His stupid macho bullshit, his ridiculous ego, and his inflated idea of what it is to grieve.

He doesn't know what to say to her. Apologize? Beg for forgiveness? Or just sit and talk; tell his mother that he misses her. He remains standing in that street, almost hoping a wayward car would take him out before he would have to make a decision.

This moment is his life, his mouth strong, his soul weak. He never wanted to make a decision, just wanted to coast, hope things were done for him, cry when they weren't. He's a coward in every sense of the word. He thinks about walking away again, right now—just keep on living alone, not apologizing, not making peace. Go back to dying alone. This is different. He doesn't know why, but he feels somewhere deeper, that he needs to be in this place. Without making peace, he would die alone, that would be assured, even if he dropped dead right on 42nd Street at midday. He couldn't live with that pain of doing the two of them wrong anymore, a pain more powerful than whatever caused him to collapse. That pain—the pain of running away from his mother and then running from Marie not too long after. He needs to take the first step.

He puts one foot in front of the other and begins to walk—a meaningful step, the first time in quite some time. She looks up from her magazine and sees him. She gets up and puts her arms around him. He hugs his mother and gives her a kiss, holding her tight for every second that he missed her. They sit down and talk outside that bistro, tell their recollections, never once speaking about the day Andrew left. A mother's compassion—the only true thing left in this world.

Andrew and his mother go for a walk, visiting a park that she brought him to when he was just an infant. Andrew weeps when he sees the tree his mother had planted for his father while he was away.

They sit in the park for a few hours, just talking.

"I feel like I'm in a dream," he says.

"What makes you think it's a dream?"

"I feel like I'm not here, even though I am," Andrew replies.

As the sun goes down, the moon makes the park glow and the two retreat home. Andrew walks into his former home to see nothing out of place, his room just the same as he left it.

All he can think is how he let this all slip away. Even through all of the shit he did to his mother, she never once stopped caring about him.

"I prayed for you every day," she says during one conversation, continuing by saying that she wished that it somehow reached him.

They talk all night. Andrew speaks of where he went, what he tried to do to let go of the pain, try and start anew. An exercise that ultimately led him back here. He speaks of every night he thought about calling her, telling her that he was on the next train or plane back to her, that he was going to move heaven and earth to try and fix things.

"Why didn't you?" she asks.

"I didn't have a quarter," he replies.

The hours reach past midnight. The teakettle rumbles when the two begin to speak truly, speaking about the earthquake that split the world apart.

The talk slows, more measured responses offered. Andrew then feels a slight twinge in his chest.

"I think...I thought...when Dad died it, you know...and all I could think of was the pain, that's all I thought about and how that pain would never go away and...I thought, you know, this is just one person and look how utterly destroyed I am...I couldn't imagine what it would be like to lose you...or Marie...I would have to die to lose that feeling, that utter hopelessness. However stupid it sounds I thought that if I have no connections, no relationships, no attachments whatsoever...it would make it easier to live. I could only disappoint myself...and frankly that ship sailed a long time ago. I wouldn't have to come home and see you be sad again or look into Marie's eyes and know that I really let her down, again and again. I felt so worthless, felt like such a drag...on people. So I checked out, I drove you away and then soon drove her away and she chased me and I beat her back at every opportunity...I was really terrible to her...but she just kept trying to push through and...I wouldn't let her. Then I got everything I ever wanted; I was truly alone, sitting on New York City corners, watching the yellow cabs scream by and cop sirens blare and people bump into each other and smelly bums on the subway sell newspapers and beg for change, surrounded by all these people who had no idea who I am...and didn't care either...had no idea how much of a loser I was, just a seat filler."

Andrew looks up to see his mother's hand on top of his.

"I know I've said this a lot tonight, but I am truly sorry for not being there for you. I was selfish; I thought my pain was more important than yours...and I'll spend the rest of my time trying to make it up to you," Andrew says.

"It's okay. I'll always love you, either way," Mary says back. Andrew and Mary drink their tea.

"Now you need to say it to her," Mary says.

CHAPTER THIRTY FIVE

Andrew wakes up in his bed. A bed. He has to think about that for a second. He hasn't had a bed in a while.

He looks through some old clothes stacked in front of his window. Stacked about ten high, shirts as old as a decade, mixed by color. Andrew pulls out a white T-shirt and a fresh pair of jeans. Throwing them on the bed, he heads to the bathroom. Taking a quick shower and brushing his teeth, Andrew washes some ugliness off himself. Returning to his room, he gets dressed and heads to the living room. It's quiet and meticulously clean, everything in its own place, save for two train tickets sticking off the end of the coffee table. He picks them up and studies them.

Andrew returns to his bedroom and takes a baseball off a bookshelf. He looks at it, spins it in his hands, feeling the stitches on his fingertips. He grips it and mimes throwing, flipping it into the air and back down into his hand. He studies it a bit longer, finally placing it in his back pocket.

Andrew grabs his father's old gym bag and packs it with clothes—a few shirts, some jeans, a dress shirt of all things. He zippers it up, grabs the train tickets off the table, a soda out of the fridge and heads for the door.

He walks into town, bag slung over his shoulder, walking like the lone gunslinger at the beginning of a western. The sun is low on the horizon, low on its overbearing nature. The landscape has cooled, a little less bright. The morning hours allowing for a brisk air to pass over this land.

Coming upon the park he sat in last night with his mother, he stops. He slowly walks over to his father's tree and gets down onto one knee. He was never much for praying; instead he mumbles some words, words only he and the tree could hear. He digs into the soil at the base of the tree, forming a cubby hole a few inches deep. Taking the baseball out of his back pocket, he drops it into the hole, using his hand to cover it with the topsoil. He buries the ball and its memories with the roots of this tree. He speaks a few more mumbled words, gets off his knee and kisses the tree.

He heads back on his way.

The street is rocky, it hasn't been paved since the winter. Andrew jumps over a pothole as he crosses the street. He looks in the large windows of his mom's shop. Different images seeping through the pane—a mother and son debating what to put on top of the boy's birthday cake, a fat man eating a donut for lunch. Andrew's mother is behind the counter, wrapping up a cake for a young couple. He continues looking through that window, like a young boy looking into a toy store. His mother hustles around the store, oblivious to the boy in the window. He walks to the door and enters, feeling the air conditioning on his face.

He catches his mother's eye, who smiles back. She finishes up with her customer and comes out from behind the counter. She and Andrew retreat to the back of the store.

"How did you sleep?" she asks, the bags under her eyes betraying what her own answer would be.

"I slept really well actually," Andrew replies.

"Good, I'm happy," Mary replies, looking down at the train tickets in Andrew's hand. "I see you found those."

"Yea, you read my mind. I was gonna come down and buy 'em this morning."

Mary nods and smiles, "Well..." she says, before pausing, "that was always gonna be your last stop."

Andrew looks back at his mother. She kisses him on the cheek and gives him a hug. The radio music drains from the room.

"I'm so happy you came back...now you can go and make peace with it all. Get back on the road and find it. I love you with all my heart."

Andrew hugs his mother a little bit harder, closing his eyes, "Thank you for always being you and never quitting. I love you and I'll see you again."

Mary smiles, "And if not... that's okay too." Andrew steps back and smiles. He then begins to weep, wiping tears from his eyes.

"I feel like I just got here, now I'm leaving again," Andrew says.

"We all leave, eventually every one of us—at least you're going somewhere cool. Go take a dip in the ocean for me...and Daddy too," Mary replies.

Andrew smiles, "He did love the beach."

"Yep," Mary says with a smile. Andrew picks up his bag and kisses his mother one more time. He walks out the front door and heads for the train. Mary watches from the window as Andrew crosses the street and disappears from view.

CHAPTER THIRTY SIX

The train is packed. Kids in wife beaters, drinking beers and screaming. A guy in a shirt and tie soaked at the armpits yelling at someone on the other end of his cell phone. It's noisy above all else. The air conditioning is broken. Andrew gets up and moves to another car, soon seeing that this phenomenon was recurring. Hot, sweating, cursing people heading into New York City on this now increasingly hot day. At each stop, people run for the doors to try and get fresh air, hoping to get just the smallest breeze or breath.

Andrew settles into one of the rear cars and tries to stay away from the windows, which are baking those closest to them like rotisserie. A guy in his 20's with a T-shirt tied around his head goes running up the center aisle, screaming about the Yankees. One of his friends follows in pursuit, yelling something about A-Rod being gay, a T-shirt also tied around his head.

An old lady across from Andrew shakes her head at the general perverse nature of the youth, silently scolding the marauding morons. The two men dodge a ticket taker asking them to quiet down and then continue their screams, soon moving onto the next car.

As the train pulls into Grand Central, the exodus begins, people running for their lives, seeking fresh air, new real estate to cool down. Andrew hangs back, watching the parade move along, breathing in the faces as they breathe in the new air. He watches the disapproving old woman slowly make her way up the ramp, at one moment swinging her cane at a young man who she finds to be annoying. Heat turns people into animals.

As the train clears and the ticket takers exit the train to their next assignment, Andrew picks up his bag and heads for the terminal. Grand Central is a zoo, almost as bad as the train. Andrew quickly moves through it, heading for the subway.

Riding the subway feels different than it had felt before. The subway car Andrew is riding is littered with earphones, books—sunglasses inside for Christ sake—all modes of turning off the person sitting or standing right in front of you. Andrew had been this way his entire life, never once looking up, his eyes tending to wander to spaces where there are no inhabitants. Sure, when a hot girl with long legs took a seat across from him, he would use his peripherals to check her out, but most of the time it's a guy with a mustard stained Giants shirt sprawled out on the subway bench. But today's different.

As the doors open to this sweaty subway car, a blind couple enters the breach. Each with their walking sticks, somewhere in their mid-40's, they float into that car and suddenly fill up that metal box with energy. Andrew's eyes gravitate to them. As the blind couple stands arm-in-arm, a gesture that might be as much function as affection, they look into each other's eyes.

They look into each other's eyes—something that is surely meaningless to someone who's blind. You can't see their eyes; you can't see the pigment, the dilation, the way they hide behind skin every few seconds. As the train makes it way down the tracks they look at each other and without saying a word, they both smile. It seemed strange, almost as if they are putting everyone on, that the walking sticks are simple props for two performance artists. The man shifts his walking stick into his left hand, currently holding onto the floor to ceiling pole, and strokes his lady's hair with his right hand. She smiles again and looks almost bashful.

A true connection that had nothing to do with khaki pants, a square jaw or some long beautiful legs. A love that had nothing to do with anything but their connection. A connection.

It truly is a connection; the couple get off at the next station. Andrew looks out through the subway window as the couple walks arm-in-arm away. A space, a bubble almost, of people forming around them. Soon the crowd envelopes them and they disappear. Andrew looks above the crowd, but they're gone.

Penn Station was just as ugly as Grand Central. Boarding his train to the coast, Andrew settles into a comfy seat and falls asleep.

In his head, images come and go—flickers of the past blown up on the movie screen. All things moving fast, a blur of moments. Some stopping quickly to show one event in complete silence. The views keep changing. Andrew feels like he's overdosing on these images. Some ugly, buried deep. The last time he saw his father. The image scrubs itself, bringing him back to the eighth grade, his father telling him to get his hands up on defense. His mother sitting by window, watering her orchids. Seeing Marie's eyes again. Her eyes when she let down her hair, when she put on that ring, when she showed up at his door with a drink. Her eyes at the diner, that last memory that he has of her. He can't remember anything after that. The film breaks, the solution tears apart the screen. It's dark again, his mind a bottomless hole. Then a train, a train and its horn. The sound of the horn grows louder, closing in on him. As if he is lying on the track, soon to be struck.

The slow rumble of the train slides into Andrew's consciousness. He awakens to see the ocean on the horizon. The blue of that infinite landscape, the possibilities of water, the cleansing it provides. Andrew grabs his bag and walks up the center aisle. The train slowly creeping to a stop, its doors opening to let in the salt water air. Andrew steps out onto the platform, looking down at the excess sand beneath his feet, brought here by the wind or wayward sandal.

He takes a breath of fresh air for the first time since home. A few people wander this waterfront town. Most are still at work, others in sixth period. Andrew stands in the street again. He doesn't know exactly where he's going. He just feels himself being pulled to the shore. He doesn't need a map; he needs to discover his destination for himself. To find her. To go home.

Andrew wanders for a few hours, not yet able to find what he is looking for. He's tired, he wants to lie down. He keeps pushing down the street. The ocean quietly easing into the coast. It has overtaken his eardrums. He takes a rest on a bench on the shore. The bench is rickety, lost from another time; it's comfortable though, somehow the wood is forgiving. It lets you look right out into the ocean. Your eyes could wander the depths of this view, that there might be something out there beyond it all. Maybe an island, somewhere you could float, rest your eyes for a bit. Maybe it was ugly, maybe the water too much, too deep, too unforgiving. Maybe if you went too far out, you wouldn't be able to make it back. There's a danger in the water, the darkness of the blue dream it provides, what's hiding under the surface ready to pull you down, let you look up at the sun through the blurry window, grasping to get back to it. Some never jump into the ocean. Andrew closes his eyes again, forgoing the view in favor of the calm crashing on the sand.

Andrew wakes up and sees a face above him. He squints his eyes and in doing so, the face disappears. He's left staring at the sky. The sand now has occupants, people on blankets, listening to the radio. He shakes his head loose and gets up off the bench. He begins to wander again, feeling the pull once more. He settles on a small block, four or five houses sitting off the sand—small, quaint, paint-chipped, sand-drenched houses. Andrew makes his way toward the last house. It looks a little beat up, the siding color a bit dulled, a black and white photo in a color roll of film. The white picket fence is broken, its door lying on the lawn. Andrew stands on the sidewalk and looks up at the house. It seems familiar enough. He feels the pulling toward the door. That wooden door.

Andrew walks up the path and then up the double stairs to the door. He knocks twice, waiting. He hears footsteps coming from the other side. Then the door swings open, Marie looks back at him.

They both stare, standing still. Marie steps to the side and Andrew enters the house. Inside was dark. A single light in the living room is the only light other than windows, even then, most of them are covered by drapes. Andrew drops his bag on the floor of the living room. He turns around and sees Marie leaning against the wall, her finger on her bottom lip.

"Thanks for letting me in," Andrew says, unsure of what Marie would say back. She nods, maybe she isn't ready to talk, perhaps a nod is enough to suffice. Marie turns and heads for the kitchen. Andrew takes a seat on the living room's couch, watching Marie disappear from view. The couch is comfortable, not as comfortable as the bench, but still pretty comfortable. Andrew looks around the room, up at the ceiling. The wood and brick of the walls, the creaky floors, the quiet living room. Andrew doesn't see a clock. He gets off his feet and heads toward a door just off the living room. Looking through the glass windows on the door, Andrew sees a path down to the beach.

Andrew pulls on the doorknob; the door jams. He yanks again and the wooden door pops open. A breeze blows in, running through his hair. It's so beautiful. It's a shame they aren't here under better circumstances. Andrew remains standing in the doorway, bits of sand blowing into the living room.

Marie returns from the kitchen and hands Andrew a mug. He looks in and then drinks, feeling it go down. Marie grabs a blanket from the den and throws it over her shoulders, returning to the doorway. She leans up against the wooden frame, her cup of coffee below her lips, sipping slowly. The view is better from here. The two stand there and watch the sun go down.

CHAPTER THIRTY SEVEN

They still haven't said much. Marie goes for a run on the beach while Andrew bombs around the house. She returns soon, sweat marking her forehead, sunburn on her shoulders. Marie takes a shower and puts her hair back up in a ponytail. Looking out the bathroom window, she sees Andrew reclined in a beach chair, eyes fixed out to sea. She doesn't know what to say to him. She doesn't know what it all means. Why he came back, why he's here. She never knew if she would ever see him again.

She starts to cook dinner, whipping butter in a bowl. She peeks out the window every few minutes to check on him, making sure he hadn't run off. As the pasta boils and the green beans steam, she peeks out the kitchen window once more. He's gone—the beach chair empty. She takes off her apron and heads for the back door. Outside on the patio she looks down toward the beach, a long expanse of nothing. She goes back inside and checks all of the rooms. Nothing. He is gone.

She grabs her coat and walks toward the front door, opening it to see Andrew kneeling by the front fence, screwing the gate back into place. He shuffles through a toolbox, looking for the right screw, then the right screw head. She quietly closes the screen door and looks out on the still oblivious Andrew, who finishes with the gate—opening and closing it, testing the once broken entry way. He turns to see Marie in the door. She waves. He smiles back. Andrew closes the toolbox and walks up the stone path to the front door. Marie opens the door as Andrew disappears through the entrance.

Dinner sits steaming on the kitchen table. Marie lights a candle. Andrew's in the bathroom throwing some water on his face, trying to wake himself up. He's exhausted, feeling like he's fading down the stretch. He slaps himself in the face, trying to jar his brain awake.

It's chicken parm and pasta. Andrew goes into the living room and flips through Marie's records. He lands on *The Freewheelin' Bob Dylan,* putting on side two; "Don't Think Twice, It's Alright" begins to echo through the house. Andrew turns the volume up a bit, the sound reaching the upstairs bedroom and escaping onto the beach. Andrew breathes in the scene—it seems perfect as all. The sounds, the smell of the food from the kitchen and the sand from the beach meeting in the living room. The moonlight blanketing the landscape, a worldwide beacon, a nightlight to the children in this town. Andrew sits down at the kitchen table as Marie strains the green beans.

Marie pours some wine as they eat. They share some glances and offer some words. The cooler wind from the windows causes Marie to grab a sweatshirt. Andrew feels the pain in his chest begin to echo. Later they do the dishes, Andrew scrubbing the ceramic while Marie clears the table. He looks up as rain begins to dot the windowsill above the sink. A gust of wind blows out the candle. He stops washing for a moment, watching as the rain starts to fall harder.

Then the sky opens up—a crashing of thunder, lightning on the ocean, crackling like a bomb blowing up the back yard, drowning out Dylan. Rain hits the shudders, knocking them against the siding. Andrew puts down his dish and closes the window, soon running around the house with Marie closing doors and windows.

As Marie closes the back door, the lights go out. It is pitch black, the only illumination coming every few seconds, and briefly, from the strikes of lightning marking the horizon. It's so loud; it feels like the storm is directly above the house, as if it is about to tear the house from its foundation, displace it to Oz. Andrew finds Marie in the living room sitting on the couch with a blanket. She looks out the unadorned window to see the storm over the ocean, the waves crashing and flying, sky as dark as she could ever remember it being. Andrew joins her on the couch and holds her and her shaking hands. She's cold, clutching the blanket close, trying to warm her goose bumped skin.

Then it quiets, the rain battering the roof soon turning to a slow drip. The moon returns, the darkness fading, *Freewheelin'* continuing to play—voicing a soundtrack to this world. Marie and Andrew stay on the couch, wrapped in the blanket.

"I hate that you ruined this," Marie says. Andrew stays looking out the window, his eyes heavy.

"Me too."

They soon fall asleep.

Andrew sees the ceiling streaked with blue, moonlight striding across the roof above his head. Marie is gone. He levels his head and sees the door to the back ajar, wind blowing onto his face. He pulls the blanket off himself and gets to his feet. Slowly inching toward the open door, he sees Marie sitting on the beach.

He begins to walk out to her, his bare feet jutting through the somehow dry sand. She's running her fingers through the sand in front of her. She keeps sweeping her hair over her left ear, for it soon to be blown back off by the wind. As he nears her, Andrew feels the pain murmur in his chest. He ignores it, doesn't care about it. All he needs to do is get to her, right now.

Andrew sits down next to Marie and kisses her on the cheek. Marie continues doodling in the sand. Andrew looks out into the ocean, the moon casting shades.

"Is there anything that you want to talk about?" Marie asks, her eyes still toward the sand.

"I'm afraid anything I say wouldn't live up to it...maybe silence will..." Andrew replies. He turns to look at her again.

"I was so mad at you for so long, Andrew. I loved you and then I lost you...twice. Do you remember the first time we rented this house? It was that hot, hot summer, we took a week off, came down...and did absolutely nothing. We wanted to do that forever, just be with each other. We did this...and it was the best week. Now we sit here...and time has defeated us."

Andrew continues looking at Marie, holding her right hand.

"I know you have to go soon," Marie says.

"I have a little bit more time," Andrew replies. Marie snickers, tears welling slowly, and finally looks back at Andrew.

"No, you don't."

Andrew's filled with sadness, the murmur in his chest growing to a wail—he grinds his teeth.

"I had to see you, try....try and make things right. At least try," Andrew says.

"Well that means a lot," Marie replies.

"I'm sorry, for everything, for hurting you and running away when all you wanted to do was heal me. I've made a lot of mistakes in my life, it was kind of my thing, but the worst was how I treated you, and I'll never forgive myself for that. I don't want you to be sad about me anymore; I want this to be the last. I want you to wake up tomorrow morning and go out and live, because believe me, one day someone will take that from you...and they won't even ask permission. Don't go out like me," Andrew finishes, dabbing his shirt in his eyes. Marie has her head bowed down toward the sand. Andrew stays looking, trying to soak up every detail, every lock of hair, every freckle on her face, her dimples.

"C'mon, let's get you back inside, it's getting cold out," Andrew says, standing up and putting his hand out. Marie grabs his hand and gets to her feet. Andrew puts his arm around Marie's shoulder as they walk back to the house.

Once inside, Andrew and Marie walk upstairs to the back bedroom. Marie gets into bed and Andrew pulls the covers over her. Marie peers up from the bed at him, her eyes glassy. Andrew grabs another blanket off the chair and drapes it over Marie. He kisses her on the forehead, looking at her and smiling. He stands next to her bed for a moment and then turns to walk toward the door.

"Andrew," Marie says quietly, sitting up in bed. Andrew turns back to Marie, sitting down on the edge of the bed. Marie puts her hands on Andrew's face and kisses him.

"I love you," she says. Andrew closes his eyes and stands up, slowly walking to the bedroom door. He turns back once more, to see Marie's eyes just above the covers edge. He closes the bedroom door.

Down the creaky stairs he goes. Returning to the living room, he spins a record, putting on "Treasure" by The Cure. Quietly it creeps through the house. He opens the brown leather notebook sitting on the coffee table and begins to write. Closing it a few minutes later, he rises to his feet and takes one last look at his home. Andrew opens the back door and heads out to the beach.

He stumbles a little bit, the pain growing louder in his chest. He keeps moving to the surf. Peeking back at Marie's window, he sees it was still dark. He needs it to be. She can't be there anymore. She doesn't have to search for him or worry or cry. When she wakes up tomorrow things would be better. Andrew reaches the water—the lip of the waves cresting over his bare toes.

Andrew looks out to the ocean, looks out at the waves and the night sky. It looks brighter, morning was coming soon. A new day. A new sunshine for everyone to be thankful for.

The pain in his chest overcomes him. Andrew falls to his knees. He looks up from the sand out into the ocean. He sees his father, standing out there on the horizon. His hair parted, a suit jacket and a tie on.

Andrew gathers one more bit of strength and gets to his feet one more time. He begins to slowly walk into the surf. As the water hits his shins, then his knees, then his waist, he feels an incredible calm come over him. The pain still simmering underneath, this new feeling seeping through him. He continues out into the water. His father smiles that big smile he always smiled. The waves hit Andrew in the chest, knocking him back a few steps. He rights himself and continues to move forward. Andrew goes under. Looking up through the dark, he sees the stars doting the sky.

Andrew disappears into the ocean.

CHAPTER THIRTY EIGHT

Marie wakes up the next morning, the sun coming through the window above her bed. She peels the covers off and walks downstairs, seeing the empty house, the quiet sound of the ocean outside. She puts on the teakettle and grabs the paper from the sidewalk. Marie opens the back door and lets the wind blow in. She sits down on the couch in the living room. Sipping on her tea, she looks out the back door out into the blues of the ocean and sky—the late summer breeze warming her skin.

EPILOGUE

John Kenney flips through a magazine. The airport around him is sweeping—a group of people go rumbling past him looking like the McCallisters when they were late for their flight to France, and sleeping—Jeff Singer curled up in a ball in the seat next to him. John looks at his watch and then up at the flight board, the words delayed marking it.

John yawns and punches Jeff in the arm, "Singer—wake up."

Jeff shakes awake, his hair sticking up on one side, his eyes bloodshot.

"Where am I?" Jeff asks, his head darting from side to side.

"Still here."

"Shit, I was hoping you were gonna be a pal and carry me onto the flight so I wouldn't have to wake up," Jeff replies, curling back into the chair and closing his eyes once again.

"I'm going to the Caribbean for my honeymoon and you're heading back to New York, there was never going to be any carrying anywhere," John says, his eyes now starting to drop, the effect of the long wait in this terminal.

"Has the snow stopped?" Jeff asks.

"Nope," John replies.

"Where did the girls go?"

"They went to get some food."

"Not hungry you fat bastard?" Jeff asks, a little laugh sneaking out at the end.

"I just didn't want to leave you here by yourself," John replies.

"Thanks a lot you fat bastard," Jeff says.

John rubs his eyes to stay awake. His eyes pan the terminal. People sleeping on top of luggage, teenagers texting back and forth, kids running off the candy their parents just bought them from the gift shop. John spots a father reading a book, his teenage son asleep next to him, the boy's head resting on the father's shoulder.

"I'm proud of you," Jeff says, still half asleep in the adjacent chair.

"What?" John replies, turning back to the slumbering Jeff.

"I'm proud of you," Jeff repeats.

"Thanks."

John looks back across the aisle toward the father and son—the father quietly flipping through his book as to not awake his son.

"Did you tell everybody? About the baby?" John asks, looking back toward Jeff, who twists in the chair.

"Not yet," Jeff replies.

"What about your parents, did you call your parents?"

"Talked to my mom...she was all excited—my dad wasn't home...which might have been a blessing because the last time we spoke we called each other 'fuckers.' I'll talk to him when I get back," Jeff says. John laughs.

"You should call your dad, I'm sure he'd be happy to hear the news," John says, slouching into the chair and closing his eyes. Jeff opens his eyes and stretches. He slaps John on the chest then looks across at the father and son.

"Watch our shit, I'll be right back," Jeff says, getting up and walking away from the overstuffed rows of bleary eyed waiting passengers.

Jeff wanders toward the terminal windows, the light snow bouncing off them, the white landscape off in the distance. He takes his cell phone out of his pocket and dials, putting the ringing receiver to his ear. Jeff runs his fingers over his lips, hearing the ring echo in his ear.

"Hey, Dad."

ACKNOWLEDGEMENTS

Woody Allen
Richard Baratta
Monica Barraza
Tom Bernabeo
Patrick Boyd
Ulric Butcher
Louis CK
Greg Colica
Chris D'Ascoli
Larry David
John DeSimone
Tara Driggs
Bob Dylan
Bob Graziano
Donald Glover
Michael Hall
Patricia Hall
Frances & Timothy Hunt
Andrew Keary
John & Nicole Keary
Kevin & Frances Keary
Kevin & Nancy Keary
Susan Keary
Jeanne & Pat Kelly
John Kenney

Molly Lambert
Gabriela Landeo
Veronique Lee
Phillip Mastrotto
Matt McDonnell
Matt Merson
Bill Murray
Phillip Orozco
Michael Pennisi
John Pepper
Derek Pinelli
Ryan Russell
Matt Shalhoub
Celeste Shelley
Jeff Singer
Steven Spielberg
Jon Stewart
Emma Taylor
Katherine Tully
Nicolette Viscusi
Christopher Wallace
Kanye West
Christie Woodside
Edgar Wright
Robert Zimmerman

WHERE TO FIND ME.

HTTP://WWW.IAMCHRISHALL.COM

HTTP://MYFORKINTHEROAD.BLOGSPOT.COM

TWITTER- @SKINNYBOYBALKI

FLICKR- HTTP://WWW.FLICKR.COM/PHOTOS/SKINNYBOYBALKI/

DOWNLOAD THE "DEATH AND OTHER THINGS" SOUNDTRACK ON ITUNES.

There's no grand plan, just things we will only, maybe, understand when we come to the end.

Made in the USA
Charleston, SC
30 August 2011